C000082767

Missing in Shanghai

To Tom

With best wishes

Jean Herod

Missing in Shanghai

Diplomatic Crime Series 3

JEAN HARROD

© Jean Harrod, 2018

Published by York Authors Coffee Shop

All rights reserved. No part of this book may be reproduced, adapted, stored in a retrieval system or transmitted by any means, electronic, mechanical, photocopying, or otherwise without the prior written permission of the author.

The rights of Jean Harrod to be identified as the author of this work have been asserted in accordance with the Copyright, Designs and Patents Act 1988.

This is a work of fiction. The events in the novel did not happen. Names, characters, businesses, places, events and incidents are either the products of the author's imagination or used in a fictitious manner. Any resemblance to actual persons, living or dead, or actual events, is purely coincidental.

A CIP catalogue record for this book is available from the British Library.

ISBN 978-0-9929971-7-5 (Paperback)
ISBN 978-0-9929971-8-2 (mobi)
ISBN 978-0-9929971-9-9 (epub)

Book layout and design by Clare Brayshaw

Prepared and printed by:

York Publishing Services Ltd
64 Hallfield Road
Layerthorpe
York YO31 7ZQ

Tel: 01904 431213

Website: www.yps-publishing.co.uk

For Jeff and Jane

Acknowledgements

It's been a long, hard year working to bring *Missing in Shanghai* to life. More than ever, I'm grateful to my sister Jane, for her unflagging advice and support, and always telling me the truth–even if it meant a lot of extra work and re-writing.

I've had the same wonderful team helping me, as well many readers urging me to get on with it. Huge thanks too to my writer friends, Fiona, Margaret and Christine, who again have been with me every step of the way on this journey.

Thanks also to Claire Waring, Clare Brayshaw, Paula Charles and John Chandler for all their work in putting this novel together.

A special thanks too to all the kind people I met in China when I lived there in the 1980s.

The events in this novel did not happen. Its plot and characters exist only in my imagination.

About the Author

Born and educated in the UK, Jean was employed as a British diplomat for many years, working in Embassies and High Commissions in Australia, Brussels, the Caribbean, China, East Berlin, Indonesia, Mauritius, and Switzerland. She has travelled extensively around the world and writes about all the countries she has lived in.

'Deadly Diplomacy', set in Australia, was her debut diplomatic crime novel, and the first of a series featuring diplomat Jess Turner and DI Tom Sangster.

'Deadly Deceit', set in the Turks and Caicos Islands, is the second in the series.

'Missing in Shanghai', set in London and Shanghai, is the third.

Jean now lives in North Yorkshire. An active contributor to regional theatre, she has written and staged several plays.

For more information about Jean Harrod and her novels, visit her website at **www.jeanharrod.com**

1

Shanghai 1984

"Communism is not love. Communism is a hammer which we use to crush the enemy."

(Chairman Mao Zedong – Revolutionary, and founder of the People's Republic of China)

Marianne glanced out the back window. The black sedan behind was like a determined hunter she couldn't outrun. It had been tailing her for weeks, and she'd never even glimpsed the face of the driver through its blacked-out windows. Why were they making their presence so obvious? To upset her? Intimidate her? She'd never experienced this level of surveillance in all her years working at the British Embassy in Peking. Why now? She would have to report this harassment to the Ambassador when she saw him later. Not that he could do much about the Shanghai secret police, but he needed to know.

Turning back, she caught sight of her Chinese driver's watchful eyes in the mirror. Another one monitoring her every move. Don't let them get to you, she thought, as she gave him a wide smile.

He just looked at the road ahead.

Relaxing into the seat, she opened the window. The air felt muggy as the watery afternoon sunshine gave way to dark clouds that hung low and heavy in the sky. These warm autumn days, and cold nights, produced some spectacular electric storms, and she could feel one coming now. She hoped it would drop its rain on the shimmering rice paddies on the far bank of the Huangpu River. If it poured down on the city, the traffic would be gridlocked for hours.

She looked up as the driver turned into Nanjing Lu, Shanghai's main shopping street, and drove towards the Peace Hotel. The Ambassador had flown from Peking and checked into the hotel earlier that afternoon. He was in the city to meet a British trade delegation at the airport and accompany them on their high-level calls around town.

Marianne checked her watch and drummed her fingers on the seat as the car inched its way along the crowded shopping street. She was due to meet the Ambassador in the Peace Hotel's Jazz Bar at 5.45pm to brief him on the programme. She didn't dare be late. He was a stickler for punctuality. One piercing stare over his gold-framed specs could set the tone for the whole evening. After that, they would travel together in the car to the Jing An Hotel, where the delegation was staying, to attend a welcoming banquet the Chinese were hosting for them. It would have been so much easier if the Ambassador had agreed to stay in the same hotel as the delegation, but he'd insisted on the Peace Hotel instead. Marianne guessed that was because he didn't want to be at the delegation's constant beck and call or feel obliged to carouse with them until the early hours, although he never said so.

A bolt of lightning streaked across the sky, making her jump. She wished the driver would get a move on before it started raining. But driving in the city couldn't be rushed.

Cars and cyclists vied for space on crowded roads. Whoever had their bumper or bicycle wheel in front seemed to have right of way. Chinese road rage was demonstrated by furiously ringing bells and honking horns. They never shouted at each other. Losing one's temper meant 'losing face' and being embarrassed was a no-no in Chinese society. To Marianne, they were the most buttoned-up race on earth.

Heavy drops of rain started bouncing off the bonnet as the car pulled up outside the Peace Hotel. 5.45pm on the dot. Marianne jumped out, held her jacket over her head, and ran up the steps to the hotel entrance.

Once inside, she rushed into the Jazz Bar and stopped in the doorway. It was empty, except for a barman arranging bottles of beer on the shelves behind the bar. Relieved to be the first to arrive, she glanced back towards the lobby. Had the Chinese surveillance team followed her in? Almost certainly, although she couldn't pick out a familiar face. It was worrying though. Only yesterday, she'd spoken again to her colleague, Justin Barber, about this constant surveillance. He'd shrugged it off in his usual blasé way. So, what? He didn't care if the Chinese *were* following him, although he didn't think they were.

Marianne had worked with Justin in the Embassy in Peking for three years before being sent to Shanghai to open the new British Consulate-General. After years of shunning the world, China was beginning to open-up, and there were commercial and investment opportunities to be had. London had chosen Marianne and Justin for the assignment because they were experienced officers and had worked together well in Peking. But now they were in Shanghai, Marianne had misgivings. To her, it was an exciting opportunity, but she wasn't sure Justin felt the same. Gregarious by nature, he seemed subdued and had been hitting the grog hard. She wondered whether to mention it to the Ambassador and ask him to have a quiet word. Except she didn't want to get Justin into trouble.

Walking over to the bar, she ordered a Tsingtao beer. She sat down at a table close by and pulled out her briefing papers for one last read through. She had to be word perfect. The Ambassador would pick apart any error or hesitation. She pulled her cigarettes out of her jacket pocket, lit one, and buried her head in the papers.

It was the sound of torrential rain hammering on the pavement outside that eventually made her look up. 'Dancing dollies' as her grandmother used to call the summer rains in the UK. Marianne smiled, remembering how much her French grandmother had loved English idioms. Instinctively, she touched the gold cross around her neck that her grandmother had given her many years ago. 'It will always keep you safe', she'd said, 'just like it kept me safe.' Her grandmother had been a remarkable woman. During World War II, she'd helped many British airmen escape back to the UK, including Marianne's grandfather. After the war, they'd married and settled in England.

Normally, the Foreign Office wouldn't accept employees whose parents or grandparents had a foreign nationality, for national security reasons. But even they couldn't refuse Marianne, given her grandmother's service to the country.

She held her wrist up to the single dull beam radiating from the ceiling light to see the time. Just after 6pm.

He was late. It was not like the Ambassador, not like him at all.

She flicked her cigarette ash into the glass ashtray and cast her eyes around the legendary Jazz Bar. Thick, stone pillars were strategically placed, as if to hold up the ceiling. Nearly everything was fashioned from dark wood: the square wooden tables scattered around the floor with their matching high-backed chairs, and the oak beams that criss-crossed the ceiling. No wonder it was so dark.

She loved its 1920's art deco theme, the era in which the hotel was built by Victor Sassoon. One of the first skyscrapers in the eastern hemisphere, it had quickly become a glamorous playground for the elite. She glanced over at the piano and other instruments, standing idle at one end of the room. What times they must have had in here.

Closing her eyes, she let her imagination wander back to the extravagant gala parties of those times. Wealthy women in their flapper dresses, shimmering with sequins and swinging tassels, tripping across the sprung wooden floor and swivelling their feet to Charleston music. Girls kicking up their legs to the music, giving anyone close to the dance floor a thrilling glimpse of stocking garter and milky white thigh.

Opening her eyes, she caught the barman staring at her from behind the long bar. Its dark wood and huge array of bottles could have come straight out of an English hunting lodge, except for the huge portrait of Chairman Mao hanging above it. The Chinese revolutionary, and founding father of the People's Republic of China, had pride of place in most public venues. Now, he was watching over the Bar to ensure people remembered the sacrifices made during the Cultural Revolution, and did not enjoy themselves with alcohol, music and dancing, she thought wryly. Not that the Chinese public were allowed in. This hotel was for foreigners only and segregation was strict. The Communist Party did not want foreigners polluting Chinese minds, or sowing seeds of discontent.

The barman pointed to the bottle of beer and glass he'd put in front of her while she'd been engrossed in her papers.

She smiled at him, poured out the beer and took a swig. The amber liquid slipped easily down her throat, although it did nothing to help her relax. She still had a lot of work to do on this visit, not least one of her most dreaded jobs – drawing up the seating plan for the return banquet that the Ambassador would host for the delegation and Chinese officials. Trying to work out who was senior to whom in this 'egalitarian' society, and seat them accordingly, was a headache. They might dress and behave the same, but *they* knew who was in charge and were deeply offended if they weren't afforded their correct status.

She took another deep drag on her cigarette and blew the smoke high into the musty air. It was already autumn, but the Chinese wouldn't put on any central heating until well into the winter, if at all. Like them, she wore layers under her clothes to keep warm. Today, she'd put on her navy-blue wool trouser suit and Chinese cashmere polo-neck sweater. With her shoulder length black hair and slim frame, she could blend easily into a crowd of Chinese without drawing any attention, at least from the back. It was a different story from the front. The Chinese were not used to seeing Westerners and were fascinated by their round eyes and bridged noses.

Marianne rested her cigarette on the edge of the ashtray, reached into her handbag and pulled out a small mirror. The circles under her eyes looked even darker than usual, especially in the dim light. She put on a slick of pink lipstick, pinched her sallow cheeks to get some colour into them, and ran her fingers through the thick, glossy hair she'd also inherited from her grandmother.

Picking up her cigarette again, she looked at the faded elegance all around her. Only ghosts from the roaring 20s and 30s inhabited the decaying building now. Yellowing paint peeled off the walls, and a thick layer of industrial grime covered the windows. China's Cultural Revolution had ended a mere eight years earlier with the death of Chairman Mao. The violent class struggle he'd engineered had been designed to wipe out the last remnants of traditional Chinese society, and privileged existence. These days, no one dared talk about the past, let alone treasure or preserve any building that reminded them of their decadent history. Only the Communist Party and its great leader were to be revered.

A movement over by the doorway made her sit up expectantly, but it wasn't the Ambassador. A handful of stooped, old men shuffled over to the instruments and sat down to play. Marianne knew from previous visits they were the original young musicians who'd first formed the jazz band in the 1930s. What changes they must have seen. Old age had crept up on all of them, but they still played regularly every evening, crooning out their favourite tunes. She smiled, and they bowed their heads politely, before studiously avoiding any further eye contact. They didn't want to engage with a foreigner and court trouble for themselves.

Checking her watch again, a creeping sense of unease settled on her. Something must have gone wrong, she thought, as she stubbed out her cigarette in the ashtray and drained her glass of beer. The Ambassador was never late for anything. Had he already gone to the Jing An Hotel, she wondered? She got up and went out to reception to try and find out.

The young receptionist smiled as she approached. "Good evening, Miss Henderson."

Marianne knew the young woman from her previous visits to the hotel. "Good evening," she said. "I'm waiting for the British Ambassador. I believe he checked in a couple of hours ago?"

The receptionist nodded without needing to check the register.

"Has he left a message for me?" Marianne asked.

The receptionist turned to the vast array of pigeon holes behind her. "No, ma'am."

"Well, can I telephone his room?"

The receptionist hesitated.

"I was supposed to be meeting him in the Jazz Bar," Marianne explained. "But he hasn't appeared."

The receptionist pointed to a bank of phones on the other side of the lobby. "He's in room 917," she said, softly. "You can use the internal phones to call him."

"Thank you." Marianne went over and quickly dialled 917. There was no answer. Had the receptionist given her the correct room number? She looked over at reception again, but the young woman was busy checking in a large group of American tourists, and Marianne didn't have time to wait.

She walked over to the lifts. As a rule, only registered guests were permitted to go up to the rooms. She glanced furtively around, then slipped into the nearest lift, and pressed the button for the ninth floor, knowing each room number started with the floor it was on. She became nervous on the way up about appearing at the Ambassador's bedroom door. It seemed familiar, intrusive even, but what else could she do?

The lift doors opened silently, and she stepped out into a small lobby. To one side, there was a window made of beautiful art deco stained glass that overlooked the street. She started walking on a well-worn carpet along a corridor, checking the numbers on the bedroom doors as she went. Brass uplighters, with marble glass shades, glowed dimly on the walls. Half way along, a red lacquer electric Chinese lantern hung from the centre of the ceiling. She stared at its hypnotic flickering light, and the grotesque dragon's head jutting out from the top.

A loud clap of thunder stopped her in her tracks.

The sound of a door creaking made her turn. It clicked shut again.

She walked on briskly until she stood outside room 917. To her surprise, the door was slightly ajar. Not wanting to barge in, she held the handle to stop the door opening as she rapped on it with her knuckles. "Evening Sir. It's me, Marianne."

There was no reply.

She pushed the door open a little and called through the crack. "Sir. Are you in there?"

Still no reply.

Her heart was pounding as she pushed open the door and poked her head into the room. It was so dark her eyes took a while to adjust. The curtains were drawn, but a chink of light filtered in through a crack in the middle where they didn't quite meet. She could hear rain battering against the windows. She went over and opened the curtains wide. Outside, the grey cloud of night had arrived with the rain, and the light was fading.

A streak of lightning lit up the place momentarily, giving her a macabre snapshot of the room, like some old black and white movie. She went back to the door and switched on the lights.

Against the wall, there was a large double bed, its covers pulled back and its sheets crumpled as if someone had been sleeping in it. On the bedside table stood two glasses and a half-empty bottle of champagne. Then her eyes fixed on an open condom foil.

She stumbled back in confusion. Was she in the wrong room? Then, she recognised the official crest on the leather briefcase on the chair. It was the Ambassador's. But, where was he?

She looked at the half-open bathroom door and went over. "Sir," she called out, her voice shaky.

No reply.

She pushed open the door and gasped.

The Ambassador lay on his back on the floor, his face drained as white as his hair. His blue eyes, now dark grey, were staring at her. A small trickle of saliva ran from the corner of his mouth, pooling on the white tiled floor.

Marianne sank to her knees beside him. Touching his hand, she could feel the warmth still on his skin. Something rolled out of his hand, onto the floor. For a split second, she stared at a small snuff bottle.

Her hands shook as she loosened his tie and opened the top button of his shirt to give him air. Pressing her fingers to the side of his neck, she desperately tried to find a pulse.

Nothing.

She put her ear to his lips. No breath.

Instinctively, she pushed his head back to open his airway. She put her left hand in the centre of his chest, covered it with her right, interlaced her fingers, and started chest compressions. Pushing hard in a steady rhythm, she counted to thirty, then stopped.

Frantically, she felt his neck again, and put her ear to his lips.

Nothing.

"Come on," she urged. "*Breathe!*" Again, she pressed down as hard as she could onto his chest, over and over.

She kept pushing and counting, pushing and counting.

"Come on!"

Her arms ached, her chest ached, but she wouldn't stop.

"Please … breathe."

But he didn't.

Exhausted, she felt his neck again. No pulse or heartbeat. She put her ear to his chest. No breath.

She sat back on her heels, shaking uncontrollably.
The Ambassador was dead.

2

> *In waking a tiger, use a long stick.*
> *(Chairman Mao)*

Head bowed over the computer, Jess's fingers flew across the keyboard. The briefing for the Chinese President's State visit seemed never-ending. There were too many subjects for the Foreign Secretary and Prime Minister to cover at their bilateral meetings, but she knew if she left anything out, it would be the one issue that was raised. Now, she was adding a page about six Chinese political prisoners being held in the wilds of northern China. They'd been found guilty of organising a public demonstration over the lack of press freedoms, and no one had heard anything from them for some time. Not that the British government could do much, except maintain the spotlight on their plight in the hope of keeping them alive.

Twisting to check the spellings of their names from a file at the end of her desk, she felt a sharp pain shoot up through her neck and into the back of her head. She rolled her shoulders to ease the tension and tried to continue typing, but the pain persisted. It was no good, her body was telling her to take a break. Not surprising really, she'd been in the office since 8am and had worked straight through lunch.

It was only now her concentration was broken that she realised it was already dark and unusually quiet. The only light in the room came from the dull beam of her metal desk lamp shining onto the computer keys. She looked at her watch with a rising sense of frustration. 5.35pm already, and she had to attend a drinks reception downstairs in Durbar Court at 6pm.

The party was in honour of a Chinese trade delegation, arriving ahead of their President, and hosted by the Permanent Under-Secretary of State, or P.U.S. as everyone referred to the Head of the Foreign Office. As the top civil servant, he was answerable to Ministers on all aspects of UK foreign policy. Jess had always been surprised by the awful acronyms still in use from a bygone era, but the title of PUS was by far the worst. It made the top man sound like infected tissue.

She looked over at the window. It was pitch black outside but then, it was the first week of December. In winter, she rarely saw daylight. It was dark when she left the flat in the morning, and dark when she left the office in the evening. If she didn't go out for a walk at lunchtime, she existed in perpetual darkness. After living for several years in the bright sunshine of Australia and the Caribbean, the British winter made her feel gloomy.

One thing *was* the same though – her office décor. Yet another battleship grey desk and combination-lock cupboard furnished her small office, along with the ever-present beige walls. A pot of purple African violets on the window sill, and the photo of Amy in a silver frame on her desk, were her only attempt to make the office feel like hers. She had planned to put up some pictures of her own but hadn't got around to it yet.

The soft tick-tick sound on the window pane made her wonder if it was sleeting outside. She hoped not. This State visit had been difficult enough to organise without the weather hampering things. She went over to the window and pulled back the grimy bomb-proof net curtain. Small ice crystals hit the window, then quickly turned to water as they slid down the glass. She shivered, pulled the thick cardigan off the back of her chair and threw it around her shoulders.

Not for the first time in the past few weeks, she wondered what on earth had made her take on the China desk. She'd been surprised six months ago when Human Resources had asked her to do it. The job was normally reserved for sinologists who spoke the language and had immersed themselves in all things Chinese for years. Jess had none of those skills. She was an experienced policy desk officer though, which helped. So, in her usual 'can do' way, she'd accepted the job. It was a constant challenge though, and she had to work long hours to get everything done. True to character, she'd thrown herself into the job and spent hours of her own time reading through all the old files to improve her knowledge. It wasn't really a hardship because the annual despatches and letters from Ambassadors to China across the years were fascinating.

She looked at her watch again and reluctantly started putting her classified papers away. She'd have to come back after the reception and finish the briefing. It had to be ready to distribute to the PM and Foreign Secretary first thing in the morning. That was her deadline, and there was no way she was going to miss it. Anyway, Protocol Department, who were responsible for co-ordinating the programme, had called a final planning meeting for everyone involved in the visit in the morning. Jess would have to attend that. Everything had to work like clockwork. This visit was too important for anything to go wrong.

Putting away her papers, she noticed a small pile of old files balanced on the corner of her desk. They were tied together with tape, with a sheet of white paper on top marked 'For Weeding'. She groaned inwardly, thinking the Registry Clerk must have slipped in and put them there without her noticing. The annual cull meant reading through the old files to decide whether they should be destroyed or kept in the archives for longer. Curiosity made her untie the tape to have a quick look at their titles. They all seemed to be about the opening of a new Consulate-General in Shanghai in 1984.

"They look interesting," said a voice behind her.

Jess jumped.

Sam Biggins smiled. "Sorry. Didn't mean to startle you. I thought we could walk down to the reception together."

Sam was the China researcher in Library and Records Department. He'd spent his entire career specialising in the country and spoke excellent Mandarin. What he didn't know about China could fit on the back of the proverbial postage stamp. Apart from a couple of postings to Peking, his job of researcher was London-based, and he'd been particularly helpful to Jess. Someone she could go to for help and information whenever she needed, and she really appreciated that.

"So, what are they, then?" he asked.

"Just some old files for weeding."

"Give them to me. I'll have a look."

Files were Sam's business. It was amazing the enthusiasm he still had for his work, and for China, after all these years. He'd joined the Foreign Office from university and was now in his early sixties. It was no secret he was coming up for retirement, although his age and grey hair belied his youthful, sometimes even boyish, appearance.

Jess tied the files back together. "I'll have a flick through first. I'm learning a lot about China from the old files."

"Haven't you got enough to do?"

"Even so…" She picked up the bundle of files and put them on the bottom shelf of her cupboard. "I'll read them after the State visit." She shut the cupboard door and spun the combination lock. Now they were safe.

Suddenly her office door flew open and banged into the cupboard. Giles Pettiford, her boss and overall Head of the China and Hong Kong Department strode in.

Jess instinctively took a step back, as she did whenever Giles appeared on the scene. Always in a hurry, he charged around the corridors like an unguided missile.

"Have you finished the briefing?" he asked.

"Almost. I'll come back after the reception and finish it."

His eyes narrowed. "I wanted to read it tonight."

For a moment, she thought he was going to throw a tantrum. He'd done it before when he hadn't got his own way. "It'll be on your desk first thing in the morning," she said, firmly.

He stared at her for what felt like a full minute. Then he gave Sam a curt nod and walked out.

When he'd gone, Sam pulled a face. "Never changes, does he?"

Jess was glad Giles hadn't kicked off. She was under enough pressure without him adding to it. "He's so uptight all the time, it's a wonder he hasn't had a heart attack before now."

"Always been the same. Lord knows why he doesn't take his foot off the pedal. He's not going anywhere."

Jess looked at Sam.

He shrugged. "I heard Human Resources want him to retire."

Jess raised her eyebrows. "He's only in his late 50s, isn't he?"

Sam nodded.

"Why retire him, then? He's good at his job, and probably knows more about China than anyone else in the Foreign Office … except you."

"No idea." Sam shrugged again. "Come on, we don't want our guests arriving before us."

But Jess was still curious about Giles. "Has he done something wrong?" she asked. "Is that why they want him to go?"

"It's hard to get through a whole career *without* doing something wrong."

She shut down her computer and collected up the stray papers strewn across her desk. "I thought Giles learnt Mandarin at university and joined the Foreign Office on fast track to become a sinologist."

"He did."

"He's had a couple of postings in our Peking Embassy too, hasn't he?"

Sam nodded.

"So, what's he done, then? Why retire him?"

He put his hands on his hips. "Someone told me you were like a terrier, Jess. When you got your teeth into something, you never let go."

"Might as well tell me then."

He sighed. "Then can we go?"

"Yes."

"Right, well, Giles was a pain in the proverbial when I first met him," Sam said, with feeling. "He was a young man in his 20s back then, on his first posting to our Embassy in Peking."

Jess nodded encouragingly.

"He was sent home suddenly without completing his full posting."

"Ah, so he *did* do something wrong." Jess was very interested now. "What?"

"I don't know."

"Oh, come on."

"Really, I don't know." Sam shrugged. "I was working in our Peking Embassy at the time too, on my first posting to China. One day, Giles was there, and the next he'd gone home."

Jess pulled a face. "That'll be a few years ago."

Sam gave a wry smile. "Over 30 to be precise."

"And in all that time you never found out what Giles did to get himself sent home?"

He shook his head.

She found that hard to believe. "Come on, old man." She ushered him out of her office and locked the door behind her. "You can tell me all about Giles on the way."

"I've told you all I know."

She gave him a sceptical look. "Giles may have blotted his copy book back then, but he survived it and went on to have a good career. Something else must have happened."

Sam shrugged. "He was once tipped for the top Foreign Office job, you know. He's always wanted to be PUS."

That didn't surprise her. Giles had a brilliant mind, but there was something about him. A mercurial personality, he could be unpredictable and difficult at times. "I still think something's happened more recently."

Sam shrugged. "Don't they always say the past catches up with you…"

Jess was struck by the sadness in Sam's voice when he said that. Or was it weariness? This State visit was stressing everyone out. The pressure to get things right, and long working hours, were causing tempers to flare. She glanced sideways at him. He looked miserable too. Perhaps his mood had nothing to do with the Chinese visit? Maybe those memories of his time in Peking as a young man made him feel old? Retiring next year would be a difficult transition after a lifetime's work.

One thing's for sure, she thought, as they made their way in companionable silence down the staircase to the drinks reception. If Sam had been working in our Peking Embassy at the same time, he would know why Giles had been sent home early. So, why wouldn't he tell her? What was the big secret? The more Jess thought about it, the more curious she became.

★

The light beaming from the glittering crystal lamps dazzled Jess as she walked into Durbar Court, a grandiose Victorian courtyard in the heart of the Foreign Office. Her eyes travelled up the three floors of columns supporting arches to the roof. Built in 1867 when the building was the India Office, the Court was originally open to the sky. Now, it had a practical atrium-style roof. Tonight, the sleet on the glass roof looked like a sprinkling of glitter. In summer, sunshine beamed down, lighting up the granite Corinthian columns and elaborate marble floor. It was a stunning sight that always lifted her mood.

Looking around, she saw drinks and canapés laid out on tables at one end of the room. At the other end stood a massive spruce decorated with glittering gold Christmas baubles, pine cones and lights. Everything was ready and waiting for their Chinese guests to arrive.

"What can I get you?" Sam asked.

"Anything soft, please. I need a clear head to finish that briefing."

Sam made his way over to the drinks, while Jess went to look at the tree. She'd been so busy in the run-up to this State visit, she hadn't even thought about Christmas. She'd have to work Christmas Eve but after that she wasn't due back until the second week of January. She was really looking forward to a break and being with Simon for the holidays. She'd hardly seen him this year, except for a couple of weeks' summer holiday in France. It was ridiculous really, he *was* her partner and a diplomat too. Simon had taken a posting to the British Embassy in Paris, so they could see each other regularly. The plan was to take it in turns back and forth on the Eurostar, and have alternate weekends together, either in London or Paris. It had seemed an ideal situation. And, loving Paris as she did, Jess had been looking forward to spending time in the city. But, as it turned out, either Simon was working and too busy to travel, or she was. They'd given up trying to see each other at weekends, and their only time together now was at Easter, their annual summer holiday, and at Christmas. She wondered how much longer this situation could go on for.

That had been on her mind more and more lately, as her body clock ticked on. If they were going to have a family they'd have to try soon, or it would be too late. She was already in her 30s. Maybe it was too late already? Did she even want another child? Her heart ached at the thought of her little Amy. Could she go through all that again? Lose another child?

And what about Simon? It had been touch-and-go with his prostate cancer. He'd been so determined to beat it. And so far, he had. And he seemed happy to be back at work. But whenever she raised the subject of children, he was evasive. 'Someday', he'd say. Was he worried the radiotherapy had affected his ability to father a child? She knew his consultant had discussed that with him before the operation. But Simon wasn't a man who talked about his feelings. He was one of life's clams. Try to prize him open and he'd shut down more firmly. Still, he'd been through a lot, and she didn't want to put him under any more pressure.

And what about her promotion? HR were urging her to take the Fast Stream Assessment Centre to get into the top ranks of the Foreign Office. It would mean taking more exams, and undergoing role plays and interviews to see if she had the right potential. It was something she'd been working towards for a long time, a real career maker. But, if she had another child she'd probably never get to a senior position because the work demanded too much time and energy. Would a top job really matter to her anyway?

"Penny for them, Jessica?"

Jess spun round to see Xiao Li, her opposite number in the Chinese Embassy. "Sorry, I was miles away." She held out her hand. "I should have been at the door to welcome you."

Xiao Li smiled and shook her hand. "This visit is causing us all too much work. But I'm sure it will be worth it."

Jess nodded. "Only three days to D-Day."

Xiao Li looked puzzled.

"The day our forces invaded Normandy to liberate France from the Germans … the Second World War."

Xiao Li's eyes lit up as she understood.

Jess liked her Chinese counterpart. She was smart and spoke good English. Even now Jess could see her brain filing away that colloquial reference to D-Day for future use.

"We all seem to be in the same state of neurotic anxiety over your President's visit," Jess joked.

Xiao Li gave a small smile, but her eyes looked troubled.

She was a pretty woman, Jess thought, with her long black hair, pale skin, and delicate features. It was difficult to tell the age of Chinese people. To Western eyes, everyone looked younger than they were. Even so, she reckoned Xiao Li was in her 30s too, or maybe even younger than her. Her tiny frame and features made her look vulnerable, but her handshake was firm. There was a toughness under that gentle exterior that Jess liked. "How are the arrangements going in your Embassy?" she asked.

"Oh, fine," said Xiao Li. "The President is a friend of our Ambassador's. She's anxious to make sure everything goes smoothly."

I'm sure she is, Jess thought. The Ambassador would be on the first plane back to Beijing if anything went wrong during the visit, or any embarrassment was caused to the President. The Chinese were sticklers for protocol. The humiliation of losing face would not be tolerated.

Jess looked around for Sam but couldn't see him anywhere. "Come with me," she said. "I'll get us some drinks."

Xiao Li touched her arm. "I need to talk to you."

Jess stopped.

"Not here." Xiao Li lowered her voice. "I need to talk to you privately."

Now it was Jess's turn to look puzzled.

"Can we meet somewhere tomorrow?" Xiao Li whispered. "Just you and me."

Immediately alarm bells started ringing in Jess's head. It was unusual for a Chinese official to want to meet and talk privately. "Where did you have in mind?" she asked.

"In a café, perhaps?"

Jess tensed. Was this going to be an approach for information? A defection even? If so, she would need to inform her boss.

Xiao Li must have sensed her unease. "I just want to talk to you about something that happened in my country a long while ago."

Jess relaxed a bit. "In that case, I think you'd be better off talking to someone with more experience of China than me. I could arrange a meeting for you with my boss, Giles."

A fearful look flitted across Xiao Li's face. "No, I don't want to talk to anyone else. I feel, well, I feel I know you, Jessica. But … well, if you can't, I would understand."

Jess wasn't sure what to do. No communist official had approached her in this way before. She'd been trained to expect it, but the request didn't seem in the least bit suspicious or threatening. Quite the reverse. Xiao Li seemed more upset than anything. "Are you coming to the final visit planning meeting in the morning?" Jess asked

"Yes."

"Well, let's walk along Whitehall afterwards. We could get a coffee in the Italian café in Villiers Street, if you'd like."

Xiao Li nodded. "We will need to go separately. I will meet you in the café." Then she looked over Jess's shoulder and went quiet.

Jess turned to see the Chinese Ambassador heading in their direction. "Good evening, Ambassador," she said.

"Good evening, Miss Turner."

Jess looked into Mrs Wu's coolly appraising dark eyes. Every strand of her sleek black hair was severely drawn back into a clasp, exposing her slender forehead and porcelain skin. For a woman who had to be in her 50s or 60s and held a prestigious Ambassadorial post, she was ageing well. Her navy woollen suit and silk blouse were business-like enough, but she drew attention to her status with sparkling diamond earrings and a chunky gold necklace. There was something about the woman, a regal air that set her apart from her colleagues. Jess didn't know Ambassador Wu very well because she'd only been in post for a few weeks. It was unusual to change Ambassadors so close to the arrival of a Head of State but, as Xiao Li had said, Ambassador Wu was a friend of the President's and influential in Chinese politics. The President obviously wanted her in London for his visit.

Jess held out her hand. "I hope you are well, Ambassador?"

"Very well, Miss Turner." The Ambassador shook her hand, with a light grasp. "Are all the visit arrangements in place now?"

Jess nodded. "I believe so. If there are any wrinkles, they'll be ironed out at our last planning meeting tomorrow morning. Will you be attending?"

Ambassador Wu shook her head. "Xiao Li will represent us. I have another engagement."

The sound of a spoon urgently rapping on crystal made everyone turn. The PUS, Sir Anthony Chalmers, a renowned Chinese scholar and former British Ambassador to Peking, stood on the marble steps at one side of the Court, ready to say a few words of welcome. He looked distinguished in his tailored suit, polished shoes, and neatly combed grey hair. Jess had met him several times, but she didn't feel she knew him. By reputation, Sir Anthony had a formidable intellect and was approachable and polite, yet he had the nickname 'Tiger' around the building. She'd once asked a colleague, who knew him well, why that nickname had stuck. "You have only to look in his black eyes," her colleague explained. "They burn into you, and only leave you once you've been devoured." Jess had laughed at the time. "No empathy, then?" Her colleague shook her head. "He's a man who doesn't care too much for other people. If you do your job well, he'll be okay with you. If not…"

Now, as Jess surveyed the guests while Sir Anthony spoke, there was a feeling in the room she couldn't explain, a kind of tension that was more than the sum of everyone's exhaustion. The Chinese trade delegation was there, as well as many well-known British captains of industry, plus all the most eminent sinologists in the Foreign Office. Even Sir Anthony was a sinologist, emphasising the importance of Sino–British relations in the organisation.

Her mind reverted to what Sam had said about her boss Giles once being earmarked for the position. Must be hard for him to watch Sir Anthony in the top job, she thought. What on earth did Giles *do* all those years ago in Peking to get himself sent home? Had he blotted his copybook for ever? Curiosity made her look around for him, to watch his reaction to the PUS making a speech. But she couldn't see him anywhere. Or Sam, come to that.

Her eyes continued scanning the assembled guests for Giles and Sam as she threaded her way quietly to the far end of Durbar Court where there were several adjoining offices. She stopped dead when she spotted the two men. They'd slipped out of the reception and into one of those offices. What on earth were they doing? With the door closed, she could only watch them through the glass window, but they were facing each other, hands gesticulating wildly. It looked like they were arguing, although she couldn't hear what they were saying. She moved closer for a better look.

Suddenly she saw Giles push Sam hard in the chest, sending him reeling back onto the floor.

She gasped as Giles stood over Sam, fists clenched. Then he hesitated, turned and stormed out of the office.

The sudden noise of the crowd clapping at the end of Sir Anthony's speech made her turn. And when she looked back, Sam had gone too.

Immediately she turned to go and look for Sam, to see if he was all right. But she felt a tug on her sleeve.

Xiao Li had followed her. "You won't forget our meeting tomorrow, will you?" she asked, anxiously.

"No … no, of course not."

Xiao Li noticed her distraction. "It's very important, Jessica." She paused. "You know I said I needed to talk to you about something that happened in my country a long time ago?" Xiao Li glanced over her shoulder and turned back. "Well, it's about the disappearance of Marianne Henderson."

Jess frowned.

"Have you ever heard the name Marianne Henderson?" Xiao Li asked.

Jess thought hard. "I don't think so."

"She was a British diplomat," Xiao Li said. "In 1984, she was sent to Shanghai to open a new British Consulate-General. Some months later she disappeared and was never seen again."

Jess stared at her. "I've never even heard of Marianne Henderson, let alone anything about a British diplomat going missing in China."

"Exactly." Xiao Li's voice was urgent. "That's why I want to talk to you. I have some information about Marianne." She hesitated. "But please don't mention it to anyone else until we've spoken tomorrow. It's very important that you don't." And then she was off, weaving her way through the guests back towards the Chinese Ambassador.

Jess watched her go, more puzzled than ever. Marianne Henderson? The name meant nothing to her. If a British diplomat had gone missing in China, she'd have heard about it, surely? Every officer who was killed, assassinated, or even in serious trouble of some kind went down in the organisation's history, like folklore. Perhaps Xiao Li had got it wrong?

Jess looked around again, but neither Giles nor Sam had come back into the room. She noticed that all the guests were chatting and laughing now, and much more relaxed after a couple of drinks. Time to go, she thought. She strolled over to the door, looked over her shoulder to see if anyone was watching, and slipped out. She'd done her duty by attending the reception. Now she had to go and finish the briefing.

As she walked back to her office, she kept turning the name Marianne Henderson over and over in her mind, but it didn't ring any bells. She would have a go at searching the electronic archives later, although she didn't expect to find anything. If the woman had gone missing in 1984, as Xiao Li said, that was before the electronic archives had been set up.

Still, there was someone who would be far more useful than any archive. Sam! If anyone would know anything about a British diplomat going missing in China, it was him. She needed to talk to him anyway to find out what that scuffle between him and Giles was all about. Honestly, what were the pair of them playing at in full view of everyone? Fortunately, all the guests had had their backs to that office window as they listened to Sir Anthony. But had *he* seen the pair of them arguing? Jess hoped not, for their sakes.

3

The cautious seldom err
(Confucius − Chinese philosopher, 551-479 BC)

Giles Pettiford stepped out of the Foreign Office and into the dark night. The freezing air, mixed with city exhaust fumes, caught in his throat and he coughed. He was feeling rather fragile this evening, as if going down with a cold. That was unusual. He never got colds. He had no time for them. Far too busy. He flung his woollen scarf around his neck and looked up at the sky. The soft sleet was slowing, but the pavement was still wet with the slushy residue. He could jump into a taxi, he thought; that would be the quickest way of getting back to his London home in this weather. But he felt the need for some air after a long day cooped up inside. A short walk across the park to St James's underground station would be just the thing to clear his head.

Turning right, he marched along the slippery pavement until he reached Clive Steps and tried to run down them in his usual way. He managed to stay upright until about halfway down when the sole of his right shoe slipped from under him. Arms flailing, he tumbled down the rest of the steps and ended up in a heap at the bottom. For a moment, he sat surprised on the wet pavement as water seeped through his trousers. Embarrassed, he looked around to see if anyone had seen him, even before checking if he'd hurt himself or not. Thankfully, he was both unhurt and alone. He sprang up and brushed himself down. Dignity restored, he crossed over Horse Guards Road and into St James's Park.

The shock of falling down the steps was nothing compared to the humiliation of being told to apply for early retirement. That conversation with the Director of HR had taken place a week ago, and Giles still shuddered at the thought of it. He'd been offered the best possible financial package to allow him to retire comfortably, and the Director had even suggested he'd help him find a well-paid job in the City. The sheer cheek of it.

Giles had refused the offer, of course, except it hadn't really been an offer. Immediately he'd said no, the Director's sympathetic expression turned hostile. Giles could either leave on the best possible terms and financial package, or he could look forward to a job that was a step down from the one he had now. The way in which the Director had set out the options came across more as a threat than a request.

Giles had been in a state of disbelief for a couple of days afterwards, which had eventually turned into a kind of numbness. That conversation, and the way it had been delivered, felt like a dagger in his back. He knew he was doing a good job. He always had. His performance and commitment were head and shoulders above others, including Sir Anthony bloody Chalmers. He should have been promoted to the top job before *him*. Now, all Giles's hopes, ambitions, not to mention a lifetime's work, had ended in one 15-minute conversation. The thought of retirement made him feel physically sick. What would he do with his time? His wife had forged her own friendships and interests while he'd been working and wouldn't want him hanging around the house. Anyway, he'd been promising her a top Ambassadorial post in Paris, or Washington, or Beijing, where she would have important representational duties too. He couldn't bear to see the disappointment in her eyes when he told her he was being put out to pasture. Couldn't bear her disappointment in him.

Now, that numbness was finally giving way to a burning fury at the injustice of it all. A hot tear slipped from his eye and mingled with the freezing sleet on his cheeks as he powered along. They were going to side-line him if he didn't go, make a fool of him. How dare they.

A scuffling noise in the darkness pulled him up short. He'd been so deep in thought, he hadn't been aware of his surroundings.

A loud hiss, followed by furious flapping, carried towards him on the breeze.

A Canada goose; those birds were aggressive if provoked, and he'd disturbed it in the dark. He stood quietly so as not to threaten the bird, until he heard it move away and splash into the lake.

As he walked out of the Park, the sleet started falling more heavily again, but he was too busy thinking and formulating a plan to notice. It was fortunate the traffic was light in the bad weather because he didn't even look before crossing the road. The fury he was feeling now fuelled rage. A powerful, all-consuming rage.

He'd been out-manoeuvred. He *knew* why. And he knew who was doing this to him.

They'd made a deal all those years ago, in Shanghai. He'd promised to keep his silence, and he had. But now he was being quietly side-lined.

Well, no one was going to do that to him.

He ran up Cockpit Steps and headed for the underground. His heart sank as lots of people milled around the station entrance reading a blackboard. He managed to get to the front, only to read that the District Line was closed again owing to signal failure.

Never mind, he thought, as he followed everyone down the packed escalator. It might take longer, but he could get on the Circle Line instead. As he stood among the crowds on the platform waiting for the train, he plotted his revenge. He had nothing to lose now. If he was forced to go, he'd take that bastard with him. The very thought of it made him feel calmer, happier even.

Now, he could feel the wind from an approaching train pushing through the tunnel. He stepped forward, anxious to get on first and find a seat.

The wind was getting stronger. He could see the train's lights looming out of the darkness.

Suddenly he felt a sharp blow in-between his shoulder blades.

He gasped as he toppled.

Oh, my God!

The realisation hit him…

All he could hear was screaming, as he tumbled forward onto the rails.

4

Study the past, if you would divine the future
(Confucius)

Jess pressed the print key on her computer and sat back with a yawn. It was just after 9pm by her watch, and hardly worth going home since she had to be back for 8am the next morning. Pity she couldn't stay over, especially on such a foul night. Still, at least the briefing was finished. That was a huge relief.

She stretched her aching shoulders and shook her hands to get the feeling back into her numb fingers. Too much typing. Or was it the cold? She got up and went over to feel the radiator under the window. Stone cold. She wriggled her freezing toes and pulled the net curtain back to see what the weather was doing outside. Staring out into the darkness, only the black sky of night was visible from her second-floor office, but at least it had stopped sleeting. She went over to the door, lifted her padded coat off the hook and put it on to warm up.

While the fifty pages of briefing printed, she started packing up her classified papers and thought about her big day tomorrow. The briefing would be distributed first thing to the Foreign Secretary, the Prime Minister, Sir Anthony, and anyone else who needed to see it. It was nerve-racking waiting to find out if that would be up to scratch, but it was the final visit planning meeting tomorrow too. She needed a good night's sleep to be ready for all that. Except, there was so much swirling around in her head, she doubted she'd get one.

And she had that meeting with Xiao Li to think about too. Why would she want to talk to Jess privately about a British diplomat going missing in Shanghai all those years ago? The thought made her uneasy. It wasn't sensible on security grounds to go and meet a Chinese diplomat alone, especially when it all sounded so mysterious. She wouldn't want to do anything to compromise the Chinese President's visit in any way. On the other hand, she felt inclined to go since Xiao Li wanted to give her information. What harm could a quick coffee do, in a public café? She would talk to her boss Giles before she went, just to be on the safe side.

She went back to her computer, typed the name Marianne Henderson into the archive search box, and waited. Not a single reference to the missing woman came up. Not surprising since it happened so long ago. She paused to count back through the years – 34 to be precise, which meant the paper files were more likely to yield results than the electronic records. She thought of Sam and all the old files in his Library and Records Department. He would certainly know if a British diplomat had gone missing in Shanghai too. Trouble was, Xiao Li had asked her not to mention Marianne Henderson's name to anyone until they'd spoken. That was a dilemma.

When the printer finally stopped, she went over and collected all the loose pages of the briefing. Checking they were all there, she slipped them into a folder and put it in her cupboard. The Registry Clerk would make photocopies and distribute a briefing pack to everyone in the morning. She shut the metal cupboard door and spun the combination lock to keep everything safe overnight.

Before leaving, she stepped out of her black high-heels and into her long boots. She was glad she'd put them on before leaving the flat that morning. Their thick rubbery soles would be perfect for the icy pavements after that sleet. She kicked her shoes under the desk and flung her scarf around her neck. Turning at the door to check everything was properly locked away, she flicked off the light and headed home.

At the main staircase, she walked down the plush red carpet, past gold-framed portraits of former Foreign Secretaries hanging on the walls. On the ground floor, she hesitated. A hot bath and bed beckoned, but she couldn't stop thinking about Xiao Li and Marianne Henderson. On instinct, she went down another flight of stairs to the basement, to see if Sam was still around. He worked late most evenings. She wanted to check he was okay after that dust-up with Giles, and to find out what they'd been arguing about. That meeting with Xiao Li was gnawing away at her too.

In the basement, she walked along the corridor, peering into dark offices as she passed by. It was silent, except for the rubbery soles of her boots squeaking on the tiled floor. Everyone had gone home, and the old building was gloomy. Of course, she'd heard the gossip about the place being haunted. Over the years, staff working through the night had reported seeing ghostly apparitions stalking the corridors. Jess had never seen anything like that, but she did feel a heavy atmosphere that seemed to wrap itself around her the minute she entered the building. Mind you, with so many people having worked there over the centuries – good people, troubled people, bad people even – they must have left something of themselves behind, surely? If she had to explain that atmosphere to anyone, she would have called it the weight of history.

She was disappointed to find Sam's office in darkness. She'd been hoping for a chat and a hot cup of Chinese tea before braving the cold. He'd adopted the habit of officials in China and kept an electric kettle and Chinese tea pot on a tray by his desk.

Like everyone else, Sam had locked away his papers and files, and left his office door open to allow the overnight security officers to carry out their regular patrols and checks. Jess pushed the door open wide to let the corridor light shine in. Sam's office was like a Chinese emporium. Apart from a map of the world on the far wall, and a detailed one of China next to it, the rest of the walls were lined with his personal Chinese paintings and scrolls. All other surfaces, even the tops of filing cabinets, were covered with Chinese trinkets. Sam called it his Chinese collection of tat, all of which he'd picked up for a song in various markets during his trips to China over the years.

Jess looked at her favourite piece on his desk, a lovely red lacquer vase that stood next to the photo of his Chinese wife and child. He'd met his wife in Peking, married her much later, and eventually brought her back to England. Their son was now grown up and at university. Not that Jess had met either of them. She just felt she knew them, since Sam talked about them all the time.

Another object Jess liked was the antique Chinese dagger that Sam used as a letter opener. It couldn't be more than four or five inches long. The sheath and handle were in black leather, with an ornate brass decoration. She pulled the dagger out of the sheath, to reveal a thin, pointed blade. There could be no doubt Sam loved all things Chinese.

She put the dagger back on his desk and sighed. There was no putting it off now. She had to brave the weather and go home.

Back on the ground floor, she walked to the main Foreign Office entrance that led into King Charles Street. "Goodnight," she said to the Security Officer as she passed.

"Night love. Take care. It's slippery out there."

The wind stung her face as she went out into the street. She pulled up the furry hood of her padded coat, which was probably made in China too, she thought wryly.

Her foggy breath led the way as she hurried along the pavement on that freezing night. The sleet had stopped, and the sky was clear. An almost full moon shone brightly. She decided to walk to the underground and get the tube home to St John's Wood, but then spotted a number 159 bus that would take her almost all the way there. She broke into a jog to try and catch it, although the pavement was too slippery to run fast.

The bus driver saw her, and kindly waited at the bus stop.

Jess jumped on, breathing hard from the exercise and frigid air in her lungs. "Thank you," she said to the driver, a small Asian man who sat so low in his seat he could barely see over the steering wheel.

He nodded and pulled the bus away.

Jess swiped her Oyster card and walked to a seat a few rows behind the driver. She pushed her hood back and stared out the window at the dark night.

The pavements were empty in Whitehall, as most civil servants had gone home hours ago. It was busier around Trafalgar Square, where people had come out for the evening to see the Christmas tree lit up. It was a cheerful sight on such a wintry night. She sat still and silent, letting the warmth of the bus and the relaxation wash over her. As the bright shop windows, decorated with fairy lights and tinsel, slid past, her eyelids became heavy, until Xiao Li popped into her head again. She sat up and pulled her iPhone out of her coat pocket. She wasn't allowed to use it in the office, for security reasons. She would search the Internet now and see if there was anything about a British diplomat going missing in Shanghai in 1984.

She typed in the name Marianne Henderson. Up came a lot of photos and Facebook accounts for women and girls with that name. She scrolled through a few before deciding that was pointless.

She typed in several other variations, such as *Marianne Henderson and Shanghai*. Nothing. *Marianne Henderson missing in Shanghai 1984*. Nothing. *British diplomat missing in Shanghai*. Nothing.

However, when she typed in *British diplomat and Shanghai 1984*, just one entry popped up.

Top diplomat in Shanghai suicide
*British Ambassador takes his own life. Guardian report ...
1984*

Jess stared at the entry and frowned. 1984 was the same year Marianne Henderson was supposed to have gone missing in the city.

She clicked onto the link. Up came 'Page cannot be reached'. She tried again and again, but it was still the same – 'Page cannot be reached'. She tried typing in a whole different set of search criteria about a British Ambassador committing suicide in Shanghai in 1984. Whichever way she tried it, nothing else came up.

Irritated, she pushed her iPhone back into her coat pocket. First, she's told a British diplomat went missing in Shanghai in 1984. Then she discovers the British Ambassador committed suicide in the same city, in the same year. Unbelievable! In the morning, she would have a word with Sam, and then talk to her boss Giles. They should have told her about this before.

Looking up, she suddenly became aware of two eyes staring at her through the reflection in the dark panel of the driver's seat. She pulled her bag closer. She wanted to look round to see who was sitting behind her, but she didn't. There were too many nutters roaming the streets of London, and she didn't want to draw attention to herself. Best ignore them. As a woman on her own in London, she was always aware of her own safety.

As the bus pulled into Oxford Street and stopped, most people got off through the middle doors. To her relief, the 'eyes' disappeared from the seat reflection. She turned to have a quick look as the doors closed, unsure if that person staring at her had got off or moved to the back of the bus. It was impossible to tell.

She stayed alert as the bus made its way north, and eventually pulled into a regular stop near Lord's cricket ground. Jess got off, went behind the bus, and crossed over the road. From the other side, she glanced back. To her relief, no one else got off the bus.

She shivered as a strong gust of wind blew in her face. She pulled up her hood again and set off along the northern perimeter road of Regent's Park. The pavement glittered in the moonlight as she hurried along to the flat she shared with Simon. It would be wonderful to get home and find him there, but she knew that wasn't going to happen. He was rarely in London these days. Still, the flat would be warm since she'd timed the heating to come on hours ago. That spurred her on.

She found herself walking along the pavement next to the open park. The grass looked white with freezing sleet, and the blackness beyond dark and threatening. She crossed over the road, to the side where apartment blocks lined the pavement and street lamps lit the way.

She looked around. Not a soul about. She wished she was already tucked up in bed after a hot bath and meal.

A soft noise behind made her stiffen. Was that a footstep?

Reaching her apartment block, she almost ran up the driveway, rummaging in her bag for her door keys as she went. As she sprinted up the icy steps to the front door, her foot slipped from under her. Arms flailing, she tumbled backwards, cracking her head on the bottom step as she landed.

Suddenly, light flooded the forecourt as the front door clicked open. "Are you okay?" a woman shouted.

Jess lay dazed on the wet ground.

The woman came out and crouched down beside her. "What happened?"

"I–I fell down the steps … hit my head."

"Can you stand up?"

Head throbbing, Jess pulled herself up onto her knees.

"Come on, let's get you inside," the woman said as she picked up Jess's bag for her. "It's freezing out here." She helped Jess to her feet, put her arm around her waist to support her up the steps and through the front door.

"Thank you," Jess whispered, as they reached the lobby.

The woman glanced outside, then shut the front door firmly behind them. "I'm Beverly," she said, cheerfully. "Although everyone calls me Bev." She smiled at Jess. "I don't think we've met before. I'm renting that flat." She pointed to an open door on the ground floor. "Why don't you come in and let me have a look at your head?"

Jess was in no fit state to refuse such kindness. "Thank you," she said, as Bev helped her into her flat.

★

Later, Jess sat with her feet up on Bev's sofa, eating a plate of Thai chicken curry. The warmth from the central heating, the spicy food and red wine were reviving her quickly.

Bev had already eaten, and sat in an armchair opposite, sipping her wine. "How's the head now?" she asked.

"Much better, thanks." Jess smiled at her angel of mercy. "That has to be an Australian accent you've got there."

Bev smiled. "Yeah, I'm from Oz."

"Which part?"

"The Hunter Valley, just north of Sydney." Bev paused. "Do you know it?"

Jess nodded. "I spent several years working in Australia, in Canberra actually."

"Poor you," Bev joked.

Jess smiled, knowing many Australians had a jaundiced view of Canberra, the Federal Capital. They didn't like government bureaucrats, paying Federal taxes, or the cold weather there. "Have you moved to the UK now?" she asked.

Bev shook her head. "Not permanently. I'm over here partly on business and partly on holiday. I've taken a six-month rental on this flat." She paused. "It's a great location, overlooking Regent's Park."

It was the first time Jess had ever been in this flat, despite walking past the front door every day. It certainly looked like a rental, with its magnolia-painted walls and beige carpet. There were a couple of prints hanging on the walls, no doubt provided by the owner, but there were no ornaments or any personal effects anywhere in the room. She'd seen a middle-aged man coming out of the flat once or twice in previous weeks, but all he could manage was a 'morning' or 'evening' whenever she'd said hello. She didn't know if he was the owner or not. No one seemed to socialise in the block.

"I went for a jog in the park today," Bev went on. "We don't get this kind of weather in New South Wales. The crisp, pale winter sky, the bare trees, the frozen earth. It's amazing. The frost on the pavement looked like a lace veil this morning."

Jess smiled. "Lethal too, if you fall over."

Bev's eyes shone as she laughed.

Jess studied her new neighbour. She looked fit, despite her slight frame. Probably from all that jogging. She wasn't young though – in her 50s or 60s maybe? Her short silver-grey hair framed a face that was lined and freckled. A weathered skin from a life outdoors in the Australian sun perhaps?

Bev frowned. "Are you sure you don't want to go to A&E and get checked out? I've got a car parked outside."

Jess shook her head. "It's kind of you to offer, but I can see straight now."

"You'll probably have a cracker of a headache tomorrow." Bev frowned. "Why were you running in this icy weather?"

"You saw me?"

Bev nodded. "I was looking out the window. The scene was so beautiful, like something out of a Sherlock Holmes movie, with the moon behind the trees and a frosty mist coming down."

"Did you see anyone behind me?" Jess asked.

Bev looked puzzled. "I saw you rush up the drive and fall down the steps. That's when I came out."

Jess shrugged. "I thought, well, I just thought I heard a noise behind me, that's all."

Bev frowned. "You mean someone was *following* you?"

Jess really didn't know what she meant. "Something or someone rattled me while I was walking along Prince Albert Road." She shrugged. "It was probably just my imagination."

Bev got up and looked out the window. "I can't see anyone out there now," she said, and snapped the Venetian blinds closed.

Jess felt comfortable in Bev's company. Like most Australians, she was down to earth and easy to talk to, with no pretence or holding back. Chatting to Bev reminded her how much she'd enjoyed living in Oz. She found herself telling Bev all about her job as a diplomat and the Chinese President's State visit. Bev listened quietly, until Jess realised she'd been talking too much about herself. "So, Bev, what do you do?" she asked.

Bev smiled. "Wine's my trade. We have a vineyard in the Hunter Valley."

"A vineyard? That sounds wonderful."

Bev nodded. "We started off just planting vines and growing the grapes for other wine producers. Now, we have a winery on the estate too, and make our own wine. That's why I'm over here, to find a UK distributor we can export to."

That explained Bev's weathered skin, Jess thought. She looked the part of an Australian farmer, in her jeans and T-shirt too. "It must be satisfying starting a business like that from scratch and growing it to produce your own wine?"

Bev nodded. "Things worked out just fine for me."

Jess noticed Bev talking about 'we' all the time. She probably had a family, although she wasn't wearing a wedding ring. But Jess didn't want to go there. Bev would then ask about her family, and Jess still couldn't bring herself to talk about Jack and Amy. The awful nightmare of their car accident and deaths still woke her up at night. Seven long years ago, and it had hardly receded from her mind. She doubted it ever would. "Well," she looked at her watch, "I'd better go up to my flat and get some sleep. I have to get up at 6 o'clock in the morning."

Bev looked concerned. "Will you be okay?"

Jess nodded. "I'll be fine after some sleep. I have a lot of work to do tomorrow."

Bev gave her something of a wistful smile. "Well, don't hesitate to ring if you need me." She got up and went over to her handbag. "Here." She pulled out a business card. "My mobile number's on there."

"Thank you." Jess pulled out one of her own cards. "Here's mine. I live on the second floor, in flat 6. You'll have to come and have a meal with me one night, when this State visit is over."

Bev smiled. "I'd like that."

"Good," Jess struggled to get off the sofa. Not because she was still feeling dizzy. She was so comfortable, she didn't want to move. "That curry was delicious, Bev. Did you make it?"

"Yes, I had a walk up the Finchley Road, to Waitrose, to get some shopping."

"Looks like you already know your way around."

Bev nodded. "You sure you're okay?"

"Yes."

They said their goodbyes, and Jess climbed the stairs to her flat. It was very late now, so she would just have a hot bath and go to bed. She felt so much better since going into Bev's. It would be great having her as a neighbour, even for a few months. At the weekends, she could take Bev around the London sights, and perhaps catch a show.

As she entered her flat and switched on the lights, a thought popped into her head that wouldn't go away. When they'd met in the lobby, Bev had immediately introduced herself, but Jess couldn't remember introducing *herself*. Yet Bev had called her Jess from the start.

How did Bev know who she was?

5

Happiness is not something ready-made, it comes from your own actions.

(Dalai Lama XIV – Tibetan Spiritual Leader)

Detective Inspector Tom Sangster felt a familiar buzz of excitement, mixed with apprehension, as the police car turned into the Embankment, on its way to the new home of Scotland Yard. He loved London – the history, the crowds, the galleries, the theatre. Spending three months on secondment to the Metropolitan Police had been the best experience he'd ever had while serving in the Australian Federal Police. His only regret was that it would all be over in a week or two when his secondment was due to end.

As the morning light cast an amber glow through leafless trees onto frosty pavements, he realised just how much he felt at home in this city. He put that down partly to the dynamism of London, and partly to family heritage. His mother and father had been born in the UK and emigrated in 1969. He'd been born five years later in Australia. He'd always felt half English, mostly because his parents talked about England all the time, and about returning to live here one day. They never did, but it was a constant longing, until they died.

There was a particular reason why he felt apprehensive today. He was going to see Jess.

When he'd found out he was coming to the UK, he'd wanted to get in touch straightaway and tell her. Yet every time he sat down to send an email, he couldn't quite think of the right thing to say. He decided that it would be easier to contact her once he was in the UK. The trouble was they'd become close during their time together in the Caribbean; too close as things turned out. In the end, she'd returned to the UK to be with her sick partner. Tom knew now that he and Jess would only ever be friends, but the nagging desire to see her persisted. Yet, even though his secondment was nearly over, he still hadn't contacted her, immersing himself in work instead.

And what a job it was – in the Met protection team. The same work he'd been doing as a Federal Agent in Canberra for the last couple of years, on the Australian Prime Minister's close protection team. It had been exciting and interesting to go everywhere with the PM as one of his bodyguards – the high life, the parties, the sporting events. Fantastic.

So, when his boss in the Met told him last night that he wanted him to take the place of a sick colleague on the protection team covering the Chinese President's State visit, Tom had been over the moon. What a great way to end his secondment. It would look good on his CV back in Canberra too. But, when he saw the list of participants attending the final visit planning meeting at the Foreign Office today, he could hardly believe his eyes.

There was Jess! Now the Head of the China Section, and directly involved in the President's visit.

Fate, it seems, had taken the decision to contact her out of his hands.

He pulled his ever-present sketchpad out of his pocket. Sketching was a passion. His colleagues in Oz all knew about it and pulled his leg relentlessly. When he'd joined the PM's close protection team, his boss came up with the code-name 'Picasso' for him. They all thought it was hilarious, and he'd seen the funny side of it too. He hadn't mentioned anything about sketching to his new colleagues in Scotland Yard though.

Last Sunday, he'd found himself with a rare day off work, and strolled around the streets of London. After lunch in a pub just off Trafalgar Square, he went into the National Gallery, a place he'd always wanted to visit. He saw, of all things, an exhibition of Australian impressionists. Those light-filled landscapes of coast and red bushland were dazzling compared to the darkness of a British winter. No wonder the Brits were such a cynical bunch, he thought. While at the Gallery, he'd been surprised to find he was permitted to sketch there. Out came the sketchpad and graphite pencil he carried constantly in his pocket, and he'd spent the entire day studying and sketching some masterpieces. He'd enjoyed it so much, he planned to go back on his next day off.

He flicked to the back of the sketchpad and pulled out the last sketch he'd done of Jess in the Caribbean. Portraits were his speciality, and he kept this one with him all the time because it was the most technically competent sketch he'd ever done. At least, that's what he told himself.

Once again, he studied Jess's eyes and smile.

They'd worked together on two murder cases now. The first, when she was the British Consul in Australia. The second, when she was the Head of the Governor's Office in the Turks and Caicos Islands, in the Caribbean.

God, what a surreal experience the Turks and Caicos had been. The Islands were beautiful, like a film set. The hurricane had been devastating though, and the murders brutal.

And Jess … well, she'd just been Jess. Persistent. Resolute. Determined to uncover the truth. How they'd both survived all that, he'd never know.

He smiled at the sketch. Now, he was really looking forward to seeing her again, but worried too. He didn't want to walk into the meeting and give her a shock. Or would it be a pleasant surprise? He hoped the latter. As he sat there mulling it all over, he regretted not getting in touch sooner. She would think he hadn't wanted to see her.

He pulled out his iPhone and found her mobile number. His finger hovered over the 'call' button. No, he couldn't ring her out of the blue now. She would probably be on her way to work or up to her eyes getting everything ready for the meeting. An email perhaps? Again, he hesitated. What was he going to say? 'Hi, see you at 10 o'clock this morning'. No, he couldn't do that either. He put his phone back in his pocket as the car pulled up outside Scotland Yard.

He'd just have to surprise her. In truth, he really wanted to see her reaction. Or did he?

6

*Real knowledge is to know the extent of one's ignorance
(Confucius)*

The note Jess found on her desk when she arrived that
morning was unusual. Sir Anthony wanted to see her
immediately she got in. The note was written by hand,
in caps, on a large sheet of white paper, with the word
'immediately' underlined. Instinctively, she knew it
couldn't be good news. In the normal pecking order, he
would speak to her boss, Giles. So why did he want to see
her? And why so urgently? She toyed with the idea that the
Chinese President's visit had been cancelled. A couple of
months ago, that would have been a blessing. Now, with all
the hard work done, it would be disappointing.

She hung her coat on the hook behind the door and
took off her boots. On waking that morning, she'd taken
one look out of the window at the frosty scene in Regent's
Park, anticipated the travel chaos, and called a taxi. That
had saved her 30 minutes. Now, finding this note on her
desk, she was glad she had.

She opened her combination-lock cupboard, pulled out
the briefing, and hurried through the connecting door into
the general office in her stockinged feet. Relief flooded

through her when she saw the Registry Clerk's coat on the back of the chair. He was probably in the communal kitchen making some coffee. That was his daily ritual. She put the briefing on his desk, with a note asking him to start the photocopying.

Her ringing phone interrupted, and she ran back into her office to answer it. "Hello?"

"Did you see my note?"

Jess recognised the voice of Sir Anthony's Private Secretary. "Yes," she said. "I've just stepped in."

"Sir Anthony is waiting."

"I'm on my way."

The phone went dead in her ear. Jess ducked under the desk and fished out her high heels. She hadn't taken her jacket off, so she was ready to go. She glanced at her hair in the mirror hanging by the door. Still tidy, thanks to the taxi ride.

Immediately, she stopped by Giles's office, hoping he might know what Sir Anthony wanted. Better to be forewarned than go into the tiger's den blind. But his office was in darkness, and that was unusual. Giles was always in first.

Jess ran down the stairs to the ground floor, walked along the corridor, and into Sir Anthony's Private Office. The cupboards were open, and the Private Secretary's desk covered with papers, but he wasn't there. Probably still going around the building leaving hand-written notes on desks, she thought. She went over to the connecting door to Sir Anthony's Office, wondering whether to go in unannounced. She peered around the half-open door.

Sir Anthony stood, hands in trouser pockets, staring out of a huge bay window onto Horse Guards Parade. The large room was gloomy on this early winter morning, the only light beaming from his desk lamp. Shoulders hunched, he looked deep in thought.

Sensing her presence, he glanced sideways.

"Jess Turner," she said, seeing his confusion. "Head of the China Section. You wanted to see me?"

"Ah, yes." He gestured to a chair by his desk and made his way slowly around the other side.

Something about the gravity in his voice was worrying. But when he sat down opposite her, and she saw the colour had drained from his face and lips, she was really on edge.

He clasped his hands together on the desk, as if to steady them. "Have you heard the news this morning?"

Jess quickly sifted through the items she could remember from the 6 o'clock radio news bulletin. Nothing especially relevant sprang to mind.

"A man was killed at St James's Park underground station last night," he went on. "Fell onto the tracks … under a train."

Jess sat very still. In the silence, she could hear nothing but the loud tick of the grandfather clock in the corner of the room.

"It was Giles," he said.

"*Giles?*"

"Yes. On his way home."

She sat stunned.

Sir Anthony sat quietly too, as if waiting for her to process the news, or perhaps still not quite believing it himself.

"I'm so sorry," she said after a while. "That's terrible." Her words sounded lame, but she really didn't know what else to say.

He nodded, as if he understood.

They sat in silence for a while longer, until Jess pictured the gruesome scene on the rail track. "Are they *sure* it was Giles? I mean … you know, if he went under a train."

"Yes. He was carrying his driving licence and other documents."

Jess shuddered, wanting nothing more than to get out of this oppressive office, with its gloomy, book-lined walls and dark, antique furniture, and away from the black pools of eyes boring into her from across the desk. She held her nerve. "How did it happen?" she asked.

Sir Anthony ran his hand over his grey hair. "The Police will tell us when they know. They investigate every suicide on the underground."

"Suicide? Is that what they think?"

He shrugged. "Does that surprise you?"

She paused for a moment. "Frankly, yes. Giles never struck me as the kind of man who would commit suicide." She searched for the right words. "He was so … well, so energetic, and purposeful in everything he did."

"People have their demons." Sir Anthony looked down at his clasped hands. "Of course, Giles was nearing the end of his career. That might have driven him to do something out of character."

Sam had told her that HR was trying to push Giles into early retirement. Would that drive a man to throw himself under a train? Possibly, but not Giles, surely? "I've heard talk about HR wanting him to take early retirement," she said, "but I find it hard to believe Giles would take his own life over that." She hesitated. "And the manner of his death was so, well, so public." When she looked up, Sir Anthony's eyes had narrowed to slits. That's when she realised *he* would have endorsed any decision to force Giles to take early retirement.

She fell silent.

The pause was excruciating, and she shifted in her seat.

After a while, he said: "You understand what this means for you, Jess, don't you?"

She looked at him. "Oh, the Chinese visit, you mean?"

"Yes." The colour had come back into his cheeks now, and he was back in control. "It falls to you in the Department to make sure everything runs smoothly." He paused. "Is the briefing ready?"

Typical, she thought. Giles was barely cold, and he was straight back to business. "Yes," she said, trying to keep the weariness out of her voice. "It's being photocopied now." Looking at her watch, she was surprised to see it was still only 8.30am. "You'll have your copy within the hour."

He nodded. "Good. I understand Protocol Department will chair the final programme planning meeting this morning?"

"Yes. At ten o'clock, in the main conference room."

"I'm sure I don't have to remind you how important this visit is, Jess."

His tone of voice left her in no doubt about that.

"We are all very sad and upset about Giles's death," he continued, "but this visit has to go on as planned. It's vitally important for our country and for our relationship with the Chinese. Nothing must go wrong." He gave her a pointed look. "It's your job to make sure everything runs like clockwork."

She looked away from those intense eyes and nodded.

"Good." He slapped both palms on his desk and heaved himself out of the chair.

That was her cue to go, and she stood up.

"I want to be kept fully informed of progress," he said. "If you have a problem, or if you're not sure about anything, talk to my Private Secretary. And if anyone steps out of line, refer them to me."

"Yes, Sir." She turned and walked to the door.

"I know you won't let me down, Jess."

There was an odd edge to his voice as he said that. Was it an attempt at kindness? Or a warning?

He gave a final nod, dismissing her.

She was glad to get out of his office, but her head was reeling. Suicide? Giles? She felt a sudden pang of sadness for the man. She hadn't liked him very much, but she wouldn't wish that on her worst enemy. His poor family would have to live with the shock of it forever too.

She walked along the corridor, hardly believing the situation she found herself in. Six months ago, she'd known nothing about China. Now, she was *the* China officer in the political department working on the most important Chinese State visit ever. Then, on the eve of the visit, the Head of Department dies under a tube train, leaving her in charge, and reporting directly to the Head of the Foreign Office. Some officers would be delighted to find themselves in the spotlight, with an opportunity to shine. But Jess couldn't shake off a deep sense of foreboding.

Still, at least she wasn't alone with all this. There *was* someone more qualified on Chinese affairs who would help her.

★

Sam Biggins's head was poised over an open newspaper on his desk, and the air filled with the scent of jasmine tea from the steaming mug standing next to it, when Jess walked into his office.

He looked up. "To what do I owe the pleasure so early in the morning?"

She slumped down on the chair opposite his desk. "Have you heard about Giles?"

The smile faded from his face.

"He died last night. Fell under a train at St James's underground station."

An involuntary shudder rippled through Sam.

"The Police think it was suicide."

Sam paled, his face as white as Sir Anthony's earlier. "How do you know?" he asked.

"Sir Anthony just called me down to his office to tell me. I came straight here."

Sam sat very still.

For a while, they just looked at each other.

Then Jess said: "I don't understand *why* Giles would commit suicide?"

Sam shrugged. "Me neither."

It wasn't the way Sam said, 'me neither', nor the nonchalant shrug he gave, that made her think he was lying. It was the way he blinked a couple of times when he tried to hold her gaze that sealed it.

"I saw you both arguing last night," she said.

A blush spread across Sam's freckled face and neck.

"Let's hope no one else did," she added. "So, what was it all about?"

Sam let out a deep sigh. "You know what sort of mood Giles was in when he came to your office earlier wanting the briefing."

She nodded, only too aware.

"He was very uptight about this visit." Sam looked at her. "It was just another of his stupid tantrums."

"It didn't look like a tantrum from where I stood," she said. "It looked more like a fight."

"It wasn't a fight."

"What was it, then?"

Sam picked up his fountain pen and started fiddling with it. "He was worried the visit was going to be a disaster. He didn't think, well, he didn't think … we could handle everything."

Now she knew exactly what he meant. "You mean Giles didn't think *I* could handle everything."

Sam shrugged. "He just thought you were a little inexperienced to be running things on the China front, that's all."

That came as no surprise to Jess. "He was right in a way, wasn't he?"

"You're doing just fine," Sam said. "Believe me, if anything, Giles was pissed off with me for not helping you more. He was reading the riot act."

Jess could well believe Giles was having a rant about her inexperience but that wouldn't have led to a physical shoving match. Was Sam holding something back? Somehow, she felt he was.

He got up, poured a second mug of jasmine tea, and put it down on the desk in front of her. "Here, drink this. You look awful."

"Thanks," she said, drily.

"I mean you look shocked. This'll warm you up."

She sipped the tea gratefully. "Sir Anthony seems to think Giles may have committed suicide because of this early retirement business."

Sam looked up. "He said that?"

"Well, not in as many words." She paused. "Giles didn't strike me as the kind of man who would commit suicide." She shook her head as if to reinforce her own thoughts. "Definitely not." She looked up at Sam, half expecting him to agree with her.

Instead he asked: "How's Sir Anthony taking it?"

"Pretty shocked. His face was deathly, and I noticed his hands trembling."

Sam nodded. "Suicide is shocking."

It suddenly occurred to Jess that everyone was assuming Giles had committed suicide. Even *she'd* relayed that message to Sam. But had he? Or was that what everyone was supposed to think? She looked at her watch again. She had to go back to her office and get ready for this meeting, but she still had a burning question she was determined to ask. "Now Giles is no longer here, will you tell me what he did to get himself sent home from Peking all those years ago?"

Sam's eyes clouded. "There's no point now in dragging that up again. It happened a long time ago."

His patronising tone infuriated her. "Tell me," she said. "What do you know about the disappearance of a British diplomat in Shanghai in 1984? And please don't tell me you don't know anything about Marianne Henderson either."

Sam looked startled, then guarded.

His reaction convinced Jess he knew exactly what she was talking about. "I've had a look in the electronic archives," she continued. "There's no reference to her in there. Not surprising really since it happened before they were created."

"Jess…"

"I need to know. I think it's important."

He looked at her.

"Please, Sam." She paused. "Or should I ask Sir Anthony instead?"

Sam sat for a while, clearly wrestling with his thoughts. Then he got up and went over to close the door. His face was grave when he sat back down at his desk. "I was told never to talk about this again, to anyone." His eyes pierced hers. "How did you find out about Marianne Henderson anyway?"

Something stopped her telling him about Xiao Li. "I read about her," she said.

It was his turn to look disbelieving.

"Look Sam." She sat forward on the chair. "I'm trying to do a job. I find myself increasingly on my own with everything. I need to know the background to what went on. I don't want to get things wrong, and I can't make a judgement if I'm being kept in the dark."

"What do you need to make a judgement about?"

She wanted to tell him about the meeting she'd arranged with Xiao Li later. Again, instinct made her keep quiet.

"Look, if I tell you what I know," he said, "will you promise to keep it to yourself? I mean it, Jess. You must not discuss it with anyone else or you'll get me into trouble."

She nodded.

He took a deep breath as if talking was an effort. "In 1984, Marianne Henderson was sent from the British Embassy in Peking, along with another colleague, to open a new Consulate-General in Shanghai. She'd been there several months and was working on the visit of a UK trade delegation to the city when … well, things started to go wrong for her."

Jess listened keenly.

"Because the trade delegation was headed by a British Minister, our Ambassador in Peking flew down to Shanghai to host them throughout their stay." He paused. "After he met the delegation at the airport, he went back to the Peace Hotel, where he was staying, to change for dinner before going to a welcoming banquet for the delegation. However, when he was back in his room, our Ambassador committed suicide."

"Oh my God!" So, the newspaper article *was* true. "Why did he commit suicide?" she asked.

Sam's voice was almost a whisper now. "Marianne found his body in his hotel room. There was no suicide note, but it turned out later he'd been having an affair." He glanced up. "With Marianne."

Jess's jaw dropped.

"Apparently, she wanted him to leave his wife," Sam went on. "When he refused, she threatened to expose the affair and ruin his career and marriage. With no way out, he took his own life."

"How awful! So, what happened to Marianne?"

"She just … disappeared."

Jess was incredulous. "How could she just disappear?" She gasped as another thought occurred to her. "She wasn't spying for the Chinese when she had that affair, was she? Tell me she didn't set the Ambassador up."

"Jess …"

"Did she defect to China *after* his suicide?"

Sam put both hands up to stop her talking. "You're getting carried away now. There was nothing to suggest that Marianne was working for the Chinese. I'm sure they wanted rid of her, just as much as we did."

"So, what do *they* think happened to her?"

"They say she just vanished, fell completely off their radar."

"Oh, come on." Jess stared at him. "She wouldn't have got out of China without them knowing about it."

Sam shook his head. "I'm telling you, no one knows what happened to Marianne. No one."

Jess persisted. "If there's no record of her leaving China, and she didn't come home, then she must still be there." She shuddered. "My God! She will have either defected under duress or been locked up in some labour camp for the past 30 years."

Sam looked glum. "She wouldn't have survived in a labour camp all that time."

"So, what are you saying? You think she's dead?"

He nodded, sadly. "How else could she have simply disappeared? It was certainly a sordid and embarrassing episode for both governments."

"And that's why it's been hushed up?"

"Yes."

"And that's why there's nothing in the files about her, or in the media come to that?"

"You've been looking?" he asked.

She nodded.

"Well please stop now I've told you," he said. "Believe me, nothing good will come of you dragging this up again, *especially* at this important time in Sino–British relations."

Jess could understand why the two governments would want to keep such a scandal quiet. It *was* shocking. But the media must have got wind of it at the time, surely? Except, of course, it was before the age of the Internet and global communications. Perhaps it was possible back then to hush up something like that and keep everyone in the dark? There were so many questions she wanted to ask, but reluctantly, she stood up. "I have to get back to the office. Perhaps we can continue this later?"

"I've told you everything I know, Jess. There's nothing more to discuss."

Yes, there is, she thought. You still haven't told me why my boss Giles was sent home from Peking. Why are you holding that back? "Look, I have to go and get ready for this Protocol meeting," she said. "Are you coming?"

"You go on ahead. I need to get my papers together. I'll see you in the conference room in fifteen minutes."

"Right." She walked to the door.

"Jess …"

She turned.

"Are we okay about this? I mean, you will stop digging and asking questions about Marianne Henderson, won't you?"

She smiled at him. "I really appreciate your honesty, Sam. In fact, I don't think I could get through this visit without your help."

He nodded. "It might seem daunting, Jess. But the Chinese President will come, and he'll go home again. These visits are meticulously planned. Everything will be fine. So, don't worry. I'm here to help. You just have to ask."

"Thanks," she said, warmly.

Looking at her watch again, she rushed off to her office, high heels tapping on the tiled floor as she went. Poor Marianne, missing in Shanghai since 1984. Was she thrown to the wolves because of an affair?

Back in her office, she went over to her bookcase and pulled out the oldest paperback version of the 'Diplomatic Service List' she could find. It was creased and dog-eared from years of being thumbed through. It listed all serving British diplomatic officers in the Foreign and Commonwealth Office and gave a full record of their postings to different countries, and the dates of their postings. She leafed through, looking for an entry for Marianne Henderson but, as she expected, there wasn't one. She flicked to Giles Pettiford – yes, there he was. He'd been working in the British Embassy Peking in 1984. She turned to Sam Biggins – he'd been there in 1984 too. *And* Sir Anthony Chalmers. So, she thought as she closed the book, all three top sinologists in the FCO had been in Peking in 1984. Surely one of them must know what happened to Marianne Henderson?

Still distracted, Jess grabbed her papers, and headed down to the conference room on the ground floor. Protocol Department was responsible for hosting the meeting, but she wanted to make sure the room had been set up properly. She still had Sir Anthony's words ringing in her ears. *It's your job to make sure everything runs like clockwork.*

She was pleased to be the first person to arrive. It was an impressive room, with a highly polished wooden conference table running along the middle, and chairs for

20 people around it. The walls were decorated with large antique paintings and tapestries. She was relieved to see that the table had been well laid out, with an agenda and draft visit programme at each setting. Glasses and jugs of water were arranged at intervals along the middle of the table, with plates of biscuits for people to help themselves. By the window stood a trolley with flasks of tea and coffee.

Although she'd enjoyed Sam's jasmine tea, she was desperate for a good slug of caffeine. She went over to the trolley and helped herself to a cup of coffee, adding a dash of milk. She gazed out of the window as she sipped it. It was properly light now, and chinks of pale blue winter sky poked through the cloud. Not such a bad morning after all. A ragged pigeon walked along the ledge outside. It stopped, stared at her through the window, then flew off.

She felt calmer standing there looking out over Horse Guards Road. What a morning, and it wasn't even 10 o'clock. As she mulled things over, another loose end suddenly popped into her head. Sam said Marianne had gone to Shanghai to open a new Consulate-General with *another* colleague. Who? Jess made a mental note to find out. And she still didn't know what Giles had done to get himself sent home from Peking all those years ago either.

She took several more sips of coffee and forced herself to forget about Giles and Marianne. She needed to focus on the Chinese President's visit, and make sure every little detail was in place. Nothing must go wrong. Those were Sir Anthony's exact words.

Through the window, she saw a car draw up in the road outside. She knew from experience it was an unmarked police car. Must be the two protection officers from Scotland Yard who were due to attend the meeting. They were responsible for protecting the Chinese President while he was on UK soil and probably knew the programme better than anyone else. They had visited every site and mapped out every movement the President would make in the UK. She smiled as the two grey-suited officers got out of the car and walked towards the side entrance. Most definitely our policemen, she thought, as she drained her coffee cup.

It was the way one of the police officers hurried along the pavement, with a sense of purpose that seemed to set him apart. That gait. That spiky, grey hair. She almost pressed her nose against the window to get a closer look.

He looked over to the window, as if he knew she was there.

The coffee cup and saucer fell from her hands.

What the hell was Tom Sangster doing in London?

7

The object of the superior man is truth
(Confucius)

"You didn't look surprised to see me when I walked in," Tom joked.

Jess just smiled. In truth, she'd been shocked to see him. For all her hasty picking up of the pieces, tiny shards of china still lay on the floor under the window from the broken coffee cup to prove it.

"You *knew* I was coming."

She laughed. "I was looking out the window and saw you get out of the car with your colleague." She gave him a stern look. "Why was *that* the first I knew about you being in London?"

He had the good grace to look uncomfortable. "Ah, yes, well, I've been here several weeks."

"Several *weeks*?"

"I've been very busy," he said, as if that was an excuse not to call. "The Met have kept me on my toes, I can tell you."

"Glad to hear it." She allowed herself to wonder if it was just the job that had brought him to London. "So, how come you're working at the Met?"

"Oh, I'm just on secondment for three months. It's great to be in London, getting the work experience."

Jess was struck by the enthusiasm in his voice. She'd never heard that from him before. He'd always seemed so self-contained. "*Were* you going to call me?" she asked.

He looked at her. "I wasn't sure if you'd want me to."

"On the contrary." She didn't want any awkwardness between them. "It's lovely to see you, Tom." He was just as lean and fit as ever, though his grey hair was receding a bit more. "London obviously agrees with you."

They moved to one side of the conference room, while everyone else milled around. The meeting had gone well. People were chatting and saying their goodbyes.

Xiao Li came over. "I'm leaving now, Jessica. My Ambassador will be so pleased everything is in place for our President's visit. Thank you."

Jess thought Xiao Li's face looked strained. She'd been mostly quiet throughout the meeting, and on the odd occasion she had spoken, her voice sounded flat. "I look forward to seeing you *very* soon," Jess said pointedly, to reassure Xiao Li she hadn't forgotten about their meeting in the café.

Xiao Li raised a small smile. "I look forward to it too." With a nod of her head, she left the conference room.

Jess picked up her coat from the back of her chair. She would much rather stay and talk to Tom, but she had to go after Xiao Li. "I'm afraid I have to dash off, Tom. I've got another appointment."

"Oh?" Tom's face fell. "I was going to ask if you wanted to grab some lunch. But, if you're busy perhaps we could get a drink after work, or have dinner?"

Jess looked at her watch, it was already 12.30. The meeting had gone on for two-and-a-half hours. "I don't know if I'll have time for dinner tonight," she said. But, seeing the disappointment on his face, she added. "Let's have a drink after work, when we're both finished."

He smiled. "That would be great. Just ring me when you're ready to leave." He pulled a business card out of his suit pocket and gave it to her. "My mobile number's on there."

"My number's still the same," she said.

"Then I've still got it," he said as he helped her into her coat. Did she imagine his hand lingering on her shoulder for just a moment? They set off together along the corridor towards the main entrance. All visitors had to enter and exit the building this way, as well as sign in and out. "I'm sorry I didn't get in touch sooner, Jess."

"It's all right." She touched his arm. "I understand."

While he unpinned the visitor's pass from his jacket lapel and handed it to the Security Officer on the door, Jess watched Xiao Li stroll across the cobbled quadrangle towards the security barrier where vehicles entering the Foreign Office had to be checked.

Jess turned back to Tom. "Ready?" she asked, then ushered him briskly across the quadrangle and past the traffic barrier. As they walked into King Charles Street, a biting wind tugged Jess's scarf from her neck, and blew it onto the pavement.

Tom picked it up and draped it gently around her neck. "See you later," he said.

"Right." Jess tied a knot in the scarf. "I'll give you a call. Might be quite late."

"That's fine." He paused. "I'm sorry about your boss, Giles. You sure you're okay about it? Only you look …"

"I'm fine," she said, quickly, "just a bit tired with all the work for this visit." At the start of the meeting she had told everyone about Giles's death, to explain why he wasn't there. It had to be out in the open. Of course, everyone had immediately spoken kindly of him. She'd been grateful for that.

Now, up ahead, she saw Xiao Li turn the corner into Whitehall. "I must go Tom. I'll see you later."

Tom followed her gaze. "Until tonight then."

"Yes." She smiled. "It really is good to see you, Tom." She turned and hurried after Xiao Li.

Turning left into Whitehall in the direction of Trafalgar Square, she caught sight of Xiao Li crossing the road at the Cenotaph. The memorial to the fallen stood in the middle of the wide road. Jess walked along to the spot where Xiao Li had crossed and stood on the kerb. She looked right, then ran into the middle of the road and stood behind the Cenotaph steps to shelter from the oncoming stream of buses. She buried her nose and mouth in her scarf to protect herself from their exhaust fumes.

She had just reached the Banqueting House on the other side of the road when she looked up and saw Xiao Li approaching the corner of Whitehall Place. Suddenly, a black limousine drew up alongside her. A man jumped out and grabbed Xiao Li's arm.

Jess stood shocked for a moment.

Xiao Li tried to resist and pull her arm away, but the man was too strong for her. She was bundled into the back of the car.

"Xiao Li!" Jess shouted, and sprinted the rest of the way, only reaching the car as it began to move away. Unable to see through the black privacy glass, she banged furiously on the boot as the car sped off. She read the number plate. It was a diplomatic plate, a Chinese Embassy car. There was nothing she could do but watch it disappear into the distance.

"Jess!" Footsteps sprinted up behind.

She turned to see Tom. "Did you see that?" she asked, breathless.

"Was that the lady from the Chinese Embassy?" He pulled his mobile out. "Who grabbed her? Did you get the number plate?"

Jess put her hand over his phone and shook her head. "No need to call it in. It was a Chinese Embassy car."

He stared at her. "Why would the Chinese Embassy want to drag one of their own people off the streets of London?"

"I think it was because Xiao Li was about to meet me and tell me something they didn't want her to."

Tom's eyes narrowed. "I *thought* there was something going on between you at the meeting. Xiao Li looked nervous the whole time, and you kept glancing at her."

"Is that why you followed me?"

"I was going to get a sandwich for lunch before going back to the Met," he protested.

Jess wasn't convinced. "Well, it looks like I can join you now." She paused. "And I think you might be able to help me."

He looked at her, warily. "If our last two encounters were anything to go by, I should turn around and walk the other way." It was said lightly, but with feeling too.

"Come on," she said. "I know just the place."

★

Tom had walked along Villiers Street several times since starting work at the Met, but he hadn't noticed this little café before. Its windows were all steamed up today. Perhaps they were always like that, and that's why he hadn't seen it. As they walked in, a blast of hot air hit him along with the welcome smell of coffee and bacon frying. The noisy chatter, and tap and hiss of the coffee machine, bounced off the plain walls and tiled floor.

Jess spotted a couple leaving a corner table and went over to claim it.

Tom followed. The café was packed, with a mix of office workers and builders from a nearby site. "Didn't think this would be your kind of place," he said, as he pulled his chair round to face the door.

She threw her coat over the back of the chair. "Believe me, they do the best coffee in London. It's owned by an Italian family," she added, as if that explained everything.

A harassed waitress, dressed in jeans and T-shirt, dodged between the tables. "Hi Jess. Latte and bacon sandwich, is it?" she asked, while clearing and wiping down the table.

"Please, Tina."

The waitress turned to Tom.

He nodded. "Sounds good to me. I'll have the same."

The waitress gave him a wide smile. "Is that an Aussie accent you've got there? We could do with some of your sunshine right now." She turned and hurried back to the kitchen.

Tom scanned the faces of the other diners. "So, Jess?" He turned back to her. "What are we going to do about your Chinese friend?"

"Nothing we can do. She's a Chinese diplomat. The British police can't arrest, or hold, foreign diplomats. They can't go into foreign embassies to investigate either. Diplomatic immunity, you see."

Tom knew that. "So, we do nothing?"

Jess looked at him with that impassive face he remembered so well. She was assessing him, in the same way he was assessing her. She'd lost some weight, he thought. And the deep shadows under her eyes looked even more pronounced against her pale, winter skin.

"No more sketches of me please," she said, drily, "if that's what you're considering."

How had she read him so well? "Who said anything about sketching?"

She raised her eyebrows. "No more sketches, Tom. I mean it."

"All right."

"Promise?"

He nodded. It seemed unreal to him, sitting in a café in London with Jess, and picking up so easily from where they'd left off. It was only then he realised just how much he'd missed her.

As if reading his thoughts, she smiled before quickly returning to business. "I'll have to report what happened to Xiao Li when I get back to the office." She hesitated. "It'll be tricky because I didn't tell anyone I was going to meet her."

Tom could see she was worried. "What's going on, Jess? First, your colleague Giles goes under a train, then a Chinese diplomat is dragged off the street into one of her own Embassy cars."

Jess said nothing while the waitress walked over and put two large cups of latte in front of them.

"Bacon sarnies on their way," she said, before disappearing again.

Jess sat forward. "Did you know my boss, Giles, had died under a train before you came to the meeting?"

Tom nodded. "We were briefed before we left the Met."

"What exactly did they say happened to him?"

"Only that he fell in front of an oncoming train at St James's underground station last night."

"Well, the police told Sir Anthony – he's the Head of the Foreign Office – that they think Giles committed suicide. Is that what you heard?"

Tom paused to think. "They just said he'd fallen under a train. A lot of people do commit suicide in that way.

Terrible thing for the train drivers to have to live with." He hesitated when she frowned. "Any reason *why* the police think he might have committed suicide?"

Jess shrugged. "Sir Anthony seems to think it might have something to do with him being pressed to take early retirement." She paused. "Giles was an ambitious man, so I can see how devastated he would have been about that."

Tom picked up the scepticism in her voice "But you don't think he committed suicide?"

Jess stared at her coffee. "I have absolutely no reason to think he didn't. I've only been in this job for six months, and I've had no social contact with Giles or his family. But, well, he just didn't seem the kind of man who would take his own life. Oh, I know that sounds ridiculous, because how could I possibly know what went on his head, or in his life. The thing is, it just doesn't make sense to me."

Tom took a sip of coffee. "My colleagues are investigating his death, so we'll find out soon enough."

Jess nodded. "And that's what I wanted to ask you, Tom. Now, please say 'no' if it's going to cause you any trouble, I won't be offended if you do." She hesitated. "It's just that now you're working inside the Met, it occurred to me that you might be able to find out what's going on with that investigation?"

He couldn't help but smile. "Ah, I see."

"Only if it's not going to cause you a problem," she insisted.

He took another sip of coffee and sat back in his chair. As a 'newbie', it wouldn't be easy to muscle in. But suicides of this kind happen, and the investigations were routine. There was nothing to stop him trying to get alongside the officers involved and asking a few questions. "I can always give it a go."

"Excellent." Jess beamed at him and took a long swig of coffee.

"As is the coffee, as you promised."

The waitress came over with the bacon sandwiches and put them down on the table.

Tom smiled. "Now they look the real deal."

"Mm."

They sat, silently eating and drinking. He'd forgotten how at ease he was in Jess's company, given that he hardly knew her. He cringed whenever he remembered the first time they'd met, in Brisbane. God, what a nightmare the murder of that British businesswoman Ellen Chambers had been. He'd bawled Jess out for walking over his crime scene, before realising she was the British Consul. And she'd been relentless in her determination to do her job and keep the victim's sister safe from the killer, which had both impressed and infuriated him.

Now, he could hardly compare the woman sitting in front of him with the Ice Queen he remembered back then. Only later did he find out that Jess's cool demeanour was her way of coping with the death of her husband and daughter in a car crash some years earlier.

While in Australia, Jess had met a new partner, another British diplomat. Was she still with Simon, he wondered? He wouldn't ask her though, not now anyway.

He picked up a serviette and wiped his mouth. "Want another coffee?" he asked.

"Please. I'm only just beginning to thaw out."

Tom caught the waitress's eye and gestured to their cups. She gave him a thumbs-up.

"Right." Tom's voice was business-like now. "So, my first job is to find out what I can about Giles's apparent suicide last night." He stopped and looked at her. "I can see there's something else on your mind."

71

Jess nodded. "This is more difficult." She wiped the remnants of sauce from her fingers. "The problem goes way back to 1984."

"*1984?*"

"Yes." Jess lowered her voice. "I think what happened in 1984 is somehow connected to Giles's death last night and Xiao Li."

Tom leant forward to hear better.

"In 1984, the British Ambassador to China committed suicide in a Shanghai hotel," she said. "The strange thing is, there's absolutely no mention of it in any of our Foreign Office files."

He shrugged. "It *was* 30 years ago."

"Even so, there should be something. The point is no one seems to know about this death. No one wants to talk about it either." She pushed her hair back off her face. "I could tell you about any other Ambassador, or officer, who's been murdered or died in the line of duty over the decades. If an Ambassador committed suicide in Shanghai, it would be part of the history of the post. Everyone would know about it."

Tom could see that. "So how did you find out about it?" he asked.

"Ah well, I was googling something else that went on in Shanghai in 1984. The Ambassador's suicide popped up instead, in an old newspaper article. The funny thing is, only the headline came up. I couldn't access the full article online." She paused. "It would have been quite a story at the time. So, I'm wondering why I couldn't access the article. And why none of the other newspapers covered the story."

He shrugged. "Because it happened so long ago, before they started their electronic archives?"

"Possibly, but they've put some of their old archives online. Why not this story?"

He nodded. "You said you were googling something else that went on in Shanghai in 1984." Seeing her glance away, he added: "For this to make any sense, I need to know everything."

"It's classified, Tom. I've been told not to talk about it." She looked him straight in the eye. "I don't want to get the source of this information into trouble. I don't want to get you into trouble either." He felt her appraising him as she asked: "Do you still want to know?"

"You know I do. *And* you know I'll keep it to myself."

"Very well." She took a deep breath. "In 1984, a British diplomat called Marianne Henderson was sent from the British Embassy in Peking to open a new Consulate-General in Shanghai. She'd been there a while and was working on the programme for a visiting British trade delegation." She paused. "Our Ambassador in Peking at the time flew to Shanghai to host the visiting delegation. He went out to the airport to meet them, then returned to his hotel room to change for dinner. While he was in his room, he committed suicide."

Tom raised his eyebrows. "Another suicide?"

Jess nodded.

"How did he kill himself?"

Jess hesitated, wondering why she hadn't asked Sam that question. "I don't know."

"Go on."

"Marianne Henderson found his body. It turns out she was having an affair with him. The story is that she wanted him to leave his wife. When he refused, she threatened to expose the affair. Ruin his career and marriage."

"And that's why he took his own life?"

"Apparently."

"Is the source of this information reliable?"

"Yes. He was working in the Embassy in Peking at the time."

Tom shrugged. "Affairs happen all the time, although one thing does seem odd." He paused. "Why would the Ambassador kill himself *before* going to the dinner? Wouldn't he wait until later? Or until after the delegation had left China and things had quietened down?"

"Exactly! And why choose to do it in an hotel room in Shanghai during such a high-profile visit, for the whole world to know about? It's the same thing that's been bothering me about Giles's apparent suicide last night. It was so *public*." She stared at him. "If I was going to kill myself, I'd crawl into bed and take an overdose."

He raised his eyebrows.

"How would *you* do it, then?" she asked.

He shrugged again. "I've never thought about it before. But, I'd probably go quietly into the woods and shoot myself."

"You'd go *quietly* into the woods. My point again. You wouldn't do it in a blaze of publicity."

He had to admit she was right. "Granted it's a bit of a puzzle, but …"

"That's not all." She stopped and looked around. "The *really* weird thing is that Marianne Henderson disappeared in China at the very same time. And she's never been seen again."

Tom frowned. "*Never*?"

"Never."

"How old was she when she disappeared?"

Jess shrugged. "In her late 20s, or early 30s."

"Which means she could still be alive."

"Yes. And locked up in some Chinese prison or labour camp somewhere. Poor woman. Doesn't bear thinking about."

They fell silent as the waitress came over with two more coffees.

Tom noticed Jess shiver. Was that from the cold? Or the thought of Marianne Henderson languishing in a Chinese prison for 30 years? "So," he said. "I take it you want me to see if I can find out anything about Marianne in the police archives too?"

Jess pushed her coffee cup to one side and sat forward, eagerly. "There has to be something about her in police records, even if she's just down as a 'missing person'. The Chinese, of course, would have carried out an investigation into her disappearance. Surely that must have been relayed to the British police?"

"True, but it was a long time ago."

"And what about Marianne's family? They wouldn't just let her disappear? They'd have been desperate to find her."

Tom was mindful of the consequences of digging around in the UK police archives. "This could stir up a hornet's nest."

"I know, and I don't want to get you into trouble." She paused. "So, I was thinking … instead of looking into Marianne's disappearance straightaway, it might be easier first to see what you can find out about the Ambassador's suicide. When a Briton dies in suspicious circumstances overseas, the UK coroner carries out an inquiry, as well as a post-mortem if the body is sent back to the UK. I assume the Ambassador's body was sent back here. Also, the coroner would have to look at the circumstances of the person's death. The Chinese police should have provided a report at least." She pushed the hair back off her face again. "That's what we need to know. What did the Chinese police and the UK coroner say? Then, we can work back from there."

That made sense to Tom, but there was another loose end. "How does your Chinese lady fit into all this?"

Jess shrugged. "I'm not sure. At a drinks party last night, Xiao Li asked to see me today, privately. We agreed to meet here for a coffee after the Protocol meeting. That's where I was going. And, well, you saw what happened to her."

Tom's eyes widened. "It's the stuff of spy movies."

Jess was frowning. "It was Xiao Li who mentioned Marianne Henderson to me last night. She wanted to give me some information about her, that's what she said." Jess looked down. "She asked me … she asked me not to mention Marianne's name to anyone until she'd spoken to me today."

Tom could see the worry all over Jess's face. "And did you?"

"I, well, I mentioned Marianne to a colleague in the office." She shuddered. "I didn't tell him about Xiao Li or that I was going to meet her today, though." She looked at Tom with a pained expression. "Oh my God. Poor Xiao Li. What have I done?"

8

> *The guerrilla must move amongst the people as a fish swims in the sea*
> *(Chairman Mao)*

Outside the Peace Hotel, Marianne had to press herself up against its granite facing to get out of the way of the bustling crowd. Shanghai had a population of 12 million people, and it felt like every single one of them was on the pavement whenever she stepped out. She closed her eyes and took several deep breaths of air in sheer relief at being outside and away from the cloying smell of death in the Ambassador's room.

Her arms felt heavy with two briefcases. She had her own in one hand. Her other hand was clamped like a vice around the handle of the Ambassador's. The police had wanted to take charge of all his possessions. She'd refused to let them have his briefcase, insisting it was British government property. They should treat it exactly like a diplomatic bag, she'd insisted. They had no right under the Geneva Convention to search or confiscate it. That was stretching things a bit, but there was no way she'd let them get their hands on the classified and personal papers inside. The Police Inspector hadn't argued about it, but she'd sensed his annoyance.

Now, as she stood there, shivers ran up and down her spine. From shock? Or from the night mist from the Huangpu River wrapping itself around her like a damp cloak? She shook herself physically. This was no time to fall apart. She needed to get back to the Consulate-General and make some urgent phone calls to Peking and London. Only she knew what had happened here tonight. It was up to her to tell everyone the shocking news.

Her eyes searched for the Consulate-General car and driver amongst the official cars and taxis parked outside the hotel. There was no sign of him. She held her watch up to the dull beam of the hotel's porch light. No wonder. It was already 9pm. He'd dropped her off three hours ago.

She desperately wanted a cigarette. But first, she would go and see if the driver was parked around the corner on the embankment known as the Bund. Perhaps the hotel concierge had moved him on? She walked the few yards to the intersection of Nanjing Street and the Bund. She heard lapping waves and the flat horns of night barges navigating the Huangpu River. She couldn't see the water through the swirling mist, just eerie lights along the Bund from the majestic buildings that had once housed international merchant banks and trading houses. The architecture was still magnificent, but inside, the buildings were run down through lack of investment by the communist state.

She gave up trying to see anything in the fog, thinking the driver must have gone back to the Consulate-General, or he would have parked the car somewhere and waited for her in the hotel lobby. She couldn't blame him for leaving. It had taken ages for a doctor to get to the hotel and pronounce the Ambassador dead. And even longer for the police to do their forensic investigation of the room and body. She'd stayed the whole time, cringing as they inspected the crumpled sheets for signs of sexual activity, and bagged the condom foil and dirty glasses for analysis. They had to do it, of course, but it felt like a terrible invasion of the Ambassador's privacy. She'd insisted on staying, to report every detail to Peking and London, however embarrassing for the Ambassador and the British government.

And it certainly was going to be embarrassing if these details got out. No doubt about that. A real scandal, especially if he'd been having an affair, or even a casual liaison. She shuddered to think of the furore if the Ambassador had been with a prostitute. She shook her head. The Ambassador would never compromise himself like that and open himself up to blackmail. Not him. Not in a million years.

Then again, he must have been entertaining someone. Why else would he have had two glasses for the champagne? And that condom foil? She shuddered. At least he'd been fully dressed in his trousers and shirt, and not naked in death. That preserved some dignity. The poor man must have been ready to come down to the Bar before collapsing on the bathroom floor. Had he had a heart attack from the exertion of sex? Perhaps he'd had an existing heart condition, and that set it off? He *was* approaching 60 and retirement. Or perhaps he'd been driving himself too hard? It was no secret he was a workaholic.

Unable to wait any longer, she put the two briefcases on the ground between her feet and reached into her jacket pocket for her cigarettes. Lighting up, she took a deep drag and blew the smoke into the chilly night air.

She was annoyed with that Chinese doctor too. He wouldn't give her the slightest indication of the cause of death. She understood the requirement for a post-mortem before stating anything officially, but why refuse to give a preliminary view? The furtive glances he and the Inspector kept giving her made her feel uneasy. From time to time, they would go out into the corridor, out of her earshot, to talk in hushed tones. Why? Did they think the Ambassador *hadn't* died of natural causes? There was no blood on his body that she'd seen. No gunshot or stab wounds. No bruises or cuts to his face. Nothing to suggest someone had attacked him. So, why were the police being so secretive?

She'd told the Inspector she didn't want the media involved. She could just imagine the lurid headlines and speculation. They had to keep it under wraps, for the time being at least. That shouldn't be difficult in a country where the State controlled every media outlet. Fortunately, the Inspector had agreed with her on that point, although it was impossible to tell from his hooded eyes what else he was thinking.

She wished she could have phoned her colleague Justin and asked him to come over to the hotel to help her. But he'd gone to Hangzhou, to attend an urgent consular case. A young British student had been involved in a bicycle accident and was critically ill in hospital with a brain haemorrhage. As Marianne had done most of the work on the trade delegation's visit, it made sense for her to stay in Shanghai and for Justin to go to Hangzhou. The town was only a couple of hours by train from Shanghai, but it seemed a million miles away at that moment.

Fortunately, it wasn't long before the fresh air and nicotine cleared Marianne's head. First, she would go back to the Consulate-General and phone the Embassy Duty Officer in Peking to report the Ambassador's death. Then she would go over to the Jing An Hotel to tell the British Minister and the trade delegation. She'd rung earlier to explain that the Ambassador couldn't make the dinner. The Minister had demanded to know what was more important. To mollify him, she'd said it was a very sensitive matter that she couldn't discuss over the phone. In truth, she hadn't told him because she didn't want him to tell other members of the delegation and start any gossip. This death had to be handled quietly, at least until all the circumstances were understood. Anyway, the Ambassador's wife and family needed to hear about it first.

Resolute, she took a last drag from her cigarette, and stamped the butt out on the pavement. As she slipped the packet and lighter back into her pocket, her fingers brushed against something hard. Frowning, she grasped the object and pulled it out.

The little snuff-bottle! She remembered it slipping out of the Ambassador's hand as he lay on the bathroom floor, but she couldn't remember picking it up and putting it in her pocket. She may have done though, in all the confusion. She held it up to the street light to get a good look. It was only about three-inches high. A Chinese temple with little lanterns hanging under its eaves had been skilfully painted on one side. She turned the bottle over, but there was nothing on the other side.

She took the stopper off the top of the bottle and sniffed gingerly. No smell. She turned the bottle upside down and tapped it on the palm of her hand to see if any snuff came out. Nothing. The bottle was just a decorative piece. An antique, by the look of it. Why did the Ambassador have this in his hand when he died, she wondered?

She pulled a tissue out of her bag and wrapped the bottle up for protection. She would hand it over to the police in the morning, in case it was somehow relevant to his death. Her fingerprints were all over it, but she couldn't help that.

Why was she worrying about her fingerprints being on it? Her stomach churned at the direction in which her thoughts were going. Had the police been right to be so suspicious?

She slipped the snuff bottle into her bag, picked up the two briefcases, and made her way through the thronging pedestrians back to the hotel. She approached a taxi waiting outside the front entrance for a fare. The driver was sound asleep inside, his head resting back on the seat, mouth wide open.

She rapped on the window then jumped into the back.

The driver stared at her, thrown by the shock of a foreign woman jumping into his taxi.

"Please take me to Yong Fu Lu," she said in Chinese.

Chinese people never expected foreigners, especially Westerners, to speak their language. Taxi drivers were used to driving the odd tourist around the city sights, but they were usually accompanied by an official guide. They were not used to an unaccompanied Western woman wanting a ride to a residential area of Shanghai. "Yong Fu Lu," she repeated.

This time he nodded, put the taxi in gear and pulled out into the traffic without a glance behind him. That provoked a furious tirade of bicycle bells, which he ignored. To him at least, his taxi had right of way over any cyclist.

Once satisfied they were heading in a north-easterly direction, to the old French concession of Shanghai where the British Consulate-General was now housed, Marianne settled back into the seat. A smell of garlic permeated the air, and it was coming from the driver. She was used to that, particularly after living in Peking for three years. There, in the cold north, they chewed garlic every day, believing it had antibiotic properties that prevented colds and flu.

She remembered buying some in the free market not long after her arrival thinking it was a bunch of spring onions, because that's what it looked like. She smiled, remembering the 'salad' she'd made with it.

Now, she could feel a tension headache starting, like a tight band around her forehead. She laid her head back on the seat and closed her eyes. But the sight of the Ambassador lying dead on that bathroom floor was too vivid, and she opened them again. She couldn't stop thinking about the condom foil and champagne glasses either. He didn't seem the type to have an affair. Still, who was the type? And what did she really know about him? Only that he was highly intelligent, and a China expert who spoke Mandarin perfectly. A reserved man who only ever talked about work. Did any of his colleagues really know him? Did his wife even?

Marianne tried to think back to when she was in the hotel lobby earlier speaking to the receptionist. Did she see any woman in the lobby she knew? She sifted through the faces in her memory, but no-one sprang to mind. If anyone had been familiar, she'd have remembered.

She sat up when the driver pulled up outside the wooden gates of the British Consulate-General, at no 244 Yong Fu Lu. She paid, got out, and watched as he pulled away quickly, no doubt relieved to have this foreigner out of his car. The cloud and mist had given way to an inky black sky, and the moon was out. A cool breeze rustled her clothes and hair.

When she opened the gates, she was annoyed to see the house and driveway in total darkness. When would the Chinese staff remember to leave the porch and security lights on?

She started up the drive. It was eerily quiet. No barking dogs, because the Chinese weren't allowed to keep them as pets. No voices either, because the Chinese all went to bed so early, to be up at the crack of dawn.

Her old blue Peugeot was a comforting sight, still parked outside the front door where she'd left it. At least she'd get home tonight. But there was no official car. Where the hell was the driver? Only then did it occur to her that he might be with the police, being questioned. Drivers tended to know more about their boss's lives than anyone else. Did he know who the Ambassador had been entertaining in his room? Would he tell the police if he knew? Of course, he would. He'd be reporting to Chinese security regularly anyway.

At the front door, she let herself in with her key, switched on all the lights and made her way to her office at the back of the house. She loved this office because the window looked out onto the garden, and an old Yulan magnolia tree. She couldn't wait for next spring to see its beautiful white flowers, and hopefully have its sweet scent waft through the open window.

Flicking through the papers in her in-tray, she found the monthly roster of duty officers in Peking. No one liked to be on duty because it meant staying at home every evening and at the weekend to take emergency calls. Anyone who couldn't be contacted while on duty would be in serious trouble. She looked through the names, hoping to find Sam Biggins on duty. He was the new China researcher, on his first stint at the Embassy. He had visited Shanghai several times to help them set up the Consulate-General. He was fun and easy to get along with.

Her heart sank when she saw the Duty Officer was Anthony Chalmers. Not that she didn't like him, she just found him heavy going. He hadn't been in the Diplomatic Service long either, but he was a 'flyer' and had already made himself indispensable to the Ambassador, much to the annoyance of Giles Pettiford, the other young First Secretary in Peking. Giles and Anthony had joined the Foreign Office in the same in-take. Both had been singled out to be trained as China specialists, and the rivalry between them was plain to see.

She found her hand shaking as she picked up the receiver to make the call.

He answered quickly. "Anthony Chalmers."

"It's Marianne."

"Oh, hello." He sounded disappointed. "I thought you were the Ambassador."

That surprised her. "Were you expecting him to call?"

"Yes. He wanted me to report the outcome of the trade delegation dinner to London tonight."

Oh, did he? she thought, knowing that was her responsibility. "Well, I have some very sad news." She paused, but there was no easy way to say this. "The Ambassador died in his hotel room this evening."

There was only a brief intake of breath. "*Died?*"

"Yes." She told Anthony exactly what had happened, but he interrupted before she could finish.

"Why the need for the police and forensics?" he asked. "What did he die of?"

"The doctor wouldn't say. They've taken his body to the morgue."

"We are talking about natural causes, aren't we? Surely, you're not suggesting…?"

"I'm not suggesting anything," she said, quickly. "I'm just telling you what happened. That's all we should do at present."

There was a pause. "I don't think you should have let the police carry out the forensic examination of the room and Ambassador's body," he said. "At least not before anyone from this Embassy got down to Shanghai."

If she had thought young Anthony a cold fish before, his reaction now confirmed it. There was no sense of shock over the Ambassador's tragic death, or sympathy for his wife and family. All Anthony's analytical brain could think about was process.

"I was there, Anthony. I witnessed his death. There was nothing else to do *but* call the authorities."

"Did you stay there the whole time they carried out their investigations?"

"Yes." Marianne felt irritated. "Listen, I'm going to dictate exactly what happened to you over the phone. Have our communications officer send it word for word in a classified telegram to London from me. This should not go over the open telex, it's too sensitive."

"You're speaking over an open phone line, Marianne."

She didn't need reminding of that. "We have no classified communications down here, as you know. Just do it, Anthony, please."

"Of course." He stayed quiet while Marianne dictated the telegram, only sucking in his breath when she got to the part about the condom foil and champagne. "That's hard to believe," he said.

"I saw it with my own eyes."

"Still…"

"I know." She paused. "Please don't add any comment to my telegram. We don't want to speculate about an affair or anything else. Just relay the facts exactly as I have dictated them to you. London will understand the sensitivities and draw their own conclusions."

There was another pause. "Should I come down to Shanghai?" he asked. "You'll need some help."

Marianne had expected that reaction. Anthony would want to be in the centre of the action, but he was the last person she wanted to see in Shanghai. "It would be better if Sam came down," she said. "He's been here several times already and knows the place."

"Sam's already there," he said. "Or rather he's in Hangzhou with Justin." He paused. "Didn't you know?"

No, she did not know. And that shocked her. What were the pair of them playing at?

"I can fly down and give you a hand, Marianne," Anthony went on.

"No. You're needed in Peking," she said. "You have to be the link with London and the media." She knew that would appeal to Anthony's sense of importance.

And it did. "Of course, I can see that."

"Good." Her next request would be more difficult. "Someone will need to tell the Ambassador's wife."

"Ah, yes."

Marianne caught the hesitation in his voice. "Perhaps you should ask Cathy to go with you to the Residence? She'll be a great help and comfort." The Embassy nurse was a gem, someone they all went to in times of trouble. "Ask her to take some sedatives with her, just in case."

"Right." He sounded a little reassured.

"Better do that quickly," Marianne said. "We don't want the Ambassador's wife finding out from anyone else." She paused. "No need to tell her every little detail. You know, about the condom foil and champagne … not just yet anyway."

"No, no, of course not." He took a deep breath. "Leave it to me."

"Thanks, Anthony."

"Ring me immediately if there's any more news," he said. "Doesn't matter what time."

"I will."

There was another pause. "Are you okay, Marianne?"

His concern took her by surprise. "I'm fine," she said. "It was a shock, I can tell you, finding him there like that. But I'm all right now."

"Good." And with that he hung up.

Marianne put the phone back in the cradle and sat back in her chair. She knew Anthony could be relied upon to do exactly what she'd asked. Now, she would ring the hotel where Justin was staying in Hangzhou and ask him to return to Shanghai immediately. And bring Sam with him. It shouldn't take the pair of them to attend a consular case, she thought crossly.

She rubbed her aching temples and opened her handbag to look for her cigarettes. She lit up and blew out the smoke. Then she caught sight of the tissue-clad snuff bottle. She pulled it out, unwrapped the little bottle and laid it on the desk. Such a pretty thing. But why did the Ambassador have it in his hand when he died?

Then an idea came to her. She laid her cigarette on the edge of her ashtray, walked over to her cupboard and pulled out the new polaroid camera she'd bought in Hong Kong a couple of weeks earlier. It was a real hit with the Chinese staff. She'd gone around the building taking snaps of everyone and producing immediate photos. Their delighted cries of surprise had amused her. She would have a lot of fun with this camera at receptions and parties.

Now, she took a snap of the snuff bottle and waited. When the photo was produced, she unpeeled the paper and there was a perfect picture of the little bottle. She would use this to do some research.

A movement outside caught her eye. She stared out the window. There it was again … a flickering light.

She got up and went over to the window. Was someone out there with a torch?

Unable to see properly, she went over to the door and switched off the overhead light. Once her eyes had become accustomed to the dark, through the window she could see the source of the light, and it was coming from the Yulan tree. A lantern was hanging from a lower branch, with a lit candle inside. As the tree swayed in the breeze, so did the lantern, causing the candle light to flicker.

Marianne frowned. She'd seen these lanterns hanging in the market, they were popular for Chinese holidays and celebrations. Normally they were red and made of silk or paper on a bamboo frame. But this lantern was white, and about a foot high. On one side, she could see large Chinese characters painted in black. She opened the window and peered closer.

The characters read 'Dàshī' in Chinese. Chills shivered up her spine as she realised their significance. This was no celebratory lantern. This was a white funeral lantern. And on the side, painted in Chinese characters, was the word 'Ambassador'.

She stood transfixed.

Suddenly, a strong gust of wind shook the Yulan tree. The lantern broke away from the branch and rose into the sky like a balloon. She watched it bobbing around in the breeze as it went higher and higher, until it suddenly caught fire. Flames shot everywhere, then went out just as quickly.

Unnerved, Marianne slammed the window shut. Then, in the silence, she heard a noise inside the house. Footsteps.

She froze as her office door opened. The light went on.

Justin and Sam stood staring at her.

"Thank goodness you're back," she said. "The Ambassador's dead."

9

If I am walking with two other men, each of them will serve as my teacher. I will pick out the good points of the one and the bad points of the other and correct them in myself.

(Confucius)

From her perch at the office window, all Marianne could see were torch beams flickering outside as Justin and Sam searched the garden. She took a deep drag on her cigarette and blew the smoke out into the chilly air. The Consulate-General heating had been timed to go off hours ago and the Shanghai night was a cold one.

Frustrated, she threw open the window. The wind blew straight into her face, and she had to hold the window to prevent it closing back on her. "Found anything?" she shouted.

Justin appeared out of the darkness. "What exactly *did* you see out here, Marianne?"

"Just the lantern." She pointed to the magnolia. "Hanging from a branch."

He looked over at the tree. "Well, there's nothing there now. Not even a piece of string over the branch. No sign of anything, or anyone."

"Well *someone* hung the lantern there and lit the candle inside. It lifted into the sky like a balloon, then caught fire. The debris *must* have fallen back down to the ground."

Justin shrugged. "That could be anywhere. Maybe we'll find something when it's light."

She nodded.

"*Sam*," Justin shouted. "You found anything?"

"Nah," came the reply out of the darkness.

"No point in staying out here then," Justin shouted again. "Let's go inside. We could all do with a stiff drink."

That was Justin's answer to everything, Marianne thought, a drink. Still, she was glad he was back. He was the kind of man who seemed effortlessly good at everything he did. He refused to worry about anything or show any nerves. With his easy charm and manner, he always got his own way, and that irked her at times. They were the same grade, neither of them senior to the other. Yet she always seemed up to her eyes in work, while he breezed through everything.

Sam gave her a small smile as he walked back into her office.

Marianne was struck by the contrast between his personality and Justin's. Fresh-faced and a little naive, Sam had only left university a year or two ago and was just starting out on his career in the Foreign Office. He was fortunate to have been taken on as a researcher, especially on such a fascinating country as China. And he knew it. He was over the moon to be serving his first stint at the Embassy in Peking, working hard and showing himself to be considerate and helpful. A real team player.

"Sorry we didn't find anything outside," he said.

She shrugged. "Probably nothing *to* find. Whoever put the lantern there is long gone. Besides, they are made of bamboo and silk, or paper even. It would have burnt out quickly."

As he nodded, Sam's brown hair flopped over his forehead, framing his freckled face. His boyish looks, and sensitive manner, made him seem vulnerable, and Marianne always felt the need to protect him, particularly from the office politics that went on amongst the other men.

As if reading her thoughts, Sam said, kindly: "Must have been a hell of a shock finding the Ambassador like that."

His sympathetic words hit a nerve, and Marianne's eyes brimmed.

He shuffled his feet awkwardly, not knowing what to say to comfort her. "I suppose you're wondering what I was doing in Hangzhou with Justin."

She nodded.

At that moment, Justin appeared in the doorway, balancing three glasses of brandy in his hands. "Let's go and make ourselves comfortable in the reception room. We can put the electric fire on in there and warm up."

Marianne and Sam followed him along the corridor and into the reception room, which served as a place to welcome visitors and have a more informal chat. It was certainly easier to deal with Chinese officials that way. Occasionally, the furniture would be removed to hold cocktail parties in there. In summer, they could open the terrace doors and spill out into the garden. Marianne loved the fact that the office was in a house, with a garden, kitchen and other facilities. Much nicer than working in an office block.

She sat down on the comfy chintz sofa.

Sam sat on the soft chair opposite, while Justin put the drinks down on the coffee table and went over to the fireplace to switch on the electric heater. He picked up his glass of brandy and went back to stand in the front of the fire to warm himself up.

They sipped their drinks in silence for a while.

Marianne felt the fiery liquid warming her. She pulled her cigarettes and matches out of her pocket and lit up.

Justin frowned at her, then lifted a glass ashtray off the mantelpiece and went over to put it down on the coffee table in front of her. "Can you tell us exactly what happened this evening, Marianne?"

She looked at him as he returned to the fireplace, brandy in hand, like the lord of the manor. His face was red with cold, or maybe the drink, his hair thick and black. He would have been handsome if it wasn't for his air of entitlement, and the fact that he wore his love of food and alcohol around his middle. You should have been here too, she thought, not in Hangzhou. Now, she could feel the brandy working, and exhaustion creep over her. She closed her eyes and put her head back on the top of the sofa. All she could see was the Ambassador lying on the bathroom floor, his face as white as his hair...

"Marianne?" Justin said.

She jumped and opened her eyes again. Earlier, when Justin and Sam had walked in, she'd hurriedly told them about the Ambassador and the lantern. They'd rushed into the garden to see if anyone was out there. Now, she needed to tell them the whole story. Slowly, she took another swig of brandy to steady her nerves and started to recount events, step by step, from the time she spent in the Peace Hotel Jazz Bar waiting for the Ambassador, to finding him on the bathroom floor, to the hours after in his hotel room waiting for Chinese police and forensics to do their work. She had told this story a couple of times now and, with every re-telling, she was becoming more focused and concise.

Justin and Sam listened quietly.

Marianne noticed Justin raise his eyebrows when she got to the part about the condom foil and champagne. Like everyone else, he clearly found that hard to believe, but he said nothing. When she'd finished, she half expected him to pick up on that point, but he didn't. Instead, he asked: "And the police actually allowed you to stay in the room while forensics carried out their examination?"

"I wouldn't leave."

He looked at her. "Why not?"

"Well," Marianne paused to think. Why had she insisted on staying?

Justin went on: "If he died from natural causes like a heart attack or stroke, why did the Chinese police call forensics in?"

Marianne frowned, trying to think back to the sequence of events. "Routine, I suppose, especially when a foreigner, and a foreign Ambassador at that, is found dead in an hotel room."

Justin nodded. "How long were they in there for?"

"*Hours*," Marianne said, with feeling.

Justin looked thoughtful. "That suggests the police were thinking the Ambassador *didn't* die from natural causes." He paused. "Did they find something unusual straightaway? Something that set off alarm bells? Something that made them want to call in forensics?"

Marianne looked away. Justin was voicing thoughts she'd been trying to push from her mind all evening. "They refused to give me any kind of read-out about the cause of death," she said, calmly. "But, of course, they could see from the champagne and glasses and, well, everything else, that someone had been in the room with the Ambassador."

Sam looked at them both, wide-eyed. His voice was just a whisper when he asked: "Are you saying someone had sex with him, then murdered him?"

Justin gave him a sharp glance, as if warning him to be quiet.

Marianne caught that glance. "I'm not saying anything. I'm just telling you the facts."

Justin shrugged. "I can't imagine the old man doing something like that. Having an affair would open him up to scandal and blackmail. He was always so careful."

Sam nodded. "A bit of a cold fish too."

Justin turned to Marianne. "Why the hell didn't you ring me earlier? I could have got back from Hangzhou hours ago."

His peeved tone annoyed her. "Just how was I supposed to do that?" she asked. "I found the Ambassador on the bathroom floor. He wasn't breathing. I tried to revive him. I called the police when I was sure he was dead. Then I stayed in the room for hours while they carried out their investigation." She'd hit her stride now. "How could I leave everything to phone you? Anyway, all I could have done was phone the hotel you were staying in and leave a message. That's exactly what I did when I got back here. By that time, you'd returned to Shanghai."

"She's right," Sam said. "I don't think I would have left the Ambassador with the police and forensics either if I'd found myself in that situation. I'd have wanted to stay to make sure they treated him properly and to find out everything I could to report to Peking and London."

"*Thank* you, Sam," she said, with feeling.

Justin looked at Sam, then he put up his hands in a show of apology. "I'm not criticising you, Marianne. You've been through enough this evening." He ran his hand through his dark hair. "It's just that this is all … crazy."

"You're telling me?" She flopped back into the sofa again.

They sat in a kind of tense silence, each with their own thoughts. Suddenly, a wailing sound echoed down the chimney, making them all jump. "What the bloody hell was that?" Justin hissed.

"Only the north wind," Marianne said. "These old houses have a ventilation system all of their own. It howls through the plumbing in the boiler room too."

Justin stepped away from the fireplace. "I'm going to get the bottle of brandy from the kitchen." He put his glass on the coffee table and left the room.

When he'd gone, Sam said: "Ignore him, Marianne. He's just annoyed with himself for not being here to help you."

She nodded. "One of you should have been here."

He looked sheepish. "I'm really sorry, Marianne. I, well, I…"

"Here we are." Justin came back into the room with the bottle of brandy. He filled up their glasses. This time, he didn't go back to the fireplace, but sat down in another chair. Resting his glass on the arm, he looked over at Marianne. "What I don't understand, is why anyone would hang a funeral lantern on the Yulan tree."

"It's a Chinese custom," Sam piped up. "They do it all the time when someone dies."

"I know *that*," Justin said. "But who knew the Ambassador was dead at that point?"

They both looked at Marianne. It was another thing she'd been turning over in her mind since seeing the lantern. Apart from the Chinese police and forensics, she was the only person who knew the Ambassador was dead. So, who'd hung it on the tree? And why?

"I've been wondering that myself," she said. "The lantern had the Chinese characters for Ambassador painted on the side. It was meant for him, no doubt about that." She hesitated. "The thing is, well, somehow I don't think it was meant as a gesture of sympathy or condolence."

Justin's eyes narrowed.

She shook her head. "It felt, well … menacing."

"Menacing?"

She shifted uncomfortably on the sofa.

Sam suddenly picked up his glass and took a long gulp of brandy. It must have gone down the wrong way because he started coughing, as if he were choking.

"For goodness sake!" Justin exploded.

"Why don't you just get him some water," Marianne said, irritably.

Justin didn't move, so Marianne went to get up.

Sam put out a hand to stop her. "I'm fine."

While they waited for Sam to clear his throat and compose himself, it didn't escape Marianne's notice that he brushed a tear from his eye.

Justin was soon back to business. "You said you have a snuff bottle, Marianne? The Ambassador had it in his hand when he died?"

She gave an involuntary shiver, re-living again the shock of finding the Ambassador on the floor. "It's in my desk drawer."

"Good. Keep it safe in there, in case the police need it."

"I tried to find a pulse," she said. "There was nothing. I put my ear to his lips. No breath. No heartbeat." Her voice shook. "I tried CPR for ages and ages. But there was nothing I could do. Nothing."

"It's okay, Marianne," Sam said. "It's okay."

Justin gave a long sigh of his own. They fell silent again, until he got up and started pacing around the room. "None of this makes any sense." He stopped and turned. "It's this suggestion that the Ambassador was having … a liaison that's getting to me." He looked at Marianne. "Do you think he was?"

"How the hell should I know?"

"Because you know everything that goes on around here," Justin said. "Nothing gets past you. Besides, you knew him better than the rest of us."

She frowned. "What makes you say that?"

"Well, for one thing, when you were working in the Embassy in Peking, he always took you to meetings and calls with him."

"Only to take the notes," she said, pointedly. "He knew I'd do a record of the conversation to send to London."

Justin ignored the barb. "He took you to receptions, too."

"Only when his wife didn't want to go. I was the token British woman, with the added advantage of speaking Chinese. Be thankful you were all spared that."

Sam gave her a small smile.

"What on earth were you doing in the Jazz Bar anyway?" Justin asked.

"The Ambassador asked me to meet him there," she said. "He wanted me to brief him on the programme first, then travel with him in the car to the Jing An Hotel for the welcoming banquet."

"Why was he staying in the Peace Hotel, and not at the Jing An Hotel with the Minister and delegation?" Justin asked.

Marianne was wondering now if the Ambassador had always planned a liaison in his hotel room. She shrugged. "I just assumed he wanted a bit of time and space away from them. It was his choice, I didn't question it."

"And as it turns out, it was an opportunity for the old man to have sex with some woman *other* than his wife," Justin said.

"How crudely put," Marianne said.

"How would you put it then?"

It was the strange look that Justin gave her, as if he were seeing her for the first time, that made her feel uncomfortable. Even Sam was looking at her with fresh eyes.

As she looked from one to the other, both men averted their eyes. Why? Then, it hit her like a thunderbolt. She understood now why they were firing those questions at her and insinuating she knew the Ambassador better than any of them.

They thought *she'd* been the woman having sex with the Ambassador in his hotel room.

10

The man of wisdom is never of two minds; the man of benevolence never worries; the man of courage is never afraid.

(Confucius)

The next morning Marianne woke early to a chink of daylight filtering through a gap in the curtains. Finally, it was morning. For a moment she lay still, listening to the roar of a plane taking off from nearby Shanghai airport. She felt calm, until the events of the previous night came flooding back.

She sighed and looked at the clock on her bedside cabinet – 5.05am. Reluctantly, she pushed the covers back and got up. She slipped on her robe and threw the curtains open wide. The soft, grey light of dawn greeted her. She shivered in the cold and went into the bathroom to run a bath. Or run a tub really, because that's what it was. Her house was a small villa, built by the Japanese. The bathroom was tiny, with a deep tub that she could stand up in, rather than a long European bath to stretch out in.

After bathing, she slipped on her robe again and went down to the kitchen to make a cup of tea. She stopped at the door of the sitting room when she heard a rattling sound coming from the kitchen. She knew what it was. Yesterday morning, the house boy had put a wire cage down to catch a rat that was coming in through the plumbing pipes to steal food. He'd laughed at her efforts to entice the rat with a piece of cheese and substituted it with a large piece of rump steak. "This is how we catch rats in China."

Marianne peered cautiously round the door to the kitchen. There, on the floor, was a huge, black rat trapped inside the cage. It had heard her and was furiously throwing itself against the wire to try and escape. She stared at it for a while, wondering how to get the cage and rat out of the kitchen. If she picked the cage up, the rat would bite her through the holes in the wire, yet there was no way she could leave it there. Its mess would have to be cleared up before she could eat breakfast too.

She went over to the back door and threw it open wide. Then she pulled out a long, thin wooden spoon from the utensil jar and approached the cage. The rat stared at her with its hard, black pits of eyes and bared its teeth. Gingerly she bent down and slotted the thin handle of the spoon through one of the holes in the wire, and out of another. She lifted the cage up, almost dropping it in fright as the rat lunged at her and locked its teeth onto the spoon. She darted through the back door and threw the cage and spoon onto the grass in the garden. She went back inside and slammed the door shut. She would leave a note for the house boy to deal with the rat. After all, he'd caught it.

Back in the kitchen she busied herself washing the floor, surfaces, table, and anywhere else the rat might have been, until the whole kitchen reeked of disinfectant. By then, the whole experience had put her off breakfast. She just made herself a cup of tea and went upstairs to get dressed.

It was still only 6 o'clock when she found herself driving out of the villa complex and taking the main road into town. Better to get an early start in the office than hang around at home, thinking about everything. Besides, she had a lot to do before she went over to the Jing An Hotel to pick up the Minister and delegation and take them to their first appointment.

Pottering along the main road at 20 mph to avoid the water-filled potholes, she'd encountered mostly lorries, official cars, and taxis at first. They were the only motorised vehicles permitted on the roads. Now, in the city's narrow streets, she had to avoid a mass of cyclists too. It amazed her what they balanced on their bicycles: cages of live chickens and ducks for the city markets, furniture, and even industrial machinery. The one in front of her now was towing a wooden platform on wheels, with a small fridge on top. The poor man was bent double over the handlebars, pedalling furiously to propel the bicycle along.

She glanced at the cramped houses as she went by. Families had spilled outside and were washing from bowls of water – the men and boys stripped to their waists for a more thorough clean. Adults, as well as children were brushing their teeth and spitting into the gutter. There was no such thing as privacy, or personal space, in this over-crowded city.

She couldn't stop thinking about the Ambassador as she drove along. In the cold light of morning, the shock and confusion had gone, and her brain was sifting through events. She kept stopping at the time *after* the Ambassador's death, when the police were in his hotel room. It was the way they kept giving each other furtive glances or going out into the corridor to speak in hushed tones that bothered her the most. She should have realised when they called in forensics that something wasn't right. She should have gone down to the lobby straightaway and telephoned the Embassy in Peking. Yet her strong instinct at the time had been to stay in the room with the Ambassador's body while the police investigated. In some weird way, she hadn't wanted to leave him alone with them. Had that been the wrong thing to do? Or, in her heart, had she already been fearing the worst? *Someone* had been in that room with him before he died, that's for sure.

A coldness crept over her. Not just because of the tragedy of his death, but also for the situation she found herself in. She'd been alone in the Peace Hotel's Jazz Bar waiting for the Ambassador. She'd been alone again when she'd found him dead in his hotel room. Of course, the Chinese police knew that. Her fingerprints would be all over the crime scene. If indeed it *was* a crime scene.

That wasn't where the real coldness stemmed from though. No, it stemmed from the realisation last night that Justin and Sam seemed to think *she'd* been having an affair with the Ambassador. What did they think happened last night, for goodness sake? That she'd slept with him in his hotel room, and then killed him, like some praying mantis?

The thought made her feel a little dizzy. She pulled up alongside the kerb and wound down the window for some fresh air. Immediately, a flurry of bicycle bells rang out. She was blocking the way. Needing more time to sort out her thoughts before going into the office, she decided to go and have a walk around Fuxing Park. It was close to the Consulate-General, in the old French Concession of Shanghai. Designed like a French park, with a lake, fountain and flower beds, she often stopped off for some exercise, or to sit in one of the Chinese pavilions and watch the world go by.

Arriving there, she parked her car and grabbed her briefcase. Ever cautious, she didn't want to leave her papers in the car. She slipped through the grey iron gates and started strolling along the wide, tree-lined boulevard. This was one of the few places in Shanghai where there were trees and grass. In her flat shoes, she walked along the concrete path towards the lake. It was wonderful to feel, and hear, the autumn leaves crunching underfoot. And to feel the breeze blowing in her face and hair. Finally, she could breathe.

She passed a group of old men playing cards and looked over at their pet birds in bamboo cages that hung from branches in a nearby tree. Even locked up in their cages, the little birds sung for joy to be out in the open and in the trees. That always made Marianne feel sad. She couldn't bear the thought of being imprisoned, locked away from society and the natural world. She'd rather be dead.

Reaching a pavilion, she went inside and sat down. Close by, a group of Chinese were on the grass performing their daily exercises together. Marianne had even joined them on some summer mornings to practise 'qi gong' with them. They never spoke to her, but they were comfortable in her presence. She smiled and relaxed as she watched them perform their slow, flowing movements and breathing exercises.

Predictably, her mind wandered back to the previous night. She really needed to write everything down, she thought, exactly as it happened, with timings and observations. A proper diary of events. She pulled some blank sheets of paper and a pen out of her briefcase and started to write. It was a relief to organise the random thoughts jumbling around in her head and put them down on paper. Occasionally, she stopped to reflect on what she'd written. She wanted to be sure she had everything right. At least it all made sense now, and she understood why she'd reacted the way she had.

Later, when she looked up, she was surprised to see she was alone. She'd been so engrossed, she hadn't noticed the exercise group leaving. Suddenly, a strange feeling came over her. It started as a shiver up her spine that told her something was not as it should be.

She checked her watch. Almost 8 o'clock. She'd been there for over an hour, writing. Now she'd be late for the office. Hurriedly, she stuffed the pages into her briefcase, slung it over her shoulder and jumped up.

There it was again. That shiver up her spine.

She looked all around, searching the bushes, without knowing what or who she was looking for.

She set off at a brisk pace. Tension filled her now, and she looked over her shoulder. Someone was following her, she was sure of it. She'd got used to that black sedan behind her for weeks, so why did it feel so threatening to think someone was following her around the park?

She was almost jogging by the time she reached her car. She jumped inside, locked the doors, and sat for a moment to get her breath back. Starting the car, she pulled into the traffic. From time to time she glanced in the mirror to see if the black sedan was there. Strangely, for the first time in weeks, it wasn't.

After a short drive, she pulled through the wooden gates, into the sanctuary of the British Consulate-General. Her relief was short-lived though. At the end of the drive, parked in front of the house, was a Chinese police car.

As the gates closed behind her, an overwhelming sense of being trapped, like those little birds hanging in their cages in the park, came over her. And there was absolutely nothing she could do about it.

11

Respond intelligently even to unintelligent treatment
(Laozi – Chinese philosopher and writer 6th – 5th
Century BC)

Marianne parked her car in her usual spot and walked towards the front door of the Consulate-General. Through the window, she could see Justin in his office, seated behind his desk, talking to two Chinese police officers. Mrs Wu, as interpreter, sat between them. The police had told Marianne last night they would want to speak to her again, but she hadn't expected them so soon. She slowed to catch Justin's eye to let him know she'd arrived, but he didn't look her way.

Once in the building, Marianne stopped outside Justin's door and listened to the murmurings inside. His smooth voice dominated the conversation, with Mrs Wu slipping in effortlessly behind him with the translation. They were an effective team.

Marianne raised her hand to knock and go in, but the image of the dead Ambassador sprang into her head again. The shock had gone, but not the sick feeling in her stomach. She dropped her hand and headed for her office at the back of the building. She needed to compose herself before talking to the police again.

In her office, she took off her coat, sat down at her desk and pulled out the diary of events she'd written in the park from her briefcase. She wanted to be word perfect when the police interviewed her. She started reading through everything again: from being followed by that black sedan on the way to the Peace Hotel, to her time in the Jazz Bar waiting for the Ambassador, to her journey up in the hotel lift, to the awful scene in his hotel room. When she got to the bit about the crumpled sheets and condom foil, she wondered how the Ambassador's wife was doing. Had anyone told her the full truth yet? Marianne would call her later, to offer condolences.

Her eyes drifted over to the window and the Yulan tree. The grey morning mist had given way to watery autumn sunshine, and she wondered why that funeral lantern bursting into flames had felt so threatening last night. Her eyes scanned the branches and mossy grass beneath the tree for signs of rope or any other debris from the lantern, but there was nothing.

Returning to her notes and reading through her description of the Ambassador's body on the bathroom floor, her eyes stopped on the sentence about the snuff bottle. She opened her desk drawer and looked inside for it. No sign. She pulled the drawer right out and shuffled everything around. The snuff bottle had gone.

She frowned, but she didn't panic. She'd mentioned it to Justin and Sam last night and told them where it was. They must have already given it to the police. Although they shouldn't have done that without asking first.

Not wanting anything else to disappear without her permission, she gathered up her notes and looked around for somewhere safe to put them. Somewhere no one would find them easily. She went over to the filing cabinet and flicked through the admin files. She pulled out one with the title 'Boiler and General Maintenance'. That would do. No one else in this post would ever look in there, she thought wryly. Taking half the papers off the file, she punched a hole through the corner of her notes, threaded the red tag through the pages and put the other papers back on top. Now, her diary of events was secure inside this innocuous file. She put the file back and closed the cabinet.

At that moment, Mrs Wu put her head around the door. "Justin asked me to get the snuff bottle for the police."

It was just like Wu to get straight to the point, without even a polite 'good morning'.

"I haven't got it," Marianne said. "I'll go and speak to them."

Wu shook her head. "No. Better you stay here."

Marianne's eyes narrowed as she looked at Mrs Wu. Her glossy hair was drawn back into a ponytail, exposing a slender forehead and porcelain skin. She couldn't be more than 22 or 23, but insisted on being called Mrs Wu, despite her youth and unmarried status. And Marianne knew why. Wu wanted to give herself an air of authority and set herself apart from the other local Chinese staff in the Consulate-General. Wu clearly thought she was going places. She already had a head start in that her father was a senior official in the Communist Party, which was no doubt how she'd got such a prestigious interpreting job in the first place. Marianne had never warmed to Wu and didn't like the way she spoke to her now. She moved towards the door.

Mrs Wu blocked her way. "Justin said you must stay in here."

"Why?"

"Please." Mrs Wu insisted. "Just wait. Justin will explain everything."

"Where's Sam?" Marianne asked.

"Justin sent him over to the Jing An Hotel to accompany the Minister and trade delegation on their programme of calls today."

Marianne was incensed. How dare Justin interfere in her work without consulting her.

Footsteps echoed along the corridor and they both turned.

Justin put his head around the door. "Where's the snuff bottle? I've told the police you found it on the bathroom floor next to the Ambassador. They want to take it away for analysis."

Marianne looked at him. "It's gone."

"You said last night you had it in here."

She nodded. "Yes, I put it in my desk drawer. But it's not here now, someone's taken it."

He looked lamely around her office. "Must be in here somewhere."

Marianne shook her head.

Justin sighed. "I'll tell them we'll get it to them later."

Marianne went to walk past him. "I'll tell them myself."

"No." He stood in front of her.

"I'm happy to talk to them," Marianne said. "They said they'd want to speak to me again."

Mrs Wu sounded officious when she said: "They're not here on an informal call."

Justin shuffled his feet nervously. "I've told them you have diplomatic immunity and will not be answering any of their questions today," he said. "At least, not until we've spoken to London."

Marianne's eyes widened. "Why?"

"Because they've just told me the Ambassador did not die of natural causes."

Marianne reeled back in shock.

Justin nodded. "His death is now a murder enquiry."

12

> *The man who asks a question is a fool for a minute, the*
> *man who does not ask is a fool for life*
> *(Confucius)*

The wind whipped through her hair as Jess stepped out of the Foreign Office into King Charles Street. 7.30pm on the dot. Fortunately, tonight, there was no sleet driving into her face or icy pavements to contend with. The sky was clear, with an almost full moon, which meant it was bitterly cold. Oh, to be back in the Australian or Caribbean sunshine, she thought. She pulled up the hood of her padded coat and held it in place as she walked into the wind.

Reaching Whitehall, she dodged between the buses and taxis and dashed across the road to the Black Swan. The warmth and cheery hubbub inside the pub on this mid-winter night lifted her spirits. She pushed back her hood and looked around for Tom. They'd agreed to meet in here for a drink and chat at 7.30pm. The place was packed with civil servants having 'one for the road' before going home. With their rosy red cheeks, some looked like they'd been in there a couple of hours and were already the worse for wear. The perishing weather outside was no incentive for them to leave their comfortable cocoon either.

There was no sign of Tom. She checked her watch, even though she knew she was bang on time. Did he know where the pub was? She pulled out her mobile to call him and realised she was gripping it like a vice. Relax, she told herself, let the poor man be a few minutes late. Walking up to the bar, she ordered herself a gin and tonic. She thought about getting Tom a drink too. But what? She'd seen him drink plenty of red wine in the Caribbean, but would he prefer a pint of beer or lager here? She looked at all the beer taps, wondering which brew he would choose.

"Let him get his own beer." The barman gave a wide grin. "His punishment for keeping a lady waiting."

Jess laughed and paid for her drink. Spotting a couple in the corner putting on their coats, she went over to claim their table, and settled down to wait for Tom. The first long sip of gin and tonic slipped down a treat, and she felt her jangled nerves relaxing for the first time that day. And what a day it had been. Surreal even. She'd arrived that morning to discover her boss Giles had died the night before under a tube train. Then, she'd seen Xiao Li being dragged into an official Chinese Embassy car. What had she wanted to tell Jess about the missing British diplomat, Marianne Henderson? Jess was worried that she hadn't reported what happened to Xiao Li to anyone, but she didn't know who to tell. Her own boss was dead and, by the time she'd made up her mind to talk to Sam, he'd gone home.

She was worried about Tom too. She should never have asked him to snoop around inside the Met. He was just on secondment from Australia. They'd suss him out in a heartbeat. She took another sip of her gin and tonic. She was going to tell him to forget she'd ever asked. None of this was his problem. Mind you, he was a difficult man to stop once he got involved in a case.

She shook her head remembering how shocked she'd been to see him today. Pleased too. But now she was nervous. The memory of their lingering goodbye kiss in the Turks and Caicos Islands made her shiver. Of course, he'd accepted her decision to return to the UK to be with her partner Simon through his illness, and they'd not been in touch since. That didn't stop her wondering from time to time what life would have been like if she'd gone to Australia with Tom. She shook her head at her own nonsense. For one thing, he hadn't even told her he was in London. Second, he would have gone back to Australia without seeing her at all if it hadn't been for this Chinese State visit. And third, he was keeping her waiting. So, not so keen after all. She smiled. They were friends, that's all.

"That's the first time I've seen you smile all day."

She jumped and looked up. "I was beginning to wonder if you were coming."

"Sorry I'm late," Tom said, in his no-nonsense way, without offering any excuse. He looked at her glass. "Another one?"

Jess was surprised to see she'd finished the first. "Please, I'll have a…"

"Gin and tonic?"

She nodded and watched him walk up to the bar. He got served straightaway, and cast his eyes around the pub and the customers while waiting for the barman to get the drinks, glancing instinctively towards the door when someone came in. That was Tom. Always alert. Always watchful.

He came back with the drinks and sat down.

Jess noted he'd bought himself a pint of lager.

After taking a long gulp from his glass, he turned to her. "So, what's the latest?"

She shrugged. "Nothing else has happened."

"Well that's a relief," he said. "What did they say in the Foreign Office when you told them about Xiao Li?"

She looked away.

"You *have* told them?"

"Not yet. I didn't really know who to tell since my boss is dead. I was going to have a word with Sam." She paused. "Sam Biggins was working in the Embassy in Peking in 1984 when the Ambassador committed suicide in Shanghai and Marianne Henderson went missing. He's the one who told me not to start raking up the past."

Tom raised an eyebrow. "Bit late for that, isn't it?"

She shrugged. "Sam went home early so I didn't get to talk to him. Anyway, while I've been sitting here, I've made up my mind to tell our PUS, Sir Anthony, about Xiao Li first thing in the morning. He told me about Giles going under that train and said to go to him if I had any problems. Let's face it Tom, I can't keep this to myself."

He nodded. "Sounds like a plan."

She shuffled in her seat. "And I want *you* to forget all about this. I had no right asking you to go sniffing around for information. No right whatsoever. I don't want you jeopardising your secondment to the Met."

His voice was matter-of-fact when he said. "Bit late for that too."

"Oh, really?" She looked at him. "What have you found out?"

"The British Ambassador's death features in the electronic archives, but only in a list of overseas deaths in 1984. All it says is that he died in Shanghai in 1984. Committed suicide in the Peace Hotel, just as you said."

Jess's eyes widened. "How?"

"With poison."

"He *poisoned* himself?"

Tom nodded. "With arsenic, apparently."

Jess sat stunned. She didn't know what she'd expected, but it wasn't arsenic poisoning. She pulled out her iPhone and started googling.

"What are you looking for?" he asked.

"To see what the symptoms are."

"I can tell you," he said. "In the final stages, the person suffers seizures and goes into shock. Then they go into a coma and die."

"Have you seen someone die of arsenic poisoning, then?"

"No, but it's textbook stuff."

Jess nodded. "It says here that arsenic is a metalloid and found all over the world in groundwater. White arsenic is made by heating arsenic ore, which produces a white crystalline powder that is soluble in water and virtually undetectable in food or drink." She glanced at Tom. "Did he eat or drink something with arsenic in it?"

"I guess so."

She frowned. "It says here too that in nineteenth-century Britain, arsenic was the poisoner's substance of choice. It was used to commit many murders." She paused. "Seems a rather ... *untidy* way of killing yourself."

"Untidy?"

She nodded. "Wouldn't it have been easier to take an overdose of sleeping tablets?"

"Perhaps he couldn't get any."

"Or hung himself at home?"

"People don't always hang themselves at home. They don't want family members to find them and have to live with that for the rest of their lives."

Jess was in her stride now. "Or, he could have just walked out of the hotel and thrown himself under a bus. Or jumped into the Huangpu River that runs through Shanghai." She returned to her iPhone. "Aha, listen to this." She read out loud: "Arsenic is a traditional Chinese medicine, dating back to 200 BC. The last Chinese Emperor but one, called Guāngxù, was poisoned with it. Scientists X-rayed through the tomb because they weren't allowed to open it and concluded the Emperor had consumed a quantity of arsenic three times a potentially lethal dose." She paused. "Now this is interesting."

"What?"

"They discovered the Emperor had been poisoned by measuring the levels of arsenic in the roots of his hair. Levels were higher near the roots, rather than the tips, showing poisoning was sudden, rather than a slow build up. That indicated he'd been poisoned." She turned to Tom. "Did they measure the arsenic in the Ambassador's hair?"

"How should I know?"

"Well, what did the post-mortem say, then?"

"There was nothing about a post-mortem."

She stared at him. "Must have been one."

He shrugged. "Perhaps the family, or the British government, wouldn't allow the Chinese to do one."

"In which case they would have done one here. The Ambassador's body must have been repatriated to the UK for burial or cremation, surely?"

"I've told you all I know from the electronic records."

Jess frowned. "The UK coroner must have held an inquiry too."

He shrugged. "We are talking about a death that occurred 34 years ago. Practices and regulations have changed."

Jess sighed with frustration. "So, all we can confirm is that the British Ambassador committed suicide in the Peace

Hotel in Shanghai in 1984, by poisoning himself with arsenic." She paused. "What about Marianne Henderson? Anything about her?"

"Absolutely nothing."

Jess snapped her iPhone case shut and slipped it back into her pocket. "That's it then. I'm going to have to ask Sir Anthony about Marianne Henderson in the morning too."

"Is that wise?"

"What else can I do? If I'm going to tell him about Xiao Li, I'm going to have to say she wanted to give me some information about Marianne Henderson's disappearance. It might all have happened 34 years ago but, well, what's really bugging me, Tom, is that the poor woman might still be alive. What if she's locked up in some Chinese labour camp somewhere?"

"That's not very likely, is it?"

"No. But only because she probably wouldn't have survived in those tough conditions for so long."

He took a long swig of beer and swallowed. "Looks like we've come to a dead end, then."

She looked sceptical. "There must be a paper file on all this in the Met's historical records, surely?"

He shrugged.

"How easy would it be to get a look at that?" she asked.

"Not easy at all," he said. "But I reckon I could give it a go."

"I don't want you to do anything that would get you into trouble."

"So you said." He smiled. "Come on. Let's brave the cold and get something to eat. Know anywhere good?"

She nodded. "Chinese or Italian?"

"Whichever is the closest?"

"We can walk to the Italian."

"Let's do that, then." He stood up and helped her on with her coat.

As she slipped her arm into a coat sleeve, she glanced up at him. "You haven't told me what else you've been doing this afternoon."

His eyes shone. "I've been out with the other guys in my protection team. We've been doing a recce of the Queen's State Dining Room, where she'll be hosting the Chinese President for dinner. It was fantastic going inside Buckingham Palace. A real privilege."

Jess smiled at his boyish enthusiasm, then she felt guilty about what she was asking him to do. "I really don't want to get you into any trouble."

He pulled a face. "No one else I'd rather get in trouble for."

She laughed as she slipped the other arm into her coat. The intervening years had faded away, and they were back to their easy friendship. She felt comfortable with Tom. Having worked with him on that Brisbane murder case, and on the horrors in the Turks and Caicos Islands, he was the one person she knew she could trust. Absolutely. And that was a relief because there was no one else in London she felt she could turn to.

13

He who knows all the answers has not been asked all the questions.
(Confucius)

It was 11pm when the taxi pulled up outside her block of flats. Jess was getting used to travelling around in style, but taxis were a luxury she could ill afford. She would have to stop this extravagance after the Chinese President's visit.

Now, full of spaghetti, tiramisu and red wine, she felt so much better. It wasn't just the food. It was great to go out with a friend, talk about old times, and take her mind off work for a few hours. It wasn't going to be a very easy conversation with Sir Anthony in the morning about Xiao Li and Marianne Henderson, that was for sure. But she had to tell someone. Sir Anthony was not only the head of the Foreign Office, he'd been working at our Embassy in Peking when Marianne Henderson went missing. He'd probably be furious Jess hadn't said something before now, but that couldn't be helped. She would put things right in the morning.

She paid the taxi driver and got out. The moon shone brightly through the leafless trees across the road in Regent's Park. A bitterly cold, but beautiful, night. She really ought to go out more, she thought. After this State visit, she would keep to more regular working hours and perhaps take an evening class. She could resume the jewellery making lessons she'd started years ago.

As she hurried towards the front door, she glanced over at Bev's ground floor flat. Her sitting room window overlooked the forecourt and the park opposite. Seeing the slats of the vertical Venetian blinds open slightly, Jess walked over and peered into Bev's sitting room to see if she was still up. It was all in darkness. There were no lights on in the hallway or kitchen beyond either.

She thought of Bev all alone in London and decided to invite her out for a meal at the weekend, or to a show. She could invite Tom too. They were both Australian and should have a lot in common. She would write a note and pop it through Bev's letterbox in the morning, on her way to work.

She was about to leave when a white glow in the corner of Bev's sitting room caught her eye. She cupped her right hand up against the window and peered closer. The light was coming from what looked like a small TV, perched on the corner of the sideboard. As Jess's eyes became more accustomed to the dark, she saw it was no ordinary TV. It was CCTV. Then, she saw her apartment block's forecourt on the screen *and* herself peering into Bev's sitting room window.

She jumped back, embarrassed to be caught snooping, and hurried over to the front door. She let herself in and started climbing the stairs to her flat. Why on earth would Bev have CCTV in her apartment, she wondered? She couldn't remember seeing it last night when she was in there. The camera was focused on the front of the building though. But why? Perhaps because that flat was on the ground floor and easier to burgle. Had Bev been watching the CCTV screen last night when Jess slipped on the icy steps? Is that why she'd come out so quickly to help?

A welcoming blast of warmth hit Jess as she went into her own flat. She flicked on the hall lights and picked up the mail from the doormat.

Her mobile bleeped. Putting her bag and mail on the hall table, she took off her coat, pulled out her phone and scrolled to the text.

Great to see you again. Enjoyed the meal and company. Just checking you're home okay. Tom x

Jess smiled. It was good to see him too, and good to have someone checking she was okay. She replied.

I'm back home and fine, thanks. Had a lovely evening too. See you tomorrow x

Great. Same time, same pub. We'll swap notes. Good luck with the boss x

Thanks, I think I'm going to need it. Don't get into any trouble on my account x

Don't worry. I won't x

Jess gave a wry smile at Tom's last text. She couldn't help but worry. The last thing she wanted was to ruin his secondment.

She picked up the mail from the hall table, walked into the kitchen and switched on the lights. As she sifted through, she spotted the usual bills and advertising flyers, but one plain, white envelope looked unusual. It was so thin, it felt like there was nothing inside and her name and address had been handwritten on it, in blue ink.

Intrigued, Jess slit open the envelope and peered inside. She pulled out an old, faded photo … of a Chinese snuff bottle.

She stared at it, thinking there must be some mistake. She looked inside the envelope again for a letter, but there was nothing else in there. Had the postman put it through the wrong letterbox? It *was* addressed to her. It had a UK first-class stamp on the top right-hand corner and a London postmark.

She stared at the photo again, angling it up to the light to see better. The pretty snuff bottle had a Chinese temple painted on it, with little lanterns hanging from the eaves. When she turned it over, someone had written 'Shanghai – 1984' on the back, in the same blue ink.

Shanghai – 1984! That's when she knew it was no mistake. Someone had deliberately sent her that photo. As she stood in the kitchen trying to make sense of things, a little ripple of fear shivered through her. Whoever had sent her the photo knew exactly where she lived. But why send it to her? What was the importance of that little snuff bottle? And what did it all mean?

14

Silence is a true friend who never betrays
(Confucius)

The next morning, Jess stood outside Bev's front door, an envelope clutched in her hand. Inside, was a note inviting Bev out on Saturday evening. As she went to put it through the letterbox, a vision of the CCTV screen in Bev's sitting room the night before made her hesitate. Something about that unnerved her. Why would Bev need CCTV? Was she watching Jess outside her front door now? Jess slipped the envelope into her coat pocket and headed for the front door. What did she know about Bev anyway? This was London, the woman could be anybody.

The purple glow of morning breaking behind the bare trees greeted Jess as she stepped outside. It might be early, but the morning traffic along Prince Albert Road was already busy. Fortunately, most of the preparatory work on her side of the State visit was finished, so she didn't have to be in especially early. That's what she told herself anyway. The truth was she wasn't looking forward to talking to Sir Anthony about Xiao Li and Marianne Henderson. She wished now she'd tried to see him last night, before she'd left the office.

Crossing the road, she headed for the bus stop. As she walked, she kept looking over her shoulder to see if a bus was coming. They weren't very frequent, and she didn't want to miss one.

A familiar figure came jogging out of the park.

Bev raised her hand in a wave and came running up. "G'day, Jess. How are you this morning?"

Jess couldn't help but smile. Bev looked so lean and healthy in her exercise gear. "That's what I call dedication. It's still dark, and you're out running."

Bev smiled, sounding almost defensive when she said: "It's important for me to keep fit."

"Oh, I wasn't criticising." Jess noticed Bev's face wasn't even red from running. Nor was she panting and puffing. "I'm full of admiration," she went on. "I think I'd be sick if I got up early and went running."

Bev laughed. "Maybe, at first. You'd soon get used to it." She paused. "Why don't we go out for a run together sometime, if you'd like to."

Jess couldn't think of anything worse, but she nodded politely. She did realise that Bev was trying to be friendly though and remembered her kindness the other night when she fell and hit her head. She pulled the envelope out of her pocket. "I was going to post this through your letterbox on my way out, but forgot," she said. "If you're not busy on Saturday night, I wondered if you'd like to go out for a meal or catch a show or something."

Bev's eyes lit up. "I'd love that."

A squeal of brakes made Jess turn. A bus was slowing as it approached. Jess stuck her arm out to request it to stop. "I must get this, or I'll be late for work. I'll give you a call about the arrangements for Saturday night."

"Thanks, Jess. See you then, if not before."

"Bye." Jess sprinted the few yards to the bus stop, arm outstretched all the way to make sure the bus stopped. As the doors opened, she turned and waved to Bev, then got on and chose a seat at the back.

As the bus made its way slowly in the procession of traffic into the centre of London, she watched the rose-pink mist of dawn through the window. On a summer morning, she would often walk through Regent's Park to the underground station at Baker Street. It could be quicker than taking the bus. She never went into the park until it was light though and was surprised to see Bev jogging around it this morning. She would warn Bev. On these dark winter mornings, the park was not the place to be. Then an odd thought came to her. Why would the woman have CCTV for security, and then go jogging in the park in the dark?

As the bus rumbled on and the London streets came to life, Jess pulled the photo of the snuff bottle out of her bag and stared at it. Why would anyone send her that? With 'Shanghai – 1984' written on the back, it had to be connected to the Ambassador's suicide and Marianne Henderson's disappearance. But how? And why send it to her home address and not her office? That made her nervous. Was the photo meant to frighten her? It seemed more like a puzzle than a threat. A challenge even. Still, she would need to be careful. Perhaps Bev's CCTV camera was not such a mad idea after all.

She pulled out her iPhone and googled 'photos of Chinese snuff bottles'. She scrolled through a photo library of beautiful specimens, mostly made of glass, cloisonné, lacquer or porcelain. Some were carved for decoration and some hand-painted. She could see how collectable and valuable they might be. Disappointed she couldn't find any resembling the one in her photo, she slipped it back into her bag.

By the time Jess reached the Haymarket, it was properly light. There was no frost that morning, just grey cloud. It was going to be one of those gloomy winter days, the cloud hanging so low you could almost hit your head on it. Still, at least it wasn't sleeting, snowing or even raining yet. She stood up and moved to the central doors to get off. She would walk the rest of the way and clear her head.

At the end of the street, she ran down the steps, crossed over the Mall and followed the path into Horse Guards Road. She was just approaching the Foreign Office when, up ahead, she saw Sam walk down Clive Steps and head into St James's Park. Bit early for a morning walk, she thought, as she watched him go. Instinctively, she went after him to show him the photo. If there was one person who would know something about that Chinese snuff bottle, it was Sam.

She followed him into the park, past the resident pelicans on their breeding ground, and headed for Blue Bridge. Sam walked so quickly, she found it difficult to catch up. She called out to him as he crossed over the bridge, but he didn't hear her. Jess glanced back towards Horse Guards Parade, where the London Eye poked up behind the old roof tops. It should have looked out of place, but somehow it didn't. As she crossed the bridge, she saw Sam heading in the direction of Buckingham Palace. Then, just as she thought she would never catch up with him, he stopped at a park bench. She stopped too because she saw someone else sitting on the bench. If Sam had a meeting, she didn't want to intrude. She screwed up her eyes to see better. Whoever it was had their back to her and wore a long, black coat and fur hat. It must be a woman, she thought, because of their small frame.

Jess continued watching from a distance.

Sam sat down at the opposite end of the bench from the woman. With a wide gap in between them, they looked like strangers who didn't know each other. That seemed odd to Jess. People were hurrying through the park on their way to work, but no one else was sitting around on this cold winter morning. If he was just passing time, Sam would have sat on one of the many empty benches along the way. No, he had to be meeting this woman. Yet, from what Jess could see, they didn't seem to be speaking to each other. Perhaps they were talking quietly? Jess strained her ears, but she couldn't hear voices.

From her distant side view, Jess couldn't see the woman's face, and walked on a few paces to get a better look. It was only when the woman sat forward slightly and looked at Sam that Jess saw the unmistakable pale, yet oriental, face …

Mrs Wu, the Chinese Ambassador.

Alarm bells started ringing in Jess's head. This looked like a clandestine meeting. Yet they still didn't seem to be talking to each other. Were they passing notes or documents? It was only when they both kept looking at their watches, and into the distance, Jess realised they were waiting for someone else to arrive.

Pulling up her hood so as not to be recognised, Jess looked around. She wanted to find a safe spot to watch from, where she wouldn't be seen. Turning back, she walked to the point where another path criss-crossed the one she was on. She took a left turn and walked some way up the path leading back to the Mall, keeping Sam and Mrs Wu in view all the time. Then she dodged across the grass, feeling the heavy dew underfoot as she went. Finding another bench almost directly behind Sam and Mrs Wu, but at least fifty yards away, she sat down to watch.

She didn't have to wait long. A man came into sight. He glanced over at Sam and Mrs Wu, then walked towards them. His pace was neither fast nor slow, he just looked like he was out for a stroll. Buttoned up in a large black overcoat, all Jess could see were grey suit trousers and a white collar and tie poking out from either end of it. But what really struck her was the way he walked which indicated an older man – assured, oozing authority. That piqued her interest even more. As he got closer to Sam and Mrs Wu, she saw his face. He looked familiar somehow, even from a distance.

For a reason she wouldn't have been able to explain, Jess whipped out her iPhone and scrolled to camera. Holding it up, she snapped the man, took another of the back view of Mrs Wu and Sam sitting on the bench, and quickly shoved the phone back into her coat pocket.

Things got even more interesting when the man approached the park bench where Sam and Mrs Wu sat. He didn't greet either of them or sit down. Instead, he turned and looked across the lake as if he was just watching the mute swans gliding by. Now, Jess could hear voices. She couldn't make out what they were saying, but the three of them were having a conversation, without looking at, or acknowledging, each other.

All manner of thoughts whirled around in Jess's head, but one stood out. She shouldn't be there watching or taking photographs. She didn't leave though, she couldn't take her eyes off the three of them.

Jess studied their body language to try to understand what was going on. They were tense, no doubt about that. From her distance, it was Mrs Wu's voice she heard doing most of the talking. Was she passing information? Working for British intelligence even? That didn't make sense because Sam Biggins was there. He was just a researcher in the Foreign Office, wasn't he?

Suddenly Mrs Wu stood up and drew herself authoritatively up to all five feet of her height. Then she turned on her heels and walked off. Everything about her stiffness and abrupt parting indicated she'd left on a sour note. Jess hadn't heard any arguing, but they'd hardly want to attract attention by shouting at each other.

Immediately, the unidentified man strolled off in the other direction, but not before glancing all around him. For the briefest moment, his eyes locked on Jess's. Her heart quickened. She bent her head forward and started rummaging in her bag to try to shield her face. Thankfully she still had her hood up. When she peered up again, he'd gone. She breathed a sigh of relief, comforted by the thought that as she didn't know him, he wouldn't know her.

Sam continued to sit motionless on the seat. Jess couldn't tell by his demeanour how he was feeling after his meeting, but she didn't dare let him see her. She stood up, dashed across the grass, and ran up the path away from him. She was too shaken by what she'd seen to confront him now, and there were so many questions buzzing around in her head. She had to give herself time to think, to try and make sense of things, before deciding what to do.

Eventually, she walked back towards the Foreign Office the long way around to avoid Sam. As she went, she pulled out her mobile and scrolled through the pictures until she found the snap she'd taken of the man. Magnifying the screen, a large, well-lined face and ruddy complexion stared back at her. She still couldn't place him. Had she met him briefly somewhere before? Or seen him in the papers or on TV perhaps?

She didn't know, but she was compelled to find out.

15

Only the wisest and stupidest of men never change
(Confucius)

Jess sat at her desk in the office replaying the scene in the park over and over in her head until every little detail was seared on her brain. It had looked like a covert meeting, something out of a Le Carré spy novel. Except it wasn't fiction. The meeting was no chance encounter either. The three of them had set it up, yet they didn't want to be seen talking to each other. Interestingly, it was Mrs Wu who'd seemed particularly annoyed when she left.

What on earth was going on? And what was Sam up to? He'd been the one to tell Jess what happened in Shanghai in 1984. He'd told her to stop her digging around in the past too. Yet here he was meeting the Chinese Ambassador secretly. Why? There could be only one reason, although Jess couldn't begin to get her head around it. Had Sam been working for the Chinese all these years? Surely not, although he had been uniquely placed in Library and Records Department to see all the classified documents. If anyone was betraying their country, she prayed it was Mrs Wu.

Jess stood up and paced around the room to try and stop her mind running riot. She had to think logically. All this began when Xiao Li asked to meet her to tell her about Marianne Henderson. Everything kept coming back to Marianne. She was the key to all this. Why had she disappeared in Shanghai in 1984? And why did no one give a damn? That was what bugged Jess the most. No one seemed to care. She tried to put herself in Marianne's shoes. Diplomats often found themselves travelling around a country, away from colleagues and their Embassy in the capital, as she had found to her cost in Brisbane when the British businesswoman Ellen Chambers was murdered. If it hadn't been for Tom…

Had anyone helped Marianne in Shanghai? Sam and Sir Anthony had both been working in the Embassy in Peking at the time, as had her boss Giles Pettiford. But who else had been working in Shanghai with Marianne? Sam said that Marianne had been sent to open the new Consulate-General with another UK colleague. Who was that colleague? Maybe they could shed some light on what happened to her?

Her thoughts turned back to Sam. She had wanted to show him the photo of the snuff bottle, but his little rendezvous in the park had shaken her confidence in him. First though, she knew she had to talk to Sir Anthony. Xiao Li's request to speak to Jess privately about Marianne Henderson, and the manner of her removal off the street, even if it was by members of her own Embassy, were weighing heavily. Jess couldn't keep that to herself any longer. Sir Anthony had told her to go to him if she had any problems. He *was* the Head of the Foreign Office. If she couldn't tell him, who could she tell?

Resolute, she picked up the phone and called his Private Secretary. She guessed Sir Anthony would be busy with engagements all day, but perhaps he could spare her ten minutes at some point? Deep down, she didn't know whether she was doing the right thing or not. She just knew it was her duty to report it, whatever the consequences.

For the rest of the morning, Jess was unable to concentrate on anything with the turmoil in her head. She would read a few things, get up and pace around for a while, then go back to reading again. This went on until, in the distance, she heard Big Ben strike one o'clock. Almost simultaneously, her stomach rumbled. She needed to get some lunch, but she was reluctant to leave her office in case Sir Anthony's Private Secretary called. When her stomach growled again, she knew she couldn't hold out much longer. She would pop down to the canteen and buy a sandwich to bring back to eat at her desk. Sir Anthony was probably having his lunch now anyway.

Picking up her handbag, she locked the door behind her and hurried along to the central staircase. She would have found the canteen even if she hadn't known where it was. All she had to do was follow the smoky haze of frying and the smell of boiled veg that hung in the stairwell.

Down in the basement, the staff canteen was anything but inviting, with its dingy walls, large melamine-topped tables, and patterned lino designed to look like red tiles. A far cry from the glittering party in Durbar Court the other evening, she thought, as she picked up a tray and joined the queue.

Large rectangular dishes of pre-cooked fish and chips, egg and chips, and other fried food, were laid out on the counter, keeping warm under heat lamps. She didn't fancy any of that, but hot food seemed more inviting now than a sandwich. She picked up an individual shepherd's pie from a tray and helped herself to a large spoonful of carrots and broccoli. She would eat quickly and go back to her desk.

Keeping her eyes down to avoid having to sit with anyone she knew, she made her way to an empty table at the back of the canteen.

While she ate, she could think of nothing but Marianne Henderson. Something was lurking in the recesses of her brain, but she couldn't quite put her finger on it. She laid her knife and fork down and looked up. She'd been too busy eating and thinking to see Sam come into the canteen but, at that precise moment, he turned away from the counter holding a tray of food. They locked eyes.

He hesitated.

She nodded at him. This was an ideal opportunity to talk to him, on neutral ground in the canteen. Butterflies fluttered in her stomach. She didn't dare tell him she'd spied on him with Mrs Wu in the park. She'd have to try and get him to open-up some other way.

He walked over, with none of his usual boyish bounce on show. "Mind if I join you?" he asked.

"Please." She gestured for him to sit down.

He put his tray on the table and sat down, heavily. "How are things?" he asked.

His grey hair looked limp and greasy, as if he hadn't had time to shower that morning. But his eyes made her start, the whites were completely blood red. "Are you, all right?" she asked.

He looked surprised at first. "Oh, you mean my eyes. Burst blood vessels. It happens from time to time. High blood pressure."

"They look sore."

He shook his head. "Looks worse than it feels. My wife says I look like I've just come off the set of a vampire movie."

She smiled. "You do."

"Thanks." He changed the subject. "Everything all right with the visit?"

She nodded. "Fine. The work's all done. Just waiting for the President to get here."

"Bet you'll be glad when it's over?"

"On the contrary. It'll be interesting with all the Chinese in town."

He pulled a face.

"I thought you'd enjoy having them around," she said. "A fitting end to your career."

He looked up, sharply. "What's that supposed to mean?"

She shrugged. "You said you were retiring soon. Relations are so much better with the Chinese these days. I'm sure you've played your part in that over the years."

He just started tucking into his fry-up.

"It might be a good opportunity to catch up with some Chinese officials you know too," she added. "Have you had a look at the list of people coming with the President? He's bringing a whole retinue."

He nodded.

"Anyone you recognise?"

"One or two."

"There can't be many top Chinese officials you don't know."

He just smiled.

She had to talk to him about Mrs Wu, but she didn't quite know how to raise the subject. Then a thought came to her. "Tell me. Did you meet Mrs Wu, the Chinese Ambassador, during one of your stints in China?"

She'd dropped that question in as casually as she could, but he immediately stopped eating and gave her a searching look. "Yes."

Jess was thrown, she hadn't expected him to admit it. "Where did you meet her? Peking?"

"Shanghai," he said. "She was employed as our Chinese interpreter when the Consulate-General first opened. Her English was brilliant, even back then."

Jess's head was reeling. Oh my God, Mrs Wu had been an employee of the British Consulate-General in Shanghai in 1984 when it opened. That means she would have known Marianne Henderson back then, and probably Sir Anthony, and Giles too. The thought made her stomach turn. Could Mrs Wu still be working for the British government? Did that explain the meeting in the park?

Emboldened, Jess reached into her handbag and pulled out the photo of the snuff bottle. This was as good a time as any, she thought, as she laid it on the table, reverse side up, so that Sam could read "Shanghai – 1984" written on the back. He didn't react until she turned the photo over to expose the snuff bottle.

His fork clattered on the plate.

His reaction startled her. "Someone sent me this photo, anonymously," she said.

"For God's sake." He stared at her. "I told you to leave all this alone. Why won't you listen?"

His hostility surprised her, but she wouldn't be put off. "This photo is obviously connected to events in Shanghai in 1984. Why would someone take a photo of this snuff bottle? Can you tell me what it means? Your reaction when you saw it tells me it *is* important."

"I'd burn it if I were you." He went to pick it up.

Jess slapped her hand down on top of the photo to stop him, dragged it towards her and put it back into her handbag. She wanted to tell Sam she'd seen him in the park with Mrs Wu that morning. She wanted to know why they were meeting and who the other man was. But he looked so shaken, angry even, she knew she couldn't push him any further right now.

That sat in uncomfortable silence for a while.

"Well, I must get on with some work," she said with a forced brightness.

He didn't reply.

"See you later, then." She got up and walked calmly out of the canteen. *Oh my God!* What a reaction! She'd never seen Sam so upset. That photo had shaken him to the core, but he wouldn't tell her what the significance of the snuff bottle was.

Still, her heart was hammering with excitement. She'd uncovered a connection between Marianne Henderson, Sam Biggins and Mrs Wu in Shanghai in 1984. Now, finally, she felt she was getting somewhere.

★

Back in her office again, Jess jumped every time the phone rang, thinking it was Sir Anthony's office. It was like an axe hanging over her head. How would he react when she told him? Throw a fit? Move her from the China desk? Refuse to allow her to take part in the President's programme? Sack her even? All these worries were getting under her skin.

Jess sighed and looked up at the window. The darkness of night had crept over the building ages ago. Only the beam from her desk lamp lit the room and cast shadows on the wall. She shivered and checked her watch. Just past 6pm. She needed to keep an eye on the time. She was meeting Tom in the pub again at 7pm.

Kicking off her shoes, she bent down and rubbed her frozen toes. She needed a hot drink to warm herself up now the central heating had gone off. She put her shoes back on and went into the general office adjoining hers. All was in darkness. Everyone else had gone home without saying goodbye, probably not wanting to disturb her. She really had been living in her own little world while working on the President's visit. When it was over, she'd take everyone out for a meal to say thanks.

She went back into her office, picked up her mug, and walked along the silent corridor to the kitchen to make some coffee. Apprehension flowed over her as she approached Giles Pettiford's old office. His had been a terrible death, under a tube train. A violent, tragic death. Still no news about whether it was suicide though. As she passed by, his office door stood half open, with only the light from the corridor shining inside. Jess couldn't bear to look in, for fear of seeing him sitting at his desk. The man was a total workaholic in life. Nothing could keep him from his papers. Would he come back to them in death too? She scooted past, eyes firmly ahead. She was being totally irrational, but Giles's strong presence still seemed to be all around, casting shadows.

It was on her way back from the kitchen, mug of coffee in hand, that she noticed the position of Giles's office door had changed. It was now pushed to, with light around the edges of the door. Someone was inside, with the light on. It couldn't be his secretary. She'd been so upset about his death, she was on sick leave. Jess's heart quickened as she tip-toed over and put her ear to the door. She heard rustling papers and a cupboard door close. She raised her hand to push the door open.

Suddenly, the door clicked shut from the inside, making her jump back. She went to grab the handle to open the door, but something stopped her. Call it an irrational fear, self-preservation, or whatever, she turned and hurried away. It was none of her business who was in Giles's office anyway. Back in the safety of her own office, she shook her head at her own folly, and kicked off her shoes again. Mug in hand, she walked over to the window and looked up at the night sky, which was all she could see from her window. Blackness greeted her. No moon, no stars, no rain, no sleet. Just blackness.

Suddenly she became aware of a presence behind her. There had been no noise, no rustling of clothes, just a sense that someone was there. She spun round, spilling her coffee down her skirt.

"Sorry. I didn't mean to startle you," a smooth voice said.

Jess stood open-mouthed, looking at Sir Anthony.

"You asked to see me," he said, "so I thought I'd take a walk up here."

That was unheard of. Sir Anthony always summoned everyone to his office. And there she was now with no shoes on, mug in hand, and coffee all over her. He, on the other hand, was impeccably dressed in his suit, with his tie knotted perfectly in place.

While Sir Anthony went back to the door and closed it, she put her mug down on the windowsill, rushed around her side of the desk, and slipped on her shoes.

"Let's sit down, Jess." He walked back and pulled up a chair to the other side of her desk.

She sat down obediently, thinking this was all wrong. *He* should be the one sitting behind a desk, not her.

"Now." He fixed his dark eyes on her. "How's the Chinese President's visit going?"

"Oh fine. All the work's done. We're just waiting for him to get here now."

"Good." He paused. "So, if that's all going well, what did you want to talk to me about?"

"Well," she hesitated. She'd been rehearsing this moment all day in her head, but he'd flustered her by coming up to her office. She took a deep breath. "I felt I should report an incident that happened the other day."

He raised an eyebrow. "Is it connected to the President's visit?"

"Yes, although not directly."

He crossed his legs and waited.

As she looked down to collect her thoughts, she couldn't help but notice his polished shoes. "I don't know how else to say this except to come straight out with it," she said.

He nodded.

"At the reception in Durbar Court the other evening, my opposite number at the Chinese Embassy asked if she could see me privately the following day. She, well, she didn't want anyone else to know about it." Jess glanced up at Sir Anthony, but he sat still waiting for her to continue. "I have to say I was surprised," she went on, "but Xiao Li looked so anxious that I agreed to meet her in a café in Villiers Street after our last visit planning meeting."

"Yesterday?" he said.

She nodded.

Sir Anthony frowned. "Are we talking about a defection here? A defection of a Chinese official?"

"No." Jess pushed her hair from her forehead. "I don't think so, but…"

"Because if we are, you were out of your depth. You should have reported it immediately." His voice was low and firm, but the tone sharp. "So, what did she want to talk to you about?"

"Marianne Henderson."

Sir Anthony didn't move a muscle. Not that Jess expected him to. He was a cool operator, a master tactician and negotiator. Only now, his eyes bored into her so fiercely that she had to look away.

"I had no idea who Marianne Henderson was at first," she continued, "until Xiao Li explained she was a British diplomat in Shanghai who went missing in 1984. Xiao Li wanted to give me some information about her."

A strange look flitted across his face for the briefest moment. Was it shock? Surprise? Jess couldn't tell.

"And you went to meet Xiao Li ... alone?" he asked.

Jess nodded. "After the protocol meeting, Xiao Li and I left separately, as she had asked. I followed her up Whitehall. Just as she approached the corner with Whitehall Place, a Chinese Embassy car drew up alongside her. A man jumped out and grabbed her. Xiao Li struggled but he dragged her into the car and it sped off."

Sir Anthony stared at her. Those eyes ...

Jess braced herself for a blast. But it never came.

"Have they found Marianne?" he asked, quietly.

Jess was thrown again. "I–I don't know. Xiao Li never got to tell me. But, well, they must know *something,* or she wouldn't have approached me in the first place, surely?"

He held her gaze for a while longer, as if trying to tell whether she was telling the whole truth. Then he sighed, deeply. "I'm glad you told me Jess. It was the right thing to do." He paused. "Have you discussed it with anyone else?"

She shook her head. She couldn't possibly implicate Tom.

He nodded. "Right, leave this with me. I'll make some discreet enquiries."

She wondered whether to mention seeing Sam Biggins and the Chinese Ambassador in the park that morning, but something stopped her. She was curious about Marianne Henderson though and compelled to find out more about her. "You must have known, Marianne," she said.

He nodded.

"I keep thinking about her going missing all those years ago. I know it has nothing to do with me, but I can't stop thinking about her." She looked at Sir Anthony. "What happened to make her disappear?"

He sounded weary when he said: "It was all a very long time ago."

"I shudder to think she's been in some Chinese prison for over 30 years." Jess looked at him. "Don't we have a duty to look for her? She might still be alive."

He shook his head. "It all happened a long time ago. And that's where it should stay. In the past."

Jess thought she saw anguish in his eyes now, but it was hard to tell what the man was thinking. "Why did she go missing?" she asked.

"Best not drag up the past."

"Please. I should like to know."

He looked at her and sighed again. "It's the age-old story of love and betrayal. Marianne had an affair with our Ambassador. Our married Ambassador. The Chinese Secret Service found out. They blackmailed him, threatening to expose the affair to his wife and family, and he passed over some classified information to them."

"Oh my God!" Sam had told her about the affair, but not that the Chinese had blackmailed the Ambassador into what could only be described as spying for them.

Sir Anthony nodded. "Racked with guilt and finding himself compromised as a man and a patriot, he committed suicide."

"With *arsenic?*"

Sir Anthony's eyes narrowed. "How did you know about that?"

Letting that information slip was a mistake since Tom had told her. "On Google," she said, quickly. "I found a newspaper article that said our Ambassador committed suicide. It didn't say anything about Marianne Henderson, or the affair and blackmail though. That's *really* shocking."

He eyed her suspiciously. "Yes, it is."

"Do you think Marianne's dead?" she asked.

He looked and sounded genuinely sad when he said: "Probably." Then he stared her. "I know all about you, Jess. I know what happened to you in Australia, and I know what happened in the Turks and Caicos Islands. You nearly lost your life on both occasions."

She stiffened.

"Don't let there be a third occasion." His voice was firm. "Things may not turn out so well for you next time."

Was that a threat?

"You're a good officer," he went on. "Don't ruin your career over this. The events in Shanghai in 1984 are an embarrassment for the British government, and heartache for the families of the Ambassador and Marianne. It will only do harm if you drag this up and the media start digging around. Our relationship with the Chinese is good, better than it has been for many years. We have trade agreements, resource agreements and many other reasons to keep them on our side." He sat forward in the chair. "Don't do anything to spoil this visit, or damage this bilateral relationship in any way, because the stakes are too high."

She bristled. "I would never do anything to compromise this country's interests. Not in a million years."

"I'm glad to hear it," he said. "Now this exchange, and what I've told you about Marianne and the Ambassador, stays firmly in this room. Is that understood?"

She nodded.

He stood up. "Decline all further approaches from the Chinese for meetings." He paused. "It's important you tell me immediately if anyone contacts you again about any of this."

"Of course."

At the door, he turned to her. "Now let this be the end of the Marianne Henderson story once and for all."

16

*By three methods we may learn wisdom. First, by
reflection, which is noblest; second, by imitation, which is
easiest; and third by experience, which is the bitterest.*

(Confucius)

"All I'm saying is that there's a discrepancy between what
Sam told me and what Sir Anthony said."

Tom frowned at Jess.

"Sam never mentioned anything about the Ambassador
passing secret information to the Chinese," Jess went on.
"He told me the Ambassador committed suicide after
Marianne Henderson threatened to expose their affair. He
never said anything about the Chinese finding out and
blackmailing him."

Tom put his chopsticks down and dabbed his chin with
a paper napkin. He was enjoying having dinner with Jess
for the second night in a row. They'd met in the pub again,
had a quick drink, and got a taxi to this Chinese restaurant
off Victoria Road – one of Jess's favourites.

He flicked his eyes around again. Why were Chinese
restaurants always so dark? The only light came from a few
lamps made to look like Chinese lanterns, suspended from
the ceiling. The furniture was modern though, and typical

of western restaurants serving eastern food. His eyes rested on a large mural on the far wall, covered with painted faces of historic Chinese women.

"Beautiful faces, but sad, don't you think?" Jess said.

He turned to see she had followed his gaze. He looked at the mural again. "Why are none of them smiling?"

"You wouldn't either if your feet were bound so tight they were killing you."

He saw her mischievous smile. "True."

She laughed.

He'd chosen a table by the window so that he could watch all the comings and goings. It made him feel more at ease. Only three other tables were occupied, with couples, but it was a cold night and not one where you'd want to come out if you didn't have to, even for great food.

He glanced out the window. The glass was tinted, which made it easier to see out than in. He tensed when he saw a grey car parked across the street. He screwed up his eyes, but it was too dark to read the number plate.

Forcing a smile, he turned back and pushed the dish of Gong Bao Ji Ding towards Jess. "Have some more of this chilli peanut chicken before I eat it all." He paused. "Great food here by the way."

She looked up. "I wouldn't take you to any rubbish restaurant."

He smiled and took another swig of beer to wash down the food.

Jess helped herself to another spoonful of chicken.

"Sam might not be trying to hide anything from you," he said. "Perhaps he just doesn't know the full story. Have you thought about that? Sir Anthony would know because he's the head of the Foreign Office. Maybe it's the age old 'need to know' principle. Sam didn't need to know everything, and still doesn't."

144

"True," she admitted, "but it's like the cork has suddenly popped out of a champagne bottle and everything's just flowing."

He frowned.

"First, my boss Giles falls under a tube train. Then, this business with Xiao Li. They may seem like random events, but they're connected to what happened in Shanghai in 1984, I'm sure of it."

Tom knew she was right, and that worried him. He hadn't told her he'd come to a road block inside the Met. After checking the electronic archives and finding nothing more about the Ambassador's suicide, he'd phoned historical records. The archivist had been friendly at first. She would check to see if they had a file and let him know. But, when she'd phoned back, her voice was officious. "Yes, they had a file on the Ambassador's death in Shanghai in 1984. It was now under the control of Counter Terrorism Command. He would need to get a letter from his superior officer requesting the file, the reason for the request, and how it linked in with any current investigation."

That sealed it. Tom knew he'd never get his hands on that file. But would Jess stop digging? She was like a dog with a bone once she got her teeth into something. She just wouldn't let go. He knew all about that, because he was just the same.

This was serious though. They would be taking on the establishment, and there was no way they could win. He had to stop her ruining her career. "Sounds like we're talking about treason here, Jess. If the Chinese were blackmailing the Ambassador and he gave them classified information, well…"

"I'm aware of that, Tom."

He tried again. "It's obviously been hushed up or you, and everyone else, would have known about it."

She nodded.

"It's going to be impossible to follow any paper or electronic trail. And no one's talking." He shrugged. "Looks like we've come to the end of the road. Anyway, it all happened a long time ago, and it's well above *our* pay grade."

She gave him a hard stare, as if reaching into the recesses of his mind. "Has someone warned you off?"

Before he could answer, they were interrupted by the waiter who laid a plate on the table with a flourish and set about theatrically carving up half a Peking duck. They watched in silence as he smeared sweet bean sauce on a steamed pancake and filled it with pieces of succulent duck, shredded cucumber and spring onion. He filled two pancakes, put one in front of each of them, and left the rest for them to assemble themselves.

Peking duck was Tom's choice, he loved the crisp skin and soft meat. He picked up his pancake and took a large bite. "Mm. Delicious."

Jess picked up her pancake with her chopsticks and took a bite. She chewed slowly and swallowed. "So," she looked him in the eye, "who's warned you off?"

She could read him like a book. He knew he had no option but to tell her what happened when he tried to get hold of the file on the Ambassador's death from historical records.

Her face lit up when he'd finished. "Ah, well, at least we know now they've got a file?"

"Apparently."

"I suppose it's not possible to make up a credible reason for wanting to see it, is it?"

He raised his eyebrows.

"No, I guess not." She sighed. "Well, we'll have to think of something else."

That's what he feared. She was so preoccupied with Marianne Henderson, she wasn't going to let go.

They continued eating, absorbed in their own thoughts.

After a while, she asked: "Who did that archivist tell you to write to, to get hold of that file, I mean?"

"The file originated in Special Branch. They merged into the Counter-Terrorism Command several years ago and they now control it."

"Ah." She put down her chopsticks. "So, Special Branch were involved at the time. Now that's interesting."

He knew what she was thinking. "I know where you're going with this," he said. "They worked closely with MI5 at the time, as do Counter-Terrorism Command now."

She nodded. "I remember a case of a foreign diplomat in London being arrested for spying some years ago. MI5 didn't arrest him, because they weren't authorised to. It was Special Branch."

He nodded.

"The thing is, Tom, MI6 would have been involved if the British Ambassador had been spying for the Chinese in China. Espionage, or intelligence gathering overseas, is their responsibility." She paused. "It would be really interesting to know what's in that file, and to find out how Special Branch got involved back then."

Tom rinsed his fingers in the little bowl of water placed on the table and wiped them on his napkin. There was one last unmade pancake which he was politely leaving for Jess.

She pointed to it. "You can have it."

"It's yours."

She shook her head. "Take it."

"Thanks." He took the pancake out of the steamer and put it on his plate. Then he tipped the remnants of the Peking duck and veg onto it, spooned over the bean sauce and rolled it up. "Maybe Special Branch went over to

Shanghai?" he said. "You know, to liaise with the Chinese Police on the investigation."

Her eyes lit up. "Of course!"

He leant across the table. "Sir Anthony said he would look into that business with Xiao Li. He told you to forget all about Marianne and leave it in the past." He paused. "Are you going to do what he says?"

"That's just it though," she said. "It's not in the past, is it? Xiao Li's rough treatment the other day by her own colleagues has to be connected to Marianne Henderson."

Tom felt rather self-conscious as she watched him eat his last pancake, and quickly wiped away the sauce dripping down his chin.

"And what about my boss Giles?" she went on. "His death is too much of a coincidence. I remember you once told me you didn't believe in coincidence?"

"Yeah, well …"

"Any more news about Giles by the way? *Was* it suicide?"

"No news yet." He rinsed his fingers again and shrugged. "It could have been an accident. Perhaps he got too close to the edge of the platform and was swept over by the crowd. It happens."

He could see her watching him carefully for a reaction when she said: "Or perhaps he was pushed?"

Yeah, he thought, maybe someone did push Giles under the train, but he didn't voice his thoughts. He wanted to stop her digging, not encourage her. Her career was on the line. If Giles's death was no accident, it stood to reason she was in danger too. He would have to be blunt. "If you don't let it go, as Sir Anthony asked, you could ruin your career. Have you thought about that?"

"If I'd thought like that in Australia and in the Turks and Caicos Islands, we'd never have got to the truth."

"Yes, but what Sir Anthony said is right. Your life was on the line in Australia and the Turks and Caicos. You survived. But it might be different this time, and the stakes are high."

She stared right into his eyes. "That's why I'm going to insist you don't get involved any further. I was wrong to tell you in the first place. This is not your problem."

Exasperated, he said: "I'm already involved."

"How so? I've not told anyone about you."

"Because of you." He sighed as he looked at her exhausted eyes and winter-pale skin. Her blonde hair was swept back and held in place by a clasp. A tendril of hair had escaped and fallen across her face. She looked so vulnerable. Yet he knew if he said anything more she'd push him away. He was worried about her safety though. Did she live alone in London? Was there someone close to help her? Now, with a sinking heart, he knew he had no alternative but to ask her about Simon and find out if they were still together.

"How's Simon doing?" he asked, as casually as he could.

Her eyes brightened. "He's fine. His cancer's in remission and he's working in our Embassy in Paris. He took the job to be as close as possible to London and me." She gave a wry smile. "We had great plans to see each other every weekend, but, well, you know how it is. Work just gets in the way every time."

It felt like a punch in the stomach to learn they were still together, but he couldn't show it.

"How about you, Tom?" she asked. "Is there anyone in your life?"

"Nah." He shook his head. "My partner and I split up around the time you and I worked on that case in Australia. I haven't met anyone since. As you say, work just gets in the way." He glanced at her. "Once I'm on a case, especially a murder, I'm like a man possessed. It's, well, it's like a puzzle that burns in my brain. I've just got to get it solved." He sighed. "Nothing else seems to matter at the time. You can imagine how good that is for relationships."

She smiled. It was a long time since anyone had smiled at him like that, and he wished he could take out his pad and pencil and capture it on paper. He knew she'd never allow it. Still, now they were talking, he felt compelled to know more about her and deflect the conversation away from his boring personal life. "Being a diplomat is a bit of an unusual career, Jess. How did that come about?"

"Oh, that's a long story."

They fell silent as the waiter came over to clear the dishes and to ask if they wanted dessert.

"The pineapple fritters are great here, Tom. Do you like them?"

Tom could see that she did. "Yeah, let's get some."

The waiter nodded and disappeared into the kitchen.

Tom looked at her again. "I'd still like to hear the story," he said. "About how you became a diplomat."

"Oh, that." Her eyes looked far away, as if she was reaching back in time. She dabbed her mouth with her napkin. "I always wanted to travel, even as a little girl. I was brought up near Heathrow Airport, you know."

"Poor you."

She laughed. "We weren't directly under the flight path. I used to stand in the garden watching the planes circling above. I dreamt of getting on those planes. It's all I ever wanted to do."

"All your dreams came true, then."

She nodded. "I wanted to be an air hostess at first. That's the only way I could think of getting on those planes. When I was doing my 'O' levels, I decided I was going to be a journalist. I even negotiated a job for myself on a local newspaper for when I left school. My plan was to work on the local paper, then become a Fleet Street reporter,

and then an overseas correspondent travelling the world."
She laughed. "Big dreams for such a little girl. Lord knows
where they came from."

Her face was open and animated as she talked. The
professional diplomat had gone, leaving Jess Turner in her
place. He had to admit he really liked them both.

"Anyway, I never did take up the journalist job," she said.
"I went on to do my 'A' levels instead. A personnel officer
from the Foreign Office visited one day and gave us a talk
on the Diplomatic Service. As soon as she started speaking
about all the countries I could travel to and the embassies
I could work in, well, that was it for me. I was determined
to become a diplomat."

"And you did."

She smiled.

Tom ordered another Chinese beer and a fresh pot
of green tea for Jess while they waited for their dessert.
He wondered if it was a good time to ask her about her
husband and child. He knew they'd died in an accident in
Jakarta when she was working in Indonesia, but he didn't
know the details. He knew he shouldn't really ask, but he
felt compelled to know everything about her. "Then you
got married?" he heard himself say.

A shudder ran through her. "It wasn't a happy ever after
story."

"I know. You told me before that they died in an accident
in Jakarta. I'm sorry I asked. You don't have to tell me the
details."

"I want to." She paused and took a deep breath. "I met
Jack in South Carolina when I was on holiday. A holiday
romance that turned into a happy marriage. Then we had
our little Amy."

She looked so sad. "You don't have to say any more," he
said.

"Amy was just two years old when I was posted to the British Embassy in Jakarta," she continued. "Jack hoped to get some work once we got to Indonesia; he was a marine biologist. He said he'd come anyway, to look after Amy and me." She bit her lip. "It was just an ordinary day. I was rushing around, trying to get ready for work. The house was like a tip. I was giving a presentation at a conference that morning and I couldn't find my memory stick."

"It's okay, Jess…"

"I dropped Amy off at a nursery every morning on my way to work. But that morning, well, I was mad with Jack for letting the house get into such a mess. We had an argument. He grabbed Amy and said he'd take her to nursery, to give me more time to get ready." Her voice cracked. "He sped off down the drive in a temper, with Amy in the back seat. I–I can't forget the sound of squealing tyres … the sound of the explosion as the car burst into flames." She paused to breathe. "Jack turned out of the driveway, you see, in front of a petrol tanker. The car burst into flames almost immediately the tanker hit it." Her eyes were brimming. "They were killed instantly, right in front of me."

He felt a lump in his throat and tried to think of the right thing to say. All that came out were the words: "I'm sorry, Jess. That's really tough."

At that moment, the waiter came back with a plate full of hot pineapple fritters. Seeing Jess's distress, he put the plate down on the table and disappeared again quickly.

Jess gave an embarrassed smile and pulled a tissue out of her handbag. "Bet you wished you'd never asked now?"

He nodded.

She dabbed her eyes and sat back in her chair. "Come on, you can tell me about yourself while we eat these fritters." She picked up her chopsticks again. "How did you become a detective?"

"Ah." He gave a wry smile. "Well that's a story too. It wasn't my first choice. I wanted to be an artist."

"I'm not surprised, I've seen your wonderful sketches."

"Yeah, well, there was no money in it. I had to feed myself, so I took a job as a court artist to add to my income."

Jess looked surprised. "That must have been interesting."

"Yeah, I sketched all the crims on trial for the courts and the media. I got interested in some of those cases. A mate of mine was in the police. He reckoned it was a good career. So, I decided to give it a go."

"And here you are."

"And here I am all these years later. But you know, Jess, I took to it like a duck to water. This job feels more like a vocation. I love it, most of the time."

They both smiled, then fell silent while they started eating again.

Tom's thoughts turned back to her husband and child's horrific accident. He would never bring that up again.

The restaurant door opened, blowing in a gust of wind along with a young couple, who were chatting away to each other. Tom noticed them choose a table close to where he and Jess sat, even though there were vacant tables further away. A very un-British thing to do.

Alert now, he looked out of the window again. That grey car was still parked across the street. He looked from the young couple to the grey car.

"Oh, by the way," Jess said, more brightly now. "I've got a new Australian neighbour in my block of flats. She's over here for a few months on business. She owns a vineyard in the Hunter Valley back in Oz apparently."

Wine was another of his passions. "What's the name of the vineyard?"

She frowned. "I don't know. Her name is Beverley."

"Beverley what?"

Jess paused and looked up. "Now you come to mention it, I don't know her surname. Anyway, she was very kind to me the other night when I fell over on the ice and hit my head." She rubbed the spot on the back of her head and winced. It was still tender.

He raised his eyebrows. "Did you get it checked out?"

"Oh, it's fine. Just a bruise. Anyway, Bev took me in and gave me supper. I've invited her out on Saturday night to see a show if I can get some tickets." She paused and asked shyly. "I wondered if you'd like to come along, if you're not on duty? You two should have a lot to chat about."

He didn't need asking twice. "That'd be great."

She nodded. "I'll text you with the arrangements if I don't see you before then." She sighed. "It's the big day at Heathrow on Monday."

"Yeah. Are you going to the airport to meet the Chinese President?"

"Yes," she said. "I'll be there with the Protocol Officer."

"Me too. I'm on duty with the guys."

She smiled. "I'll look out for you. Give you a wave."

"Uh-oh. No distractions, please."

She smiled again.

Tom was worried though. No one should have to go through what Jess had been through in her life. She'd had enough sadness, he couldn't let her jeopardise her career with this obsession about Shanghai. He leant forward across the table. "Are we agreed that you're going to drop this Marianne Henderson business?"

She leant forward to mirror him and lowered her voice. "I don't think I'm going to be allowed to."

He frowned.

"It's that photo of the snuff bottle," she said. "Someone sent it to me deliberately. They wrote Shanghai 1984 on the back because I think they want me to find out what happened to Marianne Henderson. They must think I'm in a good position to do some digging."

Tom stared at her.

"Look Tom, I haven't instigated any of this." It was her turn to sound exasperated, even though she was still whispering. "I've just been doing my job. Xiao Li was the one who mentioned Marianne to me. And Xiao Li was the one who wanted to meet up to talk about her. Then Giles died under that train, and someone sent me the snuff bottle photo. All I'm saying is I don't think I'll be able to let things go, even if I wanted to. Someone's determined to get me involved."

She was right, of course. Events were building up all around her. A perfect storm, as the Americans would say. Tom looked out the window at the grey car again.

She frowned at him. "What's so interesting out there?"

He put his right elbow on the table and cupped his chin in his hand to try to conceal his lips. "See that grey car parked across the street," he whispered. "It drew up just as we got here."

She peered out the window.

"That same car was parked in the road next to the Black Swan pub earlier."

Her eyes widened as she turned back to him. "We're being watched?"

He nodded. "I can't read the number plate, it's too dark." He swivelled his eyes back. "And don't look now, but there's a young couple sitting close by."

Jess nodded. "I've seen them."

"They're listening to our conversation or trying to."

First, he saw shock in her eyes, then understanding. "I'm *so* sorry, Tom. I should never have got you involved in all this."

He shrugged. "Well I am involved now."

She sat head bowed, deep in thought. He didn't know what was going through her mind. When she looked up again, her eyes glittered.

"That's it then," she whispered. "One way or the other, I think we're going to find out what happened to Marianne Henderson all those years ago in Shanghai."

17

> *Women hold up half the sky*
> *(Chairman Mao)*

Marianne looked over to where Justin sat, whisky glass in hand. The lamp on the table next to him shone a dull light onto his face, making him look sick and ghostly. Even Sam and Anthony Chalmers were tense and quiet as the four of them sat together in the Consulate-General reception room after another eventful day.

Marianne leant forward, picked up the teapot and replenished Sam's and Anthony's cups before filling her own to the brim.

Anthony gave her a sideways glance. "Thanks."

She gave him a frosty look in return, but he met her stare impassively. She found his intense eyes so unsettling she had to look away. What *was* it about Anthony? He had a kind of personal magnetism that couldn't be ignored, charming one minute and cold and calculating the next. Ambitious, with an almost forensic brain, he didn't suffer fools gladly. Nor did she. Now, she was getting more and more irritated with the three of them. The suggestion of

157

her having had an affair with the Ambassador had taken hold in their minds, although they would never say so. She kept getting speculative looks, the odd lingering glance, and an undisguised attempt to steer away from the subject whenever the conversation got anywhere near it. The elephant in the room, that's for sure.

It was bad enough having Justin to deal with. Now, London had insisted Sam stay in Shanghai to help with the fallout from the Ambassador's death, *and* they'd sent Anthony Chalmers down from Peking. Marianne didn't want Anthony around. Nor did Justin, if the wobbly he threw when he found out was anything to go by. But London ignored their protests. Marianne was convinced Anthony had talked London into letting him come, simply because he didn't want to be left out of the action. Still, be grateful for small mercies, she thought. Giles Pettiford would probably have been here too but for the fact he'd drawn the short straw and been moved into the Peking Embassy's Consular Section to help clear the backlog of applications for visas and new passports. The three-month wait, and resulting complaints, were embarrassing for the Ambassador and the British government. For a policy flyer like Giles, that kind of functional job was a come down, and he made no secret of his annoyance at having to do it. Of course, Giles's misfortune amused Anthony and Justin no end. Such was the competition between the three of them.

Sam was different. As a Foreign Office researcher, he could expect to spend most of his career in London. He was only in the Embassy in Peking at present to get some China experience. Being immersed in a country was the best way to do that. Of course, he would never be asked to do any mainstream job in the Consular Section like Giles or the others. Studying classics and oriental studies at Oxford had secured Sam a job for life in the Foreign Office. It also meant he was not in competition with the other three, or with anyone else in the organisation come to that.

Marianne watched Sam sip his tea while he listened politely to the conversation. Reserved, shy even, he never said much, and certainly nothing without thinking it through first. Cautious and reliable, that was Sam. Mind you, she sometimes caught him with an odd expression on his face that made her wonder what was really going on under that quiet exterior.

As young, red-blooded males, the guys talked about sex. She'd heard them when they thought she wasn't around. She'd noticed them eyeing the Chinese girls too, despite their baggy, sexless uniforms. Looking was all they could do; they'd be sent home if they ever dared take up with a Chinese woman and open themselves up to blackmail. There could be no fraternising with the locals in this alien communist country. That's why the suggestion of the Ambassador having had an affair was such nonsense. Why would he compromise himself in that way? It just didn't make sense.

She sighed, deeply. Although she was used to being the only female diplomat in Peking, she would have loved some female company right now. The Foreign Office had a long way to go to even try to close the gender imbalance.

She picked up her cup, held her cold hands around it, and took a long sip of tea. That, at least, was never in short supply in China, although buying milk to go with it was a challenge. The Chinese never drank milk, believing dairy food made people smell, and that's why flies followed foreigners everywhere.

Anthony interrupted her thoughts. "London are in a flummox," he said. "The Ambassador's death is a real blow. But *murder* … well, that's sending them into the stratosphere."

Justin raised an eyebrow. "Who've you been talking to?"

"The China Desk Officer."

"I thought we agreed *I* would be the sole contact with London," Justin said. "We don't want everyone going off at half cock. We need to keep a lid on everything."

"The lid is very firmly on," Anthony replied. "There's a complete news and information blackout in London. Only those who need to know are being kept up to date."

Justin sounded edgy. "So, what are you doing discussing it with them?"

Anthony held up his hands. "*They* raised it with me. I was just talking to them about the trade delegation."

"Refer them to me in future."

Anthony gave him a sharp look. "There won't be any leaks to the media or anyone else, if that's what you're worried about. It will come out in the end though, no doubt about that, especially if the Ambassador was murdered by a Chinese. That'll harm the relationship no end. Set it back years, I should think, whatever we do to try to contain the fallout."

Justin glared at him.

Anthony refused to be silenced. "That would be the worst-case scenario from London's perspective. China's too." He paused. "Do we know yet why the Chinese police think he was murdered?"

Justin glanced anxiously at his watch. "Wu's at the police station now trying to find out more. I wish she'd hurry up and get back. We need to know exactly what we're dealing with."

Anthony nodded. "Do we know yet which poison was used?"

Justin shook his head.

Anthony turned to Marianne. "I have to say you seem surprisingly calm, in the circumstances."

Marianne looked up quickly, spilling a little tea down her blouse. She rubbed the spot with her fingers. "What are you suggesting?"

"I'd be more worried if I was in your shoes."

Her hackles rose. "In *my* shoes?"

"You were the only one there when the Ambassador died. There's no one to corroborate your side of things."

She gave a frustrated sigh.

Sam intervened. "That's a bit insensitive, Anthony, even for you."

"Well, Anthony's got a point, Marianne." Justin reached for the bottle of whisky on the table. "You were on your own most of that day *and* when the Ambassador was killed."

Marianne's eyes narrowed. "Only because you and Sam had gone off to Hangzhou."

"You said it was okay for me to go," Justin replied.

"What else could I do? A British student had been seriously injured in the town. But if I'd known Sam was there." She stared at Sam, who was embarrassed enough to look away. "I'd never have agreed to you going too, Justin. Not with the trade delegation in town. *And* you know it."

Justin slowly poured some more whisky into his glass and screwed the top back on the bottle. "All I'm saying is that you have no alibi for that night."

Her cup rattled on its saucer as she plonked it down with a flourish.

Anthony nodded. "He's right, Marianne. You must be prepared. It's okay if you can continue to claim diplomatic immunity. But it's not going to be easy for you If you have to submit to Chinese police investigation." He turned to Justin. "Have London said anything about her immunity and whether she should help the police?"

Justin shook his head. "They've been knocked sideways by all this."

"*They've* been knocked sideways?" Marianne said.

"Look at it from their point of view," Anthony went on. "They have to tread carefully with Margaret Thatcher due out here at the end of the month for talks with Deng Xiaoping. There's nothing more important than the smooth handover of Hong Kong."

Justin picked up on the point. "London won't want to upset the Chinese and jeopardise what's been achieved in the negotiations so far."

Marianne was inwardly furious. They were talking to her as if she was an idiot. She knew the score as well as any of them. The Consulate-General was supposed to have opened last year. When the Chinese said they couldn't find a suitable building for it, everyone knew it was a negotiating tactic. As soon as the impasse was resolved, they identified one straightaway.

"I'm happy to give the Chinese police a statement," she said. "I *should* tell them what I know."

The silence in the room said everything.

"I've nothing to hide," she insisted, "and it might help them catch whoever did this."

Anthony shook his head. "London would never allow it. That would be like throwing you to the wolves."

Justin turned on Anthony again. "Do you have to be so melodramatic?"

"You know I'm telling the truth," Anthony said. "The Chinese police are a law unto themselves. The Security Services too. They arrest anyone they want to. Beat them up to get a confession. Use torture. Lock people up and throw away the key. We can't let them anywhere near Marianne."

Sam's voice shook. "*Will* you give it a rest, Anthony?"

Marianne's head swam. Anthony was right about the Chinese police, but if the Ambassador *had* been murdered, it was her duty to help them.

"Look, let's all stay calm," Anthony said, in what Marianne thought was a patronising tone. He turned to Justin. "Have the Chinese police confirmed how the poison was administered?"

"The champagne, surely?" Sam said.

Justin flashed him a dark look, and Sam clammed up again.

Why did Sam always defer to Justin, Marianne wondered? He was independent of all of them. Why didn't he stand up for himself a bit more?

Anthony put his cup and saucer down on the coffee table. "We need cool heads to plan how we're going to handle this."

Marianne stared at him. "I don't know what *you* think you have to handle."

"All I mean is that we have to be on message," Anthony said.

"Well here's a message," she said, bluntly. "I did *not* go up to the Ambassador's room in the Peace Hotel and murder him."

Justin winced.

"I'm telling the *truth*. I did not murder the Ambassador. I was not having an affair with him either." She looked from one to the other. "Oh, I know that's what you're all thinking."

"Of course, we're not," Sam said.

She only had to look at their eyes to see the doubt so evidently there. She reached for the cigarette packet on the coffee table, lit up, and blew the smoke high into the air.

"Honestly, Marianne, would you stop." Justin sounded grumpy. "You're going to give us all lung cancer the way you're getting through those things."

Irritated, she pointed to the whisky bottle. "If cirrhosis of the liver doesn't get you first."

Justin flashed back. "Are you criticising me for having the odd tipple now and again?"

"The odd tipple?" Anthony said, in a languid voice. "Come on, Justin. You've been hitting the bottle a bit hard of late. Perhaps you should ease off a bit?"

A flush rose from the base of Justin's neck to the roots of his hair. Marianne wasn't sure if he was mad with Anthony for mentioning his drinking, or mad because he couldn't conceal it any longer.

Then Anthony suddenly changed tack. "Has that snuff bottle turned up yet?"

Marianne looked pointedly at Sam and Justin.

Justin spoke first. "You're the only one who handled it, Marianne."

She kept her voice calm. "I put it in my desk drawer. Someone took it." She paused. "Only you and Sam knew about it, and where it was."

Justin shrugged. "Well I haven't seen it."

"Me neither," Sam said.

She gave an irritated sigh.

"Look," Anthony said, "this is getting us nowhere. Let's all go and get something to eat." He rubbed his hands together at the prospect. "We'll meet in the morning and decide what we're going to do then."

Suddenly, Marianne realised what Anthony had done. He'd caused a row on purpose. Now he was appearing to be entirely reasonable. She knew his game. He wanted to take control.

Except Justin wasn't playing. "You three go out for a meal." He stood up. "I've had enough for one day, I'm going home."

"Oh, come on," Anthony said. "Don't get upset. That's not going to help Marianne."

Justin gave him a piercing stare. "Don't forget who's in charge here."

Anthony looked from Justin to Marianne and then back at Justin. "You and Marianne are the same grade. So, it's not you either."

Marianne was thankful for that, but she could see Justin was about to blow up. "I'm tired too," she said to Anthony. "You and Sam go out for a meal. I'm going to finish up here and go and get some sleep."

"You need to eat," Anthony persisted.

She nodded. "I'll get something at home."

Anthony shrugged. "Well, if you're sure?"

"I am." She stood up and looked from Justin to Anthony. "And, to correct you on one small point, I wasn't alone all day. The driver can corroborate my movements, at least until he dropped me off at the Peace Hotel."

Anthony looked surprised and turned to Justin. "Haven't you told her?"

"Told me what?" she asked, sharply.

Justin gave her a sympathetic look. "When Wu telephoned from the police station earlier, she had another piece of news ... bad news, I'm afraid. Our driver passed away last night."

Marianne stood frozen.

"He was cycling home late," Justin went on. "A truck suddenly turned and slammed into him. He came off his bike and hit his head on the concrete pavement. He died instantly at the scene."

★

Later, Marianne sat at her desk in the dark staring out the window into pitch black. No moon or stars tonight, just total cloud cover. She rested her elbows on the desk, put her hands over her eyes, and listened to the old house. Its wooden doors and shutters creaked and sighed as they contracted against the cold night air. She was relieved the guys had gone and she was alone, at last. There was something comforting about sitting in the dark like this. She felt safe. Untroubled. Invisible even.

She opened her eyes and looked out at the Yulan tree. No funeral lantern tonight, just darkness. Someone had hung it on the tree and lit it up last night. Who? And why? Was someone out there now watching her? Perhaps the driver of that black sedan was creeping around, peering through the windows?

She got up and snapped the Venetian blinds shut before switching on the light. Then she went over to the gunmetal filing cabinet and pulled out the bottom drawer. She flicked through the files, looking for her special admin file. Special, because within its mundane pages talking about boilers and general maintenance lurked her diary of events since the night of the Ambassador's death. She updated it religiously every day and put it back in the filing cabinet, where she hoped no one would ever think of looking. She did it to keep everything clear in her mind. She couldn't allow any little detail to slip away.

And she hid it because she felt she couldn't trust Justin and Sam. Someone had taken that snuff bottle. It must have been one of them because only they knew where it was, and Anthony was in Peking at the time.

She reached under the desk for her handbag and pulled out the polaroid of the snuff bottle. She hadn't shown this photo to anyone or told them about it. It was that trust issue again. She stared at the photo, remembering how exquisite the little bottle had been, with its temple painted on the side and lanterns hanging from its eaves. Why did the Ambassador have it in his hand when he died? And where the hell was it now?

The snuff bottle itself might have disappeared, but she would keep a photo of it safe. She went over to her combination cupboard for her polaroid camera. Laying the photo on her desk, she pointed the camera lens at it and took a second snap.

While she waited for the camera to produce the second photo, she opened her desk drawer, pulled out a sheet of photocopy paper and her bottle of glue. She laid the original photo down on her desk, reverse side up, and covered every edge with glue. Then she stuck the photo to the photocopy paper, pressing down the edges firmly to make sure they were completely stuck to the paper. Punching a hole in a top corner, she slotted it into the file with her diary of events. She would keep everything hidden amongst the papers on this file, where they would be safe and away from the prying eyes of her colleagues.

The prying eyes of her colleagues? That thought made her feel sick.

18

What the superior man seeks is in himself; what the small man seeks is in others

(Confucius)

Marianne drove slowly along the narrow Shanghai streets in the darkness. The wipers clunked back and forth, but they ended up more smearing than clearing the misty rain on the windscreen. She really ought to get the wiper blades changed, she thought, as she rubbed the glass with the back of her hand and put the heater on full blast to clear the fog.

She was still in a state of shock over their driver's death. Accident, on his bike ride home from work. Really? First the Ambassador, then him? And on the same night. That was too much of a coincidence. Had the driver been murdered too, she wondered? If so, why? Did he know something the Chinese authorities didn't want him to know? Or seen something perhaps? She knew the poor man was married and had a child, because he kept a photo of his son on the dashboard of the official car. She'd never met his family. Fraternising with foreigners, even if you worked for them, was frowned upon in this communist state. Still, she'd try and make sure his family were taken care of.

Following the distorted tail-lights of the vehicle ahead, her mind wandered back to her conversation with Justin, Anthony and Sam. They were right. The Ambassador's death couldn't have come at a worse time. Everyone had worked hard to improve relations with China, especially during the tricky Hong Kong handover talks. Not least the Ambassador himself. London wouldn't want anything to go wrong with Margaret Thatcher's visit at the end of the month. It was too important. But murder? Christ! They'd have to cancel the PM's visit, surely?

She glanced in the mirror, but all she could make out were dipped headlights. She knew that black sedan was behind. She could feel its presence, although the last time she'd seen it was on that fateful day, on her way to the Peace Hotel. The vision of the Ambassador's eyes staring up at her from the bathroom floor sprang into her mind.

Those grey, lifeless eyes.

Her heart started pounding, making her feel hot and dizzy. She pulled the woollen scarf off her neck and threw it onto the passenger seat beside her. She was just tired out. She'd be fine after a good night's sleep. Reaching for the handle, she wound down the window. Cool air rushed into the car and blew rain onto her face. She took several deep breaths of air until her heart started slowing.

After a while, she turned into the road leading to the airport and the more rural outskirts of the city. A disgusting stench wafted through her open window. She knew exactly what it was. She was driving behind a night soil cart. In the communes, human excrement was collected up into night soil pits and transported to the fields in carts, to be used as fertiliser. Nothing could be wasted in this country with over a billion mouths to feed. The resulting methane gas was lethal. Any individual unfortunate enough to fall into one of these pits, as happened, could be overcome. Death would soon follow. Marianne wound up the window, checked her mirror and overtook the cart as quickly as possible. Only when she'd put enough distance between them did she open it again.

Murder! Her mind drifted back again to the Peace Hotel. She kept trying to remember if she'd seen anyone suspicious that night. No one had been in the Jazz Bar while she was there, except of course the barman and the jazz band. What about in the reception area? Or when she was going up to the Ambassador's room in the lift? There was nothing suspicious that she could remember, except …

A soft click…

Yes, of course, she remembered hearing it as she walked along the corridor to the Ambassador's room. It sounded like a bedroom door closing, yet she hadn't seen anyone. Had the Ambassador's killer been a guest in the hotel too?

Taking the next turning on the right, she drove into a complex of villas. Hers stood at the far end, next to an open field. She'd chosen it precisely because of its location. And it was quiet. Only foreigners could live in these newly built villas. She'd moved into hers when first arriving in Shanghai. Many were still empty, including the one next to hers. The nights were especially silent, with only cicadas in the summer and early autumn to listen to. Very few birds lived in and around the city because of Shanghai's low-lying position. There were no mountains, hills, or forests nearby either. Come the morning though, she would always hear wood pigeons cooing in the field, much like in the UK. Having been brought up in the country, that comforting sound every morning reminded her of waking up at home.

Now, standing in darkness, her villa looked lonely and desolate. Why hadn't the house boy put the porch light on? Probably to save electricity. Chinese habits were so ingrained.

She pulled into her parking space in front of the house and switched off the engine. Leaving her headlights on to light up the path, she got out, unlocked the front door, reached inside and flicked on the hall light. It was only when she returned to the car that she heard the phone ringing inside the house.

She grabbed her scarf and bag from the passenger seat, locked the car, and ran up the path to answer it.

A thought flashed into her mind, and she stopped dead. The front door had opened on the first turn of the key. Yet, she always put the double lock on. As did the houseboy. Always.

She hesitated on the threshold. She wanted to answer the phone, yet something was stopping her going inside.

An overwhelming smell of disinfectant hit her. She recoiled instinctively at the thought of the black rat that morning, with its teeth clamped onto the side of the cage.

When the phone stopped ringing, she listened for any noise inside the house.

Nothing.

"Hello?" she shouted out. "Anyone there?"

Only silence.

Leaving the front door open as her escape route if someone was inside, she put her scarf and bag on the hall table, and tip-toed into the sitting room. No one there.

She went back into the hall, switched on the landing light and crept upstairs. There was no way she could relax until she was sure she was alone in the house. On the landing, she put on all the lights and poked her head into every room. No one. She breathed a sigh of relief and went downstairs again. Shutting the front door firmly, she pushed the bolts at the top and bottom into place. Feeling secure now, she smiled at her own jitters. Stop being so paranoid, she told herself. But she still went around closing all the curtains, in case that black sedan was out there, watching her.

Not feeling very hungry, she went into the kitchen and made herself some scrambled eggs and toast for supper. She had to eat something. Then she went upstairs. It was only when lying in a hot bath in a fog of steam that her jangled nerves finally started to unwind. She was so looking forward to a deep sleep and clearing her cluttered mind.

The phone started ringing again.

She groaned. There was only one phone in the house and that was downstairs in the sitting room. She lay motionless in the water wondering whether to get out and answer it. She didn't want to move, but what if it was London? What if it was urgent? She waited, but it just kept on ringing. She climbed out of the tub, grabbed a towel, and ran downstairs.

The phone stopped ringing just as she got to it.

She stood, water dripping from her onto the carpet, waiting for whoever it was to ring again. They didn't. Shivering now with cold, she retraced her damp footprints up the stair carpet and into the bathroom. She didn't get back in the bath in case the phone rang again. She just dried herself and put on her Chinese pyjamas and robe. The feel of soft silk against her skin was comforting. The Chinese made lovely silk garments, mostly for export, but she could buy them in the aptly named Friendship Store, which was only for foreigners.

She looked at her watch. 11.20pm. Having been exhausted all day, she was now wide awake. She looked at the bedroom window. Was that black sedan out there? She switched off the bedroom light, went over to the curtain and peeked out. Complete darkness. She waited for her eyes to adjust. Then she saw something, a tiny light wafting around. A lit cigarette? She stood very still and heard a car door close quietly. She ducked back from the curtain and sat on the edge of the bed.

Yes, they were out there, watching her. They were *always* out there, watching her.

She got up and walked around restlessly, picking things up and putting them down again, more awake than ever.

There was no point in going to bed, so she went into the lounge and switched on the TV. It took a while for the old set to warm up, and it was a waste of time when it did. She groaned to see the nightly film was, yet again, a dramatization of Mao and the Long March. She, and the rest of China, had watched the communist Red Army march through China, dispossessing local warlords and Chiang Kai-Shek's nationalist government troops, so many times before. Would the brainwashing never end?

She switched the TV off with a flourish and wandered over to the new CD player that took pride of place on the sideboard. She'd bought it in Hong Kong on her last trip. A fabulous innovation, except her current music collection was in cassettes, and her cassette player was broken. Still, she'd bought a few CDs while in Hong Kong too. A real mix of music. Would the Classics Collection CD help her sleep? No, damn it, she'd choose something to annoy her watchers outside and make them wonder what was going on. She picked out a Cyndi Lauper CD, put it on, and got herself a large glass of wine from the fridge. When the track 'Girls Just Want to Have Fun' came on, she turned up the volume full blast and opened a window to be sure they could hear it outside.

Some fun this posting was turning out to be!

★

Later, as she lay in bed, it was Anthony's words that kept coming back. *I think I'd be more worried if I were in your shoes.*

Of course, she was worried. Very worried. *The Chinese police are a law unto themselves … it would be like throwing you to the wolves.*

She lay tossing and turning. *You have no alibi for the night.* Justin's words this time. *You were on your own most of the day and when the Ambassador was killed.* Of course, she was on her own, but only because *he'd* gone off to Hangzhou.

Why were Justin and Anthony being so negative? Did they know something she didn't? Had London said something? Every time she phoned them, they wouldn't discuss anything with her. Yet they talked openly about it with Justin and now Anthony. Did they think she might incriminate herself if the Chinese were recording these phone conversations, as they surely were? Did London think she was guilty? Guilty of having an affair with the Ambassador, and murdering him?

The whole idea was ludicrous.

These thoughts kept tumbling around in her head, over and over, until her eyes felt heavy and she finally drifted off into a fitful sleep.

★

Later, much later, she woke up with a start, to the sound of the phone ringing.

She looked at the clock. 3.05 am. Who on earth was ringing? She struggled up in the fog of sleep, got out of bed and ran down the stairs to the phone. "Hello?" she breathed.

Silence on the line.

"Hello?" she said again. "Who's calling?"

A click sounded in her ear as the caller hung up.

Despite her drowsiness, she realised immediately what was happening. Another turn of the screw. The secret police had overtly followed, and watched, her for weeks.

Now, they were disturbing her sleep, to play with her mind. She knew all about these tactics. She'd joined the Foreign Office during the Cold War and been trained to know what to expect. The real objective of such harassment was to find some weakness, or wrongdoing, in an officer they could exploit by blackmailing them into handing over information. Essentially, to become a traitor to their own country.

Her hands shook as the shocking realisation sunk in, and she put down the phone. She'd been right all along, the Chinese were singling her out. But what on earth did they hope to get on her to blackmail her into co-operating with them?

A sick feeling started gnawing away in her stomach. Of course, if she was found guilty of having an affair with the Ambassador and murdering him…

She put her head in her hands.

19

Political power grows out of the barrel of a gun
(Chairman Mao)

Marianne awoke the next morning to sun streaming through a gap in the curtains. Dust particles floated in the beam of light. She watched them dreamily for a while, until everything came flooding back. She wanted to just pull the covers over her head and go back to sleep. But she couldn't, she had to go to work.

Hearing wood pigeons calling to each other in the distance, her mind drifted back to her childhood, growing up in the English countryside, in a village with her grandparents. A simple, idyllic life spent exploring the surrounding woods and fields. Her grandfather had taught her to shoot and fish. Twice a year he would take her camping on the North York moors. Just the two of them. He'd tell her stories of his missions behind enemy lines in the War and how he'd fended for himself in the French countryside to avoid being captured by the Germans. Looking back now, Marianne supposed it was his way of teaching her to look after herself, and of getting the War out of his system. Now, while she found cities exciting, they were stifling too, and Shanghai was one of the busiest and most populated in the world. A sudden yearning to get away swept over her. What was to stop her driving to the airport now and jumping on the next plane out of the country? Anywhere. Just to get away. She could leave her car at the airport, and all her possessions in the villa. She wouldn't miss anything, they were just things. She smiled at her own crazy thoughts.

She glanced at the clock and sat up with a jolt. She should have been in the office 45 minutes ago. For a moment, she got into a panic, then she flopped back on the pillow. No wonder she'd overslept, with those bastards waking her up at 3 o'clock in the morning. She'd left the phone off the hook after that, and slept for five uninterrupted hours, which made her feel so much better. She'd been working hard for months now, no wonder she was exhausted. She didn't see any signs of exhaustion in Justin or Sam or Anthony, so let them get on with it for a while.

Lying there in the cold light of morning, her brain started sifting through all the facts again. Did the Chinese think she was particularly vulnerable? Flaky even? Did they really think they could blackmail her? Force her to betray her own country? Was that what all this surveillance and harassment was about?

She thought of her grandmother. What would she tell her to do? 'Tell the truth and have courage', that's what she'd always told her as a child. 'Always rely on yourself, Marianne, and trust your own instincts. They will not lie to you.'

What was her inner voice telling her now? That she was in a truly difficult predicament.

She allowed herself a moment of self-doubt. Her grandmother had believed in her. It was important to have *someone* believe in you, Marianne thought. She had no one now. Once she'd got through this, she would have to rethink what was important in her life. Meanwhile, she'd have to believe in herself, take better care of her own interests, and fight for her reputation, since others seemed happy to accept she'd had an affair with the Ambassador and even killed him. Except Sam, of course. He was the one person who was ready to stand up for her.

When she got up and drew the curtains open wide, a kind of energy zipped through her. A sense of purpose. She would come through all this. She had *not* had an affair with the Ambassador, and she had *not* murdered him. She was innocent. Trouble was, in this alien country, it felt more like people were guilty until proven innocent. Still, not only would she prove her innocence, she would do whatever she could to help the police find the Ambassador's real killer. She would never rest until he or she was found and brought to justice.

She got up, put on her robe, and went downstairs to make breakfast. There would be no more missing meals or snacking. She needed to look after herself.

As she passed the phone, she put the receiver back on the cradle.

In the kitchen, she took a box of oats out of the cupboard. The manager of the dry goods store in the Embassy in Peking had sent her a food supply from their regular shipment from the UK. Baked beans, custard power, cereals, tins of fruit and vegetables, pastas, and Vesta beef curries were the most popular. In Peking, in the dry, cold north, there wasn't much fresh food to buy. The Chinese lived mostly on rice and vegetables. Meat was very expensive and rationed. But even vegetables were in short supply during the winter's sub-zero temperatures. She would smile at the heaps of cabbages Chinese residents piled up on their apartment balconies, which they used as cold storage in the winter. In the Friendship Store, Marianne could buy locally reared pork, some fish and prawns. The few vegetables available were mostly cabbage and potatoes through the winter. Boring as hell, but that, coupled with what she could get from the Embassy store, kept her going. And she'd never been healthier in her life than on that sparse diet.

In Shanghai's more temperate climate, there were more fresh vegetables in the markets. Everything came straight from the fields and had to be cleaned, washed and prepared by hand. Even the chickens and ducks were sold live and had to be killed and plucked. The houseboy would do that for her when he came in around 9 o'clock in the morning. But, living alone, and with no convenience foods to buy, Marianne generally ate out in the local restaurants designated for foreigners. Fortunately, she loved Chinese food.

Lifting a bottle of milk out of the fridge, she set about making some porridge, and opened a tin of peaches from the Embassy store. That would set her up for the day.

She had just started eating when the phone rang. With her new-found resolve, she got up and answered.

"Where on earth are you?" Justin was in a flap.

"At home, having breakfast?"

"Do you know what time it is?"

She looked at the clock. "Nearly 9."

He was quiet for a moment. "Are you all right, Marianne?"

"I'm fine," she said, with a confidence she didn't feel.

"That's good to hear." He hesitated. "The Chinese police just rang to say they'd be here in half an hour. They want to interview you."

Marianne's stomach lurched. "How come?"

"Apparently the Chinese Ambassador in London went into the Foreign Office yesterday to update the Minister on the Ambassador's death. You can just imagine when the

Ambassador confirmed it was a murder enquiry … the shock's still reverberating around the place."

Marianne stood quietly.

"Anyway," Justin went on, "the Chinese police want to talk to you about what happened that night. You were the only one there, your testimony will be important." He paused. "Given the circumstances, our Minister agreed you should help them with their enquiries."

Marianne was under no illusion about the implication. "London have waived my diplomatic immunity?"

"Yes."

A coldness ran through her as she remembered Anthony's words. *London would never do that … it would be like throwing you to the wolves."*

So, London were going to offer her up as a sacrificial lamb. Then she chided herself for thinking that. She had to help the police find out who killed the Ambassador, it was her duty. "I can't get in for 9.30," she said. "Ask them to come at 12 noon instead." She knew full well the police wouldn't want to do that because it was lunchtime and their main meal of the day. To miss lunch in the works canteen might mean not eating at all that day.

Justin knew it too. "Better not mess them around, Marianne."

She was not going to be pushed around by anyone, not by Justin, not by Anthony and not by the Chinese police. "If they can't make 12 noon," she said, "ask them to come at 2 o'clock."

There was another pause. "If that's what you want?"

"It is."

"Very well, I'll see what they say."

She glanced out the window. The black sedan was parked just a few metres away from her own car, in full view. "Perhaps I should ask them myself," she said, drily, "since they're parked outside my house."

There was a silence down the line. "God, Marianne, I'm so sorry you're having to go through all this. Look, I'll sit with you in the interview. I'll be there every step of the way."

He sounded sincere and that brought a lump to her throat. "I don't know what everyone is thinking back in London, because they won't discuss it with me over the phone," she said, "but I'm innocent of all this, Justin. You know that, don't you?"

He gave a long, deep sigh. "I'm sorry," he said again. "I know it's awful, but the police have to talk to you and get all the facts down on paper. You must understand that." He rushed on. "Anyway, I'll see you later, when you're ready." Then he hung up.

She stood frozen to the spot. He hadn't said he believed her. He hadn't said anything to reassure her, just that he'd be there with her every step of the way. Would he? Could she trust him? Could she trust any of them?

Her hand shook as she put down the phone.

Instinctively, she touched her grandmother's little cross around her neck. 'Always rely on yourself Marianne and trust your own instincts. They will not lie to you.'

★

She drove through the Consulate-General gates at 12 noon on the dot, hoping that everyone had gone out for lunch. She wanted time alone to read through her diary of events and get everything crystal clear in her head before she spoke to the police. There could be no hesitation, no muddled thinking, and no chink in her statement for them to pull apart.

She let herself into the building and stopped to listen for voices or activity. Only silence. Good. She went into her office and took off her coat.

On her desk, she glanced at Shanghai's daily newspaper. The gaunt face of Chairman Mao's widow, Jiang Qing, stared out from the front page. The Chinese were still fascinated by her.

The trial of the Gang of Four, as Jiang Qing and her three colleagues were known, had taken place not long after Marianne had arrived in Peking, and was televised to the nation. Just one month after the death of Mao, they'd been arrested and charged with 'counter-revolutionary acts'. They were generally blamed by the Chinese government for the worst excesses of the chaos and violence that had gripped the nation during the ten years of the Cultural Revolution.

In the West, it was considered a show trial. Someone to blame for that turbulent political era in China, and probably to make sure Jiang Qing and her followers did not assume any political power after the death of her husband Mao. The trial was also probably televised to the nation as a reminder to the Chinese people of how powerful the Communist Party was, and what would happen to anyone who dared act, or speak out, against the State.

Marianne stared at Jiang Qing's wax-like face. She'd been sentenced to death, which was commuted to 'life' in 1983. And Marianne had no doubt the woman would remain in prison for the rest of her days.

She shivered. Would the Ambassador's murder trial be televised to the nation too? Would she have to stand in the dock giving testimony? If her diplomatic immunity had been waived, that could happen. Oh my God! She got up and headed straight for the filing cabinet. Pulling out her special admin file, she sat back down at her desk and re-

read her diary of events over and over, fixing every timing, every detail, every thought firmly in her brain until she was word perfect. She could not make any mistakes.

When she eventually sat back in the chair, her heart was pounding. Every time she relived that night, the shock reverberated deep inside her. It was all right for everyone else, and London, to run around saying they were shocked and disbelieving, but they hadn't been there. For her, it was overwhelming. No one had given that the slightest thought.

Still, there was someone who would be even more devastated. The Ambassador's wife. Marianne glanced at the phone and wondered whether to try ringing her again. She wanted to tell her about her husband's last moments. But every time she rang the Residence in Peking, she was told the Ambassador's wife was resting and couldn't come to the phone. The poor woman knew all the details now, including the signs that her husband had had company in his hotel bedroom. Did she also think Marianne had been having an affair with him? Is that why she wouldn't come to the phone? Or was she so upset about his death that she really couldn't talk to anyone?

Marianne sighed and looked out the window. The watery sun was still out, but a wind was rustling through the trees, blowing off dead leaves and scattering them around the grass lawn. Why did autumn always feel so sad? Glancing towards the Yulan tree, she noticed someone sitting on the garden bench close by. It was Wu, huddled up in her padded, winter coat, reading a book. Marianne watched for a moment. Every so often Wu looked up, stared into the distance, then returned to her book. She was so absorbed in it, she was unaware of Marianne's watchful eyes.

Marianne put her file back in the cabinet, put on her coat and went outside to talk to Wu. She had to offer her condolences about their driver's accident, and Wu would be the best person to liaise with the authorities about providing for his family.

Wu's head jerked up at the sound of leaves crunching underfoot. She quickly closed her book. "I didn't know you were in the office, Marianne."

Marianne smiled. "That's because you were so absorbed in your book. What are you reading?"

Wu slipped the book into the bag beside her. "Oh, nothing interesting."

"Well it had your full attention. What's the title? I might try it."

Wu pursed her lips. "It's just an old Chinese story. A stupid one really."

Marianne sat down beside her. "Sorry for interrupting your lunch break, but I wanted to talk to you about the driver."

Wu looked at her with her usual impassive eyes.

"I'm sorry about his accident," Marianne continued. "It's shocking."

Wu nodded. "Very bad for his family."

Marianne sighed. "That's what I wanted to talk to you about. He leaves behind a wife and young son. Do you know who will look after them? Do they have any other family to help them?"

Wu gave her a curious look. "Why are you so concerned about his family?"

Marianne knew only too well how it felt to lose family. "My mother and father were killed in a car accident when I was little girl."

Wu didn't express any sympathy, but she looked interested. "How old were you at the time?"

"Only three," Marianne said. "I hardly remember them at all now. I was staying with my grandparents at the time, while my mother and father took a holiday together. After they died, I just carried on living with my grandparents, until I left home."

"Oh," said Wu. "What about your brothers and sisters?"

"I was an only child," said Marianne. "How about you?"

Wu frowned at her. "I'm an only child too. You know the one child policy here in China."

"Yes, yes, of course."

"And your grandparents now?" Wu asked. "How old are they?"

While that might have seemed a rude question to foreigners, the Chinese often asked personal questions, especially how old people were. Marianne sighed. "They're both dead now."

Wu looked at her with a strange expression. "You don't have *any* family?"

Marianne shook her head. "No. That's why I wanted to discuss the driver's accident with you. It will be important that his wife and son are taken care of. I know we've got an insurance policy for the staff. Can you dig it out and find out whether we can claim compensation for them?"

Wu frowned. "He was cycling home *after* work."

Marianne hesitated. "Are you saying he won't qualify for compensation because he was off duty?"

"Yes."

Marianne wasn't surprised, it would probably be the same if something happened to her. "Well, let's give it a try anyway," she said. "We have to try and help his family."

Wu gave a slight toss of her head in a show of frustration. "Things are not the same here as in England. We can't just give things a try."

It was said in a dismissive way that irritated Marianne, but she kept her voice steady. "The law is not always watertight. There are often clauses and different ways of interpreting things."

"Maybe in your country, but the law can't be exploited for individual needs here."

There was an unusual bitterness in Wu's voice that intrigued Marianne.

"The State is in control of everything, and everyone," Wu went on, "including the insurance companies. Whatever they say should happen, happens."

It was Marianne's turn to become frustrated. "I'm not so inexperienced about your country that I don't understand that," she said.

Wu turned to her. "Have you heard the Chinese saying that 'we all eat out of the same rice bowl'? Well, that's what it's like for us," she went on without waiting for a reply. "We all eat the same food, wear the same clothes, do the same things. No one wants to be noticed, to be singled out. That's dangerous for us."

Marianne had never heard Wu talk like this. Was she trying to tell her something?

"It's all right for you, Marianne. You're a free woman in your society. You can work, you can travel, you can live where you like. You have enough money and independence to do whatever you like, whenever you like. But we can't."

Wu's voice was not only bitter now, it was almost accusing. Marianne was trying to be supportive when she said: "You have a good job here, Wu. You speak excellent English and are well educated. I'm sure many of your Chinese friends would love to work here."

Wu gave her a curious look. "It's not my ambition to work for the British Consulate-General all my life."

Marianne realised she'd offended her somehow. "I didn't mean to suggest you were destined to work here forever."

"I might work here," Wu went on, "but I don't have the privileges you have."

Marianne thought that was rich coming from the daughter of a senior and influential Communist Party official who'd probably got her the job in the Consulate in the first place. "At least you have some good family connections."

As soon as she'd said it, Marianne wished she hadn't. For the first time, the mask slipped from Wu's face, and her eyes blazed. "If you want to talk about self-interest, consider how your country has meddled in mine throughout history. England caused the opium wars to get its own way on trade and took Hong Kong for itself."

Marianne was stunned at the outburst. "Yes," she said, calmly, "but Hong Kong and Kowloon will be restored to China. They might have been given to the UK under the Treaty of Nanking, but Britain is prepared to negotiate their return to China. Things are more complicated than just handing them back. The Hong Kong people have been brought up in a democratic society, with the very freedoms you talked about earlier." Marianne glanced at her. "They don't want to lose them."

Wu sighed and looked away. "I should not have spoken so harshly," she said. "You must miss your grandparents very much. But you don't understand what it's like to be … us."

"Maybe. But from my studies of your culture and language, and having spent three years already living in Peking, I probably understand more than most Westerners."

Wu nodded. "Then you will also understand that at some time in the future, China will be the most powerful nation on earth. It is inevitable."

Inwardly Marianne thought Wu was probably right, but she didn't say so.

"We will not be invaded or pushed around anymore," said Wu quietly.

Marianne knew there was nothing she could say to appease Wu, so she decided to lighten the mood. "So," she said. "What's your ultimate career ambition, Wu?"

Wu replied without hesitation. "To join the Chinese diplomatic service and travel the world."

"Ah I see. Well, you've made a good start here." Marianne smiled. "Maybe you'll come to work in the Chinese Embassy in London one day? Maybe we'll even meet again there?"

"Maybe." Wu gave Marianne a small smile as she rose. "But I expect we'll both be staying in China for some time yet."

Marianne watched Wu go, with a sinking heart. Whatever she did, or whatever she said these days, always seemed to be wrong. She needed to get away for a while, take a break. A good walk in the countryside, somewhere to breathe in some fresh air. Or maybe she'd just go to Hong Kong for the weekend. Do some shopping, eat some western food, and get her hair done. Yes, that would help put things into perspective.

The sound of a car turning into the driveway made her look up. A police car. She looked at her watch. 2pm on the dot.

For some reason, the haggard face of Chairman Mao's condemned widow sprang into her mind again. Marianne pushed it from her thoughts, held her head high, and steeled herself for all the questions that were about to rain down on her. 'Tell the truth and have courage.' Those words rattled around in her head as she walked towards the police car.

20

When anger rises, think of the consequences
(Confucius)

Marianne, Inspector Zhang, and his police interpreter followed Wu into the Consulate-General conference room. It was really the dining room of the old house, with a long wooden table and chairs down the middle for entertaining. There would be no sociable lunch or dinner today, no happy occasion to celebrate, and no light chatter. It was set for a formal meeting.

Inspector Zhang and his interpreter took their seats along one side of the table, and Marianne and Wu on the other. Marianne had half-expected Wu to go and sit next to the Inspector, but she sat down next to her instead. This confrontational set up, and the formality of the meeting, only served to heighten the tension in the room. That was palpable. Clearly none of them wanted to be there, but only Marianne had everything to lose.

Before anyone spoke, Marianne heard a car come racing up the drive. She could tell by the squeaky brakes when it stopped that it was Justin's. Footsteps marched quickly along the hallway.

All eyes turned to the door as Justin came in. He stopped on the threshold. "Apologies for being late," he said. "Hope I haven't missed anything."

Wu gave him a sharp look. "We were about to start without you."

He walked to Marianne's side of the table, then looked above Inspector Zhang's head into the large mirror above the fireplace. He quickly smoothed down his ruffled hair and straightened his crooked tie. He put a light hand on Marianne's shoulder and whispered 'sorry' in her ear, before sitting down on her other side.

It was typical of Justin to be late, and she'd smelled alcohol on his breath as he'd leaned in. Another liquid lunch. And where on earth were Sam and Anthony?

Inspector Zhang gave a polite cough to get their attention. He was the police officer who'd attended the Ambassador's death at the hotel. Marianne wasn't surprised to see him, although she'd hoped for someone more engaging. He'd been curt and dismissive towards her the other night. Now, he was even more aloof and sat bolt upright on his straight-backed chair.

Wu, with great persistence, had managed to persuade him to take off his police hat, which seemed to annoy him. A reaction, Marianne suspected, that was more to do with his own authority than anything else. Perhaps he felt more in charge in his hat?

His interpreter, a young man with a thin, sharp face, and wearing a different uniform, sat quietly beside him. He laid his open notebook on the table and held a pencil in one hand. With the other, he kept picking imaginary fluff off his trousers. A nervous habit that Marianne found irritating.

Before the meeting, Wu had placed a black, lacquer tray in the middle of the table. On it stood five china mugs, each containing a spoonful of Chinese tea leaves, alongside a large, metal teapot full of boiling water. Wu stood up, lifted the teapot and filled all the mugs with hot water before placing one in front of each of them. Marianne watched the leaves fizz and uncurl in her mug as they reacted to the almost boiling water. The tea was far too hot to try to drink, but it was a polite custom that had to be honoured. Normally the Chinese would put a china lid on their mug and continue topping up the same tea leaves with hot water for hours, but not in meetings.

To Marianne's surprise, when they did start talking, it was Wu who took charge. She clearly wasn't going to let some junior police interpreter take precedence over her, and started translating for everyone right from the start, including the Inspector. Marianne guessed Wu was probably far more proficient in English than the young man anyway, who seemed content to leave it to her.

The Inspector started by asking Marianne to give them a full account of her movements on the day the Ambassador died, and to explain exactly what happened in his hotel room. Although both she and Justin could speak Chinese, they both spoke in English throughout the interview, while the Inspector spoke in Chinese. Then, all sides politely waited for Wu's translation each time, knowing that this was the way Chinese officialdom liked to conduct meetings. Protocol was all important.

Marianne gave a precise account of exactly where she'd been all that day, and particularly from the moment she'd left the Consulate-General to the moment she'd found the Ambassador on the bathroom floor. It was important to get everything right, and she was glad she'd kept her diary of events. She wasn't giving an official statement, of course, but it was a formal interview, and she had expected the young police officer to take notes. Curiously, he just listened.

The Inspector nodded when she'd finished. He was wearing the same stony expression as the other night. He refused to look her in the eye too and focused on a point just above her right shoulder, and out the window behind her. It was difficult to guess his age, although he had to be well over 50. The most intriguing thing about him was the unnatural jet-black colour of his hair. It looked dyed, and rather harsh against his pale skin. His fingernails were perfectly manicured too, which made her think he was more senior than his title suggested.

"Exactly what time did you arrive at the Peace Hotel?" he asked, in a perfunctory way.

"The driver dropped me at the front entrance at 5.45pm," she replied. "I remember looking at my watch because that was the exact time I was supposed to meet the Ambassador in the Jazz Bar."

"Of course, we can't ask your driver to confirm that because he's had an accident since then," the Inspector said.

Marianne nodded. "Poor man."

The Inspector nodded in a matter of fact way. He didn't offer any sympathy or even look sad, but then that was the Chinese way. They weren't given to public displays of emotion, and took the English saying 'stiff upper lip' to new heights.

"Exactly how long did you spend in the Jazz Bar?" Inspector Zhang asked.

"It was 6pm when I next looked at my watch," Marianne replied. "It had grown so dark, it was hard to see the time. I distinctly remember having to hold my wrist up to the light."

"So, you were in the bar for 15 minutes?"

"Longer than that," she said, "I waited another five or ten minutes before deciding to go and look for the Ambassador." She paused. "The barman will be able to confirm that."

"Did you see anyone else you knew in the bar?"

Marianne shook her head. "We were the only two people in there for most of the time. The jazz musicians turned up just before I left."

"What did you think had happened to the Ambassador at the time?"

Marianne shrugged. "I thought the arrangements might have changed, and no one had been able to get a message to me."

"Is there anyone who could corroborate your movements that afternoon, Miss Henderson?"

She shook her head. "My colleague Justin was in Hangzhou."

Justin nodded to confirm that but said nothing.

Wu piped up. "I was at the Jing An Hotel all afternoon checking all the arrangements for the visiting British trade delegation."

Marianne glanced sideways, unsurprised that Wu was immediately exonerating herself from any involvement. "The barman can confirm how long I was in the Jazz Bar," she said again. "One of the hotel receptionists gave me the Ambassador's room number so that I could go up to his room."

Inspector Zhang kept up his pose of looking over her shoulder. "She gave you his room number so that you could use the internal phones to call his room. People are not allowed to go up to guests' rooms unless invited to do so."

Marianne sighed. "I know, but he wasn't answering the phone. I had no option but to go up to his room to look for him."

"You could have asked a member of the hotel staff to escort you," the Inspector said.

Marianne wished she had asked someone to escort her up to the Ambassador's room. Better still, she wished she'd just gone straight to the Jing An Hotel and dealt with the visiting trade delegation on her own.

There was silence for a moment, then the Inspector changed tack: "Who set up that meeting in the Jazz Bar between you and the Ambassador, Miss Henderson?"

"The Ambassador rang me and asked me to meet him there," she said.

For the first time, the Inspector's eyes swivelled to look at her. "Was it normal for the Ambassador to ring you direct to ask you to meet him?"

Marianne knew why he was asking that question. A simple 'were you having an affair with the Ambassador' would have cut to the chase and saved a lot of time, but that wasn't the Chinese way. She answered honestly. "Sometimes," she said. "And sometimes he would ask his PA in Peking to ring and give me a message."

The Inspector shifted on his seat. Was he feeling uncomfortable with this line of questioning?

"Can you tell me, Miss Henderson, how well you knew the Ambassador?"

Again, Marianne just wished he would ask her if she'd been in bed with the Ambassador in his hotel room that afternoon, or even if she'd killed him, so that she could categorically deny it and put the record straight. She had to follow the Inspector's lead though. It would be foolish to antagonise him.

"Quite well," she answered. "I worked in our Embassy in Peking for three years before coming to Shanghai to open this new Consulate-General. The Ambassador was in Peking the whole time I was there so, yes, I knew him quite well."

The Inspector pursed his lips ever so slightly. Marianne could feel her frustration rising. She looked over his head at the mirror hanging over the chimney breast. The garden outside was reflected in it, and she could see the trees swaying in the wind. She continued to watch the trees through the mirror, while she waited for the next question.

"So," Inspector Zhang said. "We found two dirty glasses and a half-empty bottle of champagne on the bedside cabinet." He looked at Marianne. "Who do you think he was entertaining in his room?"

She tried to look him in the eye, but he steadfastly looked away. "I have no idea," she said.

He asked abruptly. "Was the condom still in its foil wrapper when you got there?"

Marianne had to think about that. The foil wrapper was open, but she couldn't remember if the condom was still inside. "I don't know," she said, truthfully, "I never looked inside the wrapper."

At that point, Wu halted proceedings by picking up her mug. She looked around the table at everyone, nodded, then took a sip of tea. That seemed to be a sign for everyone else to do the same. Marianne noticed the young police officer's hands shaking as he picked up his mug. He took a quick sip then carefully put it back down on the table. What with his annoying fluff-picking habit and his shaking hands, he seemed even more nervous than she was. Why? Was he uncomfortable in these surroundings, interviewing foreigners? Or was he afraid of the Inspector? Marianne couldn't blame him for that. The Inspector was an oppressively solemn man.

Inspector Zhang gave his little cough again, to signal he wanted to return to business. Before he could speak, Justin, who was obviously getting as frustrated with this tortuous questioning as Marianne, interjected. "So, Inspector. Can you tell us exactly how the Ambassador died? I believe the formal results of the post-mortem are ready?"

The mask-like face the Inspector had worn up until now creased slightly. He was clearly expecting to ask all the questions, not answer them.

Wu gave the Inspector a sharp nod, as if instructing him to answer.

The Inspector's eyes narrowed as they rested on Wu, but she didn't flinch. "The British Ambassador died of arsenic poisoning," he said.

"What was the evidence of that?" Justin asked.

Again, the Inspector didn't answer straightaway. Again, Wu gave him a nod.

"Arsenic produces a fatty, yellow liver." Inspector Zhang paused. "There was evidence of a sub-endocardial haemorrhage in the left ventricle, and that occurs in most cases of acute arsenic poisoning."

Justin glanced sideways at Marianne, and then back to the Inspector. "Was it a single dose of arsenic that killed him, do you think?"

The Inspector nodded.

"Administered how?" Justin asked.

"The Ambassador drank it," the Inspector said, "in the champagne."

"Ah," said Justin.

Marianne's mind was well ahead of them. Her grandmother had told her about the poisons used by agents during World War II. The 'L' pill, the lethal pill, which was given to special agents going behind enemy lines, contained cyanide. Brain death occurred within minutes and the heart stopped beating. There was skin discolouration and convulsions with that method of poisoning, just as with other poisons, including arsenic.

She looked at the Inspector and frowned. The Ambassador certainly didn't have any skin discolouration on his face or lips when she'd tried to resuscitate him, or afterwards. He didn't have any convulsions either. She remembered a trickle of saliva running from his mouth. But there was no vomit, which her grandmother had told her was often the case in poisonings.

She wondered whether to raise that with the Inspector, except she didn't want him to think she was an expert on poisons and assume it to be a sign of her guilt. She turned to Justin. "You went to the morgue to identify the Ambassador, Justin. Did you see any signs that he'd been poisoned?"

Justin gave her a strange look. "I wouldn't know what to look for."

The Inspector coughed again.

"Continue, Inspector," Wu said.

"You said before, Miss Henderson, that the Ambassador had a small snuff bottle in his hand when he died?"

"That's right," Marianne said. "It rolled out of his hand and onto the floor."

"Yet you do not have this snuff bottle?"

Marianne looked him straight in the eye, which made him quickly avert his. "I don't know how it happened, but I must have put the snuff bottle in my jacket pocket in the heat of the moment while I was in the hotel and forgotten about it. I found it there later that evening."

"Was there any snuff in the bottle?" the Inspector asked.

"No. I took the stopper off and tipped it upside down to check if there was anything inside. It was empty. I just assumed it was a trinket for display, an antique maybe." She shrugged. "I don't know why the Ambassador had it in his hand. It's a mystery."

"Then the snuff bottle disappeared?" Inspector Zhang said.

Marianne caught the scepticism in his voice. It was the first time he'd changed his tone and revealed any sentiment throughout the interview.

She glanced at Justin. "I put it in my desk drawer, in my office. When I came in the next morning it had gone."

"Very strange," the Inspector said. "Tell me, Miss Henderson, are you sure the snuff bottle existed at all?"

Marianne felt her temper rising. Why would he think she'd made up some story about a snuff bottle? It didn't make sense since he'd already said the arsenic was in the champagne. "Quite sure," she said, swallowing her anger. She reached down to her handbag, pulled out the polaroid photo of the little bottle, and slapped it down on the table in the front of him. "That's the bottle," she said. "I took a photo of it that night, before it disappeared."

Marianne felt a frisson of surprise around the table that went from Wu to Justin to the Inspector. Producing that photo had stunned them all, and that made Marianne feel so much better. She was telling the truth, for God's sake. Perhaps they would believe her now?

As they sat in silence, a familiar wailing sound came down the chimney breast and echoed around the room. Inspector Zhang jumped, and looked over his shoulder. His poor interpreter looked shocked.

Marianne smiled. "It's only the north wind blowing through the old house."

The Inspector looked at her as if she was the she-devil. He picked up his hat from the table and put it carefully on his head. "I think we have asked enough questions for one day," he said.

Enough? All she'd done was give him the same information she'd given him the other night at the hotel.

He hadn't asked her anything else. She hadn't had a chance to deny anything either because he hadn't asked her the right questions.

"I should like you to come to the Central Police Station tomorrow to give a formal statement," he said.

Marianne felt her stomach turn. Now she understood why the young man wasn't taking notes. They were just going through the motions. Tomorrow, they would do it all over again, for real.

"We would like to take your fingerprints and samples of your hair, nails and blood too," Inspector Zhang said.

Marianne stared first at him, then at Justin, who looked very uncomfortable.

"Maybe you should go along with it," Justin whispered, quite sure the Inspector couldn't understand English. "That way they can eliminate you from their enquiries and that'll be the end of it."

"This is ridiculous!"

Justin shrugged. "It's up to you."

"It's not up to me, is it?" she whispered back. "The Chinese police want me to go to the station to give a formal statement and they want fingerprints, hair, nail, and blood samples. Why, I don't know. I've already said I was there in the room. I touched the door, the curtains, the light switches, the bathroom door and I gave the Ambassador CPR for ages," she said, sharply. "Have you ever done CPR, Justin?"

He looked away. "No."

"Have you even learnt?"

"No."

"Well it's exhausting pumping hard down on someone's chest for as long as I did. I might have dropped hairs and fibres of my clothes all over the place."

"Exactly." Justin said. "All the more reason to identify what you might have left behind, and what might belong to, well, to the killer."

"He's right, Marianne," Wu said, quietly.

Marianne sighed deeply. She knew there was no point in being awkward. That would only make the Chinese more suspicious. She might as well agree to go to the station and give a statement and samples. Get it over with once and for all. "All right," she said, in a flat voice. "I'll go to the police station in the morning."

Inspector Zhang pushed back his chair and stood up. "We would also like to search your office and your house, Miss Henderson."

Marianne's jaw dropped.

"It's just routine," the Inspector said.

Marianne knew it was anything but routine and her heart started pounding.

Justin stood up. "You can't search this Consulate-General. The building is covered by the Vienna Convention. It's the territory of the United Kingdom, and inviolable."

The Inspector gave a curt nod, clearly expecting that reply. "Very well, but we would like to search Miss Henderson's house. We would like to do that with her agreement," he went on, "but we can always get a warrant."

Justin looked helplessly at Marianne.

Annoyed and incredulous, she stood up too. How could they believe she had anything to do with the Ambassador's death? It was unthinkable. As she looked from Wu, to Inspector Zhang, to the police interpreter, she saw on their faces that that was exactly what they were thinking. But it felt like a punch in the stomach to see the same expression on Justin's face.

"Very well," she said, drawing herself up to her full height. "Go ahead and search my house. I have nothing to hide." She paused. "In fact, I'll come with you and let you in."

Inspector Zhang shook his head. "I do not want you there during the search Miss Henderson."

Justin stepped in. "Give me the keys Marianne, I'll go with them and make sure everything's all right."

Wu jumped up. "I'll come too, in case there are any problems."

Marianne stood frozen to the spot as they started filing out of the room. It felt like a hand had gripped her heart, and she could hardly breathe.

Now, the nightmare was beginning for real.

21

Do the difficult things while they are easy and do the great things while they are small. A journey of a thousand miles must start with a single step

(Confucius)

Marianne sat staring into space in the reception room. It felt like her mind and body were somewhere else, as if she was floating in a parallel universe. Like in a dream, where things happened that were all jumbled up and made no sense. As a child, shortly after the death of her parents, she started having a recurring dream, where someone was chasing her, but she couldn't move or get away. She would try to run, try to scream, but she couldn't, because she was completely paralysed. The sheer terror used to wake her up in panic.

That's what it felt like now. Except she wasn't asleep, and she wasn't dreaming.

In the house, she could hear nothing except the wind rattling the ill-fitting wooden window frames behind her. The rest of the Chinese staff had disappeared, as if vaporized. All that was left of them was the smell of their lunch of rice and boiled vegetables. They were probably hiding from the police in the old boiler room out the back. They tended to use it as a staff room because it was so warm, and often met in there to chat over a mug of tea. One thing was for sure, they wouldn't want to be drawn into the police investigation in any way.

She picked up her pack of cigarettes from the coffee table with shaky hands and lit up. When the nicotine started coursing through her veins, the fog in her head cleared and she came back to reality. Now, she could hardly move her toes and fingers because of the numbing coldness, and the shock.

Search her house? For goodness sake, what on earth did they expect to find in there?

She got up, flicked on both bars of the electric fire and stood over it to warm herself up. Her head was reeling. It hadn't been a proper interview at all. Inspector Zhang had just been going through the motions. Why? Why bother to interview her at the Consulate at all? Why not just ask her to come to the police station for a formal interview and give the blood and other samples they wanted? The other thing really troubling her was that at no point had the Inspector asked her if she'd been the woman sleeping with the Ambassador in his hotel room, or even if she'd killed him. Of course, they were sensitive questions, but she would have expected to have been asked so that she could deny it. So, why hadn't he? Because he assumed she was guilty? Or was he playing with her, trying to get her flustered? Well, she thought defiantly, if he expected her to change her story at the second interview tomorrow, he was very much mistaken. She'd already told him the truth.

As she started pacing around the reception room, puffing on her cigarette and blowing smoke into the chilly air, she kept coming back to one thought. Everyone was too quick to assume she'd had an affair with the Ambassador and killed him. The more she thought about it, the more she felt like a pawn in a much bigger picture. From the moment she'd arrived in Shanghai, and long before the Ambassador's death, she'd been targeted by the Chinese secret police. She walked over to the mirror that hung over the fireplace. This is a house of mirrors, she thought. Everything's a reflection, the reverse of what it should be.

In the mirror, she noticed how pallid her skin looked, and how dark the circles were under her eyes.

Trust your instincts, Marianne. They will not lie to you.

As the thoughts crystallised in her head, her stomach churned.

"You've been set up, Marianne," she told her reflection in the mirror. "And you never even noticed it happening."

The thought seemed ridiculous, some imaginative plot in a thriller. But why else would everyone keep focusing only on her?

Even her colleagues seemed to want to point the finger at her. She reeled back in shock at the way her mind was working. Except it was the only thing that seemed to make any sense. They had made sure she was alone on the day of the Ambassador's murder, and that she went alone to meet him in the Peace Hotel. Now, Justin and Wu were out at her house with the Chinese police searching through all her things, her personal things. She'd given them access to her private sanctum, believing they were trying to help her. The thought made her want to heave.

Right, she thought, while they were searching her house, she would search *their* offices. She didn't know what she was looking for, but there was something weird going on and she might find some clues among their things.

She went out into the hallway, slipped into Justin's office, and closed the door. His office was always untidy, and she wasn't sure where to start looking. She tried the handle on his combination cupboard, where he kept all his sensitive and personal papers, but it was locked. She glanced out of the window to make sure no one was watching outside, then she went over to his desk and started searching all the drawers. They were full of rubbish, which made it time-consuming, but she went through every one of them methodically. Nothing struck her as unusual. She searched the tray of unclassified papers on his desk too, scanning them all quickly to see what he was working on. Again, nothing suspicious.

She was just on her way out, when she noticed his overcoat hanging on the back of the door. He loved that coat and wore it all the time. It was made of herringbone tweed and had a little black velvet collar. In his rush to go with the police to her house, he'd forgotten to put it on. She felt the inside breast pocket. Nothing. She plunged her hand into another pocket and felt something. She pulled out what looked like an old train ticket. Going over to the window to get more light on it, she saw it was his return ticket from Hangzhou on the night the Ambassador was murdered.

Except … it wasn't for an evening train, as Justin had said. It was for a lunchtime train, the 1.05pm from Hangzhou. That would have got him into Shanghai by mid-afternoon, and well before the Ambassador was killed. She stared at the ticket. It had been clipped on the corner by the train guard, which proved it had been used on that day, and on that train.

Had Sam been on that train too?

Slipping the ticket into her jacket pocket, she dashed into the spare office at the side of the building that Sam and Anthony were sharing temporarily. Each of them had a desk and a combination cupboard in which to store their papers. Marianne had set both combinations when the cupboards had arrived from the UK. She had given both Sam and Anthony the combination numbers and the special 'Allen' key to slot into the locks to allow them to change the numbers. But had they changed them?

She headed straight for Sam's cupboard and tried the handle. Locked. She listened carefully for any sound outside indicating Sam and Anthony might be coming back. All quiet. She started spinning the combination to the right, then to the left, stopping on the original numbers she'd set, hoping that Sam hadn't bothered to change them. He hadn't, and the lock clicked open. Quickly she opened the cupboard door and started searching the shelves. There were just the usual papers and files, until she got to the bottom shelf. Right at the back, she spotted what looked like a parcel. She pulled it out. It was covered in brown wrapping paper and tied up with string. It didn't look particularly interesting, but it was the address and name of the person the parcel was being sent to that piqued her curiosity.

It was Sam's own name and home address in the UK.

Marianne laid the parcel on his desk and tried to untie the knot holding the string in place. She picked at it with her fingernails for what seemed like ages until it eventually gave way. She pulled the string off and unwrapped the brown paper. Inside was something tightly packed in layers of tissue paper. Unfolding it, she found a small cloisonné bowl inside. It was made of blue and white porcelain, with what looked like lotus blossom painted on the side. Exquisite. She turned the bowl upside down, and there were the tell-tale red Chinese characters painted on the bottom to indicate the bowl's provenance. The Qing dynasty. And a red wax seal indicating it was an antique and could not be exported out of China. As she went to put the bowl back in the tissue, she noticed a receipt.

She studied it carefully. The bowl had been purchased in a shop in Hangzhou, on the day of the Ambassador's murder. She frowned. Was Sam going to post the piece to himself in the UK when he knew damn well it was illegal to take it out of China? Is that what he was up to, smuggling this antique out of China? She could hardly believe it.

Quickly she wrapped the bowl up again and put the package back where she'd found it. Then she realised she'd forgotten to put the receipt back in the parcel. She didn't have time to unwrap it again, so she slipped the receipt into her pocket. She hunted around his desk and drawers for a bit longer but found nothing else of interest.

She glanced at Anthony's desk and cupboard. He hadn't been in Shanghai at the time of the Ambassador's murder. She went over to his cupboard anyway in the hope of searching it, but it was locked. She tried the original combination she'd set, but his cupboard wouldn't open. Trust Anthony to change the combination. She had a quick look in his desk drawers. In contrast to Justin's, everything was arranged neatly. She couldn't find anything suspicious, but then, Anthony was too smart to leave anything incriminating around.

Her head was spinning as she came out of their office. She was caught up in the middle of something awful. She had no one to turn to. No one to trust.

Passing Wu's office, she stopped at her open door. The thought of Wu watching while the Chinese police searched her house filled her with anger too. The woman was just as complicit as Justin, Sam and Anthony in Marianne's eyes, but somehow it felt wrong to go searching Wu's office. Still, Marianne pushed the door open and went in. She'd never really lingered in Wu's office before, and she looked around. There was nothing of a personal nature that she could see. No family photos on her desk, no plants or flowers on the windowsills, no pictures on the walls. Marianne thought back to their earlier conversation in the garden. Was that because Wu never intended to stay long in the Consulate-General? Was this job a quick stepping stone on her way to greater things? Or perhaps Wu didn't keep anything personal in here because she didn't want anyone to know the real woman underneath that driven exterior?

Still, Marianne thought, as she sat down at her desk. Wu's life couldn't be easy in this crowded country, where individual rights and freedoms mattered much less than the power and survival of the State. Wu was a small cog in a massive wheel, trying to forge out the best life she could for herself in the circumstances.

Marianne flicked through the papers in Wu's in-tray. Nothing of interest. She went over to her bookshelves and was surprised to see a whole array of English classics. They looked like new books too. Where on earth had Wu got these from? Marianne had never seen them on sale in China before.

Back at Wu's desk, Marianne had a quick peek in the drawers, feeling more uncomfortable about invading her privacy. She was just about to leave when a book in the bottom drawer caught her eye. She could see by the cover it was the one Wu had been reading earlier in the garden. The one she had shoved quickly in her bag when Marianne asked what it was.

Intrigued, Marianne pulled the book out and laid it on the desk. It was in Chinese, but Marianne could read and understand Chinese characters and instantly knew the book. *The Butterfly Lovers*. It was like a Chinese version of *Romeo and Juliet*. A romantic love story, of star-crossed lovers, set way back in the Eastern Jin Dynasty. Why would the practical and ambitious Wu read something sentimental like this?

She opened the inside cover and there on the first page was her answer. In black ink, someone had written a message in Chinese characters …

When you catch someone's heart, you will never be apart.

It was just one simple line, no name or signature, but it said everything. Well, well, well, Marianne thought, Wu did have a boyfriend. He must have given her this book. Who was he? Did he live in this city too? Pity if he did, she thought, because Chinese lovers had a long wait to get married in Shanghai. They had to be at least 27, because there was nowhere for them to live. Whole families, with children, lived in just one room, so what chance was there for new couples starting out.

Marianne closed the book and put it carefully back in the drawer.

Needing to be on her own to sort out her thoughts, she went quickly upstairs to the part of the house that was being renovated for the Consul-General to live in when he came out to take up his post. She went into what would be his sitting room. The heat rose in the old house, making this room the warmest in the building. She flopped down on a sofa covered with dust sheets and stared out of the window at the treetops while she waited for Justin and Wu to come back from searching her house.

It was clear to her now that her colleagues were lying. Justin had been back in Shanghai by mid-afternoon on the day of the Ambassador's murder. She'd bet her last pound Sam had been on that train too. The pair of them were as thick as thieves. Why would they lie about it? She hardly dared answer her own question, because she was thinking only one thing.

They lied because they were involved in the Ambassador's murder.

She sat there turning everything over and over in her head until darkness began to sweep in. Suddenly the porch and driveway security lights flashed on. A car was coming up the drive. It sounded like the official car, so it had to be Sam and Anthony coming back from wherever they'd been.

Marianne got up to go and see them. But, hearing their voices in the hallway below, she hesitated. She felt so wretched at the thought of them lying to her, she could hardly bare to lay eyes on them. What was she going to say? What was she going to do?

She sat down on the top step and listened to their voices floating up the curved staircase.

"Is she in her office?" Anthony's clipped vowels were unmistakable.

"No, I can't find her," Sam replied.

"Lord knows where she is."

Sam sighed. "She can't have gone far, her car's still in the driveway. She's such a loose cannon. Who knows what she'll do next."

A loose cannon? Marianne could hardly believe those words came from Sam.

"Oh, I don't know," Anthony went on. "She's holding up pretty well if you ask me."

"Yeah, well, you sound like the old man now." Sam's voice sounded unusually harsh. "He had the hots for her too."

"Can't blame him for that," Anthony laughed. "Must be her French genes."

Marianne's temper flared. How *dare* they talk about her like that? How the hell did Anthony know about her grandmother anyway?

"Do you think she was having an affair with the old man, then?" Anthony asked.

"Justin says he's seen them together," Sam said. "He's in no doubt there was something going on."

Marianne couldn't believe her ears.

"She wouldn't kill him though," Anthony said. "Marianne's not a killer."

"Who knows what people will do when they're driven to it." Sam sighed. "Maybe she didn't mean to."

"Whoever poisoned that champagne meant to do it," Anthony said. "That's a fact."

"Yeah, well I wouldn't want to be in her shoes," Sam said. "She's never going to get out of this country if the Chinese find her guilty of murder."

It was Anthony's turn to sigh now. "And that's a fact too. I can't believe London would waive her diplomatic immunity."

"They must think she did it, then," Sam said.

Their voices tapered off as they walked into their office.

Marianne was left reeling at the top of the stairs. Sam! The one person she'd thought of as a friend. And how the hell did Anthony know that champagne had been poisoned? Inspector Zhang only confirmed it during the interview that afternoon.

Her legs wobbled as she stood up. Did everyone think she'd had an affair with the Ambassador and killed him. London too? Is that why they'd waived her diplomatic immunity? The shock was indescribable, and she could hardly move, or think straight. That's when she decided she had to get out of there, away from this nest of vipers.

Creeping down the stairs, she went to her office, grabbed her bag and coat, and slipped out of the building. Please just let me get out of here, she prayed over and over, as she closed the front door as quietly as she could.

She ran across the gravel on her toes to make less noise. Reaching her car, she opened the doors and jumped inside.

Her heart was pounding even harder when she fired up the engine, reversed quickly and set off down the drive.

In her mirror, she saw Anthony come rushing out of the front door. He sprinted down the drive after her. "Marianne," he shouted. "Stop!"

But Marianne wasn't stopping for anyone.

22

London, Present Day

*Music produces a kind of pleasure which human nature
cannot do without*
(Confucius)

Jess watched as Bev took another sip of white wine. The
light from the candle on the restaurant table made her look
radiant, with her silver-grey hair and skin glowing from yet
another run in the park. Her long, sparkly earrings reflected
the light, making colourful patterns on the tablecloth. Bev
must be in her sixties, Jess thought, but she was still an
attractive woman, especially her dark brown eyes. Her
rather enigmatic eyes. It hadn't escaped Jess's notice that,
when she spoke, Bev never looked her in the eye for long
before looking away. Was Bev just shy? Or deliberately
guarded? Either way, Jess had to admit she was enjoying
this woman's company. Bev could chat about anything,
from politics to cooking roast beef. For the first time in
ages, Jess found herself relaxing.

The pair of them had dressed themselves up to go to the
theatre and were both looking forward to Carole King's
musical *Beautiful*, especially Bev who declared it to be
music from her 'era'. Jess smiled to herself to think of her

own pasty skin under the make-up she'd put on to go out on the town. Bev was way older than her, yet she looked so much fitter and healthier.

While Bev chatted away, Jess kept her eye on the door. Outside, Christmas shoppers hurried along the pavement, heads bent low against the wind as if they were searching for something on the ground. Jess was watching for Tom to arrive, but that wasn't all. Since that grey car had followed them to the Chinese restaurant the other evening, along with that eavesdropping couple, she'd kept a constant eye out. So far, she hadn't seen either the car or the couple again, but that didn't mean they weren't there. Of course, Tom might have been mistaken. It could have been sheer coincidence that the same car was outside both the Black Swan and the Chinese restaurant. That couple sitting near them might have been innocent too. One thing was for sure, the experience had sobered her up. She'd been careful since then to do, and say, nothing about Marianne Henderson's disappearance or anything else to do with Shanghai. In fact, she'd decided to do exactly what Sir Anthony had told her to, leave it in the past. She knew that's what Tom wanted too, although he never said as much. Anyway, what could she do about Marianne on her own? Absolutely nothing.

She looked at her watch. 6.15pm. They were in a small restaurant around the corner from the Aldwych Theatre, where *Beautiful* was playing, for an early pre-theatre dinner. Surrounded by gold tinsel adorning the pictures on the walls, and a small Christmas tree with fairy lights in the far corner, Jess was reminded that she hadn't even thought about the holidays, yet alone made plans for her and Simon. All they'd agreed was that he would be home for Christmas. She would phone him soon and nail things down. This evening, though, she was determined to enjoy herself.

Their table had been laid for three, with a candle and a single-stemmed rose in a vase in the middle. Tom hadn't arrived yet, and Jess was beginning to worry. They only had enough time for a quick two-course set menu, because they had to be seated in the theatre by 7.30pm. The restaurant was already filling up too, which meant the service would be slower. "I think we'd better order," she said to Bev. "Tom must have got held up."

Bev's eyes twinkled before she looked away. "You haven't told me anything about this man. Is he someone special in your life?"

"Oh, no," Jess said, quickly. "Well, I mean … he's a very good friend, over from Australia."

Bev looked surprised. "He's Australian?"

"Yes, I thought you two would get on, both being Australian. And he absolutely *loves* wine."

Bev gave a small smile. "Is he in the trade too?"

Jess laughed. "No, he just loves to drink it. He's a policeman, over here on secondment to the Metropolitan Police for a few months. In fact, he's heading back to Oz after he's finished working on the Chinese President's visit." Even as she said it, Jess felt a twinge of sadness that Tom was leaving so soon. Why hadn't he got in touch earlier?

Bev's eyes clouded. "What's an Australian policeman doing working on the Chinese President's visit?"

Jess laughed. "Does sound odd doesn't it? He was a member of your Prime Minister's protection team in Australia. I guess he's a good fit for a similar job here."

Bev still looked puzzled. "You were telling me about this Chinese visit the other evening. How's it all going?"

"We're all ready now for him to get here on Monday, thank God."

"These visits must be a lot of work."

Jess nodded. "You don't know the half of it. I've only been on the China desk for six months and I've been flat out the whole time. Actually, I've been in the office today…"

"On Saturday?" Bev admonished.

"Oh, I had a lie in, and went in late."

"I suppose you wanted to clear the decks. Get your papers and head organised before it all kicks off."

"*Exactly!* I have to say the whole process has pepped me up. I feel energised. I'm even looking forward to the visit."

"Are you going out to the airport to do the meet and greet?"

"Yes."

Bev smiled. "Well I wish you the best of luck. I hope it goes well for you."

It was said with such sincerity, Jess was grateful. Apart from Tom, it was the first kind words she'd had from anyone about the visit.

The waiter came over and took their orders. Jess wondered whether to get something for Tom. Steak was on the menu, and he liked that. But would he make it in time? In the end she decided not to.

"So," Bev said. "*Do* you have anyone special in your life, Jess? Or does work take up every waking hour?"

Jess hesitated. She didn't like to talk about Simon, although there was no reason for her not to.

Bev picked up on that and sat back in her chair. "Sorry. Ignore me if I ask too many questions."

"No, it's okay." Jess was annoyed at herself for being defensive, especially as Bev was just making conversation. "My partner works in the British Embassy in Paris. He's a diplomat too. He took the posting to be close to London, so that we could see each other often."

"Wow." Bev raised her eyebrows. "The Foreign Office *is* accommodating."

Jess nodded. "They weren't always. Women weren't allowed to join until 1946. And, when they did, it was on one cruel condition – that they never married."

Bev just nodded.

"Men could marry and take their wives and children with them on postings around the world," Jess went on, "but women had to spend a lonely life travelling the world on their own, without the love and support of a family." She shook her head, sadly. "The marriage bar for women wasn't lifted until the 70s. When the Sex Discrimination Act came in in 1975, that made it illegal to discriminate on grounds of sex or marital status, thank God."

Bev gave a wry smile. "Different age now, isn't it?"

"Sure is."

"And *do* you?" Bev asked. "See your partner in Paris often?"

Jess shook her head. "Not as often as we would like. Work does seem to take up every waking hour."

"Well don't let it. You should put yourself and your own happiness before any organisation."

Jess was intrigued by Bev's tone. Perhaps it was time to ask *her* a few personal questions. "Do you have a family, Bev?" As soon as she'd opened her mouth, Jess wished she hadn't. Bev would only ask her the same thing and talking about Jack and Amy would make her sad. Tonight, she was determined to enjoy herself.

Bev hesitated, then she reached into her bag and pulled out a small photo wallet. She opened it and handed it to Jess. "Here are my two kids. Well, I say kids, but as you can see they're both in their twenties now."

Jess looked at the photos of two identical young, bronzed Australian boys, hair bleached by the sun, and smiling openly. "Twins?" She looked up at Bev.

Bev nodded. "And all grown up now, with minds of their own."

Jess smiled. "They look great. Are they following you into the wine business?"

"Absolutely." Bev smiled fondly at the photo and put the wallet carefully back in her bag. "How else do you think I can spend months over here?" It was said lightly, as if joking, but then she asked: "Do you have any children, Jess?"

There it was, the question Jess had been dreading. Why on earth had she brought it up in the first place? She looked at Bev, and hesitated before saying, "I was married once, with a child, a little girl." She paused for breath. "My husband and daughter were killed in a car crash, in Jakarta."

Bev looked shocked at first, then her face was full of kindness. "I'm *so* sorry, Jess."

Jess was thankful Bev didn't have the usual embarrassed expression on her face that Jess got on the rare occasion she mentioned Jack and Amy. And for that, Jess warmed to her. In fact, at that moment, she felt comfortable with this woman. Perhaps that was why she reached inside her bag and pulled out the photo of Jack and Amy. It was displayed in a miniature silver frame that went everywhere with her. "Here they are." She showed it to Bev. "Jack and Amy."

Bev stared at the photo and said simply: "What a pretty little girl."

Jess nodded. She didn't want to talk about the accident and how Jack and Amy died. All she said was: "They weren't destined to be in my life for very long, but it was, well, it was wonderful while they were."

Bev nodded, without saying anything more, but Jess noticed her eyes glistening. Was that in sympathy? Or something more?

When the waiter came over and put their smoked salmon starters in front of them, Jess glanced at the door for the umpteenth time.

Bev watched her. "Is everything all right?"

"Yes, I'm fine."

Bev persisted. "It's just that, well, the other night when you fell over outside our flats, you thought someone was following you." For the first time, she gave Jess a penetrating stare that made her feel uncomfortable.

Jess frowned at Bev. In many ways, *she* was more watchful than *her*. Bev looked round whenever the door opened too, and she had that CCTV rigged up in her flat. Why did she need that? But Jess didn't want to admit to snooping through Bev's blinds. "I'm just a bit worried about Tom, that's all," she said. "It's not like him to be late and not send a message."

Bev nodded, and they were silent for a couple of minutes.

Bev was the first to put down her knife and fork. "Oh, talking about your Chinese visit, I meant to tell you I read in the newspaper the other day that one of your Foreign Office colleagues had a tragic accident at the tube station the other evening." Her voice was soft and low. "They said it looked like suicide."

Jess was surprised Bev had seen the article, it was just a snippet in the inside pages. But then Jess had told her about the Chinese President's visit the other evening; the article must have resonated. "Yes. Giles Pettiford was my boss."

Bev looked surprised. "Oh, my goodness." Then she went on. "He must have been working on the Chinese President's visit too, and under a lot of strain. Poor man. Was that the problem, do you think?"

There was something about the way Bev asked that question that made Jess think it was no casual enquiry. Had Bev deliberately brought Giles into the conversation?

Jess was not going to be drawn into any discussion about her dead boss. "Who knows what goes on in other people's heads?" she said. "It was a terrible shock. We've just had to get on with things without him."

"Suicide is so terrible," Bev went on, "especially for families and, of course, colleagues."

Bev seemed so genuinely sad about Giles that Jess wondered if she'd experienced a similar situation at some point in her life. Was that why she was so interested in him? Jess wasn't going to ask though, she didn't want to talk about Giles any more this evening.

But Bev continued. "Do they know *why* he committed suicide? Seems a rather odd time to do it. I mean *before* the Chinese President's visit."

Jess thought the timing was strange too, but she never said so. "The police are still investigating. They haven't confirmed it was suicide yet, as far as I know."

Bev was about to say something else when Jess's mobile pinged with the sound of a text message arriving. She pulled it out of her pocket and read eagerly.

Sorry. Got caught up with a last-minute briefing for the visit. Won't make it to restaurant in time. Hope to meet you in the theatre foyer at 7.15pm Tom x

Jess was surprised at how disappointed she felt. She really hoped Tom would make it to the theatre. They didn't have much time to spend together as it was. He was due to finish his secondment at the end of the Chinese President's visit and be back in Oz for Christmas. "He's got caught up," she said to Bev, and put her phone back in her pocket.

"Oh dear! Is he not going to make it?" Bev sounded almost hopeful.

That's when it occurred to Jess that Bev might have preferred for just the two of them to go out on the town together.

Jess shook her head. "He's not coming for the meal, but he hopes to meet us at the theatre at 7.15pm."

"Oh good," Bev said, although she didn't look pleased.

★

Tom paced around the foyer of the Aldwych Theatre, both annoyed and worried, as he waited for Jess. That afternoon, the team's final meeting about the Chinese President's programme had gone very well. Every tiny detail had been discussed to ensure everyone knew exactly what they had to do. After the meeting, Tom felt confident, buoyed even, until he'd been called to another meeting with his boss.

He hadn't expected anything other than a routine meeting, until he'd got to his boss's office and been directed into an interview room along the corridor. He'd sat alone at the table until his boss appeared, with another man, whom he introduced as Inspector Dawson from Counter Terrorism Command.

Alarm bells flashed in Tom's head. He was in the shit, and he knew why. The questions he'd been asking about the British Ambassador's death in Shanghai and Marianne Henderson.

Now, shuffling around the foyer with his eyes fixed on the door for Jess, he replayed the interview in his head. First, they'd asked him about his relationship with Jess, which just confirmed to him that the grey car and couple *had* been following them. Despite his annoyance at being questioned in this way, Tom had kept his cool and good humour. He'd explained about his friendship with Jess, and about the murders they'd worked on together in Australia and the Turks and Caicos Islands. He'd got the distinct impression from his superiors that they already knew and were just testing him. That's when he decided to tell them everything, the whole truth. He could do that, of course, because he had nothing to hide.

He'd got especially annoyed when they'd asked if the relationship was romantic or sexual. What bloody business was it of theirs? Again, he'd just smiled. "We're just friends. We probably wouldn't have seen each other at all if I hadn't got this job on the Chinese President's protection detail." On the face of it, of course, that was true.

Then they'd asked why he'd been looking for information in the archives about the British Ambassador's death in Shanghai in 1984. Of course, he'd had no option but to tell the truth. They would have sussed him, if he'd tried to cover his tracks. So, he explained that Jess had mentioned the Ambassador's death to him. She'd found some reference to it in the Foreign Office files, but surprisingly little detail. She'd asked him if the Met would have kept a record. He'd told her he'd find out, and that's why he'd been looking.

"And what information did you find?" Inspector Dawson asked.

"Nothing." Tom was being truthful. "I discovered it was a restricted file, and not held in the main archives." He'd shrugged and looked at them. "When I explained that to Jess, that was the end of it." Then he'd turned the tables on his interviewers. "Why do you ask? Is there a problem?"

Inspector Dawson had stared at him for a moment. The man was nobody's fool, but he was obviously not going to push things. "When does your secondment end, Tom?" he'd asked.

"Immediately after the Chinese President's visit. I'm going back to Australia, for Christmas."

Then, Inspector Dawson advised him in no uncertain terms to get on with the job in hand, and not to make any more spurious enquiries into the Ambassador's death, or anything else that went on in Shanghai in 1984. It was not his concern. Although they'd never mentioned Marianne Henderson's name once in the interview, Tom knew they meant her too. And, when he left that interview room, he was under no illusion that he'd been read the riot act, in a very British way.

He was still smarting from that, but now he was sure there'd been a cover up. And he'd been warned off asking any more questions, as had Jess. But why? He sighed as he pondered that question, thinking they would probably never know the truth. Still, it was all a long time ago and there was nothing more he could do about it. He'd sensed Jess had reached the same conclusion after being told by the Head of the Foreign Office to leave it all in the past.

It was Jess's blonde hair catching the entrance lights that he noticed first. He went over to where she was being checked through security. It comes to something when you can't even go to the theatre without going through metal detectors, he thought, sadly.

When she saw him, Jess's eyes lit up, and his annoyance melted away.

She rushed over and greeted him with a friendly kiss on the cheek. "You made it," she said. Then she turned and beckoned a lady over. "This is Bev."

Tom saw Jess's friend was quite a bit older than her. She looked innocuous enough, with her grey hair and slim frame. He held out his hand and smiled. "Good to meet you, Bev. Jess tells me you're Australian, and in the wine trade."

Bev shook his hand with a firm grip, but the smile she gave him didn't quite reach her eyes. She looked away as she said: "Yes, we run a vineyard."

"In which part of Australia?"

"The Hunter Valley."

"Not far from my hometown," he said. "I grew up north of Sydney, on the coast."

Bev just nodded.

He'd expected her to ask him which town he was from, but she didn't. Instead, she changed the subject and started talking about how excited she was to be seeing this musical. Carole King's music was part of her history. "It's got some great reviews," she said. "Slick and beautifully played, according to *The Times*."

Jess turned to Tom. "You must be starving."

"A bit peckish," he had to admit. "I'll get something to eat after the show."

"I'll get us some drinks while you two have a chat," she said. "I'll try and get you some crisps or popcorn to keep you going, Tom. What can I get you both to drink?"

"Glass of red wine, please," Bev said.

"Same for me," Tom said.

Tom watched Jess make her way over to the bar, then he turned to Bev. "So," he said, "tell me about this vineyard you run. I might know it. What's it called?"

Bev gave him an appraising look, but eyes were cool when she said: "Sam Talbot's Vineyard."

"Is that your family name?"

"Yes."

"So, you are Bev, or should I say Beverly, Talbot?"

"Yes." She looked over to Jess at the bar, excused herself, and went over to help her carry the drinks back.

For the next five minutes, Jess did most of the talking, chatting away happily to them both while they drank the large glasses of wine she'd bought. Gone was the pinched, anxious look she'd had on her face for the past few days, Tom thought. It was good to see her happy and enjoying herself for a change. He wasn't sure about Bev though. She kept giving him furtive glances as if trying to work out where he fitted into the picture.

Soon, they were in the theatre and up went the curtain. Tom was sitting at the end of a row, and Jess in the middle of the three of them. It was typical of Jess to think of his long legs and get him an aisle seat, although the seat was still too small. Made for midgets all those years ago, he thought. He tried to keep to his own seat, but his hip kept coming back to touch Jess's in the seat next to him. She didn't move away, so he started to relax too.

As the music started, he was amazed to find out just how many well-known hits Carole King had written, way before she was famous. The wine on an empty stomach was kicking in too. A warm fuzziness came over him, and he found himself humming along to the tunes. Every so often he would glance at Jess. Her face shone more and more as she got into the story and the music. Conscious of him looking at her, she would turn and mouth: "Okay?"

He would smile and nod.

It was just as the second half was about to start, and he looked around the theatre before the lights dimmed, that he was jolted back to reality. At the back, in the far corner, there were two familiar faces apparently enjoying the show too.

The couple from the restaurant the other evening.

He felt a coldness grip him. When he looked back, he happened to catch Bev's eye. She had quietly followed his gaze and looked over at the couple at the back too. The icy stare she turned back on Tom was enough to freeze his balls off. What the hell was wrong with her?

A few minutes later, when he glanced sideways again, she and Jess were giggling, and singing along to one of the songs.

That was the precise moment he decided to find out more about Sam Talbot's Vineyard. He'd never heard of it, but that didn't mean anything since there were some 150 vineyards and wineries in the State of New South Wales. He would ask his Australian police colleagues to come up with a legitimate reason to do a trace on them.

His only reason was that he didn't care much for Beverly Talbot.

23

The man who moves a mountain begins by carrying away small stones

(Confucius)

The cold, north wind whipped right through Tom's woollen overcoat as he stood on the tarmac, outside the VIP Suite at Heathrow. He stamped his feet ever so gently to keep the circulation going. He wasn't allowed to wear a hat on duty, which was just as well as the wind would have blown it off. He stared into the distant sky in the twilight of a British mid-winter day, hoping to see the lights of the Chinese President's plane before he froze to death.

Under his coat, he felt the familiar and reassuring presence of a gun in its holster. As a member of the British police team designated to protect the visiting VIP, he and his colleagues were armed. It was the first time Tom had held a gun since leaving his last job in Australia, on the Prime Minister's protection team. Quite some difference in the weather and working conditions here, he thought, as he looked at the grey tarmac merging with the grey sky and grey buildings. A fleeting longing for the sunshine of Australia came over him until he pushed it firmly away. He'd be back home soon enough, and he was having the time of his life in London, working for the Met. He never dreamt he'd be assigned to the protection team working on the Chinese President's visit and have access to Buckingham Palace, the British Parliament and other historic venues around London. It was an amazing opportunity, and he didn't want to cock it up.

And that's what was worrying him. That interview with his boss and Inspector Dawson had rattled him. Were they still watching him, he wondered? They had to be. It was no coincidence that that couple were in the same theatre as him and Jess on Saturday night. Now, he wished he'd told Jess the couple were there, and about the dressing down he'd got from his boss and Counter Terrorism Command for asking questions about Shanghai.

He hadn't said anything at the time because he didn't want to start her off digging into the past again. That had been the wrong decision though. He would tell her the minute he got the chance. He wouldn't phone, in case their phones were being tapped, which was a reasonable assumption if they were being watched. And that was the reason he'd bought two new 'pay-as-you-go' mobiles on Sunday morning, from different providers. He'd registered them both with his details, but only one was for him. The other he would give to Jess, to be able to talk to her privately. He knew he was being ridiculously cautious, but it was good to have a back-up plan, and communication was key. The problem was, he had to find an opportunity to update Jess and hand over the phone.

All the while his mind was racing along, his professional eyes scanned the surrounding area. There was nothing grand about the Royal VIP Suite, and certainly nothing to indicate the importance of the guests who transited through it. Passengers would walk straight into a functional lounge to await their flight. They would then leave through a back door and get into sleek black limousines to take them direct to the steps of their plane.

Tom had seen Jess arrive half an hour ago in a limousine with a couple of colleagues. She didn't wave or draw any attention to herself, but he noticed her glance around for him. She smiled when her eyes locked onto his and disappeared inside the Suite.

Tom glanced over at his mate, Robin Drummond. The pair of them were the advance team and had been at the airport for hours, making sure the whole place had been checked and locked down for the President's arrival. Now, they had their eyes peeled for any sign of unauthorised vehicles or people on the tarmac.

Robin nodded at Tom, and they both walked slowly to the door of the Suite and stood either side of it, like sentries.

"You okay, mate?" Robin asked.

Tom nodded.

"Talk about brass monkey weather." Robin rubbed his hands. "Her Maj has done the right thing waiting for her guests at Buckingham Palace."

"Smart lady." Tom replied.

Robin stamped his feet. "Reckon they'll be here in another five minutes."

All the while they spoke, their eyes darted around.

"Did you work on any Chinese VIP visits while you were on your PM's protection team in Oz?" Robin asked.

"Nah." Tom glanced over. "We had the American President while I was there, and the Japanese." He couldn't help but notice the dewdrop hanging from the end of Robin's red nose. He'd had a stinking cold for a few days and standing out in the freezing weather wasn't going to make him better. He wasn't a young man either. Perhaps in his late 40s. Since Tom had known Robin, and admittedly that wasn't long, all he ever talked about was his retirement and final package. Obsession was the word that sprang to mind.

"Have you done any Chinese visits before?" Tom asked.

Robin shook his head. "My old man has though."

"Was he in the Met too?" Tom asked.

"Yeah, and a bit of a China hand."

"A specialist?"

"Oh, no. He just worked on a few Chinese-related issues in the Met. He was in a protection team guarding a Chinese visitor once. He went out to China on an investigation too."

"So, you're following in the old man's footsteps?"

"You could say that."

That gave Tom an idea. "That Foreign Office bloke that went under the tube train the other night was a China specialist. Bit of a shock that?"

"I'll say."

"What do you make of it?" Tom said. "Reckon it was suicide, like they're saying?"

Robin put his hands behind his back, and Tom knew why. They were wired, with radios on their cuffs so every member of the protection team could talk to each other. Robin clearly didn't want the others to hear what he was about to say. "Doesn't look like suicide," he said. "That's the word anyway."

Tom made a soft whistling sound that only the two of them could hear.

Robin nodded. "I was talking to my old man about it last night when he brought Mum round for dinner." He paused. "He reckons it was murder."

Tom had to lean sideways because Robin was speaking so quietly. "Murder?" Tom repeated, to be sure he'd heard correctly.

"Yeah. He knew that bloke from way back."

Tom's jaw almost dropped. "Your Dad *knew* him?"

"It was *years* ago. My Dad went over to Shanghai to help investigate the death of a British Ambassador in an hotel there. He says he met that bloke, Giles I think his name was, while he was there."

Tom could hardly believe his luck in striking up this conversation, although he knew better than anyone that police memories were better than any records in the archives.

"It was a rum do, Dad says. When him and his mate got there, the Shanghai police had already done the investigation *and* the post-mortem. They said the Ambassador committed suicide by poisoning himself with arsenic." He glanced at Tom.

"Arsenic?"

Robin nodded. "Can you believe that?"

"Does sound weird."

"Too right." Robin whispered. "Dad says he couldn't do any kind of investigation. The Shanghai police wouldn't let him, and our lot were more obstructive than helpful." He paused. "Dad thinks there was a cover-up."

"A cover-up?" Tom tried to sound surprised.

"They wouldn't co-operate with him on the investigation. He interviewed our lot in Shanghai and then went up to the Embassy in Peking. That's where he met that fella, Giles. Dad said none of them were helpful."

"What happened then?"

"When he got back to London, Dad did a report on the whole sorry story. It found its way into Special Branch and MI5, and that's where it stayed. He never saw it again, and no one would ever discuss it with him."

Tom frowned. "Never?"

"That's what Dad says. He reckons there was some funny stuff going on over there." He glanced over. "You know … spying. Why else would the Security Services keep a lid on it all? Dad just had to let it go in the end. Except …"

Tom looked at him.

"Except he always wondered what happened to the British lady who was working in Shanghai at the time." He paused. "She just disappeared."

"*Disappeared?*"

Robin nodded.

They heard a voice crackling through the radio.

Robin lifted his sleeve and spoke back into the radio. Then he turned and looked at Tom. "Here we go, mate."

They both looked up at the sky and saw the lights of the Chinese President's jet looming on the horizon.

Tom had just a minute to ask Robin another question, without seeming too keen to know the answer. "What does your Dad reckon happened to that British lady in Shanghai?"

Robin shrugged. "He doesn't know. The word was she'd had an affair with the Ambassador. When he wouldn't leave his wife, she'd threatened to expose their affair to the papers and ruin his career. They say that's what made the poor bloke top himself."

"Does your Dad believe that?"

"Nah." Robin shook his head. "She was the one who called the Met from Shanghai in the first place to report what was going on. She said she was being framed for the Ambassador's murder and was convinced she'd be killed like him." He sighed. "That's Dad's one real regret. He couldn't do anything to help that poor woman. He tried over the years to find out what happened to her, but he came to a dead end every time."

24

Life is finite, while knowledge is infinite
(Zhuangzi – Chinese Daoist Philosopher)

Back in the office, Jess made herself a cup of tea and sat reflecting on the Chinese President's arrival. Everything had gone exactly to plan. His wife had looked wonderfully elegant in her purple coat, her pale skin and dark hair swept up in a chignon. It was interesting that she chose to wear purple on arrival. It wasn't an important colour in China but was often considered the colour of royalty overseas. The President had worn a Western suit, again perhaps signifying his willingness to engage with the West, and with the UK. Jess was pleased to have been introduced to them by the Chinese Ambassador. They were a striking couple and had been gracious towards her.

So far, so good, Jess thought with some relief.

Welcoming pleasantries over, the Chinese visitors had been taken to Buckingham Palace where they would stay as The Queen's guests for their entire time in the UK.

For the rest of that first day's programme, at 6pm there would be a welcoming reception at Lancaster House for a wide array of guests, from business to the arts, followed by a State Banquet at Buckingham Palace. Everyone wanted to meet the Chinese President, it seemed.

Jess looked at her watch, almost 5 pm. She'd been invited to the reception at Lancaster House, but not to the State Banquet afterwards. She glanced over at her velvet, knee-length dress hanging on the hook on the back of the door. It was a lovely royal blue colour and had flecks of gold thread all over. She'd brought it with her to change into to go to the reception, rather than just wear her work suit. She looked up at the window. Pitch black outside, but at least it wasn't raining or snowing. That was something.

Locking the door, she changed into her dress. While re-applying her make-up, she heard the door handle rattle. Someone was trying to get in. "Just a moment," she shouted and went over to unlock the door. There was no one there. She peered along the corridor. Empty.

Immediately she thought of Sam. She hadn't seen him since that chance meeting in the canteen over lunch when she'd shown him that photo of the snuff bottle. His reaction had been unbelievable. She'd never seen him angry before, he just wasn't that kind of man. After that, she'd been reluctant to go and seek him out, except he was the only one who might know anything about the snuff bottle. It wasn't just that though. His meeting in the park with the Chinese Ambassador was really bothering her. Jess hadn't told Sir Anthony about it, and she hadn't got any further in finding out who that other man was either.

She knew Sam had been invited to the Lancaster House reception too and wondered whether to go and look for him. They could walk along the Mall together. She was upset with Sam, but then he had helped her a lot with her job and this visit. Perhaps she should go down to his office and make the peace? It would be good to clear the air. On the other hand, maybe it would be better to see him in a more social environment, like the reception. Break the ice that way. Yes, that's what she'd do. Find him at the reception and go over and chat as if nothing had happened.

Her other disappointment was that Xiao Li hadn't been in the greeting line at the airport. She should have been, which meant things were clearly not back to normal at the Chinese Embassy either. Jess had plucked up the courage at the airport to ask the Chinese Ambassador where Xiao Li was. Ambassador Wu had said the poor girl had been working too hard and was taking a long-needed rest.

Jess was annoyed the Ambassador took her for such a fool. She wanted to blurt out that she'd seen Xiao Li being dragged into a Chinese Embassy car, but she didn't. That wouldn't help Xiao Li one bit. Anyway, Sir Anthony had said he would have a word with the Chinese Ambassador, so Jess had to leave it to him.

Mrs Wu had given Jess a puzzled look and said: "You mustn't worry about Xiao Li. We're taking good care of her."

That only needled Jess. It was on the tip of her tongue to mention that she knew Mrs Wu had worked as a Chinese interpreter in the British Consulate-General, Shanghai, many years ago. Something stopped her. Instead, she said: "I'd like to visit Xiao Li."

The Ambassador shook her head. "She's not up to having visitors at present."

"I see." Jess looked the Ambassador in the eye. "Well, she's done so much work on this visit, it's a shame she can't be here to take part. We'll have to have a little get together for her when she's better, to say thank you." That was Jess's way of letting the Ambassador know she wasn't going to forget about Xiao Li. "In fact," Jess went on, "I'll ask Sir Anthony. I'm sure he'll want to do something."

Ambassador Wu's eyes looked wary for a moment, then she'd simply walked off to talk to someone else.

That wasn't the first time Jess had experienced a kind of hostility from the Ambassador. It was the way she sometimes looked at Jess, as if she resented her somehow. Or perhaps resentment wasn't the right word. Everyone said the woman was only in London as Chinese Ambassador because she was a political ally of the President, and he wanted her around for his visit. That made Jess watch closely as Mrs Wu greeted the Chinese President. She wasn't surprised to see real warmth between them. They knew each other well, no doubt about that. How well, she couldn't help but wonder?

Jess slipped on her padded winter coat and looked at her feet. Walking over to Lancaster House was going to be a problem. She couldn't wear her clunky boots with her velvet dress. She looked up at the window again. Still no rain. She'd wear the navy-blue high heels she'd brought in with her and hope for the best.

Stepping outside, the damp air hit her. She pulled the hood of her coat up and set off for the Mall. She immediately switched on her mobile phone to get her messages.

There were several, all from Tom. "I must talk to you urgently. Don't phone. I'm on duty at Lancaster House. I'll find you there. *Please* be careful."

Jess frowned and pushed her mobile back into her bag. Tom sounded stressed and that wasn't like him. Something had happened. That put her on edge as she made her way along the Mall towards Buckingham Palace.

She shivered with the cold. To her left, a damp mist hovered over the lake in St James's Park, giving the whole scene an eerie feel and making her walk faster. The further she got down the road, the fewer people were about. The only cheerful sound was the tinkling of Chinese and Union flags flapping in the breeze on the flag poles that decked out the length of the Mall. They were there in readiness for the Chinese President's and The Queen's ride from the Palace to inspect the troops on Horse Guards Parade the following morning.

Suddenly a black Mercedes slowed and drew up alongside her.

Jess stopped dead, remembering how Xiao Li was dragged into a black limousine.

The driver opened his window and threw out a cigarette butt. Then he answered his ringing mobile.

Looking back to check nothing was coming, Jess darted behind the Mercedes and crossed the road to the other side. She was annoyed with herself for being jumpy, but that didn't stop her powering on, high heels tapping along on the concrete pavement, until she was almost jogging.

It was with some relief that she turned into Stable Yard and saw Lancaster House, a mansion house close to St James's Palace that had once been part of the Palace complex. It was a cheerful sight on this dark night, with all its lights blazing. She knew the building well, since it was managed by the Foreign Office and used for government receptions and conferences. Not many people knew the government wine cellar was stashed in the basement, although she'd been lucky enough to see it.

Standing directly in front of the majestic building, she looked at her watch. 6.10pm and guests were crowding around the entrance. Immediately her eyes searched for Tom on patrol. She couldn't see him, but she saw another face which made her jolt.

That lined, ruddy complexion…

Quickly, Jess pushed her way as politely as she could through the milling crowds and followed the man through the entrance and into the stunning Grand Hall. Its sweeping staircase led up to the state rooms on the first floor, where the reception was being held. Annoyingly, she had to check her coat into the cloakroom while he just headed up the stairs to the reception. She practically threw her coat at the young attendant, grabbed the ticket, and rushed back out.

Looking up, she couldn't see the man anywhere, but another face caught her attention.

Tom was standing on the first-floor landing, watching all the guests entering the front door. She could see by his smile that he was relieved to see her. She wasn't allowed to speak to him while he was on protection duty, so she simply smiled back and walked up the staircase. Her heels sank into the deep pile of the red carpet, and she looked at all the magnificent paintings hanging on the walls as she went. The place was ablaze with crystal chandeliers and, at the very top of the house, an atrium provided a window onto the starry night sky.

The Chinese President and his wife stood at the entrance to the State Drawing Room, greeting guests. Jess was too impatient to join the queue waiting to meet them. Instead, she walked close to where Tom stood on the balcony.

Opening her handbag, she dropped it on purpose, so the contents would fall out at his feet. "Sorry," she said.

He bent down to help her pick up her things. "I've got to talk to you, urgently," he whispered.

"I've just seen the man who met Sam and the Chinese Ambassador in the park," she whispered back.

Tom frowned.

"He walked in here just ahead of me. Came straight up the stairs." She turned and stared at the greeting queue. "Big man. Greyish white hair. Big red face. Can't see him now though."

Tom glanced over at the greeting queue, then back at her. "Meet me in the Long Gallery in fifteen minutes." He nodded in its direction.

Jess already knew the layout of the building. The Long Gallery was the room adjacent to the State Drawing Room.

"I can't move from here until all the guests are inside the building," Tom said. "Then the front door will be closed and guarded."

"Okay." She checked her watch. "See you in fifteen minutes." She picked up the last of her handbag contents and looked around. Having already met the President and his wife at the airport, she decided to avoid the queue and greeting party. Instead, she walked along the landing, then slipped into the Long Gallery, to check out her rendezvous with Tom.

The long room had once housed a great art collection, and still had some wonderful paintings on the walls. It was empty and quiet in there now, with low lighting. A good place to meet Tom for a private chat. She walked quietly up to the door that connected the Long Gallery to the State Drawing Room. Hearing all the hubbub coming from the guests on the other side of the door, she opened it slightly, and peered through the gap. Quickly, she slipped into the State Drawing Room and closed the door behind her. People were too busy drinking and chatting to notice her unorthodox entry.

She stood for a while, scanning the faces, but she couldn't pick out the man she'd seen in the park. A waiter stopped to offer her a glass of champagne from a tray, which she accepted gladly. Then she wove her way through the guests, stopping occasionally to say hello and exchange a few words with people she knew. When she finally got to the other end of the room, the man wasn't there either. Where'd he gone?

Standing for a moment to sip her drink, she realised she hadn't see Sam either. Had he decided not to come?

She caught sight of the Chinese Ambassador suddenly thread her way through the guests to the other end of the room. The Ambassador glanced over her shoulder and slipped out into the Long Gallery, through the same door Jess had used.

Where was *she* going, Jess wondered? Like a magnet, she was drawn to follow her and find out.

It was quiet in the Long Gallery, as she closed the door behind her and stood to allow her eyes to adjust to the low lighting. Then she heard whispering coming from an alcove at the far end of the room. She walked silently down one side of the room, towards the alcove.

As she got closer, Jess recognised Ambassador Wu's voice, even though she was speaking in Chinese. It was the man's voice, replying in Chinese, that made her start.

Then, she saw their reflections in the window against the dark sky.

The man in the park!

Suddenly, the lights blazed full on and a security man in uniform appeared in the doorway. "Can I help you Ma'am?" he shouted.

Jess cringed.

Ambassador Wu and the man walked out of the alcove.

Recovering quickly, Jess beamed at the security man. "I'm just having a look around this wonderful old house," she said. "Stunning, isn't it?"

"You shouldn't be in here." He frowned at her, then at the Chinese Ambassador and her companion. "You all need to go back into the State Drawing Room."

"Of course," Jess said, politely. She looked over at the Ambassador and the man as if surprised to see them. "Oh, good evening, Ambassador." She smiled. "Everything seems to be going very well, don't you think?"

Mrs Wu looked startled.

Jess looked straight at the man and held out her hand. "Jess Turner," she said, with a smile. "I don't think we've met."

To do anything else but shake her hand and introduce himself would have been impolite. This man was clearly not that.

"Justin Barber." He shook her hand, with a firm grip. "Good to meet you, Jess."

Oh my God! Jess's head spun with confusion. She knew that name very well indeed.

Justin Barber was the Deputy Chief of MI6.

She smiled widely, to cover her shock in finding out who he was. He gave her the ghost of a smile, which suggested he had some idea. Her first instinct was to beat a hasty retreat. She didn't do that. Instead, she said boldly: "I'm sorry for interrupting you both. You were, well, you were so deep in conversation."

Justin Barber frowned. "You weren't interrupting anything. We were talking about the Chinese President's programme of meetings, that's all."

Unconvincing, Jess thought. "So," she said, lightly, "you must be a sinologist too. I heard you speaking in Chinese."

He gave a nod.

Jess felt her head buzzing as all the pieces started to fall into place. "Have you served in our missions in China?" she asked lightly, as if just trying to make conversation.

He nodded.

"Peking or Shanghai?"

"Both."

"Ah, you'll be old acquaintances, then?" She looked from him to Mrs Wu. "Perhaps you met at the Consulate-General in Shanghai in the 1980s?"

Mrs Wu's face turned to stone as she realised Jess knew about her being their Chinese interpreter in Shanghai all those years ago.

Justin Barber kept a small smile on his lips. "Your knowledge is surprising, Jess, given that you've only been on the China desk for six months."

So, he knew all about her too. "I'm afraid it's not as good as it should be," she said, "but I'm learning fast."

"Indeed, you are." He looked at his watch. "I'm sorry," he said to them both, "but I have to go."

"Of course," the Chinese Ambassador gave him a sweet smile.

He bowed his head. "Good evening, ladies." And, in a flash, he'd walked past the security guard and out of the Long Gallery.

And just like that, the Deputy Chief Spymaster disappears, Jess thought, wryly.

Mrs Wu glared at Jess, then walked back to the door and into the reception in the State Drawing Room.

The security man glared at Jess too. "You too, Ma'am."

That's when Tom appeared, almost from nowhere. "It's okay, mate," he said. "I'll escort her back to the party."

The security man looked at them both, then disappeared back out the door.

"Jess," Tom said softly.

"Oh my God, Tom. The man I saw in the park meeting the Chinese Ambassador and my colleague Sam was the Deputy Chief of MI6, Justin Barber." She paused. "I believe his title is Director of Operations, but he's the right-hand man of the MI6 Chief. He was just in here having a private meeting with Mrs Wu again."

Tom's face paled visibly. "Listen, Jess." He took her arm and pulled her into the alcove. "I've got to tell you something."

She was shaken into silence by the gravity in his voice.

"It was Marianne Henderson who rang the Met Police all those years ago to tell them what was going on in Shanghai."

"What?"

"She told them that she was being framed for the British Ambassador's murder and feared for her life."

Jess frowned. "Murder?"

Tom nodded.

"Oh my God." Jess's heart was in her mouth. "What happened to Marianne?"

"Nobody knows. The Met police went over to Shanghai to do an investigation. By the time they got there the Shanghai police had done a post-mortem on the Ambassador's body and concluded it was suicide by arsenic poisoning. The Shanghai police simply closed the investigation."

There was a pause.

"That explains why there was no post-mortem in the UK. They'd already done one in Shanghai," she said.

"Exactly. The Met police officer came back and did a report. It ended up in Special Branch and MI5, and he never heard another word about it. The case was just closed."

She thought for a moment. "That explains why there would have been no coroner's inquiry in the UK either." She stared at him. "So the Chinese said it was suicide. Yet Marianne rang the Met Police to say it was murder."

Tom nodded.

"How on earth do you know all this?"

"Because the Met officer who went to Shanghai is my mate's father."

"Is he still alive?" she asked.

"Sure is. Retired, of course. He says all the British diplomats in Shanghai and Peking were unhelpful at the time. They wouldn't co-operate with his questions. He spoke to them all, even to your boss who went under that train the other evening."

Jess's stomach turned. It was exactly what she had dreaded all along. A conspiracy. A cover-up.

"That's not all," Tom whispered. "You remember that grey car outside the Chinese restaurant the other evening, and that couple?"

She nodded. How could she forget?

"Well they were definitely following us." He paused. "That couple were in the theatre on Saturday night, sitting behind us."

"On Saturday night?" Jess's eyes narrowed. "Why didn't you tell me?"

He looked embarrassed. "You were so happy that night, I didn't want to spoil your evening."

She glared at him.

"And I didn't want you to start digging into the past again and put yourself in danger."

She was indignant now. "I think I should be the judge of that."

"You're right. I'm sorry I didn't say anything before. It's just that, well, I'd been given a dressing down by my boss and an Inspector Dawson from Counter Terrorism Command earlier that evening. That's why I didn't make it to the restaurant."

Concern flooded her face. "A dressing down about what?"

"Looking for information in the archives about the British Ambassador's death in Shanghai." It was Tom's turn to look indignant. "I was told in no uncertain terms not to poke my nose into things that don't concern me."

Jess looked worried now. "Oh God, Tom. I'm sorry. It's my fault, I should never have asked you to do that."

"No harm done," he said. "At least I don't think so." He pulled a mobile phone out of his pocket and pushed it into her hand. "Here, I've got you a private mobile to use to phone me in an emergency. I've got a new one too, and my number's the only one programmed into your phone."

She frowned. "Why do I need that?"

"If they're still following us, they'll be monitoring our mobile calls too." He sighed. "Humour me, Jess. I know it's a bit over the top but, well, you never know." He paused. "Only use it to phone me in an emergency, nothing else."

She nodded and put it in her bag.

"I've got to get back to work." He looked over his shoulder. "How are you getting home?"

"I'll get a taxi."

"Well, make sure you do." And with that, he was gone.

Jess's mind was whirling, but she was excited too. Now she understood how Justin Barber fitted into the picture. She'd always believed Marianne wouldn't be the only British diplomat opening the new Consulate-General in Shanghai. Justin Barber had just admitted serving in Shanghai, as well as Peking. Jess didn't have to be a rocket scientist to work out that Justin must have been the other officer sent down with Marianne to open the new Consulate-General.

And that's where he'd first met Mrs Wu, the Chinese Ambassador, with whom he was obviously still well acquainted.

So, why were Mrs Wu, Sam and Justin meeting in the park the other day? Were they still covering up that Shanghai conspiracy? If they were, what did they know? What part had they played in events back then?

Her head was going around and around with all these questions. One thing was certain, Ambassador Wu had been working as the Chinese interpreter in the British Consulate-General back then. Was she still working for the British? Was she a traitor to her own country? Or was it the other way around? Was Justin Barber the traitor? Sam even?

And how did Sir Anthony fit into all this? Only now did Jess realise she hadn't seen him this evening either. She'd expected him to be at the Chinese President's welcoming reception; he'd certainly been invited.

★

At around 8.30pm, Jess's head was still spinning as she stood outside Lancaster House shivering. She'd been waiting twenty minutes for the taxi she'd ordered to take her home, and there was still no sign of it. She phoned the company again, but they just said it was on its way. It clearly wasn't. She pulled her padded coat tighter around her, wishing she'd worn a cardigan over her velvet dress to keep warm. The night air nipped through her thin tights, freezing her legs and feet. She would have been much better off in her business suit, thick tights and boots.

All the other guests had disappeared now, their cars and taxis arriving one by one. Even Tom had gone off to Buckingham Palace to be on duty at the State Banquet. She looked back at the front door of Lancaster House as it slammed shut, and even heard the lock turn from the inside, as staff closed-up for the night. The glittering reception, and hordes of guests, were now just a memory.

Tired of waiting in the cold, she decided to walk up St James's Street in the hope of flagging down a taxi on the way. She pushed her mobile into her pocket and set off. Her feet were so cold, she could hardly feel her toes. At one point, she stopped in a shop doorway, slipped off each shoe in turn, and rubbed her toes to defrost them.

All the while her head was reeling. So, it was Marianne who phoned the British police for help before she disappeared. The poor woman must have been desperate. That made Jess feel sick to the stomach. Then the anger rose.

None of her colleagues were telling her the truth. They must have all known, even her boss Giles. Oh my God, her heart quickened at the direction her thoughts were going in. Had he been about to reveal the conspiracy, and was killed before he could?

Even Ambassador Wu knew the truth.

The real shock was the realisation that her colleagues were all involved in this Shanghai conspiracy in some way. Marianne had been framed for the Ambassador's murder and left in Shanghai to her fate. Why frame her? To cover up who really killed him? Had it been one of them? If so, why would they all be so ready to cover it up? It didn't make sense.

Jess continued along the pavement, glancing into shop windows as she passed by, still deep in thought. So deep in thought, she didn't see or hear the car coming. It's headlights, on full beam, were the first sign, then she heard the roar of an engine, and the car accelerated towards her.

Blinded, she held her hand up to her eyes.

The car mounted the pavement, heading straight for her. She looked around in panic. There was no way out, nowhere to hide on this narrow pavement. She couldn't run, couldn't avoid the oncoming car, except …

She threw herself into a shop doorway.

The car whizzed by, sparks flying as it clipped the doorway's stone pillar.

She lay on her side on the ground. Pain seared through her ankle. She touched her throbbing head and felt warm liquid on her fingers. Was that blood?

She heard squealing brakes, and a clunk as the car was put into reverse. The engine revved up again.

She struggled to get up, to defend herself. Her head spun with dizziness.

She heard shouting and screaming. Was that her?

25

Shanghai, 1984

> *The hardest thing of all is to find a black cat in a dark room, especially if there is no cat*
> *(Confucius)*

Marianne gripped the steering wheel as she hurtled along the Shanghai streets without any thought as to where she was going. Her head was buzzing and her heart pounding, with all kinds of thoughts and emotions rippling through her. She was hurt, angry, and afraid. A potent combination that made it hard to think straight. All she knew was that she had to get away. Away from her treacherous colleagues. Away from the ruthless Chinese police. And away from that bloody black sedan.

She slammed on the brakes, turned sharp left and looked in her mirror. Pressing down on the accelerator, she raced to the bottom of the street while holding her fist on the horn to alert cyclists and pedestrians to get out of the way. A cyclist, with two crates of live chickens balanced on the back, wobbled and shook his fist at her. "Sorry," she shouted into the air. She slammed on the brakes again, and this time turned right. She looked in her mirror.

No black sedan.

Had she shaken it off at last? She accelerated hard again to the end of this street. She hadn't a clue where she was, but she kept accelerating and turning, accelerating and turning. Eventually, breathless and shaking, she pulled up at the side of a kerb, and looked in her mirror.

Still no black sedan.

She let out a relieved sob and laid her forehead on the steering wheel. Finally, she was alone. After a minute or so, she looked at herself in the mirror. Her pale face and black eyes made her look mad, demented even. And this had all happened so quickly.

You've been set up, Marianne. That thought just kept spinning round in her head. Why hadn't she realised it before? It had been so well orchestrated. For a start, she'd landed all the preparatory work in the run-up to the trade delegation visit because Justin had been travelling in the region so much. On the day of the Ambassador's murder, he'd gone to Hangzhou, supposedly on a mercy mission to help some young British student in hospital, ensuring she was alone in Shanghai. She now doubted there was a hospitalised student. Then he'd said he returned to Shanghai on an evening train. That was a lie. The ticket she'd found in his pocket confirmed he'd caught the 1.05pm train back from Hangzhou, and the journey was, at most, three hours. That would have placed him back in Shanghai well before the Ambassador was murdered. Had he killed the Ambassador? It didn't bare thinking about, but what other explanation was there?

Her stomach turned at the thought of Sam being complicit in all this. What was it she'd heard him say about her? *She's a loose cannon. Who knows what she will do next?* Sam of all people, the one person she thought was on her side. Now it looked like he was nothing but a fraud, parcelling up Chinese antiques and illegally sending them to himself in the UK. There was no doubt in her mind that Sam was in league with Justin.

So, everything had led up nicely to her going to the Peace Hotel alone to meet the Ambassador, and to the scene of his murder. She could kick herself now for going up to his room to look for him. Why didn't she just go straight to the Jing An Hotel and deal with the trade delegation on her own? Except, anyone in her shoes would have done the same thing. Justin *knew* she'd go looking for the Ambassador.

And what about that door she heard close in the hotel corridor before she went into the Ambassador's room? Was that Justin and Sam too? Did they have a room in the same corridor? It would have been easy to slip along to the Ambassador's room from there and murder him.

She was in a terrible predicament, but who could she ask for help? Anthony? He was in Peking on the night of the Ambassador's murder. She knew that for a fact because he'd been Embassy Duty Officer and she'd phoned him. Could she trust him? Could she trust any of them?

The focus of her anger turned back to Justin. He was responsible for all this. He'd manoeuvred her into this situation. Now, he was at her house with the police searching through all her things. What did they hope to find? A phial of arsenic? The whole idea was ridiculous. She sat up straight. Or was it? Perhaps, that's why he volunteered to go to her house with the police. It wasn't to help her, but to plant evidence to implicate her?

She had to stop him. Looking in her mirror, she put the car in gear and drove off. She wasn't sure exactly where she was, but she could see the watery sun setting on the horizon and headed in its direction. In fact, the sun was so low in the sky she had to pull down the sun visor to be able to see where she was going.

The roads were clogged with trucks, bikes and pedestrians at this hour, as everyone made their way home. Weaving her way around all the obstacles, she headed back to her villa. Her fury with Justin increased with every mile. She wondered again if he'd killed the Ambassador? The thought made her feel sick. Was Justin capable of doing something like that? He didn't seem like a killer, but then who did? He was clever. Very clever. That pulled her up sharp. She couldn't just confront him and accuse him of murder. No, she had to be smarter than him.

By the time she arrived at her villa complex, her head was clearer. She pulled up outside the compound and parked her car in the visitors' car park, well away from her villa, and in-between two other cars, to make it stand out less. She sat for a moment, surveying the scene. The sun had gone down, and the light was fading fast. It all looked quiet. Then two women come out of the general management office. She sat back and watched them retrieve their bicycles from the rack. They were chatting so loudly to each other, they didn't even glance in her direction. She waited until they'd gone, and then got out of the car.

Caution had replaced rage now she was back at the villas. There was no sense in bursting into her house with all guns blazing while they were searching it. What good would that do? No, she had to tread carefully. They had her house keys anyway, she couldn't get back in without them.

Instead of following the road around to her villa, she walked the other way so as not to be so visible. Crossing the central communal gardens, she felt her feet sinking into the soggy grass. One of the gardeners was still at work. He looked over and gave her a wide grin. They often chatted about the flowers and plants; he was teaching her their Chinese names. She didn't want to stop today though. She smiled back and continued walking. Further along, she looked back to check she was out of his sight, then headed towards the open field running alongside her villa. From behind its hedge, she hoped to be able to see what was going on inside, without the police or Justin seeing her.

Finding a gap in the hedge, she squeezed through and found herself standing in the muddy field. Her feet sank into the recently ploughed earth. Groaning, she rolled her trouser bottoms up as far as she could and made her way along the hedge to her villa. Her shoes squelched in the mud, which was soon up to her ankles. In the end, she had to take her shoes off and hold them or lose them forever.

Coming up alongside her villa, she stopped and peered over the hedge. There were two police cars. One parked on the drive and the other on the road outside. Justin was leaning nonchalantly against the car on the drive, talking to Inspector Zhang.

Suddenly the front door opened, and Wu emerged holding a bag, which she handed over to the Inspector. Marianne wanted to march over and snatch the bag from her. How dare Wu take things from her house, for that's what it looked like she was doing. Wu said a few words to the Inspector, and ushered Justin towards the police car parked in the road. Wu seemed to be completely in charge here too.

Not only was Marianne incensed at the sight of all this going on in her villa, with her possessions, the shock of seeing Wu removing things from her house and commanding everyone made her heart quicken. She'd under-estimated the woman. Wu might be young but, if this was anything to go by, she wasn't just an interpreter at the British Consulate-General. No, that was just her cover. She was more than that. Marianne's gaze hardened as she watched Wu get into the car with Justin. Was she involved in setting Marianne up for the Ambassador's murder too?

A movement made her look towards her villa front door. The houseboy opened it, and stood on the threshold, as if unsure what to do. He glanced in Marianne's direction. She ducked down. Had he seen her from an upstairs window?

She poked her head up again once she heard the police cars leave. She saw the houseboy walk out of the villa, leaving the door slightly ajar. Walking down the drive, he glanced in Marianne's direction, and nodded. The poor boy's face looked pale with fright as he hurried away. He had seen her and left the door open for her. A warm feeling of gratitude flowed through her. Someone at last had done something to help her.

She went back to the hole in the hedge and squeezed through. Running to her villa in her bare feet, and covered in mud, she went inside and slammed the door shut. Then she dropped to her knees, with a sob. It was hopeless. If they wanted to frame and convict her for the Ambassador's murder, there was nothing she could do to defend herself against such powerful forces. She curled up into a ball on the floor. She wanted to scream and cry, but no tears came. She was strangely calm, perhaps because she knew there was nothing she could do. Soon she would be charged and convicted of the Ambassador's murder.

Even darker thoughts bubbled up. Or would she be murdered like him? A shiver ran up her spine. That would make everything so much simpler for them, rather than keep her in a Chinese prison for the rest of her life and risk western government and media scrutiny for decades.

The more she thought about it, the angrier she got. They may have decided she was an easy target to set-up, but she would not roll over easily. No, she would make it as difficult for them as she could. And one day, she would make Justin, Sam and Wu pay for this.

She dragged herself up and looked at her watch. 5.35pm. Justin and Wu would just be getting back to the Consulate-General, only to find her gone. They were sure to come back here looking for her. Well, if they were determined to frame her for murder, they'd have to catch her first.

She bolted up the stairs and into the bathroom. She turned on the taps to fill the bath, then ran into the bedroom and tore off her muddy clothes. Grabbing her Chinese rucksack, she packed a change of clothes. Just one pair of jeans, a shirt, a warm jumper and a change of underwear and socks. She started to look around to see what Wu and the police had taken from her house, then stopped. She didn't care. The photos of her parents and grandparents were still on her bedside cabinet. She collected them up and put them in her rucksack. Then she rummaged in the drawer for the Swiss army knife, an heirloom from her grandfather, and threw that in too.

There was one big problem. Her passport was in her cupboard in the Consulate-General for safe-keeping. There was no way she could go back there and get it. Still, did it really matter? She wouldn't be able to use her own name and passport to get out of the country anyway. She'd be a marked woman.

She pulled everything she needed out of her handbag, including her purse and credit cards. She would need to take her stash of Chinese yuan, or foreign exchange certificates, with her. That would be the only way of paying for most things in China.

She ran back into the bathroom, opened the cupboard door under the sink and found an old washbag. She was elated her currency stash was still where she'd hidden it. She went back into the bedroom and stuffed the notes into her rucksack. Back in the bathroom, she stood in the bath to wash the mud off her feet and stepped out again.

There was no time for anything else. She picked up her travel washbag, ran back into the bedroom and shoved that in the rucksack too.

Strapping her watch back on her wrist, she saw she'd already taken over 15 minutes. She had to go. Quickly, she threw on a clean pair of black jeans, another shirt and a jumper. She dug her light walking boots out of the wardrobe and put them on, tying the laces tight. Downstairs in the hallway, on the coat rack by the door, she found the blue, padded Chinese coat that she'd worn in Peking to keep out the cold, and a blue matching Chinese cap. She would blend in better out on the street in them. Quickly, she put on the coat and hoisted her backpack up and over her shoulders. She put on the cap and pulled the peak down over her eyes.

All the time she'd been in the villa, she hadn't put on a light. Now, she opened the front door cautiously and peered out. No one around. She slipped out of the house and shut the door behind her.

It was already getting dark, and she looked over at the field. She wouldn't go back that way – too muddy. She had to be careful though in case the police had posted someone at the gate of the villa complex to watch for her. She crossed over the road, slipped down the driveway of the empty villa opposite, and went around to the back garden. She opened the gate in the fence and peered out. No one. She slipped out, into the communal garden, and ran across the grass over to the general management office, which was now all in darkness.

Pressing her back against the wall, she inched towards the edge and peered round into the carpark. She could see her car still parked between the same two cars. She scanned the whole area but saw no one.

Quickly, she ran to the car, opened the back door and threw her rucksack on the back seat. Then she jumped into the driver's seat, pushed the key in the ignition and started up the engine.

The reliable old car sprang to life. She reversed out of the space, drove out of the carpark, and turned left in the direction of town. That was the only way she could go. To turn right would have led her to the airport, and she couldn't go there without a passport. No, she would head for the railway station, and get a train out of Shanghai, away from her tormentors. If they wanted her, they'd have to catch her. And she was not going to make it easy for them.

She touched the little cross around her neck to give her courage. *Always rely on yourself, Marianne, and trust your instincts. They will not lie to you.* That was her grandmother's mantra. "Help me, grandma," she whispered.

26

To be wronged is nothing, unless you continue to remember it
(Confucius)

Driving steadily into town, Marianne prayed she wouldn't pass the police going back out to the villa to look for her. They would recognise her car immediately. The throbbing pain in her head was excruciating now, and she could see a jagged light in the corner of her left eye. It was ages since she'd had a migraine, and she hoped she wasn't getting one now. She hadn't had time to think about bringing medication with her.

She glanced again in her rear mirror. No sign of that black sedan. She wasn't convinced she'd shaken it off. It would be lurking somewhere. She just hoped she could get away. That's all she wanted to do. Everything had happened so quickly, she just wanted to rest and have a chance to think. She pressed down on the accelerator, then immediately eased off again. Speeding would only attract attention.

Fortunately, darkness was closing in. That would help with her escape. Escape? If she'd stopped to think about what she was doing, she'd have known what a hopeless plan it was. With rigid State control, an extensive security apparatus, the People's Liberation Army, police networks, and communist officials watching everyone, it was impossible for anyone to move around China secretly, let alone a foreigner who would stick out like a sore thumb.

Except Marianne *wasn't* thinking straight. Her mind was spinning with all kinds of jumbled thoughts and images. One minute she would see the impassive faces of Inspector Zhang and his nervous colleague, then the deceptive Mrs Wu, and the treacherous Justin and Sam. Why were they doing this? Did *they* kill the Ambassador? If so, why? That was the burning question. Why?

The image of the Ambassador lying on the bathroom floor flashed into her head now, his face as deathly white as his hair. Her eyes glistened in the dark. If they could kill him, they could easily kill her too.

It wasn't cold, but she could hear her teeth chattering. She tried to focus on all the usual landmarks along the way to distract herself from such terrifying thoughts. This was her daily route to work and she knew the road well. Except her destination wasn't the British Consulate-General this evening, it was the Old North Railway Station, located on East Tianmu Road. From there, she'd get the first train out of Shanghai, wherever it was going. It didn't matter where, just away from Shanghai.

She kept looking nervously in the mirror, and all around her, as she drove along. There was no way she could tell if she was being followed. All she could see were headlights. It was risky going into town, but Chinese railway stations were always built in city centres. And Shanghai was no exception.

She turned up the heater. The autumn nights were getting chilly, reminding her that winter was near. She would head south, where the winter weather would be milder. She might even get as far south as Guangzhou, and the South China Sea coast. If she stood any chance of getting out of China, it would be down there on the border between China and Hong Kong.

For goodness sake! She looked in her mirror and pulled a face. She was crazy to think she could get all the way down to South China, let alone out of the country with no passport.

On the outskirts of town, she expected police cars to come screaming along at any moment and stop her. Until they did, she would just keep going.

On and on she went …

Her heart soared when she saw the station arches rising above the building tops. Almost there.

Where was she going to park the car? Somewhere where it wouldn't be found immediately; she needed time to buy a ticket and get on a train.

Then she remembered a hotel close to the railway station. It was a small, unremarkable place with no special architectural features but, for some reason, the communist elite favoured it, and held lots of banquets and receptions there. She'd attended some of them, that's how she knew about it. Perhaps other things went on in the hotel that she didn't particularly want to know about? She drove straight there and pulled into its car park around the back. It was usually busy, and she had planned to tuck her car in amongst the others. Except, as luck would have it, the car park was empty today. Still, there was nothing she could do about that. She had to leave the car somewhere.

She parked and looked at herself in the mirror. Tucking her hair up under her cap, she pulled the peak low over her eyes, got out of the car and swung her knapsack onto her back. Swiftly, and without a look back, she walked around to the front of the hotel as if she was going in through the main door, in case anyone was watching on security cameras. Then she suddenly darted across the main road and headed straight for the railway station.

She didn't have far to walk but, as ever on the crowded Shanghai pavements, it was slow-going dodging the swarm of pedestrians. No one gave her a curious glance. They took her for just another Chinese woman under her cap and coat. She smiled to herself, relishing the anonymity. Would the police spot her inside the station? By now, they'd almost certainly know she was missing.

Her legs felt wobbly as she neared the railway station. She hesitated and stopped. Could she do it? Could she really run away? Suddenly, she was swept along in a wave of people flooding through the archway and entry doors and found herself inside the concourse. The huge space, with its high glass ceiling, was teaming with people wearing blue Mao coats like hers, peppered with a few soldiers in their green army uniforms. Everyone was rushing towards the sound of trains coming and going from distant platforms.

She struggled free from the crowd and stood to one side, to get her bearings. The stark lights bounced off the glossy floor, making her blink. By now, the jagged light in her left eye had moved across both eyes, blurring her vision. She rubbed them hard, but it was no good. The jagged light would only go when it had run its course.

With as much confidence as she could muster, she went over to the departures board to look at the train times. She'd promised herself she would get the first train south. So, where *was* that going?

Her spirits lifted when she saw it was to Hangzhou, and the train was due to leave in 15 minutes. She liked the town, with its beautiful West Lake. At least she would be able to go walking there and breathe. She might even be able to get up into the mountains.

That's it then. First stop south – Hangzhou!

Hurrying over to the ticket office, her heart quickened when she saw two policemen standing close by. She hesitated. They seemed to be watching all the passengers. Were they looking for her? Don't be ridiculous! They won't be that organised, not yet. Looking down at the floor to keep her face hidden, she walked straight past them, half-expecting to feel a hand on her shoulder. None came. In the queue for tickets, she fidgeted with impatience. For God's sake, hurry up. But the queue moved quickly. Everyone was keen to get on their way.

Reaching the head of the line, her knees almost buckled. Would the woman behind the counter start questioning her? The Chinese could be very officious if they wanted to be.

"One ticket to Hangzhou," Marianne said in Chinese, "hard class". She had thought about going 'soft' class, but the comfortable, padded seats were usually for foreigners or communist party officials. To be less conspicuous, she would travel 'hard' class on the wooden seats, with the rest of the masses.

Fortunately, it was quite normal for Chinese people not to look each other in the eye. And, to Marianne's relief, that's exactly what happened. The woman in the ticket office just nodded, punched the destination into her machine, and out came the ticket. She pushed it towards Marianne without so much as a glance. It was difficult to say whether the woman was bored, exhausted, or just on auto-pilot. To Western senses, her behaviour would be considered rude, but that's how the Chinese often dealt with each other.

Marianne knew she was not out the woods yet. She only had 'yuan' notes, in the form of foreign currency exchange certificates, to pay for the ticket. They were in general circulation, but only foreigners used them, because the local Renminbi currency was not convertible on foreign exchange markets. Marianne held her breath as she pushed a note gingerly across the counter.

She need not have worried. The woman wasn't in the least bit interested. She simply took the note and threw some coins back in change.

Marianne grabbed the ticket and coins and walked away before the woman could say anything. A wave of relief flowed over her as she headed for platform 6, and the Hangzhou train. According to the huge station clock next to the departures board, she only had a couple of minutes before it left. She wanted to run, but didn't dare, for fear of drawing attention to herself. There would be security cameras everywhere. She had to behave as any other ordinary Chinese person.

She walked quickly, without looking round to see if anyone was following. Nearing the platform, she saw the train was in the station and the passengers already on board. The guard was about to raise his flag to signal to the driver to pull away when she slipped onto the platform. Seeing her, he stood still, to allow her to get on.

She slipped her rucksack off her back, sprinted over to the first carriage and jumped on, slamming the door shut behind her. Out of the window, she saw the guard raise his flag. Almost immediately, the train pulled away.

Her head swam, and she grabbed a nearby rail. It wasn't to steady herself because of the train's movement. No, it was with the shock of what she'd done.

She'd got away from Shanghai!

She pulled herself together when she got strange looks from the Chinese congregating in between the carriages. But her heart sank at the same time. If they were standing there, it meant there were no spare seats and she would have to stand for all three hours of the journey to Hangzhou.

She swung her rucksack onto her back again. She would walk through the carriages anyway and try to find a seat.

Chinese trains were configured much like British trains, with long carriages, and seats arranged in groups of four, two seats facing forward and two backwards, with a table in-between. The first carriage was 'soft' class, and almost empty. She longed to take seat in there, but she kept going, in the direction of the 'hard' class carriages. They were typically packed with people and luggage. She trudged through them, without success, and resigned herself to sitting on the floor in the space between two carriages. But, luck was on her side that night. A woman tapped Marianne on the hip, then lifted a small girl from the seat next to her and onto her lap. The woman gestured to Marianne to sit down.

A man standing in the aisle eyed the seat and made a beeline for it. Marianne knew he would bundle her out of the way to get it if he could. There was no chivalry in China, it was every man for himself. In a scene reminiscent of musical chairs, Marianne slipped her bottom onto the seat first, before he could get his onto it. Defeated, the man just moved on, without a word.

"Thank you." Marianne said to the woman in Chinese.

The woman nodded and looked away. But her little girl was intrigued. Dressed in layers of clothes to keep out the cold, she was a cute bundle of padding. Her black hair was cut in a straight bob with a fringe, and two button-like, inquisitive eyes stared at Marianne's face. No Chinese cap and coat was going to fool this little girl, she'd obviously never seen a foreigner before. Marianne smiled at the girl, who just continued to stare. Then Marianne glanced at the two men on the seats facing her. They were already slumped down and fast asleep.

She waited for a few minutes, to be sure she'd secured her seat from the mob and looked up at the luggage rack. It was full of bags and shopping. Two seats along, a string bag full of huge brown crabs, their legs and claws sticking out, dripped water onto the passenger's cap below. No one said anything. Marianne stood up, pushed a few bags along, heaved her rucksack onto the space above her and sat down again.

The two little eyes had watched her every move. She smiled again at the girl, who still didn't react.

Marianne laid her head on the seat back and closed her eyes. The musty, moth-ball smell that seemed to permeate Chinese clothing was all pervasive, along with the more pleasant smell of Chinese tea. Every so often she would hear a loud belch or smell a fart. That was also normal in China. Occasionally someone would clear their throat noisily, then get up and spit out the contents into one of the enamel spittoons at each end of the carriage.

Marianne was used to all that and tuned it out. She found it hard to relax though. She expected the police to appear at any moment and arrest her. She jumped when the carriage door slid open, but it was only the tea lady. She carried an enormous aluminium kettle and went through the train pouring boiling hot water over tealeaves in the mugs standing on the tables in front of each passenger.

As she filled Marianne's mug to the brim, she gave her a curious look. That's when Marianne knew she'd made her first mistake. She was a foreigner, and looked like a foreigner, whatever she was wearing. She would be remembered on this train as the foreign lady in 'hard' class with all the Chinese. If she'd gone into 'soft' class, no one would have batted an eyelid because it was normal for foreigners to travel in that carriage.

She picked up the hot mug and wrapped her cold hands around it. The warmth seeped through her fingers and up through her arms. She put the mug to her lips to take a sip of the scalding liquid.

'Hot tea', a little voice warned in Chinese.

Marianne smiled again at the child and nodded. The tea was indeed too hot to drink. She put the mug back on the table and closed her eyes again. The jagged light had gone now, and the throbbing eased. Her head was still full of jumbled thoughts, and she forced herself to think of happier times.

And that was her childhood, on the North York moors. In her mind now, the sun was shining. White fluffy clouds scudded along in the breeze. She imagined filling her lungs with unpolluted air and seeing grouse scuttle around in the purple heather. She'd loved those camping trips with her grandfather. He'd taught her to fend for herself and be self-sufficient. She thought of him in his plane being shot down during the War, and then him falling to earth by parachute. He'd survived and gone on to escape from occupied France and make it back to Britain, with her grandmother's help.

Thinking of them inspired her, and she opened her eyes. Did she have their courage? Could she survive on her own and make it out of China? Then the gloom set in. Even if she did get out, where could she go without a passport? She'd be arrested wherever she went.

She looked at her reflection in the window as the train trundled through the night towards Hangzhou. Her gaunt face and black eyes stared back. What would her grandparents think of her now? She shut her eyes again to blot out her reflection. How could she have been so blind? Her own colleagues had set her up. The very people she should have been able to trust.

After a while, the rocking motion of the train and the soft hum of the engine somehow soothed her jangled nerves. She might be alone and among an alien race, whose lives and culture bore no resemblance to hers, but she felt at ease with them. They seemed comfortable in her presence too. That's what really surprised her. No one said anything. No one questioned her, or even looked her way. Then, as the hours ticked by, she was able to think more clearly.

Whichever way she looked at it, she was in this predicament because of Justin. He was responsible. Sam too. But what about their Chinese interpreter, Wu? Marianne had seen the authority she had over Inspector Zhang, and the way she'd taken charge of searching Marianne's villa. Wu had to be working for the Chinese Security Service.

A shiver crept up Marianne's spine. Was it possible that Wu had set a trap for them all?

27

Hangzhou, 1984

We should feel sorrow, but not sink under its oppression
(Confucius)

Throwing open the curtains to let in the new day, Marianne
stepped through the balcony door and sat down on a cane
chair. In the distance, the red glow of dawn was peaking
over the mountains, reflecting in the lake's mirror-like
water. There was not a breath of wind. Only the ripples,
made by cormorants or kingfishers diving for breakfast,
disturbed its surface. The chilly autumn air made her shiver
and she pulled her padded coat around her shoulders. This
had become her morning ritual, to sit and watch Hangzhou
come to life and the wildlife flock to its lovely West Lake.
She could not have found a more perfect spot to spend a
few days of freedom.

Perched on a hill, overlooking the lake, this spartan guest-
house suited Marianne. Only foreigners were permitted
to stay, so she blended in well with tourists from all over
the world, as well as overseas Chinese back to visit their
homeland. She told the staff she was a Canadian writer,
called Susan Gray, and that she wanted a few days of quiet

to finish the book she was writing on China. They were delighted when she told them that Hangzhou would be included in the story for its beauty and didn't bat an eye that she spent most of the time in her room. She did go out every day, but only at the busiest time so as not to stand out, and that was generally in the afternoon.

Her biggest problem was that she had no passport or ID, not that she could have used hers in her own name anyway. She'd checked into the guest-house by saying her handbag had been stolen in Shanghai, with her passport inside. She was waiting for the Canadian Embassy in Peking to send a replacement passport to her in Hangzhou. Every morning, she would ask the receptionist if there was an envelope for her from the Canadian Embassy. The poor girl would shake her head sadly and say, 'perhaps tomorrow'.

Marianne knew she couldn't hold off the inevitable. It was the law for hotels and guest-houses to report ID details of foreigners staying in their establishments to local security officials. They would be in trouble if they didn't. Marianne sighed. This peaceful place had saved her sanity, and she wanted nothing more than to stay on. But she couldn't. This was already her fourth morning, one day more than she'd planned. Tomorrow, she would move on.

Bird song coming from the willow tree in the garden distracted her. She looked over and smiled. There it was again, the little bird with a white body and black throat. She'd dearly love to know what it was called. It came every morning around this time to sing its heart out and entertain her with its melodic call before it had to compete with the chorus of bicycle bells that punctuated the early morning silence. However early Marianne got up, the Chinese were always earlier.

As she closed her eyes to enjoy the peace of the morning, a delicious smell wafted up from the kitchen windows.

The breakfast buffet was already underway, and the smell of dough sticks deep-frying, and the fragrant pork and shrimp-stuffed buns, made her feel hungry.

She laid her head back on the cane chair. This was such an alien country, but she was comfortable here. She'd slipped easily into a daily routine, and it felt surprisingly normal, whatever normal was going to be in her life from now on. At first, she couldn't sleep, and was on tenterhooks when out on the street, for fear of being arrested. As the days slipped by, she began to relax a bit. Last night, she'd drifted into a deep sleep and felt rested this morning, for the first time in a long while. Her head had finally stopped throbbing too. She wasn't under any illusion though. They would catch up with her soon. Even if they didn't, she'd already decided to go back and face the music at some point. There was nowhere in the world she could go without a passport, even if she could get across the Chinese border secretly. She hadn't done herself any favours by running away, but she'd had time to digest everything, think things through. She was resigned to her fate. Not that she wouldn't fight them. She would, every step of the way.

She sighed again and stood up. She would get a shower before the other guests got out of bed and used all the hot water. There was never enough for everyone. Anyway, the boys would soon be around to get the sheets off the bed to send to the laundry, and she didn't want them to catch her undressed. There were no locks on the room doors, for the simple reason there was no crime in China. Swift and severe punishment would be meted out arbitrarily to anyone who committed any. 'Shot at dawn' was a truism. So, no one saw the need for keys and locks. That meant anyone could walk into any of the rooms at any time, including Marianne's. The guest-house staff did it all the time, to clean and do whatever they had to do. Still, she understood them. With whole families living on top of each other in one room, the Chinese had no sense of personal space or privacy, or ownership.

Marianne walked back into her room, which was surprisingly large. Before the revolution, this guest-house had been an old mansion house for rich folk. Now, it was used for putting up travelling foreigners. Nothing had been done to it. The decorations were faded, the paintwork was chipped and yellowing, and the curtains and rug threadbare. The old iron bedstead made her wince when she first saw it, but the mattress was comfortable. Apart from the bed, the only furniture was a battered wardrobe, a small bedside table, and a writing desk and chair. She loved the desk and spent hours every day writing up what had happened to her. She didn't know what she was going to do with this record but, as she'd left her diary hidden in the files in the Consulate-General, she had to start again and record every little detail. She must not forget anything.

She glanced at the photo of the little snuff bottle that lay beside her exercise book. It was the only evidence she had to corroborate her account of those awful events. She tucked it into the small shoulder bag she'd bought in the market yesterday to keep her money and credit cards safe. She had nothing else of any value with her, but that didn't bother her. In a country like China, where everyone dressed the same, ate the same, and owned nothing, personal possessions seemed irrelevant.

The bathroom suite was as ancient as the bedroom furniture. The sink and bath were stain-ridden with age, and the tiles were cracked. She didn't mind a bit. There was a charm about this old house. It had been majestic at some point in the past, no doubt about that. Turning on the creaky shower taps, she peeled off her clothes and stepped under the steamy water. The hot water pipes in the ceiling made a knocking sound as the water poured down. She'd make this shower quick anyway; she wouldn't deprive other guests by using too much hot water.

As the water revived her, she found herself looking forward to her breakfast and a walk around West Lake in the afternoon. She'd pop into the bookshop in town too and try to do some research on that snuff bottle.

★

Later, in the autumn sunshine, she'd spent a couple of hours wandering the temples and gardens around the lake. Now, she sat at on a wooden seat in one of the pagodas, staring out at the water. Surrounded by mountains on three sides, streams and waterfalls flowed down to the freshwater lake, making it look more like a lagoon. It looked so lovely and peaceful, a feeling of sadness that she had to leave tomorrow swept over her.

She slipped off her comfortable Chinese slippers, another purchase in the market. With their velvet upper and rubber sole, they were the most comfortable shoes she'd ever worn. She looked at her watch – almost 4 o'clock. What would those treacherous bastards in Shanghai be doing now? How had they explained her disappearance to London? By running away, she'd left them clear to concoct whatever story they wanted to about her and plant any evidence to point to her guilt in murdering the Ambassador. That's why she had to go back and try to defend herself.

She pushed all negative thoughts out of her mind and watched a mandarin duck paddle through the massive lotus leaves that floated on the surface of the water. Fascinated by the bird's amazing multi-coloured feathers and helmet-shaped head, she was lost in her own thoughts.

A sudden rustling of leaves nearby made her sit up. She looked over her shoulder. Was someone in the bushes?

Immediately, she jumped up, and set off down the path back towards town. She had planned a stroll through the bamboo grove, but now she decided to head straight for the safety and cover of the shops and buildings.

Her heart hammered as she walked. Occasionally, she glanced over her shoulder to see if she was being followed. She couldn't see anyone, but chills shivered up her spine. She could *feel* someone behind her.

Crazy thoughts flooded her head, then panic. Would they kill her now, in the open air? Or would it be more like the Ambassador's murder? Because to kill her would be the easiest solution for them. They could pin his murder on her, and there would be no one to defend her. No one to challenge their version of events.

She was almost jogging now and cursing herself. Why had she stayed so long in Hangzhou?

Back on the main road, she headed for the shops, where she thought she had a better chance of losing her pursuer. She stopped suddenly at the bicycle shop and walked around the row of bikes displayed outside on the pavement, as if choosing one to buy. That gave her an opportunity to glance back, to see who was coming up behind her.

She couldn't see a familiar face in the crowd, but she just knew someone was following.

A feeling of dread swept through her.

She started walking on again. Lengthening the strap of her shoulder bag, she slipped it over her head to rest across her body, in case she had to run. All the while her mind was spinning. How could she get away?

Fortunately, she knew her way around this town now. Suddenly, she darted across the road, took the next turning on the right, and dodged into the local bookshop.

"Hello." The young man behind the counter gave her a friendly smile.

She'd been a good customer in the short time she'd been in Hangzhou. He was probably looking forward to practising his English with her again, and to more book sales. She said hello back to him, and dived behind a rack of books, from where she could watch the door.

It opened. A Chinese woman came into the store.

Marianne peered over at the woman from behind the rack and realised the shop assistant was giving her an odd look. She smiled at him again and started browsing the books. She picked up one on Chinese calligraphy and flicked through it, while keeping a watch on the door.

She was just putting it back on the shelf when her eyes fixed on a familiar cover. She picked the book up, a copy of *The Butterfly Lovers*. That same book Wu had had in her office.

When someone catches your heart, you will never be apart.

That loving dedication someone had written to Wu inside the front cover. In Chinese characters, in black ink.

Marianne froze with shock as its significance hit her. Could one of her colleagues be Wu's lover? She remembered the champagne and the condom foil in the Ambassador's hotel room. Had Wu been *his* lover? No, the Ambassador was too smart and long in the tooth to fall for that. His murder could have been set up to look like that though. That was a distinct possibility.

The more she thought about it, the more certain she became that the Chinese had infiltrated the mission. Was Wu the honeytrap? London had trained them all to expect and deal with this kind of approach, leading to entrapment and blackmail. If It wasn't the Ambassador who'd succumbed to Wu's charms, it must have been one of her younger colleagues. But who? Justin or Sam or even Anthony?

Had the Ambassador found out what was going on? Is that why he'd had to die?

Marianne shivered as she realised the scope and danger of the deception. She had to phone someone for help, tell them what was going on. Then, she had an idea. She waited for the woman to leave and went up to the counter.

"Do you have a telephone in your shop?" she asked the young man in English.

"Yes."

"I should like to make an international phone call to London, if I may? It's urgent."

She saw hesitation, then confusion, in his eyes. She smiled at him, reassuringly, as if it was an everyday request. "Of course, I will pay you well for the call." She put several yuan notes on the counter, "and buy another book."

He looked at her, then at the foreign exchange certificates. "Come through to the back office," he said.

★

Marianne felt a huge sense of relief when she put the receiver back in its cradle. She'd unburdened herself, and it felt good finally to tell someone.

She peered through the connecting door to the shop, but the young man was alone. She picked up the copy of *The Butterfly Lovers*, paying him handsomely for it.

"Will you come again tomorrow?" he asked.

"Certainly." She nodded. "I look forward to seeing you again, then."

She pulled her cap into position, then slipped out of the front door. She sprinted up the street to a small hotel, where she was relieved to see a taxi waiting outside. She jumped in the back and asked the driver to take her to her guest-house. She was going to pack her things and head back to the railway station immediately. She wasn't ready to hand herself in just yet. She sat low in the taxi, with her face obscured, as it pottered along at 20mph.

At the guest house, she paid him for the short journey, then asked if he would kindly wait while she picked up her bag and then drive her to the railway station.

He was only too happy to oblige. It would be good money, a day's wages in one fare.

She walked quickly inside and asked the receptionist to make up her bill now. Her plans had changed. The Canadian Embassy wanted her to collect her passport in person in Peking. So, she had to leave early in the morning, to catch a flight to Peking.

The receptionist must have thought that was plausible because she nodded and collected up the receipts in the pigeon hole for Marianne's room. She started adding up the totals on her abacus. Then she turned. "Did your friend find you?"

Marianne felt like a cold hand had gripped her heart. "My friend?"

The receptionist nodded. "He came here, asking for you. I told him you were out, and that you liked to walk by the lake."

Marianne was furious with herself for being so indiscreet. "Is he here?"

The receptionist shook her head. "He said he would come back this evening."

Marianne's hands shook as she paid the bill with her foreign exchange certificates. She thanked the woman and walked slowly to the staircase.

Once out of the woman's sight, Marianne darted up the stairs, and along the top corridor to her room. She had to get her things and get the hell out of there as quickly as possible. She had stayed too long.

Reaching her room, she turned the knob and rushed inside. It was only when she was through the door and inside the room that she realised her mistake.

"Evening, Marianne," a familiar voice said from behind the door. She went to scream, but a hand clamped down tightly over her mouth, and the door slammed shut. She was trapped.

28

Firstly, do not fear hardship, and secondly, do not fear death
(Chairman Mao)

Jess stared at the closed cubicle curtains in St Thomas's Hospital A&E, eyes lingering on all the faded and frayed spots. They'd seen better days, but at least they gave her some privacy. Not that they could cut her off from the chaos all around, especially the coughing, sneezing, and groaning from the other casualties brought in off the streets of London that cold, December night. There was no escaping the competing smells of sick and disinfectant either.

She checked her watch, as she lay on the bed waiting for the doctor to come back with the results of her head X-ray. Ten minutes past midnight. If they kept her there much longer, she'd go home sicker than when she'd arrived, with this flu outbreak sweeping the capital.

Closing her eyes again, she shivered as she remembered those headlights coming straight at her. Blinding her. If she hadn't dived into that shop doorway, the car would have hit her for sure. It was as if the driver had no fear, of CCTV, of anyone.

Hit and run was how the hospital had recorded it. Jess had been too dazed at first to say much. Paramedics, who'd arrived swiftly on the scene, reported that a couple coming out of a nearby restaurant had seen everything and called an ambulance. The police had pitched up too, but the doctor had asked them to come back later to talk to Jess. They hadn't reappeared yet.

Jess sat up and pushed the rough, grey blanket off her. She looked sorrowfully at her velvet dress lying on the chair next to the bed. What a state. The hem was ripped, and dried spots of blood splattered the right shoulder. She put her fingers gingerly to her right temple and felt the stitches on her hairline. She remembered hitting her head on a stone pillar as she jumped out of the way of the car. The wound was more superficial than serious. Her hair would cover up that spot if she brushed it forward. Thankfully, she was feeling much better, and just wanted to go home.

She swung her legs over the side of the bed and gingerly put one foot down on the shiny floor, then the other. She slid her bottom off the bed and was relieved to find she wasn't even shaky. She took off the hospital robe and slipped her dress back on. She bent down and picked up her high heels. They were in a sorry state too, with one heel completely snapped off.

The curtains swished open, and she looked up.

"Crikey, Jess." Tom looked pale with shock. "What the hell happened?" Without waiting for a reply, he came over and gave her a hug. "When they said you'd been hit by a car and were in hospital, I thought, well, I thought ..."

"I'm okay, Tom," she whispered.

He sat her gently back down on the bed. "Really?"

"Yes, really." She touched her head. "Just a few stitches, that's all."

He tilted her face gently to one side and looked at the wound.

"I cut my head when I dived out of the way of the car," she explained. "It looks worse than it is."

"Tell me exactly what happened," he said, face grim.

"Well …" She rubbed her forehead.

"It's all right," he said. "Take your time."

She frowned with concentration. "I was trying to get a taxi home. I started to walk up St James's Street as I thought I'd have a better chance of getting one along there." She hesitated. "I crossed over the road. Suddenly a car came speeding down…"

"From which direction?"

"From Piccadilly." She paused. "Then it swerved and mounted the pavement. It drove straight at me." She looked at him. "I dived into a shop doorway to avoid it. I didn't have time to think about it, it was just an instinctive reaction. I cracked my head on a stone pillar."

He pushed her hair back from the wound. "What kind of car was it? What make?"

"All I saw were blinding headlights coming at me in the dark." Her voice shook now. "The driver slammed his brakes on after missing me." She looked at him. "Then its reverse lights came on."

"It was coming back?" Tom's voice was incredulous.

She nodded. "I heard screaming. To be honest, I don't know if it was me or someone else. The paramedics told me a couple called the ambulance. They were just coming out of a restaurant and saw the whole thing. Perhaps it was that woman who screamed?"

"What happened to the car?"

"It just drove off."

"Did you get a look at the driver?"

She shook her head. "I couldn't even tell you the make of the car, let alone who was driving."

Tom sighed. "Well, at least you're okay."

"Yes." She stood up again, and slipped her feet into her shoes, one at a time.

"Where are you going?"

"Home."

"Has the doctor said you can?"

"Not exactly. He was waiting for my head X-ray to come back. That could take all night, they're so busy."

"Ah," said a voice from behind her. "I see you're feeling better." The young doctor walked into the cubicle and smiled at Jess.

"Yes, much better, thank you."

"That's good to hear. Well, I've had a look at your X-ray and it's clear. No fractures, I'm pleased to say."

Jess smiled. "That's great. Is it okay for me to go now?"

He nodded. "As soon as you're ready. You may want to take it easy for a day or so."

"Oh, I'm fine now," she said. "I assume the stitches will just dissolve over the next week or two?"

"Yes, but concussion can be delayed after a trauma to the head. So, if you start feeling dizzy, or sick, or get some pain, go to your doctor straightaway."

She nodded. "I will."

Tom intervened. "Don't worry, doctor. I'll make sure she takes it easy."

"Good." The doctor nodded. "The police know what happened and will want to talk to you. We've given them your address and details."

"Thank you."

"Good. Well take care of yourself," he said, and disappeared back to his other patients.

Tom picked up her coat from the chair and brushed the mud off as best he could. Then he helped her put it on and picked up her handbag. "Come on," he said, offering her his arm. "We'll go home in a taxi."

"Thanks." She took his arm, and then almost immediately pulled away again. "How did you know I was in hospital? I didn't ring you."

"No, but you should have," he said. "As it happens, we were just finishing up after the State Banquet when my mate said he'd heard one of the guests at the Lancaster House reception had been knocked down. A hit and run in St James's Street." He looked at Jess with a pained expression. "I just knew it was you. We did some checking and found out you'd been taken here."

She smiled and took his arm again. "Thanks for coming."

He squeezed her hand, and they walked together in silence to the front entrance, where a taxi stood waiting for a fare.

The ride across London to St John's Wood, where Jess lived, was almost magical in the clear night. The roads and pavements were deserted in the early hours, and a full moon and stars lit up the way. Even Nelson's Column looked ghostly in the moonlight as they swung around Trafalgar Square. The Christmas tree, all lit up, looked cheerful too.

"Temperature's dropping fast," the taxi driver said. "There'll be a hard frost in the morning."

Tom nodded distractedly, while all the time looking around, his eyes darting everywhere in case some maniac came at them from out of the blue. That's what he did for a living, Jess thought, protect people. He'd been working all day, taught as a wire, ready to pounce or react. He looked so tired, and now he had to keep an eye on her too. She felt guilty about that.

She hooked her arm around his and whispered. "I'm sorry, Tom."

He looked at her. "What for?"

"For dragging you into all this."

He gave her a small smile. "You didn't drag me into anything. I'm here because I want to be." He shook his head. "Can't say I'm not worried, though."

She was worried too, scared even, but she tried not to show it. "Let's talk when we get home." She paused. "Look, it's really late. Why don't you stay over tonight? I've got a spare bedroom. It'll be like old times." She smiled at him. "You know, in the Governor's Residence in the Turks and Caicos Islands, when you came to stay."

"Crikey, yes. Don't remind me. Sitting up all night with that bloody hurricane raging all around."

"We survived it though, didn't we?"

"Just about." He squeezed her hand again. "I'd like to stay over tonight and keep an eye on you. Just in case – well, you know."

She knew what he meant. In case that bastard came back to finish the job. The irony was she'd decided to drop all that Marianne Henderson business anyway, but it was obviously too late. Someone had her in their sights, which meant she must have been getting close to the truth.

She glanced over at Tom again. He'd been with her during terrible times in Brisbane and in the Caribbean. Now he was helping her again. He was a good man, and a good friend. She was so glad he was in London. "You're welcome to come and stay with me for the rest of your time in the UK, if you'd like to," she said. "It's up to you, of course, no pressure."

He nodded, without hesitation. "I'd like that, thanks." Then he paused. "Simon won't mind, will he?"

"Oh no, he'll be fine about it," she said. "That's settled then. You can pick up your things from your rental tomorrow and bring them over to the flat."

They lapsed into silence for the rest of the journey, although Jess noticed the taxi driver give Tom an approving wink in the mirror.

As the taxi drew up outside her apartment block, Jess noticed Bev's lights were on. She climbed out of the taxi and hobbled across the forecourt on one flat shoe and one high heel. Opening the front door with her key, she waited for Tom, who was paying the taxi driver.

Almost immediately Bev came rushing out of her apartment in her pyjamas and robe. "Jess!" She sounded breathless. "Are you okay? I saw you limping."

Jess was startled to see Bev at first, then she looked down her own shoes. "I've had a bit of an accident. One of my heels snapped off."

"An accident?" Bev stared at Jess's head. "Oh, my goodness, what happened?"

"I'm all right." Jess couldn't exactly tell Bev someone had deliberately tried to run her over. "I was almost knocked over by a car," she said. "I, well, I sort of fell and hit my head."

Bev looked at her strangely.

"I've just spent the last few hours in A&E." Jess pointed to her head. "Having a few stitches."

Bev looked shocked.

"I'm all right," she assured Bev again. "It looks worse than it is. Nothing's broken."

Bev continued to look anxious. "Is there anything I can do?"

Tom came running up the steps and into the lobby. "There's nothing," he said. "I can look after her."

Bev nodded "Well, would you both like to come in for … a nightcap perhaps?"

Tom shook his head and pressed the button for the lift. "We'd better get Jess up to her flat. She needs to rest."

Bev nodded again. "Well, ring me if you need anything." She pointed to her front door. "I'm just here."

"Thanks, Bev," Jess said, kindly. "I'll ring if there's anything."

"Goodnight, then." Bev looked dejected as she walked back into her flat.

"Night, Bev," Jess said, as she got into the lift with Tom. Once the doors had closed, she turned to him. "Why don't you like Bev?" she asked.

He bristled. "I didn't say I didn't like her."

"It's clear you don't."

The lift stopped on the second floor. Immediately, Tom got out first and looked around. Then he took the front door key from Jess. He opened the door and looked cautiously inside, before flicking on the hall lights.

Jess followed him in and closed the door. "Welcome to my London pad," she said, with a flourish.

He immediately put his finger to his lips to signal her to be quiet.

Jess stood still, while he went into every room to check there was no one in the flat, closing the curtains and switching on the lights as he went. He came back and said with some relief: "Okay. No one here but us."

Jess took off her coat and hung it on the stand. "I'm starving," she said. "Have you had anything to eat?"

"You sit down," he said, ushering her into the sitting room and onto the sofa. He pulled a small stool over. "Put your feet up."

"I'm all right, Tom," she said. "Really."

"Stay there while I get us something to eat." He turned to her. "What have you got in the fridge?"

"Um … there's some home-made leek and potato soup in there. And some crusty bread from the local bakers in the bread bin. Or some eggs."

"The soup will do nicely," he said. "Warm us up." With that he went off to the kitchen. Every so often he would shout through to ask her where the saucepans were, or the cutlery. It didn't take him long to find his way around, and the questions soon stopped.

Jess looked at her watch. Almost 1 o'clock in the morning and they were having supper. Now she was out of A&E, she didn't feel in the least bit tired. She picked up the remote and switched the TV on to the BBC News Channel to get the hourly bulletin.

Tom popped his head around the door. "Do you feature in the news?"

She scowled at him. "I want to see what they're saying about the Chinese President's visit."

He smiled and went back to the kitchen.

Jess was watching the news when Tom came back in with two steaming hot bowls of soup on a tray, which he put down in front of Jess on the coffee table. Then he went back for the bread.

"There's a bottle of wine open in the fridge," she shouted.

He came back balancing a plate of bread, the wine and two glasses. "Never could see the point of white wine," he said, with a grin.

"I know red's your choice." She pointed to the bottle. "But that's a good white wine, and it is Australian."

He looked at the bottle. "It's not," he said, indignantly, "it's a Sauvignon Blanc from New Zealand."

"Is it? Well, just try it."

He poured two glasses, handed her one, then took a good swig from his own glass. "Hmm, not bad. Dry and subtle, with just a hint of bladder."

"Well, that's settled then. If you think my wine's a load of old pee, then you can buy it while you're staying here."

"It's a deal." He smiled and sat down on the chair opposite the sofa, picked up his bowl and started eating his soup. "Mm, this is good. Did you make it?"

"Yes. I can just about do that."

He looked around. "Great flat you have here. Nice location too, overlooking the park."

"Yes, we like it."

"You've got a Chinese theme going on in here too. Blue and white patterns on the curtains, and sofas. Even the lamps look Chinese."

"From Hong Kong, actually. Simon bought them while he was over there."

She switched her gaze back to the TV. "Oh, they're showing clips of the Chinese President's arrival at Heathrow." She paused. "Look, Tom, it's you, you're on the news."

He looked up. "Where?"

"Standing by the red carpet, just outside the VIP lounge."

They lapsed into silence as they watched the rest of the news and ate their soup. When they'd both finished, Tom said: "We need to talk." He leant over, picked up the remote and turned the sound up on the TV.

Jess frowned.

Face serious now, he came over and sat next to her on the sofa. "If your flat's bugged, they won't be able to hear us over the noise."

She nodded. He was so close now, she could feel the heat from his thigh touching hers, and the warmth of his breath of her cheek.

"What are we going to do, Jess?" He whispered. "This is way over our heads. Anything can happen now we know MI6 is involved." He paused. "Look at your boss, Giles."

Jess shivered. "We don't know for sure he was murdered," she whispered back. "He may have committed suicide."

Tom shrugged. "Will we ever know?"

"And I was supposed to be next." The words caught in her throat. "I think it was Justin Barber's doing. That car tonight, I mean. I don't think it was a warning either."

"Why would he see *you* as such a threat?"

She sighed. "Because I saw him in the park, meeting the Chinese Ambassador and my colleague Sam. I knew at the time his face looked familiar, but I had no idea he was the Deputy Chief of MI6." She paused. "The thing is, he saw me that day in the park, I'm sure of it. And tonight, well, I saw him meeting Mrs Wu secretly in the Long Gallery." She glanced at Tom. "Really close together they were."

He raised his eyebrows. "How close?"

"*Very* close." She paused. "You see, I think I've worked some of it out. What happened in Shanghai in 1984, I mean."

"Really?"

"Yes. I think Justin Barber was the other diplomat with Marianne Henderson opening the new British Consulate-General in Shanghai, all those years ago. The young Mrs Wu was their Chinese interpreter."

"You think so?"

"I know so. Justin admitted to working in Shanghai, as well as in Peking. It must have been him. And, well, they were all young officers at the time." She gave Tom a coy look. "What if he'd had a relationship with Mrs Wu back then? An affair?"

He shrugged. "It's possible."

"What if they're still lovers?"

"For over *30* years?"

"I know it sounds bizarre, and it's obvious they haven't been living together, or constantly in each other's lives. But, well, they could still be *involved* with each other. That's perfectly possible." She sighed. "In many ways, that's even more worrying."

He looked puzzled.

"What has their relationship meant for our country's security?" She stared at Tom. "Our country's secrets?"

He looked startled. "You think they've been passing classified information to each other for all that time?"

She shook her head. "It's more likely just one of them is spying for the other side. Either Mrs Wu is passing Chinese secrets to British Intelligence. Or Justin Barber is passing our secrets to them."

"For over 30 years?"

"I know. It doesn't bear thinking about, does it?"

"It would be explosive!"

"Exactly! And what better reason for wanting me out of the way." She shuddered. "Perhaps that's why the British Ambassador was killed in that hotel in Shanghai all those years ago. The pair of them wanted him out of the way too."

"Except his death is recorded as suicide." Tom paused. "Mind you, no one thinks arsenic poisoning is credible."

"Perhaps the Ambassador found out what was going on, and he confronted Justin?"

Tom stared at her. "That would mean Justin was the guilty party, of working for the Chinese, I mean. What other motive would he have had for getting rid of the Ambassador?"

Jess sighed. "The Ambassador would have had him sent home. Justin would have been charged with treason. Or if not, he would have defected to China and lived out his days there, rather than return to a life sentence in the UK. Much like our British spies, Philby, Burgess and McLean, ran away and defected to Moscow."

Tom flopped back in the sofa. "We're getting way ahead of ourselves here, Jess, with all this conspiracy theory."

"It sounds a good enough reason to me for Justin to want to kill the Ambassador. It might sound surreal, but who would have thought Al Qaeda would hijack American planes and fly them into the World Trade Center towers? That's the stuff of fiction too."

Tom was quiet for a while. "Well, I suppose Justin *could* have got away with it, so long as no one else knew what he was up to, of course."

"Ah, but I think someone else did know what Justin was up to, and still knows." She looked at Tom. "My colleague, Sam Biggins. That's why he was at that meeting with Justin and Mrs Wu in the park the other morning. They've been covering this up for years. Sam was shaken to the core when I showed him the photo of the snuff bottle."

"You reckon he's been in the pocket of the Chinese all these years too?"

She nodded.

"What about Marianne Henderson? What's your theory about her?"

"I reckon they framed her for the Ambassador's death, to create a distraction from them. Poor Marianne probably died in China, in some labour camp or prison. The Chinese would have been complicit in all that, especially if they'd turned both Justin and Sam into agents for them. What an investment, complete access to British secrets for all these years."

"The Ambassador and Marianne paid with their lives?"

"Yes." She paused. "That's what I think anyway."

"Still, it's all supposition at present. I mean…"

"But it fits, Tom. Don't you see?"

He was silent for a while. "If you're right, it means you can't stay here. It's too dangerous. You need to leave first thing in the morning, take a break until it blows over."

"Blows over?" She looked at him. "It's hardly going to blow over. What about the Chinese visit? It's my responsibility."

He shook his head. "You've done your bit. You don't have to stay here. Others can see the visit through."

Jess knew he was right, but she didn't want to run away. She couldn't, not without telling someone. She had a duty to put the record straight, if her theory about Justin, Sam and Mrs Wu was right.

"Jess," he said, gravely. "Someone has you in their sights. If it's Justin Barber, you can't fight MI6. The only thing you can do is get away for a while." He sighed. "Have you rung Simon? Does he know about any of this?"

She shook her head. "What can he do from Paris?"

"He could come back." Tom sounded exasperated. "Help you deal with it."

Jess said nothing. She deliberately hadn't told Simon because she didn't want to involve him and put him in the frame too. Anyway, what if she was wrong about Justin Barber and the Chinese Ambassador? She would be willing to ruin her own career, but not Simon's too.

"Even better," Tom went on. "You should go over to Paris and stay with him. You've done your work on the President's visit, you don't need to stay here. You'll be safer over there."

She knew he was right.

"I'll put you on the Eurostar to Paris in the morning," he said. "It's that simple, Jess."

It was then that the realisation hit her. "I don't want to go to Paris and be with Simon. I'd rather stay here." She was going to say, 'with you', but she didn't dare. She'd been shaken up tonight and her emotions were all over the place. "I'm just, well, I'm just feeling comfortable here ... now."

There was a pause.

He picked up his glass and emptied it. Then he looked her in the eye. "Well, why don't you come over to Australia with me when I go back at the end of the week?"

At that moment, she could think of nothing better. She loved Australia and a break in the sunshine would do her good. But what about Simon? He was supposed to be coming home for Christmas. She needed to talk to him. They needed to sort out their future once and for all. Even more than that, she knew she couldn't just run away and disappear. She had to face this and tell the authorities what she knew.

"I'm sorry, Tom," she said, sadly, "but I can't just disappear without telling anyone what I've found out."

He stared at her. "Oh, come on, Jess. Who are you going to talk to?"

"Sir Anthony. He is the Head of the Foreign office, after all."

"But can you *trust* him? He was in Shanghai in 1984 too. Isn't he part of the conspiracy?" Tom sighed with frustration. "What are you going to tell him anyway?"

"I don't know if I can trust him or not." She hesitated. "I feel I must tell someone about Sam, Justin and Mrs Wu meeting in the park, and about Mrs Wu and Justin this evening, and what happened to me. Somebody did try to kill me."

"For Christ's sake, Jess, is that really a good idea?"

She sat forward, resolute. "I've made up my mind. Tomorrow, I'm going into the office. I'm going to tell Sir Anthony everything I know, then I'm going to the Lord Mayor's dinner for the Chinese President at the Guildhall. I want to make it look like everything is quite normal. After that, I'll leave straightaway for a break."

He took her hand and stared into her eyes. "And where will you go?"

"I must talk to Simon, first," she said. "I really must."

He nodded. "Well, I'm scared to death, Jess."

"I know," she said, softly. "I'll be all right. I'll ask Bev to give me a lift to the office tomorrow. I'll be safe there. I'll even ask her to take me to the Guildhall and pick me up again. And I won't go anywhere else."

"Why *Bev*?"

"Because she lives downstairs and she's got a car parked outside." She gave him a curious look. "I asked you earlier why you don't like Bev. You didn't say."

He shrugged. "Something's not right about her. I can feel it."

"Well why don't you check her out? She is Australian, after all."

He didn't reply, but there was something about his expression.

"You already have, haven't you?" she said. "You've checked Bev out."

He nodded.

"And?"

He sighed. "There is a vineyard called Sam Talbot's in New South Wales, so that's true. The owner is Sam Talbot, and he runs the business with his two sons. There's nothing about a Beverly Talbot connected to the business."

"She's the boys' mother," Jess explained. "She showed me a photo of them, they're twins. Oh, honestly, Tom, you're so suspicious of everyone. Maybe she hasn't been active in the business because she's been bringing up a family."

"Mm. Well, I've asked one of the guys to do a full check on her and send me a photo. I'll only be satisfied when I've seen that."

He got up, switched off the TV and all the lights. He went over to the curtains and peered through the crack.

"Anyone out there?"

"Not that I can see." He turned back. "Doesn't mean they aren't there though." He came back to the sofa. "Look, I'm going to tell the guys at the Met what happened to you tonight."

"No Tom."

"I am going to tell them. Definitely. The hit and run's already been reported anyway. I need to get you some protection."

"Can you just wait until I've spoken to Sir Anthony."

"Well…"

"I'll ring or text you straightaway and let you know what he says."

"Oh, all right." He sounded reluctant. "Have you still got that pay-as-you-go phone I got you?"

"Yes, it's in my bag."

"Good. Well, ring or text me on that immediately you come out of his office."

"Right."

"And if you must ask Bev for a lift, I want you to text me just before you leave this flat, and again when you get to the Foreign Office. Once you're inside that building I'll know you're safe, and I can stop worrying."

She gave him a smile.

"I don't think you should go to the Guildhall dinner either. I really don't."

"We'll see what happens," she said. "I'll take my dress to the office with me just in case."

"If you do go, how would you get there?"

"In an office car, with the Protocol Officer. Or with Bev."

He folded his arms in a stubborn way. "I understand why you want to go to the Foreign Office to talk to Sir Anthony. That makes sense, although I'm not sure it's the wisest thing to do. I really don't think you should go anywhere else, and especially not to the Guildhall. It's a public place, and there are over 100 guests going. You would be an easy target."

"It will look odd if I *don't* turn up. I've accepted the invitation, and I'm sitting on the top table with the Chinese President and the Lord Mayor. I'll be missed if I don't go."

"I can see that. But you'd be safer not going."

"You'll be on duty there, Tom, won't you? I mean, watching the Chinese President."

"Yes, but I won't be able to keep an eye on you too."

She laid her head wearily on his shoulder. "I understand your concern, Tom. I won't do anything stupid. I'll text you with my every move."

"Promise?"

"Promise."

"Good." He put his arm around her in a comforting way. "Everything will be all right. We'll get through this."

Jess wished she felt as confident, but she was scared. Really scared. Not just for herself, but for Tom too. Why on earth had she put him in this position? It was unforgivable.

29

To rebel is justified
(Chairman Mao)

Jess sent Tom a text on her new mobile to say she was in Bev's car, getting a lift to work. '*Take care*' came his immediate reply. She slipped the phone back into her bag, satisfied it was working, and relieved to know he was there.

Those blinding headlights last night flashed before her eyes again. She pulled the visor down and looked in the vanity mirror. Not to check her appearance, but to look for that car. Irrational really, since she hadn't even seen the make or colour, let alone the driver. Still, she would stay alert for anything unusual. Being constantly on edge was tiring though and made her realise just how difficult Tom's job must be.

She smiled to think he'd be back in the flat later. It was great having him around. His reassuring presence last night had helped her relax and get some sleep. Waking up to the smell of coffee this morning had been lovely too. She'd listened for any noise like the clattering of crockery or the shower running, but he'd already gone to work. That was disappointing, but he'd left a note to say she'd been so deeply asleep when he'd popped his head around the door, he hadn't wanted to disturb her. He'd also set out a detailed account with exact timings of where he'd be all day, in case she needed him urgently. He'd finished with a couple of sentences written in capitals, and underlined, imploring her to stay inside and keep him informed by text of her every move. Along with the note, a jug of coffee was standing on the hotplate, and a bowl of chopped fruit on the table. She'd poked her head into the spare bedroom to find the bed made up, and everything neat and tidy. Even in the bathroom, the only sign he'd had a shower was the lingering steam.

The sudden noise of windscreen wipers swishing through melting ice made her jump. She glanced over at Bev, who was rubbing the back of her hand over the inside of the misty windscreen. Outside, the coating of hard frost on the black Fiat's bonnet shimmered like crystals in the winter sunshine. It had been a freezing night, resulting in a sparkling morning under a clear blue sky.

"Chilly, isn't it?" Jess said.

"That's an understatement!"

Bev wasn't her usual chatty self this morning, Jess thought. She seemed tense, her knuckles white on the steering wheel as she gripped it. Her usually radiant skin looked dull too, making the wrinkles around her eyes and mouth more pronounced. Not for the first time, Jess wondered how old Bev was. "I hope I'm not putting you out?" she said.

"No worries," Bev said. "I'd planned to do some sightseeing today anyway. I might hang around for that ceremony on Horse Guards Parade you were talking about."

"For the Chinese President?"

"Yes. I assume I can watch from St James's Park with the rest of the public?"

"You can, but it doesn't start until 11 o'clock."

"Will you be going?"

She wanted to, but Tom's warning to stay inside was in her head. "I'm afraid I won't have time."

"No worries. I'll park the car somewhere and go for a wander in the park before it starts."

Jess glanced in the vanity mirror again, then looked over her shoulder.

"You're like a cat on hot coals this morning," Bev said.

Jess knew she was jittery, but she couldn't tell Bev the reason why. "I never did like being a passenger," she said. "I prefer to drive."

At that moment, a grey car came up on the inside of them, its windows all blacked out. Jess saw the driver's window start to descend. "Lock the doors!" she hissed at Bev.

Bev reacted like lightning, pressing the door-locking button. "What is it?"

Jess tensed as she watched the grey car overtake them on the inside and drive on. "Sorry. That grey car spooked me." Now she felt foolish. "Can't be too careful in the city. Anyone can jump in the back or open the doors and grab your bag. It happens all the time."

"In Australia, too." Bev looked concerned. "Is there something wrong, Jess?"

"No, I'm fine."

"How's your head this morning?"

Jess looked in the mirror and pulled back her hair. "The stitches sting a bit. If I brush my hair forward, they're not so visible."

"You still haven't told me how you did it."

"I guess I wasn't looking where I was going. I jumped out of the way of a car." She shrugged. "I fell over in my high heels and cracked my head on a stone pillar."

Bev raised her eyebrows.

They fell silent, as Bev navigated her way through the morning rush hour traffic. She wove in and out of the traffic with ease and dodged down the back streets to avoid traffic lights and bottlenecks. That, surprised Jess. "How come you know your way around the streets of London so well?"

Bev glanced over. "I've been driving around the centre since I got here, learning all the road names and seeing the sights at the same time. It's the only way to really get to know a city."

Jess frowned at her. "*Walking* is the only way to get to know a city. I'm surprised you don't get around more on foot since you like to keep fit."

Bev smiled, then nodded at Jess's dress carrier laid out on the back seat. "What are you wearing to the Guildhall this evening?"

Had Bev deliberately changed the subject, she wondered? Or was Tom's suspicion of Bev rubbing off on her too? "It's a black-tie event. I'm wearing a long dress. A slinky, black number."

Bev laughed. "Is your policeman going with you?"

Something about the way she said 'your policeman' irritated Jess. Did Bev dislike Tom as much as he seemed to dislike her?

"He's working," was all Jess said, and they lapsed into silence again.

"I can take you to the Guildhall tonight, if you'd like."

"Oh, I couldn't ask you to do that," Jess said. "Really, I couldn't."

"It's no trouble. I'm not doing anything else this evening." Bev steered the car across Oxford Circus, and into Regent Street. "I reckon this should be the quickest route to Whitehall this morning. The roads around Buckingham

Palace and the Mall will probably be closed off, ahead of the parade later."

Approaching Piccadilly, Jess leant forward and stared through the windscreen. "There's that grey car again."

Bev nodded. "I've seen it." She followed the grey car through Piccadilly, into the Haymarket. Then, without any warning she swung the car across the road and turned right. Racing along the street, she came out in Lower Regent Street.

Jess sat pinned to the seat.

Eyes glued on the road, Bev turned right into the one-way traffic system, sped along a hundred yards or so, turned left down Jermyn Street, then into St James's Street. Parking in-between two cars, she looked in the mirror. "Have we lost it?" she asked.

"Bloody hell, Bev." Jess stared at her. "Where did you learn to drive like that?"

Bev shrugged. "You said that grey car was following us." She paused to look around. "Can't see it now. Can you?"

"No, you've lost it." Well and truly lost it, she thought but didn't say.

Bev let out a pent-up sigh. "I went on a special driving course in Australia. They were teaching women how to look after themselves on the roads. You know, if you were being harassed or followed." She smiled. "Good course, it was."

Jess gave Bev a strange look. "You could get a London cabbie's licence with your knowledge of all the streets."

Bev didn't laugh. "London's a great city. I've done loads of sightseeing since I've been here. All the historic buildings, the galleries and museums." She sighed. "We don't have anything like it back home. I envy you, working in a building like the Foreign Office."

"Yes, well, I found it a bit intimidating when I first joined. I was only young." Jess laughed. "I soon lost that." She paused. "I love Durbar Court in the Old India Office part of the building, and the grand, sweeping staircase up to the Foreign Secretary's Office, and all the portraits and pictures."

"Must be wonderful." Bev sounded wistful as she put the car into drive. "Might as well head for the Mall now we're on this side of the park and see if it's open."

To Jess's relief, it was. "Turn left," she said. "Drive along the Mall, through the traffic lights, then turn right."

Bev followed her instructions.

"That's Horse Guards Parade ground, where the ceremony will be," Jess said as they drove past.

Bev nodded.

"Just pull up here." Jess pointed to Clive Steps. "These steps will take me into King Charles Street. The main Foreign Office entrance is a hundred yards or so along there."

"Is that the only entrance?"

"Nowadays, yes. Well, that's not strictly true. There are four or five different entrances around the building. They're all locked up now. Everyone must enter and exit through the main entrance. Security, you see."

Bev nodded. "Lots of that, I expect?"

"Absolutely. Barriers, metal detectors, the lot."

"Even for employees?"

"Yes."

Bev shrugged. "Different world now, isn't it?"

"You're right there." Jess turned to her. "Thanks Bev, for the lift. I really appreciate it."

Bev smiled back. "Do you want me to come back this evening and take you to the Guildhall?"

"Oh no." Much as she would have loved Bev to come back and give her a lift, Jess couldn't impose any more on her. "Thanks for the offer though."

"That's okay. Thanks for your friendship. I've really appreciated that too."

Jess smiled. "It's been good having you around." It was said with honesty, having a friend in her apartment block was a real bonus. "Right. I'd better get on." She jumped out of the car, opened the back door and pulled out her dress carrier. "Enjoy the parade," she shouted and slammed the door.

Bev waved and drove off.

Jess paused and looked around for the grey car, but it was nowhere to be seen. It clearly hadn't been following them. Bev's quick reaction had been amazing though; worrying too. No one would react and drive like that normally, would they? And Bev knew her way around London too well. Jess felt herself becoming as suspicious as Tom, and that was a dilemma because she liked Bev.

Walking quickly up Clive Steps and along King Charles Street, she stopped outside the Foreign Office main entrance and pulled out her mobile to text Tom.

Just going into the Foreign Office. Will have to turn phone off now for security reasons. Will be inside all day. Jess

She kept looking around, wondering if it was safe to wait for a reply. It only took him a minute to respond.

Glad you're safe and at office. Still don't want you to go to Guildhall – Tom

Will see how things go when I've spoken to Sir A. Let me know if you get any info from Oz on Bev – Jess

Why? Anything happened? – Tom

Thought a car was following us on way here. Bev shook it off like a pro – Jess

Did you get the number plate? – Tom

No, sorry – Jess

Don't leave the office. Speak later – Tom

Jess switched off the phone and walked towards the security officer at the main entrance. "Morning." She manoeuvred her handbag and dress carrier through the metal detector and felt in her coat pocket for her staff pass. It wasn't there. She opened her coat to see if it was already around her neck. Not there either. Once her bag had passed security, she searched it. "Sorry," she said to the Security Officer. "I must have left my pass at home."

He gave an apologetic shrug. "I'm afraid you'll need to go into the office and get a temporary one."

Jess knew the ropes. She'd only forgotten her pass once before and it had been a pain going through all the security questions to get a temporary one. She trudged wearily up the steps and into the security office.

Later, she came out with a temporary pass and headed straight for Sir Anthony's Office. She wanted to see him immediately and get it over with. She was nervous as she walked along the corridor, partly because she didn't know if she could trust him, and partly because she knew what she had to say would sound bizarre.

Her stomach churned as she stood outside his door. She took a deep breath and walked into his outer office.

His Private Secretary looked up. "Morning Jess."

"I'd like to see Sir Anthony. It's urgent."

The Private Secretary pushed his owlish glasses firmly up the bridge of his nose. "He wanted to see you too. I left a note on your desk."

"I haven't been up to my office yet."

"I'm afraid he won't be back until after lunch now, he's at a conference in the QEII Centre." He hesitated, then gave her a piercing look. "He was in a right mood when he left here earlier. What have you done to upset him?"

She was surprised at his tone. "It's … it's *personal*."

The creases in his forehead deepened when he frowned. "Can I help? Do you want to talk to me?"

She shook her head. "I'm sorry. I can't do that."

He shrugged. "Well, I'll phone you when Sir Anthony gets in, probably around 2.30pm."

He gave her a sympathetic look that told her she was in for a rough ride. Sir Anthony was notorious for it. She tried humour to compensate for the sinking feeling in her stomach. "Do I need to bring my hard hat?"

He gave her a small smile. "Sir Anthony will give you the news himself. I'm sorry, Jess."

That didn't bode well, but there was nothing more she could say at present. "I'll wait for your call, then. Around 2.30pm."

She felt totally deflated as she walked through the building to her office. She'd geared herself up for telling Sir Anthony everything – all about Justin and Mrs Wu, about them meeting in the park, about them meeting again at Lancaster House, about their closeness, their probable treachery over 30 years, and about Sam's complicity. She was going to tell Sir Anthony about the attempt on her life too. Everything. Now, she was in two minds. If he was that upset with her, would she get a fair hearing? He'd warned her to forget all about Marianne Henderson, and not to ruin her career over it. That's what she *had* decided to do, but someone was determined to involve her. Someone had sent her that snuff bottle photo. Who though?

The Private Secretary's sympathetic smile and manner were playing on her mind too. Why did he say he was sorry? What did he have to be sorry for? *Sir Anthony will give you the news himself.* That's what he'd said. Her heart sank. It could mean only one thing. Sir Anthony was going to sack her. Did *no one* care about what happened to the

Ambassador and Marianne in Shanghai, for God's sake? Was she the only one who wanted to know the truth? If she couldn't discuss this with Sir Anthony, who *could* she talk to?

At the staircase, she found herself going down to the basement, rather than up to her office. She would talk to Sam, have it out with him. She was sure he knew everything. She would get the truth out of him. She strode along the corridor to his office. Strangely, he hadn't turned up at the reception last night. Why? Would he be in today?

She had her answer even before she'd reached his office, the scent of jasmine tea wafting through the corridor. She stopped outside his half-open door. Through the crack, she could see his head bent over a newspaper on his desk, a mug of tea next to it. His daily routine. Suddenly she felt herself simmering with rage at the sight of him enjoying his tea and newspaper. He'd been carrying on a great life, with a lovely family, for over 30 years, while the Ambassador and Marianne's lives had been snuffed out.

He looked up as if he sensed someone was outside.

Jess shrank back. Should she confront him in her frame of mind? Her resolve faded, and she ran back to the staircase on tiptoe, to stop her shoes making a noise. Be sensible, she told herself. First, she had to talk to Sir Anthony.

She ran up the stairs to her office, hesitating as she passed Giles's silent room. She wanted to feel sorry for him, but her heart was hardening against the lot of them. If Sir Anthony wasn't going to give her a fair hearing, did that mean he was involved in the cover-up too? Had they all played a part in this conspiracy, if only with their silence?

Feeling ghosts all around her, she ran into her office and locked the door. She went over and locked the inter-connecting door to the Registry Clerk's office too. She looked all around her. This room had been her second home, her refuge, the place she had spent all her working life. This morning, it felt different. Hostile even. She should be able to trust her colleagues, especially Sir Anthony, but they were all lying to her. Everything about this China job seemed tainted with death and deceit. A rot that had eaten its way into the very fabric of the organisation over the past thirty years.

She hung her dress carrier on the peg behind the door, along with her coat. She sat down at her desk and put her head in her hands. It felt like a watershed moment. A day of reckoning. If Sir Anthony was going to sack her, as she suspected, and this was going to be her last day in the office, she would put all her affairs in order and leave with as much dignity as she could.

Resolute now, she set about sorting out her office and papers. She started by lifting the large storage box off the top of her cupboard. She gathered up all her personal effects, photos, pictures, and books, put them in the box and stood back. It was only half full. Was this the sum of her working life? If she walked out with this box today and never came back, no one would give a damn. Someone else would be sitting at her desk by the end of the week.

The handle of the inter-connecting door turned, followed by a knock on the door. "Are you in there, Jess?"

It was Tim, her Registry Clerk. Jess went over, unlocked the door and opened it. "Sorry. I'm just having a clear out."

The thin, young man looked at her. His mop of unruly black hair only heightened his pale skin. He was a quiet soul at the best of times and liked a bit of peace himself. "I just wondered if you wanted a coffee?"

"Please," she said.

He came in, picked up her mug from the desk and looked around. "Wow. You mean business." He turned to her quickly. "You're not going anywhere, are you? I mean, you're not leaving us?"

A sudden booming noise cracked through the air. She jumped. Was that a bomb? Then came a second, and a third.

"It's the 41-gun salute," Tim said. "Over in Green Park … for the Chinese President."

She looked at her watch. 12.10. She'd been so preoccupied with clearing out her office, she hadn't noticed the time.

"I thought you'd be going out to watch the ceremonial welcome on Horse Guards Parade," he said.

She could hear the disappointment in his voice when he mentioned the ceremony. She'd been so caught up with herself, she'd forgotten about him and all the work he'd done on the visit. "Quick," she said. "You go and watch."

His eyes brightened. "Can I?"

"Yes, of course. Hurry up!" She grabbed her mug back from him. "Go!"

He ran over to the door and threw on his coat and scarf. "Won't be long," he said, and ran out.

She smiled at his enthusiasm, remembering how she used to love to watch ceremonies and parades. She went down to the kitchen to make herself some coffee. She'd got so down about everything, she was losing perspective. Pull yourself together, she told herself as she made her way back to her office. Maybe things won't be as bad as you think.

30

Before embarking on a journey of revenge, dig two graves
(Confucius)

At 1.30pm, Jess put her ham sandwich back on the plate, unable to eat for the sick feeling in her stomach and the nauseous smell of boiled cabbage. She'd come down to the canteen for a change of scene, not because she was hungry. Up in the office, she'd felt like a condemned woman pacing around her cell and wanted to do something to distract herself. She also thought she might see Sam down there. So far, he hadn't appeared. She looked at her watch. With another hour to kill before Sir Anthony was due in, she decided to go outside into the quadrangle and get some fresh air. She could switch her mobile on out there and see if Tom had been in touch.

The freezing air caught in her throat as she stepped outside. She shivered. Across the cobbles at the main entrance, she saw two security officers checking under VIP cars waiting to come through the barrier and ushering people on foot through metal detectors. How different from when she'd first started at the Foreign Office. Back then, staff could just duck into whichever entrance was nearest and show a pass. The world had changed so much.

She pulled her new mobile out of her bag. There were three text messages from Tom…

Are you okay?

What happened with Sir A?

My mate in Oz says there is a Beverly Talbot. They are sending photo.

Jess felt bad for not contacting him sooner and replied instantly.

Sorry, got carried away clearing out my office. Sir A not here this morning. Will speak to him at 2.30pm. Think I'm going to get the sack. Let me know about Bev soonest – Jess

The sack? Surely not? Let me know what Sir A says. Leave your mobile on. Hate being out of touch. Chin up – Tom

She put her phone on silent. These were extraordinary circumstances, and she did need to keep in touch with Tom.

Okay. Phone on silent now.

Chin up? She was going to need to do more than that to get herself out of this hole. Going back into the building, she went up to her office, and found a message on her desk. The writing, in capitals, was unmistakable. 'SIR ANTHONY WANTS TO SEE YOU NOW.'

This is it! She brushed her hair and put on some lipstick. She pulled her suit jacket off the back of her chair. She felt more professional wearing it. Just tell him everything you've found out, she told herself, as she checked her final appearance in the mirror. Then, it's up to him, and the powers that be, to deal with it. There's nothing more you can do. She stopped on her way to the door, went back to her handbag and pulled out the photo of the little snuff bottle. Tucking it into her jacket pocket, she pulled her hair self-consciously over the stitches before setting off.

She couldn't stop her heart pounding as she walked down to his office. This wasn't going to be an easy meeting.

His Private Secretary had already indicated that. She poked her head around the door, but the Private Secretary wasn't at his desk. She went inside and walked over to the inter-connecting door with Sir Anthony's office. She listened, then pushed the door open and peered inside.

There was Sir Anthony, standing by the far window, staring out onto Horse Guards Parade, with his hands behind his back.

Jess's high heels sunk in the deep green pile of the carpet as she walked up behind him. Through the window, she could see only discarded paper bags and sandwich wrappers blowing across the parade ground now. The welcoming ceremony for the Chinese President had finished ages ago. He and The Queen should be safely back in Buckingham Palace by now, tucking into lunch.

"You wanted to see me?" she asked.

His face turned to stone when he saw her. "Sit down." He pointed to the chair by his desk.

She sat down.

He walked around behind his desk, but he didn't sit. He pulled a file off the top of his tray, opened it on his desk, and leant forward to read it.

Jess was sitting close enough to see that it was a personnel file, and to read the name at the top. It was *her* personnel file.

Sir Anthony's fierce black eyes bore into her. "What I told you about Shanghai in 1984 was in strict confidence. I said it should stay between us. I also said that our conversation had to be the end of the Marianne Henderson story once and for all. Do you remember that?"

"Yes."

"I specifically asked you not to damage the bilateral relationship with the Chinese, or anything else to do with this visit."

Jess nodded. "I'm not aware I have done anything."

"Then why did the Chinese Ambassador phone me to complain about you?"

Jess frowned. "Complain?"

"Don't get smart with me, Jess. She said you've been making a nuisance of yourself. You've been following her around and demanding to see one of her staff who is on sick leave."

"*Following her?*" Jess almost laughed with astonishment.

That riled him. He almost bared his teeth as if he might leap across the table and sink them into her. "It's no laughing matter. You're a diplomat, not a private detective. You should know how to behave. If you don't, well, there's no place for you in the Foreign Office."

It was a long time since she'd been spoken to like that. She felt like a schoolgirl in the headmaster's office. Why was he behaving like this? To put her in her place? Frighten her?

"I warned you not to ruin your career over this," he said. "You ignored me."

She opened her mouth to defend herself, but he put up a hand to silence her.

He looked back at her personnel file and untagged a piece of paper from the top. "Here." He pushed the paper towards her. "This is an official notification of your immediate posting to Mexico City."

She stared at him. *"Mexico City?"*

"The Management Officer has been on sick leave for some time and will be returning permanently to the UK tomorrow. *You* are to replace him in Mexico City, with immediate effect."

Her jaw dropped. "But I don't speak Spanish," she said, lamely.

"Speaking the language is not necessary in the job you've been assigned." He paused. "You can pack up your office and leave the China desk today. Your work on the President's visit is finished. You are to be in Mexico City by the weekend, to start work next Monday morning."

She was astonished. He wasn't sacking her, he was banishing her. Getting her as far away from China and London as he could. There could be only one reason for that. Sir Anthony was in league with Justin, Sam and Mrs Wu. They were all involved in the cover-up. That must have been why none of the Foreign Office staff in the Embassy in Peking or Shanghai would co-operate with the British police when they went out to investigate all those years ago.

Suddenly, the simmering rage she'd felt outside Sam's office bubbled up again. The injustice of it all. The lies. The deceit. "What if I refuse to go to Mexico City?"

"You know full well there's a mobility clause in your employment. You must go wherever you are sent."

"And if I don't?"

"You will be considered unfit to continue in the Diplomatic Service and transferred to a home Civil Service Department." He closed her file and put it back on the top of his tray with a flourish. He looked at her as if to say 'game, set, and match.'

She stood up to face him. "It seems I'm not even entitled to a fair trial. You've judged me guilty without even hearing my side of the story. If you'd been willing to listen, I would have explained that Mrs Wu's complaint is a load of old tripe."

"Sit down!"

Jess gave him a level stare. "I haven't been following Mrs Wu around. I just happened to be walking through St James's Park the other morning and saw her having a meeting with Justin Barber and Sam Biggins." She paused. "Then, last night, I saw her having a private conversation with Justin Barber, secretly hidden in an alcove in the Long Gallery at Lancaster House." She paused. "That's what Mrs Wu is so upset about. The fact that I saw them."

Sir Anthony shrank back as if she'd prodded him with a hot poker.

Jess was in full flow now. "I assure you I have kept your confidence about what happened in Shanghai in 1984." That wasn't exactly true, she'd told Tom, but she knew she could trust him absolutely. "I agreed with you that I would let the matter rest, and I did. Except…"

He stared at her.

She pulled the photo out of her jacket pocket and slapped it down on the desk in front of him.

He paled visibly when he saw it.

"Except someone sent me this photo of a little Chinese snuff bottle. It was sent anonymously, to my home address. On the back were written the words 'Shanghai – 1984.' She could feel her legs shaking, but she wasn't going to crumple or show any weakness. "I don't know what it means, but I can see by your face that you do."

"What are you implying?"

"That Marianne Henderson was framed. She did not have an affair with the Ambassador in Shanghai in 1984, and she was not responsible for his death. What's more, no one believes he committed suicide by poisoning himself with arsenic." She was going to add, not even the police, but she didn't want to go that far and implicate Tom or anyone else.

Sir Anthony slumped back in his chair.

Suddenly the door opened. His Private Secretary poked his head in and looked anxiously at them. "Everything all right? Only … only I heard raised voices."

"Everything's fine," Jess said sharply. She picked up the photo and walked to the door. She turned to Sir Anthony. "At least in Mexico City, I'll only have drug barons to watch out for."

She brushed past the Private Secretary, who stood with his mouth open, and hurried out of the office. She was shaking like a leaf as she walked along, hardly able to believe what just happened. She'd had a row with the Head of the Foreign Office. The Tiger. The man everyone feared. Now, she'd blown her job and her career right out of the water.

★

Back in her office, Jess sat staring into space for what seemed like hours. She replayed the scene with Sir Anthony over and over in her head and came to the same conclusion every time. It wouldn't have mattered what she'd said, he was going to get rid of her anyway. She understood why he hadn't sacked her though. She could have taken him to an industrial tribunal where everything would have come out. No, he'd chosen to send her as far away as he could. If she refused to go, he would have every right to move her out of the Foreign Office. He was a wily operator, everyone knew that.

It was only when the light had completely faded that she stirred. She switched on her desk lamp and looked at her watch. Almost 5.30pm. Stiff from sitting in one position for so long, she rose wearily from her chair.

Her immediate shock, then anger, had given way to a more philosophical frame of mind. The irony was that she *had* kept Sir Anthony's confidence. Apart from Tom, she hadn't said anything to anyone about Marianne Henderson. She *was* letting it rest, just as Sir Anthony had asked her to, but she hadn't been able to control things. The genie was already out of the bottle, or the snuff bottle, she thought.

She sighed and went over to her cupboard. She would clear it out and be out of here this evening. Sir Anthony had made it easier to decide which papers to keep and which to get rid of. She'd ditch the lot. Gathering all the stray classified papers into a pile, she started tearing them up, and shoving them into a confidential waste sack. The process of ripping them apart felt good, like she was purging herself of China, and her deceitful colleagues.

Next, she gathered up all the current files she'd been working on and piled them up on her desk to give to the Registry Clerk. He could put them away in the archives. When she crouched down to clear out the bottom of the cupboard, it was like a proverbial light bulb moment. She sat back on her heels in surprise.

There was the bundle of historic files about opening the new Consulate-General in 1984. He'd given them to her days ago for weeding. For God's sake, why hadn't she looked at them before? Surely, they'd contain the names of all the officers working in Shanghai back then.

Eagerly, she carried the files back to her desk and unwrapped the tape holding them together. The dust on them was so thick, she had to wipe it off with a tissue. Her enthusiasm was dampened when she saw they were all admin files. She flicked through the first, entitled 'Furniture'. Nothing but internal notes and letters between London and Shanghai about furniture shipments, and copies of bills of lading. She felt a twinge of sadness when she saw Marianne Henderson's signature at the bottom of letters. Always in blue ink, and with strong, forward-sloping strokes of the pen. After 34 years and no sightings of her, the poor woman had to be dead.

Jess checked all the letters from Shanghai to see if Justin Barber had sent any to confirm her suspicion that he'd been the other diplomat in Shanghai with Marianne at the time. There was nothing from him, or anyone else, on that file. Jess worked her way through the second file, which was all about office machinery. Again, everything seemed to come from Marianne. She'd done all the routine work.

When Jess picked up the third file, called 'Boiler and General Maintenance', she noticed it was much thicker than the others. What could be so interesting about boiler maintenance? She leafed through, looking for Justin Barber's name on any letters. Halfway, she came across several pages of hand-written notes. All in blue ink, and in Marianne's handwriting.

A shiver of excitement rippled through her when she turned the page and saw a photo of a snuff bottle! It had been stuck to a piece of white paper and put on file. Jess stared at the image. It was faded with age, but there was no mistaking it. She pulled the photo out of her jacket pocket and compared the two. The same!

Quickly, she went back to the first page of notes and started reading. It was a diary of what happened on the night of the Ambassador's murder, and the days after. She couldn't believe it. Marianne had recorded everything. It was all here, for everyone to see. But why had Marianne put this in a file like 'Boiler and General Maintenance'? Who was going to see it in there? Unless … unless, Marianne didn't *want* anyone else to see it. Perhaps she wanted to hide it from her colleagues in Shanghai? Why? Was she already suspicious of them?

Jess read every word Marianne had written over and over, shaking her head in disbelief from time to time, or murmuring 'Oh my God'. Now, she knew exactly what happened on the night the Ambassador died. It looked like he'd been sleeping with someone in his room, with the crumpled sheets, the champagne and condom wrapper. Suspicion had immediately fallen on Marianne, despite her strong denials. The Shanghai police had begun a murder investigation straightaway, with Marianne as the prime suspect. They'd accused her of murdering him by spiking the champagne with arsenic because he wouldn't leave his wife. In the diary, Jess discovered the Ambassador had been holding the snuff bottle in his hand when he died. That was its significance. But why was he holding it?

She frowned. If the Shanghai police thought the Ambassador was murdered and started a full investigation in China, how did that turn into 'death by suicide' in UK police records? That didn't make any sense.

Jess frantically turned the pages of the file, looking for more of Marianne's notes. There were none. She picked up the last file and flicked through. No more notes. Marianne's diary had ended abruptly on day 3 after the Ambassador's death. What happened after that? What happened to Marianne?

Jess flopped back in her chair with frustration. Then she sat forward again, rigid with shock. She picked up her photo of the snuff bottle again and looked at the writing on the back. 'Shanghai – 1984.' That handwriting, that blue ink …

It was the same as in Marianne's diary! Her heart fluttered with excitement. Was Marianne still alive? Did she send her that photo? She slipped Marianne's notes off the file, folded them up and put them in her handbag. Tying the files together again, she put them on the pile for the Registry Clerk.

She checked her watch. Oh my God – 7.15pm! She'd been locked in her office all that time. She looked at her new mobile. There were several texts from Tom asking what happened with Sir Anthony and if she was going to the Guildhall dinner?

Jess picked up her handbag to go out into the quadrangle to phone him. She stopped at the door and slipped on her coat. It would be freezing out there at this time of night.

★

Outside, Jess looked up at the sky and took a deep breath of air. It was clear, with no cloud cover. A huge moon lit up the cobbles in the quadrangle. She looked around all four sides of the rectangular building. There were no office lights on; everyone had gone home.

She pulled out her mobile. She wasn't allowed to phone Tom while he was on protection duty, only when he was resting. She hoped he'd be able to take her call now, she dearly wanted to talk to him. First, she texted: *Are you free for chat on the phone?*

His reply came back quickly. *No. In car with principal.*

Jess knew that meant he was physically in the car travelling with the Chinese President and couldn't chat. She didn't want to text him with the news of her meeting with Sir Anthony. She couldn't face everyone at the Guildhall dinner either, not now she'd been dismissed from the China desk. Still, they'd soon fill her seat at the top table when she didn't turn up, just like they'd replace her on the China desk. No one was indispensable. Not even Sir Anthony. There were plenty of officers breathing down his neck for the job.

She texted back. *I'm not going to Guildhall tonight. Will take a taxi home and tell you everything later.*

Right-o. You okay? – Tom

I'm fine –Jess

Of course, she wasn't fine. She was anything but fine. She looked around again, sadly. This might be the last time she ever saw this wonderful old building from the inside.

Suddenly a movement in the far corner of the quadrangle caught her eye. A dark shadow darted across the cobbles and walked quickly up the steps to the entrance diagonally opposite to where she stood. There was something familiar about that black coat and walk.

The figure stopped at the top of the steps and looked nervously over their shoulder. The moonlight shone down brightly, lighting up that face...

"Oh my God!" Jess stared with surprise, then the penny dropped. "*Marianne!*"

She darted back inside the building and ran around the corridors to the other side of the building, where Marianne had entered. No sign of her. Where would she go? Think, Jess, think.

Sam! Jess ran back to the staircase and down to the basement. She had to warn him.

Reaching the end of his corridor, she stopped. It was deathly quiet. Except ... she saw a light shining into the corridor from Sam's doorway. He was a night owl and always worked late. Tonight though, he wasn't alone, another voice came from inside his office.

Heart quickening, Jess tip-toed along to his office door, which was pushed to.

A strangled cry came from inside ... from Sam.

Jess put her eye to the crack in the door.

There was Bev, towering over Sam menacingly while he sat at his desk.

Except it wasn't Bev, it was Marianne! Back to take revenge on those who'd framed her all those years ago and left her to rot in China.

Face contorted with rage, Marianne picked up the small Chinese dagger that Sam used to open his mail and drew it from its sheath.

Sam sat frozen, his face white with shock.

Marianne darted behind his chair, put one arm around his neck in a strangle hold and held the tip of the sharp blade to his throat with the other. "Tell me why I shouldn't kill you right now?" she hissed.

"I–I knew this would happen one day." Sam's voice shook. "I knew you'd come for me. I just knew it."

"Why did you do it, you bastard?" she spat. "I was the only one who ever stood up for you, protected you. You all framed me, then you left me to the mercy of the Chinese security police."

"I'm sorry, Marianne. Truly sorry."

"Why?" she spat. "Why?"

Sam was wide-eyed with fear.

Still holding her arm tightly around his throat to stop him moving, Marianne switched the dagger to her other hand. Then she quickly picked up his treasured lacquer vase from his desk and hurled it at the door.

Jess ducked back as the vase smashed into the door and shattered into pieces on the floor.

"No, Marianne," Sam begged. "Don't. Please."

Peering through the crack again, Jess saw Marianne grab a cloisonné bowl from the top of the bookcase behind and smash it on the floor. Then a Chinese figurine, then another. Smashing up all the beautiful things Sam had in his office.

He sat like a rabbit in the headlights. Shocked. Paralysed. Petrified.

Marianne pushed the point of the dagger into his throat again. "Do you think I didn't know about your little scam. Buying all those antiques in China and smuggling them out of the country. You knew it was illegal. You knew you'd be sacked and prosecuted if you were found out. Yet you did it anyway. And I know how you did it. You posted them by mail to your address in the UK. Or you asked other members of the Embassy, innocent members of the Embassy, to post parcels for you whenever they visited Hong Kong."

"I'm sorry," Sam kept saying over and over.

"What else have you done, Sam? You've been in the pocket of the Chinese for over three decades. What else have you given the Chinese? You, treacherous scum!"

"H–he made me do it." Tears slipped from Sam's eyes now.

"Who?" Marianne shouted.

Sam shuddered, saying nothing.

"Well, you're going to tell the truth now," she hissed. "You're going to tell the police the Chinese discovered you smuggling antiques out of the country illegally in 1984. They blackmailed you and you've been in their pockets ever since. An agent of China. A spy!"

"I can't do that, Marianne. I can't. I don't care about myself. Really, I don't. You can cut my throat with that dagger now. God knows, I've been expecting you all these years. You can't imagine what it's been like."

"*I* can't imagine. I've been on the *run* for 34 years. Banished from my country, my home, my friends, my career. Everything I held dear was trashed by you lot. Don't expect me to feel sorry for you."

"You don't understand … they'll kill my wife and my son if I say anything. They've told me over and over. I can't do it, Marianne."

"You will," she shouted. "You will stand up in court, and you will tell everyone how you all killed the Ambassador and framed me for his murder."

"No. No. That's not right. I didn't kill him, Marianne." Sam was whimpering now. "I just gave Justin an alibi for that night. I said we were in Hangzhou together at the time of the murder. That's all."

"Who did kill the Ambassador, then? Justin?" She dug the point of the dagger into Sam's throat until droplets of blood trickled down his neck.

"It wasn't Justin either. It was Mrs Wu." Sam was broken now. "She p-put the arsenic in the champagne. She k-killed the Ambassador because he'd found out *she* was having an affair with *Justin*. The Ambassador c-confronted Justin, told him to stop the relationship immediately." Sam's words were coming out in short bursts. "Justin wanted to, but Wu had such a hold over him. She wouldn't let him go. She *made* Justin help her kill the Ambassador. They had a room in the hotel, just along the corridor from the Ambassador's. That's how they did it. It was Mrs Wu who turned Justin into a spy for China. I've had to do what they've told me to, all these years. They threatened to kill my wife and son. I did it to protect my family, don't you see?"

As she finally heard the full truth, Marianne slumped down as if someone had punched all the air out of her. Her grip on the dagger slackened.

That's when Sam took his opportunity. He jumped out, barged Marianne out of the way with his shoulder and made a dash for the door.

Jess jumped out of the way as he came hurtling through it.

Marianne picked herself and the dagger up from the floor and ran after him. She was so focused on Sam, she stared right through Jess.

"*Marianne,*" Jess shouted after her. "I heard everything. I heard Sam confess. You aren't alone with this any longer. Bev … Marianne … *please, stop!*"

But Marianne wasn't stopping.

Jess ran after them, and up the staircase to the ground floor. Sam must be heading for the exit, to get out of the building, she thought. But no, he just kept running up the stairs, with Marianne following.

Jess went after them, but she was nowhere near as fast. Her padded coat was slowing her down. She thought about stopping to take it off, but she couldn't. Marianne was going to kill Sam. Jess had to try and stop her. She pushed the strap of her handbag over her head and across her body. Now her hands were free, she used her arms to propel herself up the stairs.

Up ahead, she could see Sam reach the top floor. He turned right and ran down the corridor. Marianne followed. So did she. On her right now were offices overlooking Durbar Court. Where on earth was Sam going?

At the end, he turned the corner. *Oh God!* The offices in that corridor had balconies. *Now* she knew what he was going to do. She had to stop him. Stop Marianne.

Jess reached the corner to see Sam burst through an office door at the far end, with Marianne following.

When Jess reached the door, she was breathing so hard she was almost bent over double. She stood to adjust her eyes, then heard voices on the balcony. She rushed over to the open, glass doors and looked outside.

Sam had climbed up on the stone balustrade, and was holding onto a marble column, getting ready to jump.

Jess gasped and went out onto the balcony. "Don't do it, Sam." She tried to keep her voice low and calm so as not to upset him. "We can talk about this, work things out."

She looked at Marianne, hoping she would say something to persuade him to come down.

Marianne just stared at Sam.

"I can't talk about this," he said. "I can't confess. Justin told me he would have my family killed if I do. I believe him. He's so powerful now. So is Mrs Wu. No one can stop them. No one."

"You're wrong, Sam," Jess said. "You'll be protected if you give evidence. The police can protect your family too, give them new identities, a fresh start somewhere."

Sam gave a harsh laugh. "The police are hand-in-hand with the Security Services. I won't survive that." Looking exhausted and defeated, he slumped down to sit on the balustrade. He was facing Jess and Marianne, with his legs dangling over the side. If she could just grab his arm, Jess thought, she could pull him to safety.

He looked over at Jess, then at Marianne. His face was ghostly, as if he was already dead. Perhaps he'd been dead inside for a long time. All those years of treachery and deceit. Blackmailed to betray his country, over what? A few Chinese antiques. That was the hook. Then he was trapped for life, fearing for those he loved the most – his wife and son.

"Come on, Sam," Jess said. "Talk to us. We can work things out." Even as she spoke, her words sounded hollow. She knew he would spend the rest of his life in jail for what he'd done.

He gave her a sad smile, as if reading her thoughts.

He turned to Marianne, eyes full of grief. "There hasn't been a single day over the last 34 years that I haven't thought of you, Marianne. It's been torture not knowing what happened to you. In my nightmares, you were locked up in a Chinese prison, and dying with no one to help you. It's been too much to bear. I beg you to forgive me. *Please!*"

There was a pause.

Then Marianne let out a strangled sob and reached for him.

Sam was too quick. He opened his arms wide and fell backwards over the balustrade.

Jess stood in shock, time suspended, until she heard a thud on the ground below. She gasped and ran to look over the balustrade.

Below, Sam lay spread-eagled, face down on the ground. A trickle of crimson blood flowed from his head, snaking across the white marble.

"Sam," she whispered. "Oh my God, Sam."

When she turned, Marianne had gone.

Jess looked over the balustrade at Sam again, then ran to the door. "Come back, Marianne," she shouted. "It's over. You don't have to run anymore."

Her words just echoed around the empty corridor. That's when she realised Marianne was not yet finished.

Jess ran back to the staircase in time to look over the banister and see Marianne reach the ground floor and turn right. Jess knew where Marianne was going. She ran down the steps as fast as her feet could carry her. Down and down she went, head spinning, lungs bursting. At the bottom, she turned right, and headed for Sir Anthony's office. She was sure that's where Marianne was going.

Running through the corridor alongside Durbar Court, she saw Sam lying on the marble floor. Could he still be alive? She hesitated, then dived through a door and fell onto her knees beside him. "Sam," she whispered, hoping he might stir. She reached forward and slipped her fingers around to the side of his throat. No pulse. She felt desperately around the area. Still no pulse. She put her fingers to his left wrist. Absolutely nothing. She looked up at the balcony. No one could survive a fall like that onto this hard marble floor.

"Hey!" A voice shouted out from above. "What's happened?"

Jess saw a security officer on evening patrol leaning out of one of the office windows.

"Call an ambulance," she shouted. "He's just thrown himself off the top balcony."

"Christ Almighty," came the response. The security officer ducked back into the office.

Jess dragged herself up and ran on towards Sir Anthony's office.

She barged through the door. His outer office was all in darkness. "*Marianne!*" she shouted, as she ran into Sir Anthony's room.

Then she stopped dead in surprise.

Marianne did not have Sir Anthony in a headlock. Nor did she have the Chinese dagger at his throat. She was sobbing in his arms.

Sir Anthony's eyes glistened as he held Marianne and stroked her hair.

Jess stood staring at them both, until Sir Anthony gestured to her to come in and shut the door.

Jess did as she was told.

"Come on Marianne." Sir Anthony helped her over to the sofa to sit down. Then he went around closing all the curtains so that no one could see in.

"Get her a brandy, Jess." He pointed to a drinks cabinet in the corner.

Jess went over, found the brandy and poured some into a glass.

Sir Anthony glanced at her. "You look like you could do with one too. I know I certainly could."

Jess nodded and poured out two more glasses. Balancing them in her hands, she went over and gave one to Marianne, and then one to Sir Anthony.

He was sitting next to Marianne on the sofa, stroking her face. "I can't believe you're alive." His voice choked with emotion. "I thought after all these years you must be dead. I, well, I thought you hadn't made it out of China." He pulled a handkerchief out of his trouser pocket and blew his nose. "I've always blamed myself for not escorting you safely out of the country."

Marianne stopped sobbing and looked up at him. "You've got nothing to be sorry for, Anthony. You saved my life. It's taken me all these years to come back and say thank you."

Jess couldn't believe what she was seeing and hearing. She swigged back her brandy in one go, almost choking as the fiery liquid seared her throat.

Marianne looked over. "I'm sorry, Jess. I involved you in all this without thinking through the consequences. Now I've got you into trouble." Her words caught in her throat. "I know what happened last night. I know someone tried to run you over."

Sir Anthony's eyes narrowed as he looked at Jess. "Why didn't you tell me this earlier?"

"Would it have made any difference?" Jess lifted the hair back from her face. "I'd been at the Lancaster House reception for the Chinese President. I was walking up St James's Street when a car mounted the pavement and accelerated at me. I dived out of the way and hit my head." She pointed at the stitches. "These, are the result."

Sir Anthony downed his brandy, then got up and poured himself another one.

"This is all my fault," said Marianne. "It was news of the Chinese President's state visit that got to me in the end, and Mrs Wu's appointment as Chinese Ambassador to London. I just had to come back."

Jess nodded. "I found the old 1984 files from Shanghai. I read your diary, Marianne. I know what happened on the night the Ambassador died. Your diary suddenly stopped after three days. Why?"

Marianne sighed. "When I realised I was being framed for having an affair with the Ambassador and murdering him, I was terrified. The police went out to search my house and I thought they'd planted evidence to make me look guilty. When London waived my diplomatic immunity, I realised I would be charged and tried for murder. That's when I knew there was no hope for me. So, I ran away. I had planned to go down to the border with Hong Kong to try and get across, but I was desperate, not thinking straight. I had no passport or other ID with me. Anyway, I caught the train out of Shanghai. My first stop was Hangzhou." She looked over. "That's where Anthony found me."

He gave Marianne a small smile. "You always said the West Lake at Hangzhou was your favourite spot in China. I guessed you'd be there, somewhere. And you were."

Jess turned back to Marianne, with a burning curiosity. "How did you get out of China? How did you get away?"

Marianne sighed. "Anthony gave me a new British passport in Hangzhou, issued by our Embassy in Peking."

"Surely all the ports were on alert for you?" Jess said.

"They were," Marianne said. "But they weren't looking for Beverly Simpson. That's the name my new passport was in."

Jess stared at Sir Anthony. "A false passport?"

He nodded. "Giles Pettiford was working temporarily in the Consular Section of the Embassy at the time. I got hold of Marianne's details, date and place of birth, mother and father's names to issue her with a new passport, but when it came to it, we knew she wouldn't get out of the country using her own name. So, we made up a fictitious passport application in the name of Beverly Simpson. Giles issued a genuine passport and put a photo of Marianne in it. We had one of her on file, you see."

Jess raised her eyebrows. "That was illegal."

"Yes, but I didn't believe for one minute that Marianne had had an affair with the Ambassador," he said. "You wouldn't have either, if you'd have known him."

"Who else knew what you'd done?" Jess asked.

"No one else. Only Giles and me." He shook his head as if he didn't quite believe what he'd done himself. "We knew we had to get Marianne out of China as quickly as possible," Sir Anthony went on. "If the Chinese police had arrested her and charged her with murder, she'd have had no chance. She'd never have got away. We had to do it, you see." He turned to Marianne. "Don't tell me you've been in England all this time?"

She shook her head. "I flew out of China to Hong Kong. From there, I went to Australia. I'd only planned to go for a year or so but, as things turned out, Beverly Simpson started a new life in Australia. She met her Australian husband, Sam Talbot, and became Beverly Talbot and eventually an Australian citizen." She smiled. "Sam and I started a business together. A vineyard. A very successful one too. We have two children."

Sir Anthony beamed with delight. "I wish I'd known," he kept saying. "I've worried about you for the past 30 years, Marianne. My goodness how I've worried. I couldn't bear the thought of you being caught in China and imprisoned." He shook his head. "I'm so glad you got away. So glad you've had a good life." He frowned. "Why have you come back, after all this time?"

Marianne gave him a dark look. "I told myself I would come back and find out the truth, but my desire for revenge is greater. I wanted to confront those who framed me in Shanghai."

Suddenly, alarm bells screeched out all around the building.

Sir Anthony jumped up. "What's going on?"

"Oh God," Jess said. "Sam Biggins jumped off the top floor balcony when Marianne confronted him. One of the security officers found his body. He must have raised the alarm."

Sir Anthony frowned. "You confronted Sam Biggins? About what?"

"Framing me for the Ambassador's murder," Marianne said, harshly.

"No." Sir Anthony went over to the door and locked it. "Sam can't have. That's not right."

"It *is* right," Jess said. "He just admitted it before he killed himself. *And* he said it was Mrs Wu who put the arsenic in the Ambassador's champagne in the Peace Hotel."

There was a banging on the door from outside. "You all right, Sir," a deep voice shouted.

Sir Anthony put his finger to his lips for Jess and Marianne to be quiet. "Yes." He shouted back. "What's going on out there? When I heard the security alarm, I locked the door for safety."

"Nothing to worry about, Sir, it's just a precaution. We've got a casualty out here, but we're dealing with it. Keep this door locked until we sound the all clear. Just routine, you understand."

"Very well. Phone me when everything's secure."

"Yes, Sir."

Sir Anthony started pacing around his office. He looked at Jess and Marianne. "I don't understand what you're saying about Sam Biggins. And what's Mrs Wu got to do with it?" He paused to marshal his thoughts. "The Ambassador was having an affair in Shanghai, with a Chinese woman, although we never found out who the woman was. It was a honeytrap, set up by the Chinese government. They blackmailed the Ambassador into passing over some classified documents."

Jess frowned at him. "The Chinese police launched a murder enquiry when he was found dead in the Peace Hotel, didn't they?"

"Yes."

"And Marianne was accused of having an affair with the Ambassador and murdering him when he wouldn't leave his wife. Right?"

"Yes."

"So, how did that become death by suicide?"

"Ah that." He looked down at his shoes. "I'm ashamed to say we struck a deal with the Chinese. A damage limitation exercise." He sighed. "We believed the Chinese had the Ambassador killed because he was going to confess what he'd done to the British government. The thing is, neither we, nor the Chinese, had anything to gain by him doing that. Quite the reverse. How would it have gone down in the UK if everyone had known the Ambassador was effectively spying for China? It would have damaged the reputation of the Foreign Office." He shuddered at the thought. "And if everyone had found out that the Chinese killed him, well, that would have damaged our bilateral relationship irreparably." He shook his head. "Both sides agreed that the death should be officially recorded as suicide, and that we would cover up the whole unfortunate episode." He started pacing again. "It made sense for the Ambassador to commit suicide anyway, after what he'd done. Just imagine if the media and public had found out. That was *unthinkable*."

"You've got it all wrong," Marianne said, crossly. "You've been taken in by them too."

His black eyes bore into her.

"I knew I'd been set up my colleagues," she said, "but I didn't know who'd done it." She looked at him. "I couldn't be sure it wasn't you either."

He looked taken back.

"Don't you see," Marianne said to him. "The Ambassador *wasn't* having an affair at all. Not with anybody. And he was *never* a spy. It was *Justin* who was having the affair, with Mrs Wu. She was working in the British Consulate-General in Shanghai at the time as our Chinese interpreter. It was indeed a honeytrap set by the Chinese government, but not involving the Ambassador. Involving Justin. The Ambassador found out and confronted Justin. That's why Justin and Mrs Wu killed him. It was Mrs Wu who put the poison in the champagne bottle." She paused. "So, you see, it *was* murder, Anthony. It was Mrs Wu who actually killed him."

Sir Anthony stood frozen to the spot.

Marianne went on. "Mrs Wu turned Justin into a spy for China all those years ago, and she wasn't about to let him off the hook. No, she wanted him trapped for life. That's why the Ambassador had to be silenced. The only way to do that was to kill him." She shook her head. "Justin's probably been the most prolific British traitor since Philby, Burgess and McLean. Except, he's been spying for China, rather than Russia."

Sir Anthony went over to his drinks cabinet and poured himself another brandy. "And this has been going on under our noses … under *my* nose … all this time." He glanced over again. "How does Sam Biggins fit into all this?"

Marianne sighed. "He was smuggling Chinese antiques, mostly porcelain, pottery and snuff bottles, out of the country while on a temporary posting to Peking. The Ambassador must have found that out too. That's why Justin and Mrs Wu put that snuff bottle in the Ambassador's hand while he was dying. They wanted to make sure Sam was implicated too, for life."

Sir Anthony put his head in his hands.

"Anyway," Marianne said. "Sam said Justin blackmailed him into giving him an alibi on the night the Ambassador was murdered. Justin and Sam were in Hangzhou earlier on the day of the murder. They'd been there buying more antiques. The truth is they both returned to Shanghai well before the murder." She shook her head. "I believed Sam when he said wasn't involved in the murder, but he was still complicit in framing me. He admitted it before jumping off that balcony."

Jess nodded. "I heard it all too. Sam also said that Justin pushed Giles under that tube train the other night."

"B–but why?" Sir Anthony stuttered.

"Because Giles was going to the police," Jess said.

"Oh, dear God!" Sir Anthony sat down at his desk. "This is all my fault. I was pressing Giles to retire. He had onset early dementia, you see. The doctors were telling me he would only get worse. Except, well, he didn't want to go."

"Why did Giles get sent home from Peking on his first posting?" Jess asked. "What did he do wrong."

"He didn't do anything wrong." Sir Anthony gave a deep sigh. "He had a nervous breakdown. He was always a little, well, eccentric, even as a young man. He could be mercurial, unpredictable, but this was a full–blown collapse. It just happened one day. He couldn't even get out of bed. We arranged for him to be sent home for rest and recuperation. Back then, of course, there was a stigma attached to mental health issues. We knew Giles would never be able to pick up his career again if people knew the full extent of his illness. That's why we never told anyone."

"So, the suggestion of early retirement must have really upset him," said Jess.

Sir Anthony nodded. "He was angry, resentful. You see, we'd always been competitors along the way, Giles, Justin and me. "Well, Giles said if I made him retire, he would expose me and tell everyone we'd deliberately issued a murder suspect with a false passport to leave Shanghai and escape justice. He wanted to ruin my career in the same way he thought I was trying to ruin his." He frowned.

"How on earth would Justin have found out about my conversation with Giles?"

Marianne looked horrified. "Your office is probably bugged by MI6."

Sir Anthony stood up. "You have to go now, both of you. I can't guarantee your safety." He turned to Marianne. "Go back to Australia. Go back to your life, your husband and family, where you'll be safe. *You* can't stop Justin Barber or Mrs Wu, but *I* can. It's going to take time and cunning, and a lot of surveillance, to get the evidence to convict them. While I have any breath in my body, I'll make sure they're both brought to justice for what they've done." He turned to Jess, with a pained look in his eyes. "I'm sorry, but you have to go with Marianne."

Jess shook her head. "I'm not running away."

"You can't stay in the UK. You *must* leave, for your own safety."

She hesitated. "I could go and stay with my partner in Paris for a few weeks. I've cleared my office and papers."

He looked at her, sadly, and shook his head.

"Why not?"

He went back to his desk and picked up her personnel file. He pulled a photo from the file and handed it to her.

Jess's stomach lurched. There was Simon, with another woman. They were holding hands, and kissing. The Notre Dame Cathedral was clearly in the background, which confirmed it was taken in Paris. Pulling the photo closer, she recognised the woman, and looked up at Sir Anthony.

He nodded. "I'm sorry, Jess. It started in Washington when she worked for him as his secretary. He ended the affair when he came back to London for his cancer treatment. But, well, she applied for a secretarial job in the Embassy in Paris when she knew he was there. HR, in their wisdom, agreed to it."

Jess's hands were shaking as she handed him back the photo. The shock was unbearable, but it all fitted. That's why Simon was so cool about the future, and so conflicted about having a baby, at least with her. Why hadn't he told her? Why did she have to find out this way?

Marianne came up and looked at the photo over Jess's shoulder. She put her arm around her in sympathy.

The sound of sirens wailing in the distance filled the night.

"They're coming," Sir Anthony said. "You have to go, before anyone sees you." He went over and switched off the lights. Then he went to the large sash window overlooking Horse Guards Parade, drew back one curtain and pulled up the window. "The building will be in lockdown by now. Go out of this window. No one will see you."

Marianne reacted quickly and gave him a big hug. "Thank you, Anthony … again."

Jess shook her head. "I'm not going. I'm not running away."

"You *must*," he said. "You can't fight them, and this is going to take some time to sort out. I will do it. I promise you. Until then, it's too dangerous for you to stay here." He pushed her towards the open window. "Go!" he ordered. "Get of the country as quickly as you can. Both of you."

Marianne didn't need persuading. She climbed out the window first, with ease.

Jess sat on the windowsill and looked back at Sir Anthony. Could they really trust him to stop Justin and Mrs Wu? Bring them to justice?

"*Go!*" he hissed.

She stared into his eyes. "I *will* be back." She rolled sideways out of the window, landing on the grass outside.

Marianne pulled her to her feet. "Quick. Let's climb over the railings and get out of here."

They ran over to the railings together.

"Here," Marianne said. "Take my hand. I'll help you over. I'll always be there to help you, Jess."

31

Wherever you go, go with all your heart
(Confucius)

"*Hurry up!*" Marianne was pacing around Jess's flat, looking at her watch. "We've been here too long."

Jess pulled jeans, shirts and jumpers out of the wardrobe, and threw them into her overnight bag. She grabbed several changes of underwear and flung them in too. "What do I need to take?" she shouted.

Marianne walked into the bedroom. "Just a change of clothes. We can buy whatever you need once we're out of the country." She went over to the closed curtains and peeked out.

"Anyone there?" Jess flopped down on the bed, wearily.

"No." Marianne turned. "What *are* you doing?"

"I'm sorry, Marianne. I can't leave."

"For goodness sake. You heard what Anthony said. We both need to get away until this is all over."

Jess shook her head. "I'm going to drive you to the ferry, make sure you get safely away. But I'm not letting them force me out of the country. Besides, I've got to talk to Simon."

"Simon?" Marianne gave her a horrified look. "Forget him. He doesn't deserve you."

"I don't want him back. It's just that, well, we need to sort things out. This flat to start with. It belongs to both of us. I can't just up-sticks and run away."

"Oh, Jess." Marianne walked over and cupped her hands around her face. "Please understand. They'll kill you if they catch you. Me too. Justin will face a life sentence and public disgrace if all this gets out. He'll do anything to avoid that. Anything."

"There must be a way." Jess frowned. "I know some investigative journalists … we could give them the story."

Marianne shook her head. "Leave it to Anthony. He promised to get them, and I believe he will."

"You have more faith in him than I do."

"I do." Marianne pulled her to her feet. "Come on. We must get out of here."

Jess stood up, reluctantly. "Why the Hull ferry anyway?"

"That was always my escape route," Marianne said. "I've got tickets for the car ferry to Zeebrugge tomorrow morning. You can easily come too."

"But why Hull?"

"Because I'm betting Justin won't think of that. They'll stake out Heathrow, Gatwick, London City Airport, and maybe some of the regional airports, and the Eurostar. They may even watch the ferries from Dover, or Folkestone." She shrugged. "They won't be expecting us to head north."

"You've thought it all out, then?"

Marianne's eyes turned steely. "I've had *many* years to plan this. What I didn't plan for was compromising your career and safety. I'm sorry, Jess." She ran her fingers through her hair. "You must come with me. You can't stay here without protection."

"I've got Tom."

"What? And put him in danger too. Ruin his career? Please Jess, I feel responsible enough as it is. I involved you. I put you in danger. At least let me help you escape."

"Why did you involve me anyway?"

"I read about you in the Australian papers when you were the British Consul in Canberra. You helped catch the killer of that businesswoman in Brisbane." Marianne paused. "I couldn't believe my luck when you were given the China desk job in London. *Finally*, I thought, someone with some integrity and determination. Someone who would want to dig out the truth."

"I'm flattered," Jess said, drily. "But that's exactly why I don't want to leave the country."

Marianne wasn't listening. "I found out where you lived. I rented the ground floor flat in this block to be near you, to get to know you."

"At least I know now why you had that CCTV camera rigged up in your flat."

Marianne frowned. "You saw that?"

Jess nodded. "Through your sitting room window late one night."

"Then I'm sure you also realise that it was me who sent you the photo of the snuff bottle."

"Yes."

"It was the only thing ... the only piece of evidence I brought out of China with me. You were my last hope. And you didn't disappoint me." Marianne's voice cracked. "I'm so sorry, Jess. I never thought it would come to this. Never."

"And Xiao Li," Jess asked. "What about her?"

Marianne's shoulders slumped. "I didn't mean for her to get involved." She sighed. "I sent Mrs Wu a photo of the snuff bottle too. I wrote 'Shanghai 1984' in blue ink on the back, just like the one I sent you. Except, on hers, I also wrote 'Marianne Henderson is alive and well'. She looked at Jess. "Sometimes you don't have to do much. You just let people know you're onto them and they do themselves in. They get jumpy, start contacting people, get out of their routines." She shrugged. "That's all it took."

"God, Marianne."

"That's one of the reasons I came back, because of Mrs Wu." Marianne had a far-away look in her eyes. "You see, I was in the garden of the Consulate-General one afternoon after the Ambassador's death, still blissfully unaware they were trying to frame me for his murder." She shook her head. "I remember it so clearly. I was talking to her. Even back then, as a young woman, she wanted to be called Mrs Wu. It was to give herself authority but even I didn't understand how dangerous she was. She told me quite confidently that she would be the Chinese Ambassador in London one day. Well, you can just imagine my reaction all these years later when I saw on the BBC website that she was being appointed Ambassador here. That was the final straw. I just had to come back."

"So, why did Xiao Li come to me? Why did she want to tell me?"

Marianne shrugged. "I don't know what went on inside the Chinese Embassy. Xiao Li must have found out about it somehow. Perhaps she saw the snuff bottle photo? Perhaps she had the job of opening the Ambassador's mail. I don't really know how she got involved."

Jess frowned. "She must have talked to her Ambassador, Mrs Wu, about it. That led to Mrs Wu contacting Justin and Sam. They met up in the park. I saw them." She looked at Marianne. "Then I saw Mrs Wu talking privately to Justin in a small alcove at Lancaster House, during the President's welcoming drinks. They were standing close to each other, intimate even. Well, that set alarm bells ringing."

Marianne beamed. "It flushed them all out."

"Xiao Li must have worked out that something wasn't right with Mrs Wu. Perhaps she was just a nightmare to work for. I can imagine she would be, and that's why Xiao Li wanted to tell me about Marianne Henderson being alive." Jess sighed. "Perhaps she has a conscience and thought what they did to you was wrong."

Marianne nodded.

Jess sighed. "Well, at least now we know the truth. We know who killed the Ambassador in Shanghai and why. We know the part Sam Biggins played, and he's dead. But we're no nearer to nailing the real killers – Justin and Mrs Wu. And we're no nearer to exposing Justin for the traitor he is – the Deputy Chief of MI6, for God's sake." She stared at Marianne. "We can't just disappear and let them get away with it."

"We *won't* let them get away with it," Marianne said. "Anthony knows the truth now. He's an influential man, *and* a force to be reckoned with. I believe him when he says he'll get them both, over time."

Jess wasn't so sure. If *she'd* worked things out in the six months she'd been on the China desk, why hadn't *he* in the past 34 years? But then, he probably hadn't wanted to know, because that would mean him owning up to the murky part he played in providing Marianne with a false passport and a way out of China to avoid a murder charge, even if it was trumped up.

Marianne grabbed her arm. "We must go. *Now!*"

Jess picked up her handbag and pulled out her mobile. "I can't go without telling Tom. I gave him a set of keys last night. I'm expecting him back later."

"No!" Marianne put her hand over the mobile to stop her. "No police. They're not going to do anything to help."

"Oh, come on…"

"They won't." Marianne protested. "I rang the Met Police from Shanghai. I told them everything. I asked them for help. And did I get any? No, I did not." She shook her head, fiercely. "I have no faith in any police. None whatsoever. They're the leakiest organisation going, too."

Jess shook her head. "Tom is totally trustworthy. I wouldn't be here now if he hadn't saved my life in Brisbane. And that's the truth."

Marianne pulled a face. "You'll have to leave your mobile behind. They can track you on that."

"Not on this one they can't." Jess held up her second mobile. "Tom bought it for me, to contact him in an emergency. It's pay-as-you-go. They won't know about this one." She looked at the phone and raised her eyebrows. "Oh, there are several texts from him already." She went quiet as she read them, then looked up at Marianne. "Every text says the same thing." She turned the phone towards Marianne.

BEVERLY TALBOT IS MARIANNE HENDERSON!

Marianne's face turned white. "How the hell did he find out?"

Jess gave a wry smile. "He thought something wasn't quite right with you and checked you out with his Australian colleagues."

"They don't know."

Jess shrugged. "Then he's probably worked it out for himself."

The phone rang in her hand, making Jess jump. She looked at the number: "It's Tom."

"Don't answer!"

Jess ignored her. "Tom?"

"Jess," he whispered. "Put your mobile on speaker so that Marianne can hear this too. Then just listen, we don't have much time."

She frowned and did as he said. "Go ahead."

"I know you and Marianne are in your flat at present, and I know you're getting to ready to leave."

"How on…?"

"Please just listen, Jess." He took a breath. "That grey car is parked on Prince Albert Road, just along from the flat. It's waiting for you to come out."

Marianne gasped.

"There's another MI6 surveillance car parked in Martin Street, alongside your flat. You must *not* go out the front door of your apartment block or get into Marianne's black Fiat."

Jess gave Marianne a look of despair.

"Listen, Jess," he said. "I'm parked in a dark blue Audi Q3 in Morgan Street, a block back from your flat. You know where I mean?"

"Yes. Whose car is it?"

"I hired it earlier, to get around more easily. Now, this is what you must do," he said, authoritatively. "Go down the staircase and exit through the *back* door of your building, into the courtyard. You'll have to climb over the wall, into the garden of Duchess Court. That's the apartment block behind yours." He paused. "Can you do that?"

"Yes." Jess and Marianne said in unison.

"I'm going to walk along to the front door of Duchess Court now. It's close to where I'm parked. I'll ring all the buzzers until someone lets me in. Then I'll go through to the back door and let you both into the building."

"What if no one lets you in?" Jess asked.

"They will, I'm a police officer."

"Oh, Tom."

"Don't worry, it'll be fine," he said. "Now go on. Do it. I'll let you into Duchess Court. We can exit through the front door, jump into my car, and drive away."

"Right." Marianne was already on the move. "Let's go, Jess."

"Hey, Jess…" Tom paused. "See you on the other side." And with that he was gone.

Jess hung up and looked at Marianne.

There must have been real sorrow in that look because Marianne's face was full of pain. "There's no turning back now, Jess," she said, softly. "They're onto us … both."

How the hell had it come to this, Jess wondered? All she'd ever done was the best job she could. Now she was being forced out of her flat, out of her life, and out of the country she loved.

"Jess…?"

She gave a resigned sigh and picked up her overnight bag. In the hallway, she laid her old mobile on the table, and looked around her flat for the last time. Her heart squeezed with sadness. "Goodbye Simon," she whispered.

Marianne gave her a sympathetic hug.

Jess opened the front door and peered out. All clear. She stepped out, followed by Marianne, and closed the door firmly behind her. "Right. Follow me, I know the way."

She looked over the bannister into the stairwell. All quiet. She crept down the stairs, followed by Marianne. Every few steps she stopped to listen. Only their own footsteps and nervous breathing echoed back.

She stopped on the ground floor and peered round at the front door. No sign of anyone in the lobby. She beckoned Marianne to follow her.

Quickly, they went out of the back door. Freezing rain blew in Jess's face and she shivered. She looked up at the wall dividing the grounds between the two blocks of flats. It was much higher than she remembered.

Marianne was already pulling one of the wheelie bins over to the wall. "If we climb up on here, it'll be easier to get over."

It still looked too high to Jess. "You go first. You're fitter than me."

"Right-o." Marianne quickly hoisted her rucksack onto her back and clambered up onto the bin. She was able to pull herself up onto the top of the wall and straddle the top. "Hand me up your bag."

Jess pushed her overnight bag up towards her.

Marianne grabbed it, then lowered it down the other side, letting it fall the rest of the way. Then she lowered herself down the other side. "I'm down," she whispered. "Your turn."

The wheelie bin was slippery in the rain, and Jess couldn't get a grip. She looked around and found an old beer crate. Pulling that over, she stepped onto it to help her climb onto the bin and grabbed the top of the wall with both hands. She winced as the sharp edges of the bricks cut into her hands, but she managed to haul herself up onto the top. As she swung one leg over and straddled the top, she could just glimpse the street where the surveillance car was parked.

"*Stay down*," Marianne hissed.

Jess lay flat on the top of the wall, swung her other leg over, and started lowering herself down the other side.

Marianne grabbed her legs and pulled her down quickly.

Suddenly a security light lit up the back garden. They stood paralysed. The back door of Duchess Court opened. "Jess!" a familiar voice called.

"*Tom!*"

"Come on," he beckoned.

They ran into Duchess Court.

"You okay?" he asked Jess, as he closed the door and took her bag.

"Relieved now you're here." She gave him a hug.

"Don't hang around." Marianne was impatient to get going.

They hurried through Duchess Court, and out of the front door into the dark night.

Tom stopped to look all around. "This way." He set off down Morgan Street, and they followed him to the car.

Unlocking the Audi, he ran around to the driver's door, and they all piled in. "Where to?" He started the car.

"Hull," Jess said.

"*Hull?*"

"Yes, we're going north," Jess said, "to the port of Hull to catch the ferry to Zeebrugge. That's in Belgium."

"Then we're getting flights to Singapore," Marianne said. "Then on to Australia."

Jess fastened her seat belt. "The problem is Marianne already has tickets for her black Fiat and herself on the ferry, but we can't take that car now." She glanced at him. "Will you drop us at King's Cross. We'll have to make our way north by train."

"*Drop* you?" He shook his head. "I'll take you."

"You can't drive us all the way to Hull," Jess said. "What about work in the morning?"

"My stuff's in the back. I'm coming with you."

Jess looked horrified. "You can't, Tom."

"I'm not leaving you to deal with this by yourselves." He put up his hand when Jess started protesting again. "It's decided. I'm coming too."

"Oh, Tom. You'll ruin everything … your career."

"No, I won't. I only had one more day of the Chinese President's visit to go, then I was due to go back to Australia. I'll come on the ferry with you two."

Jess looked at him. "Oh, I'm not going. I just want to make sure Marianne gets away safely."

"You have to come with me," Marianne insisted. "Tell her, Tom. It's for her own safety."

He looked at Jess. "You know she's right," he said, softly.

"Look, can we just get going," Jess said. "Before anyone sees us."

Tom drove swiftly to the next crossroads, turned right in a northerly direction, away from Prince Albert Road, and away from the surveillance cars. At every turning, Jess gave him directions. "We're heading for the Finchley Road, then following the signs for the M1," she said.

Tom nodded. "Hull, here we come."

For a long while, the three of them were tense and silent. The only communication came from Jess, giving Tom directions as necessary. He kept looking nervously in the driver's mirror. Marianne, in the back, constantly turned to look out the window. All they could see were headlights. Later, as they got onto the M1 and Tom set the cruise control just under the speed limit, they started to relax a little. The traffic was light at that time of night and they were making good progress.

Tom was burning to know everything that had happened and kept asking questions. Marianne sat in the middle of the back seat, doing all the talking, updating him about everything.

Tom frowned. "Let me get this straight." He glanced in the driver's mirror. "Are you saying that Sir Anthony really believed that the Ambassador had been caught in a honeytrap. That he'd had an affair with a Chinese woman and been blackmailed into handing over secret papers."

Marianne nodded. "It's been a particularly successful way some security services have operated for decades. They find people's weaknesses, or something they've done wrong. Then they blackmail them into doing whatever they want, by threatening to expose them."

Tom nodded.

"At the time, the Foreign Office believed the Ambassador had been murdered by the Chinese," Marianne went on.

"Of course, the Chinese would never have admitted it. Their original intention was to kill him, or rather for Mrs Wu to kill him, and frame me for his murder. That's why they launched a murder investigation immediately. But when I disappeared, they had no one to blame and put on trial. No show trial to televise to the nation and exonerate themselves." She paused. "So, the British and Chinese governments agreed to cover it all up."

"You've lost me." Tom gave her a puzzled look in the mirror. "Why would the British government cover something like that up? What did they have to gain?"

"Oh, come on, Tom." Marianne sounded exasperated. "If the British Ambassador in Shanghai had been exposed as a spy for the Chinese, just think of the media frenzy there would have been in the UK. The embarrassment for the Foreign Office, and the British government. There would have been enquiry after enquiry for years, and everyone's names dragged through the mud for allowing this to go on under their noses. Careers would have been ruined, both for those at the top of the Foreign Office and Ministers. No, that wouldn't have done." She paused. "Why do you think the Cambridge spies were able to flee to Russia? Because relations were so bad with the Russians, the government knew it would be easier all round to let them disappear into the wilds of Russia. They would have no power, and no influence over there. More importantly, they would never be allowed back into the UK. And that was much better than having them put on trial and in prison in the UK, with all the public scrutiny that would entail."

"I suppose."

"And what if the media had found out that the Chinese murdered the Ambassador? My God! That would have destroyed the UK/China bilateral relationship forever," Marianne said. "The British government would never want that. China is too big and important a country."

Tom looked pensive. "Would the two governments have actually sat down and written up some formal agreement to cover it all up."

"Hardly." Marianne gave a harsh laugh. "It would have been agreed with the Chinese by the Head of the MI6 station in Peking perhaps, or by the next Ambassador. Of course, those at the top of government would have known. There might even be a document somewhere in the Intelligence archives recording everything. That won't ever see the light of day."

"Stinks, doesn't it?" he said, quietly.

"Good and proper," said Marianne. "Don't forget the times back then. There was no Internet. No global communications. No social media. No mobile phones. Nothing like that. Secrecy and cover-ups were so much easier to deliver. No one could get away with that now." She paused. "At least I hope not."

He glanced over at Jess. "What about your boss, Giles, then?"

"Giles is my big regret," Marianne said from the back seat. "I didn't have the opportunity to thank him for helping me escape from Shanghai." She sighed. "He was working in the Consular Section of the Embassy in Peking at the time and had access to British passports. He made me a new passport under the name Beverly Simpson and used a photo of me from my personnel file. He would have prepared everything meticulously, passport application and supporting paperwork. That was Giles. He was a brilliant man, if a little … eccentric."

Tom was deeply interested in how Marianne had escaped from Shanghai and how she'd managed to start a new life in Australia without any official sanction. The pair of them chatted on and on about it for a long time.

Meanwhile, Jess sat in silence in the front passenger seat. Her head was reeling. She thought about Simon, in Paris with that woman. Why hadn't he just told her he wanted to be with someone else? They could have sorted things out ages ago. Why drag things on? Then she thought about Sir Anthony. Would he be able to bring Justin and Mrs Wu to justice? Hard as she tried, Jess didn't have Marianne's faith in him. In MI6, Justin was in a powerful and covert position. He wasn't subject to the same levels of scrutiny and could get away with much more.

What about her own career? She'd just blown it apart. If she left now, would she ever be able to come back? But what would happen if she stayed? What could she do? Not much, unless she took her story to the media. That was a possibility, but would they be brave enough to publish the story without any evidence of what happened in Shanghai in 1984? Even if they did publish the story, would that compromise Sir Anthony's room for manoeuvre to nail Justin and Mrs Wu? And what about Marianne and her new life in Australia? Her cover would be blown, and maybe even worse – she had a family to protect now. As the car sped north, into the night, those questions just kept rolling around in Jess's head. Whichever way she looked at it, she was being forced to leave her whole life behind. Desolate at her situation, she slumped down in the seat and closed her eyes.

★

"Wake up, Jess." Tom reached over and shook her knee. "We're coming up to the last services on the M1 before we turn off on the M18. Do you want to stop?"

Jess opened her eyes and sat up. She wasn't asleep, she just didn't want to talk.

He glanced in the mirror again.

"Everything all right," she asked.

"Impossible to tell in the dark," he said. "All the headlights look the same."

"I need the bathroom," Marianne said.

"Me too," Tom added.

"We'd better pull in then," Jess said. "We'll get some hot drinks and food to keep us going too."

Tom slowed as he approached the exit for the services, then took the slip road off the motorway. He drove into the car park and looked in the mirror.

"Anyone following?" Jess asked.

"Not that I can see." He parked the car in-between two vans for privacy.

"We can't all go in together," Jess said. "You two go first. I'll go when you come back. I'll bring us back some food and coffee too." She looked out the window. "Looks like it'll have to be hamburgers, from the Golden Arches."

"That'll be fine," said Tom. "Come on Marianne."

"Let's get one thing clear before we go." Marianne put on her woollen hat and pulled the brim down over her eyes. "You must call me Bev from now on. That's who I am, Beverly Talbot."

He nodded. "Come on Bev."

Jess kept her eyes peeled on the other vehicles in the car park while Tom and Bev walked quickly up the steps and into the building. She tapped her foot with impatience. She felt exposed parked here and wanted to get back on the road as soon as possible.

Tom returned first and jumped into the driver's seat. "You go now." He smiled at her encouragingly. "It's real quiet in there."

She zipped up her padded coat, pulled the hood up over her head and got out. Her nerves jangled as she went inside, but she tried to behave as normally as possible. As she went into the bathroom, Bev was coming out. They glanced at each other, but that was their only acknowledgement. CCTV cameras were everywhere.

While waiting for the assistant to make up her take-away order of hamburgers, chips, and coffee, she started feeling uneasy. It was just a feeling. *Come on!* The assistant was so slow.

Jess glanced nonchalantly around at the few people eating or waiting for food. She locked eyes with a young woman, sitting at one of the tables drinking coffee. It was the way the woman immediately looked away, then started tapping on her mobile phone, that made Jess suspicious. Jess grabbed the paper bags of food from the assistant and walked out quickly. Running back to the car, she jumped in the passenger seat. "Go!" she said to Tom.

He reacted immediately, started up the car, and sped out of the services and back onto the motorway. "What happened?"

"A young woman was watching me get the food. It was the way she looked quickly away when I caught her eye. Then she got on her mobile." She sighed. "It could be innocent … I don't know."

He looked grim. "Right, hold on. I'll shake off anyone following."

"Tom…"

"I'm trained for this." Tom put his foot down and moved into the outside lane.

"Don't forget we're coming off at the next junction onto the M18," Jess warned.

"I know." He was doing 90 now in the outside lane, well over the speed limit. "Don't take any lids off that coffee." He sped on until the sign for the M18 was clear. One mile ahead. He didn't slow down. Half a mile ahead. He got right up to the turnoff, then suddenly dived across the lanes, skidded up the slip road and off the motorway. Then he slammed on the brakes.

Jess and Bev sat pinned to the seats in their activated seat belts. "Bloody hell, Tom," Bev said.

"There." He looked in his rear-view mirror. "If there was anyone behind, they'll be on their way to Leeds now." He drove on, setting the cruise control for just under the speed limit.

Once her nerves had settled down, Jess handed him a hamburger and passed his coffee to him whenever he asked for it.

"What time did you say the ferry left?" he asked.

"6 o'clock," said Bev from the back seat.

He looked at the dashboard. "It's 2.45am now. How long to Hull?"

"Another couple of hours at most," Jess said. "We need to get on the M62 for Hull. We shouldn't hit any traffic at this time of the morning."

"We have to get to the ferry 90 minutes before departure," said Bev. "The gate for foot passengers closes at 5 o'clock."

Tom shook his head. "We'll turn up just before the ferry sails. We don't want to hang around in the terminal for long. Too exposed."

"No," Bev said, anxiously. "We'll be too late. They won't let us on."

"Yes, they will. I'm a police officer." He glanced at Bev in the mirror. "Are we still agreed we're going on board as foot passengers and leaving the hire car in the car park at the terminal?"

"Yes." Jess and Bev replied in unison.

"Be days before they find it," he said. 'I'll ring the hire car company when we get back to Oz."

Jess looked at him but said nothing. She was very unhappy about running away. It didn't feel right. It went against everything she stood for.

They settled back in the car, quietly eating and drinking while Tom drove on. The wipers clunked back and forth hypnotically, clearing sleet off the windscreen. There was no way Jess could doze off. Her head was still buzzing with the decision she had to make. Should she go? Or stay?

The time ticked on.

★

At 4.55am precisely, Tom pulled into Docks Road, at the Port of Hull, and headed for terminal 2. As the car turned a corner, a huge, white ferry loomed up in the distance like a ghost ship in the misty darkness.

They all stared at it.

"Great driving, Tom." Bev sounded overcome with relief. "Now hurry up and park. The boarding gate closes in five minutes."

"We don't want to attract any attention." He drove slowly along to the passenger terminal and pulled into the multi-storey car park. Heading straight up to one of the upper floors, he parked the car and switched off. Then he relaxed back into the seat with a deep sigh and rubbed his weary eyes. "Never thought I'd be driving to Hull tonight."

Bev was anxious to get on board. "Come on. We've still got to get the tickets."

"Wait." He warned. "Let's sit here for a while. See if we've been followed."

"But the gate closes…"

"Relax, Bev." He looked in the mirror. "It'll be all right."

She sighed with frustration and sat back in her seat.

"Right," he said after a few minutes. "Let's go."

They jumped out of the car, put on their coats and grabbed their bags. Walking quickly down the stairs, they hurried out of the car park and across to the ferry terminal. It was completely empty inside. All the other passengers and cars were already on board.

"I'll get the tickets." Bev ran over to the ticket office.

Tom went over to talk to the security officers at the departure gate.

Jess stayed with their bags. She looked back at the door, then over at Bev. She'd come along initially to make sure Bev caught the ferry safely. A big part of her wanted to run back out that door and go home.

Tom came back. "It's okay," he said. "Everyone else is on board, but they will allow us through the departure gate." He gave a satisfied nod. "We'll be the last passengers on board."

Then he looked at Jess's face and tensed as if he could read her mind. "You can't stay here, not until this all blows over." He hesitated. "I'm sorry about Simon," he said, softly.

She raised her eyebrows.

"Bev told me when we stopped at the motorway services."

She looked away. "It was a shock at first, but not really a surprise, if that makes sense. I knew something was wrong."

He took her hand. "We need you in Oz," he said, softly. "*I* need you in Oz."

She smiled. "I wish it was in better circumstances."

"There are no better circumstances than this." He pulled her close and kissed her, gently. A long, lingering kiss that left her in no doubt that he meant every word. "Come with me, Jess. We'll have a good life together."

"*Oi*, you two." Bev shouted over. Then she got a sense of what was going on and hurried back. Alarmed, she looked at Jess. "Please don't tell me you're staying here. *Please!*"

"Well, Jess?" Tom's voice cracked with emotion. "Are you coming to Australia with me? Or staying here?"

Jess looked from Bev to Tom. She didn't want to leave like this. Every part of her wanted to stay and fight Justin and Mrs Wu, but she knew the score. What could she do on her own? She had to leave it to Sir Anthony. She saw by the expression on Tom and Bev's faces that they both cared for her. But in Tom's eyes, she saw more, and that sealed it. "All right." She picked up her bag. "I'm coming with you."

Tom beamed and hugged her tight. "You won't regret it. I promise." He took her bag off her. "Come on."

Together, they hurried over to clear passport control and security.

"All set?" Bev asked once they were through.

"Yep." Tom took Jess's hand. The three of them walked quickly over the footbridge and onto the ship. The departure gate closed firmly behind them. "You two go and find your cabins," he said. "I'll have a nose around the ship, just to make sure."

★

Later, Jess stood alone on deck, watching as the ferry pulled away from her country, her home. It was still dark at 6 o'clock and the lights from the port twinkled in the distance. She pulled up the hood of her coat, making no attempt to wipe away the tears mingling with sleet on her cheeks. The waves pounded onto the hull of the ship and the wind howled around the decks, tugging at her hair and coat. She was giving up everything and everyone she had ever loved. The overwhelming sense of desolation and loss made her feel weak, and she had to hold on to the railing to prop herself up. This was all down to two people. Justin Barber and Mrs Wu. They had exiled Marianne, and now they were doing the same to her, some 34 years later.

Out in the open sea now, the ferry shuddered and swayed in the turbulent waves. An announcement came over the Tannoy instructing passengers to stay below decks for the next few hours until they'd sailed through the worst of the North Sea weather. Jess didn't move, she just held on tighter to the railing. The longer she stood there being battered by the wind, the angrier she became. An anger, or rage, that she'd never experienced before. She could not, would not, let them get away with it. If Sir Anthony didn't deal with them, she would come back, whatever the consequences.

She jumped as a hand slipped into hers.

Bev stood beside her, looking just as grief-stricken at the fading lights in the distance. "I was so happy to be back in London, running around the park, seeing all the sights again, going to the theatre with you," she said. "I was home at last, after 34 years. I felt a happiness so deep inside that I wouldn't be able to explain it to anyone."

Jess turned to her. "I can only imagine what it must have been like for you in Shanghai, all alone in an alien country. I couldn't do this without you and Tom."

"I wasn't completely alone. Anthony helped me and, of course, poor Giles. If it hadn't been for Anthony I would never have got out of China. They would have framed me for that murder and executed me. Or imprisoned me for life in a Chinese jail." Bev hesitated. "One way or the other, I would be dead now."

Jess had no doubt that was true. "I wish I had your confidence in Anthony. I'm not sure he'll be able to nail Justin and Mrs Wu. They're too smart. Too powerful."

"What else can we do but hope he does?"

Now Jess's eyes glittered with a steel-like resolve. "I tell you something. I'm going to give Sir Anthony time, but if he doesn't do it, then I'm coming back." She sighed with frustration. "Just imagine all the classified information Justin's been handing over to the Chinese. Doesn't bear thinking about."

Bev nodded. "It'll be explosive when it gets out."

"*If* it gets out. I have my doubts. Even if Sir Anthony *does* stop them, he's not going to come out of it very well. All that going on under his nose, and he never knew about it. He won't get his seat in the Lords with all the rest of them. Might even lose his knighthood," Jess said, bitterly. "No, I think it'll probably be another cover-up. Easier all round that way."

"Oh, don't say that, Jess."

"Well…"

"I'm really angry when I think about Mrs Wu too," Bev said. "What a heroine she must be in Chinese eyes. She's been successfully running a spy ring in the highest reaches of the British establishment for over 34 years."

Jess turned to Bev. "That seals it then. If Sir Anthony doesn't do it, I'm coming back to expose Justin Barber for the traitor he is."

Bev squeezed Jess's hand. "I'll come too, and finish what I started."

They smiled sadly at each other and turned back to watch the lights of their homeland disappear completely from view.

32

London

The Daily Echo, Thursday 21 December

CHINESE AMBASSADOR TO RETURN TO CHINA

Following the Chinese President's highly successful State visit to the UK, the Chinese Ambassador, Wu Ling, has announced her own departure. She will be returning to China to take up a new position in the Central Politburo of the Communist Party of China.

"The Chinese President's visit was a milestone in the history of our bilateral relations," she told reporters today. "China and Britain have begun a vibrant, new chapter in our mutual co-operation and development. I am honoured to have been able to contribute to the State visit, and to this close and productive relationship that is set to go from strength to strength in the coming years."

In her new position, Wu Ling will be one of only two women to sit in the Central Politburo, making her one of the most influential women in Chinese politics today.

33

London – 20 months later
The Daily Echo

BRITAIN'S TOP DIPLOMAT DIES
IN ROAD ACCIDENT

Dorset police are appealing for information to help them find a motorist after Sir Anthony Chalmers, distinguished sinologist and Head of the Foreign and Commonwealth Office, was killed in a hit-and-run crash earlier this morning. Sir Anthony, a keen cyclist, was staying at his holiday home in Weymouth and was out for a bike ride at the time.

The crash happened around 6am in Puddle Lane, Weymouth, with Sir Anthony suffering serious head injuries in the collision and the motorist failing to stop at the scene.

Emergency services arrived shortly after the crash but were unable to revive Sir Anthony.

So far, no witnesses have come forward. Anyone with any information should contact the Dorset police, or Crimestoppers.

34

To see what is right and not to do it, is want of courage or of principle
(Confucius)

Sydney, Australia – Two days later

"Dad … dad … dad." The baby sat in his buggy grinning at his mother from under the brim of his sun hat.

Jess Sangster squeezed a bit more suntan cream out of the tube and rubbed it all over his face and chubby arms. The Australian sun was fierce, even though it wasn't yet summer. She took a sip of coffee and looked around the café in Circular Quay. She was sitting at a table outside, where she could watch the path leading back to the ferry terminal and up to the glittering shell-like roofs of the Opera house. It had become a habit when back in the city to choose a place where she could merge with other people or watch her surroundings. Being constantly on guard was tiring, but she was determined to protect her son. Soon though, the tourists would arrive and mill around in their droves, making that job more difficult. But, at this time of the morning, thankfully, it was quiet. Just the way she liked it.

She pulled the sunshade down to protect Daniel from the sun and rocked the buggy back and forth in the hope he'd fall asleep. He was teething and had kept Tom and her up most of the night. Poor Tom. He'd gone off to work exhausted. Still, he never complained. He spent every moment he could with them whenever they were staying with him in the city. He adored having them at home, even though he was anxious the whole time. This morning, he'd cross-examined her about where she was going and urged her to stay in the flat. She'd told him she couldn't stay locked up inside for ever. She had to go out. Daniel had to go out too. To ease his mind, she said she would keep in constant touch. Now, true to her word, she sent him a text message to tell him she was in the Circular Quay café. He knew exactly which one, because she'd told him her movements before leaving.

Pushing her sunglasses up the bridge of her nose, Jess looked at the sparking blue water and up at the majestic steel harbour bridge. Cars were flooding across from the swanky houses and apartments on the north shore into the central business district. She always enjoyed her visits to the city, especially just sitting in this café, watching the world go by. Who could tire of this spectacular view?

Looking back at Daniel, she saw his head droop. He was going to sleep at last. Breathing a sigh of relief, she checked the path in both directions, and opened the *Sydney Morning Herald* to scan the political headlines and foreign news. A soft, cooling breeze blew all around her, lifting the edges of the newspaper. She had to hold it down with one hand, while never taking the other off the buggy handle. This was her daily routine, to scour the media for news of the UK.

This morning though, something really worried her. She pulled the article she'd printed from the UK *Daily Echo* out of her bag and read it again.

Sir Anthony Chalmers had been killed in a hit-and-run crash near his holiday home in Weymouth.

Every time she read the article, she felt a cold feeling in the pit of her stomach. So many thoughts and images flashed into her head. She could see Sir Anthony pacing around his office before helping them to escape, the terrifying surveillance cars outside her London flat, the blinding headlights of a car trying to run her down on the streets of London, and Sam's arms outstretched as he fell back off the balcony balustrade. She shuddered at the sight of his crumpled body lying on the marble floor of Durbar Court and closed her eyes.

When she opened them, she glanced again along the path. This time, she smiled and waved at the approaching figure.

A squeal of delight came from the buggy as Daniel opened his eyes and spotted his aunt. He tried to wriggle out of the straps to greet her.

Bev bent down and squeezed his cheek. "Hello little man."

He reached out his arms for her to pick him up.

She looked at Jess. "May I?"

Jess groaned quietly inside. Now he would never go back to sleep. "Go ahead," she said, knowing that Bev loved him almost as much as she did.

Bev unbuckled him, lifted him high into the air, and twirled him around while he giggled uncontrollably.

When that ritual had been repeated several times to Daniel's satisfaction, Bev strapped him back into his buggy and looked at Jess. "I'll be glad when your annual leave is over. We're really missing you at the vineyard."

"You sound like Tom. He loves us being with him in the city, yet he can't wait to get us back up–country again."

"He's only worried about you and Daniel," Bev said. "It's not safe in the city."

Jess nodded.

"*I* worry all the time you're here too. At least when you're living with us at the vineyard, we've got so much security we can keep an eye on you both. *I* can keep an eye on you both."

Jess smiled at her. "It's good for Daniel and me to spend more time with Tom. He misses us."

Bev nodded. "We have a selfish reason for wanting you back too. Our annual accounts need sorting."

Jess laughed.

"I'm going to get a coffee," Bev said. "Want another one?"

"Please."

While Bev went off to get the drinks, Jess went back to the *Sydney Morning Herald*. There was the usual domestic political wrangling, and problems over North Korea and the Middle East.

She folded the paper up when Bev came out with the drinks and pushed it into the buggy alongside the now sleeping Daniel.

Bev sat down and glanced at Jess. "You sounded worried on the phone."

Jess unfolded the newspaper article and handed it to Bev. "Anthony's dead," she said. "Killed in a hit-and-run."

Bev nodded without even reading the article.

"You knew." Jess stared at her. "So, when were you going to tell me?"

Bev looked away. "I was going to wait until you got back to the vineyard." She sighed, deeply, and pulled her iPad out of her shoulder bag. "You'll probably see this before you get back anyway." She scrolled to the BBC website and handed Jess the iPad.

Jess took it and started reading the article Bev had put up on the screen.

★

MI6 APPOINTS JUSTIN BARBER AS THE NEW HEAD

The latest Secret Intelligence Service Chief served as right-hand man to former head, Sir Michael Rutherford.

Justin Barber, a distinguished career intelligence officer and formerly Britain's top spy in the Middle East, has been Deputy Chief and Head of Operations in the Secret Intelligence Service for the past three years.

He will take up his new post next month, it was announced on Thursday.

★

Jess heard the blood pounding in her ears as she looked from the iPad to her son. Her heart fluttered as she stroked his soft, fine hair and watched his chest rise and fall in sleep.

When she eventually looked up at Bev, she saw a familiar steeliness in her eyes. An unshakeable resolve.

She took Bev's hand and squeezed it.

Together, they sat in silence in the sunshine, staring out across the sparkling water of this stunning harbour, in the country that had become their much-loved home and refuge.